storm of
fortune

Books by Austin Clarke

SURVIVORS OF THE CROSSING

AMONGST THISTLES AND THORNS

THE MEETING POINT

WHEN HE WAS FREE AND YOUNG AND HE USED TO WEAR SILKS

STORM OF FORTUNE

storm of fortune

a novel by
austin clarke

little, brown and company
boston / toronto

FIRST EDITION

T04/73

Library of Congress Cataloging in Publication Data

Clarke, Austin Chesterfield, 1932-
    Storm of fortune.

    The second vol. of a trilogy; the first vol. is
The meeting point.
    I. Title.
PZ4.C5973St3 [PR6053.L325]   813'.5'4   72-12805
ISBN 0-316-14700-1

First published in Canada
by Little, Brown & Company (Canada) Limited

PRINTED IN THE UNITED STATES OF AMERICA

To Marjorie DaCosta Chaplin

part one

Violence and fear at the base

Dots was sweating when she arrived at Bernice's apartment. Sleep, and a few yellow grains that looked like sand, were still in her eyes, testifying to the fact that she, like her husband and her employer, Mrs. Hunter, had stayed up most of the night talking about the brutal beating the two policemen had given Henry.

Henry did not say where he was when he was beaten by the policemen ("Man, it is a damn shameful thing," he had told them, when he dragged himself from the car which he had left parked in the middle of the road in Rosedale, where Dots worked. "It is a damn shameful thing when the police have to beat up people. Not that they was one, two or three — it must have been four or five big blasted police who kicked me like if I was a dog. I don't mean that the beating is a shameful thing, I don't mean that at all. I mean that it is shameful that me, a big strong-arse black man not quite turned forty, would let three, four goddamn white cops put such a licking in my arse! That is what I mean. And man, if they didn't *jump* me, if they weren't hiding, if they didn't gang-up on me, like they did . . . because they're blasted cowards when they's walking about, individually, one at a time. And I tell you, Boysie, I tell you Dots, be-Jesus Christ, if they wasn't cowards, and if they had just come at me one-by-one, goddamn, it would have been one big nasty race war in Toronto this morning. But this is a lesson to me. Whenever, or wherever, I meet one o' them policemen, cop, detective, civilian in mufty, god-blindme! it is licks I putting in his arse!'").

And this was what Dots had on her mind this morning. She had heard Henry's side of the story: she didn't know that the beating had been intended for her own husband; and Henry said nothing about it. She didn't know either, that he was beaten because of Brigitte, her husband's lover and the woman whom she had come to regard as her close friend. She knew none of these things. Still, this morning, late in summer, she bounded into Bernice's apartment in such a rage that Bernice herself became frightened.

"And when that poor man relate to me this morning," she went on to say, "even before I got outta my bed, before I even got out of my second sleep, how them four or five police dragged him outta the car, the car that Boysie lent him to go up to Hamilton in, to meet a friend of his that had come in from Barbados, and how they treated him, a human being, after all! a human being, gal, tell me if it is any wonder, I asking you now, is it any wonder Bernice, that I could never bring myself to like these blasted people in this place? Is it? And I am going to tell you something else. From today, from this morning I am a different-thinking person. I can't tell you how different I am thinking at this precise moment, because I haven' work it out completely yet. But I know I bound to think different towards Canada from today.

"I just gave that whore I works for my notice! I leffing her! Yes. I told her straight to her face, in the presence o' Boysie and Henry who was still there bleeding, while we

was putting cold towels on his face, Jesus God Bernice! his
eyeballs like they was ready to drop outta his head, from
the amount o' blows his head sustained . . . and . . . and
in a time like this Bernice, in a time like today, we have to
see ourselves in a new sperspective. This ain' no time for
quarrelling and bickering 'gainst one another, no matter
how much I might have cussed you, or you cussed me behind my back — because Brigitte told me everything — but
don't let that come between you and me, 'cause that is life.
I left my job and you have to leave yours, too. I am not
going to stop nagging you, Bernice, so help me God, till you
give Mistress Burrmann your notice. We have to unite over
Henry's tragedy. So, make up your mind by the end o' the
summer when she come back from Mexico."

Bernice remained very quiet. She was not fully attentive.
She could have told Dots many things about Henry's beating. But she had neglected to say them when Dots arrived,
and now she felt she could not disclose them. She didn't
even tell Dots that her sister, Estelle, was in the Toronto
General Hospital recovering and being treated for a "mis-
carriage." In the first place, she had neglected to tell Dots
that Estelle was pregnant.

"So what you have to say to that, gal?" Dots asked her.

"You got a point."

"*I got a point!* Is that all you can say, I got a point?"

"Work is very hard to find, Dots."

"Did I tell you different? I haven' just emigraded here,
Bernice! 'Course, I know work's hard as hell to find. And
for us, it harder still. But is it more harder to find than
pride? Could it ever be harder to find than *that?* You tell
me, because *you* is the Black Muslim."

"Well, I don't mean it that way," Bernice said, feeling
trapped. She was wondering how much Brigitte had told
Dots about Estelle and about Henry.

"Anyhow, I waiting. I waiting to read them papers, the *Star* and the *Globe*. Normally they have a damn lot to print and say 'bout negroes living in this city. I waiting to see *their* story concerning this violence, this blasted racial injustice that we negroes have to live with, day in and day out. And so help me God, if Henry don't get satisfaction, well . . . I have something planned for the Mistress Hunter, the Mistress Burrmann, the mister policeman, for *everybody* in this place." Her hostility seemed to exhaust her, and she remained quiet for a while.

Bernice had tidied the apartment. And she was glad she had thought of doing it before Dots came. She had already put the soiled, blood-stained sheets from Estelle's bed into the dirty clothes hamper.

"But where *she* gone to so early in the morning?"

"Who? Mistress Burrmann?"

"What the hell would I be inquiring 'bout Mistress Burrmann for? Is Mistress Burrmann and me any friends? I mean Estelle!"

"Oh! Estelle? . . . well, you should have met her at the corner. You didn't see her at the corner? . . . well, she must have gone in Agaffa's motor car then . . ."

"So Estelle socializing with Agaffa, eh?"

"Just left."

"In a motor car?"

"They just this minute turned the corner there, by Marina Boulevard and Eglinton. Not five minutes ago."

"At nine o'clock in the morning?"

"Child, even I was surprised to see Estelle wake up so damn early, in almost six months that she's been living here with me. First time Estelle get out of bed before mid-day noon."

Dots shook her head in that characteristic way when she wanted to express deep and unpronounceable sorrow. Then she looked Bernice straight in the eye, and said, "How long we been friends?"

"Friends? Well, Dots, it's a long time! If you really want me to count the time, this month coming would be thirty-three, thirty-four months. Almost three years."

"Right! Three years. Three years I've been trampling up here at your every beck and call. Three years. Three Christmases! Every time you feel bad, every time you feel depressed. Every time you get a headache, every time you want to go to church and you don't want to be the only black person to be riding by yourself on that streetcar. Every time your period comes and you can't do Mistress Burrmann's kitchen-work, I have come and help you, I been answering your call. Right? And now, good Jesus Christ, Bernice! you mean to say you can't be honest with me, for one minute? You call that friendship? Well, let me tell you something. Agaffa just dropped me here! In her motor car, with her man Henry, and Boysie. With Henry in the back seat bleeding like a pig and crying like a dog. Now, is there two Agaffas that we know?"

"Well, I don't know, Dots. That is what Estelle told me."

"Estelle is a liar!"

"Well, I don't know."

"I have always tell you, Bernice, that Estelle is a lying bitch. She is your sister, and I am your friend . . . *was* your friend. And still I say to you, she lie like hell! Now you can do what the hell you like."

"Well, that is Estelle's business, not mine."

"Well, that is Estelle's business, not mine!" Dots said, aping Bernice. "And that is all you have to say?"

"Well, that is what Estelle tell me."

"Well, that is what Estelle tell you! Did she tell you she was running round all over Toronto with a married man?

Did Estelle tell you that? And that the married man is a white man, to boot? Did she tell you that? And did she tell you that the same white man she was running round with, *the same man* mind you, did she remember to tell you that that man was, or is, your very own employer, Mr. Burrmann?"

"But Dots . . ."

"Don't but-Dots me! Jesus Christ, woman, we is womens, grown women, not kids! I am trying to be honest with you. I made a effort to tell you all this, all this nasty scandal making the rounds round Toronto the last time I came up here in the hot o' that summer day. You didn' even want to answer the 'phone or the door. I had was to go over by Brigitte to see if you was there or if you was really home. And I didn' well sit down in that whore's, in Brigitte's place, before she didn' expose both you and the Estelle to me. I had was to cuss Brigitte like hell after she told me all them things 'gainst you and 'bout Estelle. Be-Christ, and what made my belly burn me was that you entrusted such personal things as that to a stranger. And a white woman at that! To a complete, complete stranger. Never mind that Brigitte would bring a imported German beer over here and sit down with you and laugh and smile and cuss her employer Mistress Gasstein and yours, Mistress Burrmann, with you. That isn' friendship, Bernice. That is not sincereness. I thought I was your friend. But I see that nowadays you forgetting the Black Muslims and you gone overboard, contrary-wise the other way."

This struck Bernice hard. She didn't know who to trust now: not even Dots, who was bringing this new "sperspective" to her; and to think of it — that she had recently put Brigitte at the top of her friendship list, not more than a week ago.

"I swear to you, Dots, I swear to you this Friday morning, I swear to you . . . you have me wrong."

"Listen to me, Bernice," Dots said. She made herself comfortable on the chair, and she took out a package of cigarettes, plain tips (a habit which Bernice didn't know she had), and she made a great performance lighting one. She offered one to Bernice, but Bernice shook her head in disdain and in disgust. "I am going to tell you something now that is going to take you as a big shock. I know more about your business than you think. Yes." She inhaled the cigarette. She closed her eyes. She exhaled. She opened her eyes and then she said, "Last night or this morning, whichever it was, that you called me, and wake me up outta my bed, well I put two and two together, and be-Christ I did know that something was wrong. Something had to be wrong that you would call me that hour o' the night. Foreday-morning? Boysie been creeping in my bed all hours, three, four, five, six o'clock. And in all that time, Bernice, do you think that my eyes was shut? You really think so? When every blasted night I am seeing all kinds o' blonde hairs and long hairs on Boysie jacket? Bernice, my hair isn' blonde. Is my hair blonde? Be-Christ, it never was, and never will be! And I'm only telling you all that to tell you this, that I haven' been sleeping whilst Boysie was out screwing-round with Brigitte. I haven' been sleeping whilst Estelle your sister has been running round with Mr. Burrmann. Bernice, Dots was not dozing whilst you been talking my name to that German whore, Brigitte. 'Cause, look! I is a married woman. And a married woman could see things that no damn single gal could ever see and comprehend. You ain' know that? Marriage, Bernice, marriage is the best high school and college I know on this Christ's earth. So before you could come to me with any more lies, either 'bout you or Estelle, just let me remind you that my name is *Missis*, you hear? *Mistress!* And even in this cruel country, that means a damn lot."

After this, nothing more was said, either by Dots or by Bernice, who in the first place could not find much to say. Bernice felt now the same way she felt when she saw the violence through her window; and when she realized it wasn't Boysie, but somebody else. And hearing Dots talk this way, so frankly that it was upsetting, she wondered whether she could not have been more honest with herself; whether she should not have gone downstairs last night, after the policemen had driven away; whether she should not have looked into the car to identify who was the man beaten.

She thought of it now, trying to relive the tension and the fear and the violence of a few hours ago; a night which began with the car and then the other car, and then the violence, and which ended with Estelle bleeding as if she was a pig killed by an amateur butcher; she thought of Brigitte; and she remembered the ambulance screaming across respectable Marina Boulevard where motor cars didn't even sound their horns, nor children dare to ring their bicycle bells too loudly; nor domestic servants and nursemaids to call out to one another, as they most surely would do back in the West Indies. And all that time she had to wait in the hospital; and the evil abusive looks from Nurse Priscilla *that same bitch who came in here that night when Estelle arrived from Barbados, and cocked up her fat backside and drink my drinks and eat my eats, my curry-chicken and souce, that same short-memory whore, Priscilla* . . . She wondered whether Brigitte had really told Dots everything about Estelle, or whether Dots was making it all up.

"Bernice? Bernie?" Estelle had said in her delirium only

a few hours ago. "Hold my hand, Bernie. I am so 'shamed, and I have disappointed you so much I don't know what to do. Don't forget to post the letter to Mammy for me, and don't forget to remind me that Sam Burrmann ask me to go to the Immigration on Bedford, first thing Monday morning, 'cause he already fixed it up with a friend who works there. But Bernice, I really brought my pigs to find market this time, eh? I come all this way up here from Barbados to Toronto, and spoil things for you, and me, in nearly no time at all, in merely six months . . . but I have to put this one down to experience. And Mammy always used to say that experience never killed anybody, that you have to experience a bad experience one more time to correct it, that only the weak in spirit and intelligence . . . but I have gathered my experience from this experience. If I tell you how this whole thing happened, if I told you all the things that that man told me 'bout his wife, Mrs. Burr-mann, how she can't do this and how she can't do that, that he isn' happy with her, if I tell you everything that that man promised to give me, merely because he could work-up his behind on me and feel like a man for once in his life, Ber-nice you yourself would be ashamed. I am so ashamed of myself, so 'shamed that I brought shame on your head and on Dots heads. . . . But there is one thing that I want you to understand. Bernice, one thing. And that is that I didn't let that white man do anything to me that I couldn't pre-vent him from doing. And I want you to understand that. You and Dots and everybody who would have something to say about this, although they don't know one damn thing about my business. The only reason he succeeded in doing what he did to me was that I had less love in my heart than he had hate in his. And to-besides, I treated him like a man. And this is what got me frightened now. A great fear has come over me, Bern, a great fear. But I am not going to

embark on any vengeance scheme. There ain' going to be
no hatred from me, although, be-Christ, as you would say,
the white man ain' have no blasted right expecting nothing
from us save hate and hatred and bloodshed . . ." And it
was at this point that she had fainted on the stretcher, from
the exhaustion of her body and blood and thoughts — or
was it while she was on the bed? Perhaps, it was on the bed
where they had put her by this time.

It had been confusing and terrible amidst the screams of
the ambulance and the crying of Estelle, and the shame,
the shame; for Bernice had been muttering all the time
during the drive down to the hospital, "My own sister, my
own sister tonight have crowned my head with a crown o'
thorns and shame"; and she was shaking her head in sorrow
as she said this, "Estelle have succeeded at last in making
me a princess o' shame and sorrow" — perhaps they had
already put her into her bed, in the public ward, by the time
she had made this confession. Yes, she said all that on her
hospital cot; "and there ain't no better place to confess or
tell the truth, if in a lifetime a person had find it too hard
even to talk to God or whisper something in His ear. There
is no better place. But God have mercy on you, Estelle. God
bound and 'bliged to have pity on you because what you
have done, you did it in ignorance 'gainst the knowledge o'
white people and 'gainst the knowledge o' white people in
their actions to you, a black person. So God have a heavy
penalty to pay himself, if he don't help you."

That was what Bernice had said, leaving the hospital,
herself still under shock from the ambulance and the emergency, before Freeness (who drove taxicabs when there was
nothing doing in the way of crap games and parties) found
her walking in a daze, east along Gerrard, crossing Yonge
Street, going in the wrong direction for Marina Boulevard.
Just before Freeness recognized her, Bernice had remem-

bered something: she had forgotten to take the 45 rpm record which Estelle had held tight in her hands, all during the long drive down to the General Hospital. It was Estelle's favourite record: *I Lost Someone,* sung by James Brown. She played it everyday, particularly after she had found out she was pregnant.

Freeness stopped the cab and waited until Bernice drew alongside. He then ordered the drunk he was taking home to "Get to hell outta my cab, man, before I call the cops for you!" and although the man couldn't understand why he was being ordered out, he hastily climbed out, hitting his head twice on the top of the back door. Freeness took Bernice home. He did not charge her one penny. He had had to drive with the meter ticking, registering money, because the regulations said so. It was a four-dollar-sixty-cents ride. And in all that time, he did not once ask her what was wrong, why she was walking the streets so late at night. He assumed it was a madness that came with loneliness and by being away from home. And when Bernice was able to piece all the jigsaws of her confusion together in the hours since she got home, she decided to get Freeness's telephone number from Henry, to thank him personally. But she quickly forgot all about it when Dots arrived.

Bernice looked at Dots and began to hate her the same way she hated Mrs. Burrmann. Dots knew too much about her troubles: Mrs. Burrmann did too many unkind things to her and brought about these troubles. There was the same wall of noncommunication between herself and Dots as existed for over thirty-four months between Mrs. Burrmann and herself: and whereas Mrs. Burrmann never did know how Bernice felt about anything important (and probably didn't care) because of Bernice's smile and her apparent contentment with her employment, which were mere defences erected to prevent Mrs. Burrmann from ever getting at the truth, and to prevent herself from ever having to tell the truth to Mrs. Burrmann; now, she was using this same silence, this same dumbness, this same stubbornness against Dots, which she hoped Dots would interpret correctly and make her decide to leave. Bernice had no desire to talk this morning. But Dots was persistent.

"But why would a police come right outta the blasted blue and beat up Henry? That is a thing I see happening on television in the South. I didn' know it could happen in Canada. And I don't even know if in the South, a police could come out of the blue and pour licks in a man *just because* that man is a black man, or a negro, or a nigger, as they call them in the South, and get off scotch-free."

"I don't know either, Dots, I just don't know."

"And Henry say he didn' do that blasted police nothing." She sighed, and added, "Just like that?"

"I don't know, Dots. Some funny things does happen in this place, Toronto."

"But Christ, not like that, though! Not for doing nothing, at all. It is the same case as that coloured gentleman in the motor car accident I witnessed four years ago at the corner o' Bloor Street and Sherbourne."

"Child, I don't know," Bernice said. She got up and started moving her favourite memento, an artificial waterfall in the likeness of Niagara Falls, dusting the spot on which it had stood for three days without being dusted; and then she replaced it; and she did the same thing with the other porcelain figurines and false forests of deciduous and coniferous trees which decorated her centre table. Now that Estelle was in the hospital, she had replaced the plastic cover on the chesterfield with the Mexican spread which Mrs. Burrmann had given her a long time ago, as a present from one of her Mexican vacations. Bernice had picked up the habit of covering the chairs and the chesterfield in her apartment with plastic, just like Mrs. Burrmann, who protected all her new and expensive furniture in this way, until one night, Mr. Burrmann came home drunk and horny for sex (Estelle had had her period), and knowing he couldn't make love with his wife, and unable to find any unfaithfulness on her, unable too, to find any fault with her housekeeping, screamed at the plastic slipcovers on the furniture and ripped them off.

In his mind, he was ripping off his wife's nightgown. "Take those fucking things off, you cheap Jewish bitch!" he screamed.

(Bernice had heard his voice from her apartment on the third floor and had winced.)

"I see you want to get rid o' me, so I going, gal," Dots said.

"It's not that. Just that I'm busy this morning."

"The mistress still on her vacation?" Dots asked. "Where she gone this time?"

"Mexico."

"And he? Where he gone?"

"Last time I rested my eyes on him, he say he was heading north. But I don't know if he gone north or if he gone south, or if he gone at all. I can't bother myself tracking-down Mr. Burrmann." Bernice wasn't looking at Dots as she was talking, but continued to discover dust on the centre table; and by the time Dots was opening the door, Bernice was inspecting the dressing table, moving a bottle of cosmetics, wiping the ring on which it had sat with the side of her hand, replacing it, and moving on to the next bottle which contained complexion lightener.

"If you're not too busy later on, phone me. I gone." And she was gone.

Bernice didn't tell her good-bye. In her mind she wished her good riddance. Since there was no need to pretend fur-

ther, she sat down on the chesterfield. A great loneliness
shook her body like a spasm. She was alone now; really
alone. Alone in the world, it seemed. And she was frightened. It was a closer fear than the fear she felt that afternoon when the letter which she had sent to Mammy came
back from Barbados, ADDRESSEE UNKNOWN. At least then,
Mrs. Burrmann was in the house. Brigitte was there across
the street, still a friend; and Dots was down there in Rosedale, a telephone call away, and as a friend. Now, she was
friendless. They had all deserted her through their insin-
cerity.

The letter, the letter; she was thinking of the letter from
Lonnie. "Where I put that letter? Where I put it?" She
searched in the drawers of her dressing table, and it was
not there; she searched under the linen white plains with
the West Indies skies of blue and the green coconut palm
trees and red coconuts and other fruits of the tablecloth
which Mammy had sent up to her two Christmases ago,
and it wasn't there. She peered under the large old-fashioned
radio which Mrs. Burrmann had moved out of the basement and had placed in her room. Then she remembered
that the letter was in her dress, the dress she had on when
she took Estelle to the hospital. There was blood on the
dress. Many blotches, made in motion. The things that
must have been said by those nurses when they saw her
with so much blood on her dress; and by the people when
she was walking the street afterwards! A policeman in a
cruiser had missed his light as he watched her and tried to
make up his mind. Then he roared through the red light.
The blood covered from her chest down to her waist; and
there it must have been in two minds, because it left out
the space which represented her abdomen; and it continued
uninterruptedly in dots and dashes, all down its way morse-
coding the terrible experience of her sister's unsuccessful at-

tempt to have an unprofessional abortion. Brigitte had given the instructions for the unsuccessful abortion, after having convinced Bernice that she was "good at these things." The letter was in this blood-stained pocket of this blood-stained dress. But the letter was unblemished. She wiped away the tears that came with the memory of the dress and the blood, and she started to read the letter. *"People building new buildings, almost everybody — but me — have a new car that they buy on the time-payment plan, and a lot of American ships in the harbour and the whole town full with those blasted noisy Yankee sailors. . . ."* This was the second page where she had stopped when she first began to read Lonnie's letter. Remembering, now, that it was a letter to inform her of what Estelle had done to Mammy, by putting her into the care of the government, in St. Peter's Almshouse, before she left Barbados to come up; and because too, it was a letter, so far as she could remember, in which Lonnie said something about wanting to come up to Canada, before he became an old man, to be with her; and because she was alone now, with the fear of this loneliness so heavily upon her, that she thought the world was against her, she decided to read the letter from the beginning.

She went back to the chesterfield. Lonnie, her boyfriend, and the father of her child, Terence, was saying from Barbados: *"Darling Bernice, love, This is Lonnie. I am pining after you real bad these days. I was going to write you long long time before now, but since I had to look after the business you ask me to look after, I could not write before this time. I visited Mammy. She is in the Poor House, all right. But I think it is a good thing that Estelle put her there, because after I had a talk with Nurse Forde who is the charge nurse in charge of Mammy, Nurse Forde told me that Estelle was right to put Mammy there. Mammy*

*put on weight and she fat. Nurse Forde say not to worry.
Mammy is in good hands in the Poor House. Nurse Forde
say she remember you. The island looking like New York
these days. People building new buildings, almost everybody — but me — have a new car that they buy . . ."* (she
realized she had just read this passage the second time, so
she skipped it and continued further on). *"But with me,
things bad as usual. Rough, rough as hell, if you ask me.
But I am not going to ask you again to send for me, because that is a decision that only God could make you decide. But for old times sake, I begging you to send down a
few dollars because St. Matthias Church having the annual
outing, and I am naked as a bird's arse. I need a new suit.
So see what you could do. Your loving man, Lonnie. PS.
Roses are red / Roses are blue / My love is true / Until I
dead. Lonnie."*

Bernice held the letter in her hand for some time, refusing to think of what Lonnie meant, and of what he
thought of her; refusing to admit that the power of his profession of love had actually hit her; refusing to permit this
power of his love to make her feel as Lonnie wanted her to
feel, as he said her absence made him feel. She folded the
letter and held it in her fist, and she waited. She moved to
the window and she waited. In the broad daylight, she
looked at the burning road, the scene, the alleyway where
only a few short hours ago, Henry had been beaten up by
two policemen. She felt no compunction at all for her silence as Henry was being beaten, the same silence which
she had come to regard as immoral in Mrs. Burrmann, and
in Mr. Burrmann. It was as if she had dreamed about
Henry being beaten in a dream that was not too clear, a
dream which was so undramatic that she could have either
forgotten or remembered it the next morning, without feeling elation or disappointment. Henry himself was now very

far from her mind. She felt depressed. She was just about to go downstairs to have something to do, for the habit of being a domestic was like a custom of washing dishes ("Wait! but there ain' one blasted dirty dish in this place! Hey, imagine that! nobody at home: *he* probably up north already, fishing and drinking like a fish, the children still at camp, and Mistress Burrmann of course, 'way down in Mexico . . . that bitch couldn' even take me to Mexico with her, and even Dots mistress took her once to North Bay . . . the house empty. The house empty this morning. And the morning, afternoon and night belongst to me, and I here thinking about servanting . . ."). And then she saw Dots coming from the house where Brigitte worked. Dots was walking fast, as if she had something important to do. She looked up anxiously at the window where Bernice was sitting, but didn't see her. Bernice thought she noticed that Dots appeared less anxious after deciding that nobody saw her coming from Brigitte's house. But there was something in Dots's manner which caused Bernice to fear. She had a presentiment that Dots was coming back to abuse her, or to beat her. Bernice moved away from the window just as Dots was about to cross the street. She tied on her apron, and went from her apartment, leaving the door open. She entered the kitchen to make herself a cup of tea, boiled twice to make it strong as she used to drink it back in Barbados; and she was going to do it for the first time in Canada now that Mrs. Burrmann wasn't home.

She had just turned on the electric stove when she heard Dots calling out at the side door, "Bernice! Bernice, come, open this door! Come come!" Bernice started to tremble. "Open-up, open-up! I know you in there!" And when the door was open, Dots burst inside, held Bernice by her hand, as if she was a child crossing a busy street, and led her upstairs, back into her apartment.

When they reached the apartment, Dots closed the door, adjusted the night latch, came back, stared Bernice in the eye, and said, "Sit your arse down, girl!" And Bernice sat down. She didn't know what was going to happen, but she knew it was something terrible. "You're sitting down?" Dots asked her, although she could see that Bernice was. "Good!" she said; and she sat down too. For some time, she said nothing; and Bernice could hear the cars passing outside in the morning rush, and she thought she heard children's voices playing. A truck screeched across the boulevard. Otherwise, everything was as silent and dramatic with the silence waiting for violence as last night when Henry got beaten, which she was thinking about now. And she tried to think fast of what Dots had in mind: there wasn't anything Dots could say to her concerning Boysie and Brigitte was there? Brigitte certainly couldn't tell Dots that Boysie was her lover; besides, Dots said she already knew. Brigitte couldn't tell her anything about the beating without thereby implicating herself, could she? The only thing Brigitte could tell Dots was that Estelle was now in the General because of an attempted abortion; and she couldn't even tell her that, because that too would implicate her in a crime.

All the instructions had come from Brigitte who said she had learned about them during the war, when she had to help out friends in the nursing corps of the German army. "Darlink, this is nothing at all to perform." Bernice and Estelle had both heard something about German technology even while they were growing up in the West Indies.

"Would I be right, Bernice," Dots said, "to call myself your friend? Right?" She did not permit Bernice to answer. "And not only are we friends, Bernice, but we are from the same place, hundreds o' miles down in the Wessindies, to come up here to work in white people kitchens as domes-

tics? Right? Well, tell me now, Bernice, what kind o' Black
Muslim, or black nationalist-woman you walking 'bout Toronto telling people you is, what kind o' conscience-thinking
woman you admit yourself to be, to me, that you would
leave me, a friend, the same black woman as you, and go
'cross that road there, and present your problems to a
woman like Brigitte? Eh? Are you drunk as hell, Bernice?
You think that because the same Brigitte smiles with you
today, that tomorrow morning you have any guarantee she
is going to smile again with you? Bernice, do you call that
wisdom?"

"But I still don't understand what you mean."

"I mean Estelle!"

"Estelle?"

"The abortion."

"What abortion?"

"You had no right at all, at all, at all, whatever, to go to
a woman like Brigitte and ask her cooperation in a abortion
for Estelle! Jesus Christ, Bernice, are you out of your blasted
mind, or something? Suppose me and my husband Boysie
had a man-woman fight, and I call-in the police, and the
police come. Knowing the police in this place is white
mens, don't you see that I would be bringing a foreign
body in a black-man black-woman secret? That police cease
to be a police, *in my mind,* the minute he tamper in my
man-woman affair with my husband! You don't see it that
way? Going to a white woman with a thing as personal as
that? A blasted *white woman?*"

"Now, listen to me, Dots. Brigitte isn' no blasted white
woman! Brigitte is a friend."

"A *white woman?*"

"I regards Brigitte as my friend. And when I look at Brigitte I do not see a white person, I sees a friend."

"With a abortion?" Dots was on her feet. She was shaking with rage. She was standing close to Bernice now. "You mean you couldn' call me? And you calling *her* your friend? When it is that same DP-whore who just done telling me all your nasty business? You still regard the Germans as your allies? Your friend?"

"But what did Brigitte tell you? Anyway, the fact that Brigitte tell you about it don't mean that she betrayed me. Do it?"

"You really want to know? Well, I will only tell you *only* the best things 'bout yourself that she told me. The best. Not the worst. I will leave the worst for you to imagine."

Tears had already formed themselves in Bernice's eyes. This was a complete shock, a complete shock of fear and isolation.

"Your *friend* just tell me again that Estelle breeding for Mr. Burrmann." And she added, "that Mistress Burrmann gave Mr. Burrmann five hundred dollars to get the abortion. And that he gave it to you. Brigitte told me that, those very words, so help me God! That not once or twice, nor three times, Mr. Burrmann took Estelle down in Jarvis Street where the worst whore in Toronto won't go, and there he screwed her. Every time he do it, every time he *fooped* Estelle your sister, your *friend* told me that he give Estelle fifty dollars for her body, and you and she benefit therefrom. Your sister! Breeding for Mr. Burrmann. Your employer! Your friend. Exposing you to me. Jesus Christ, Bernice, have Canada turned your blasted head behind your back? It do these things to you, so quick, to make your eyes blind and your ears deaf?" Dots began to cry.

"Mr. Burrmann do that? Mr. Burrmann give her money?"

"You know how I feel right now? You know what I feel like doing with you? I have a blasted mind to knock you down to the ground! With my hand! You don't know

no longer restricted by her large brassiere. And she slid
down off the bed like a seal sliding into water, and went to
Bernice, and shook her hand. She also embraced Bernice.

Looking back at Estelle, who could not move around so
easily because she was still bedridden, Mrs. Macmillan said
cheerfully, still heaving from unexplainable laughter and
from the exhaustion of walking, "So this is Estelle's sister! You look just like Estelle, you hear me, darling? Identical as twins, you hear me?" Bernice was not only blacker
than Estelle, she was obviously less beautiful. But the strong
bond of friendship which had formed between the two con-
valescing women had failed to permit Mrs. Macmillan to
see or to recognize this obvious difference. "Estelle there,
she's been making me wet my pants with laughter. From
the moment she came out of that coma she was in, two or
three days ago."

Estelle had climbed off Mrs. Macmillan's bed by this
time. She limped over, and showed Bernice to her own
bed, with Mrs. Macmillan following them. Estelle had not
yet introduced her to Bernice, by name. "This is . . ." she
began. But Mrs. Macmillan beat her to it.

"The name is Macmillans," she told Bernice. "Gloria
Macmillan." She grabbed Bernice's hand, and shook it as
strongly as a man would. Bernice tried to present a pleasant
face. She smiled and said, "I am Bernice. Estelle's sister. I
am pleased to make your acquaintance." Mrs. Macmillan
beamed. She admitted, "Darling, had it not been for Estelle here, this sister of yours, you hear me, darling, well I
tell you, this slaughter-house . . . I call it a slaughter-
house because every bitch you see on this ward, every single woman except those two over there, the one in the pink
housedress and the other one there lying down talking to
her bloody self as if she is off her bloody rocker, every *single* woman except those two have been under the doctor's

knife . . . or else they wouldn't be here, would they now, eh, darling?" Mrs. Macmillan then gave Bernice a guided tour of the illnesses and reputations and social positions of every woman in this ward. She talked about every woman except Estelle, whose medical history she presumed Bernice to be already acquainted with. There was a woman, "a Catholic I think she is, because when I sneaked up on her bed to read her history off her chart, I find out that she is this big and proper Catholic person, a real going-to-mass type, too — judging by the number of rosaries she keeps under her bloody pillow. Well, I laughed like hell, you hear me, darling? Ask Estelle, here. I find out that that woman already have ten children in thirteen years!" And the woman in question, apparently now fagged-out and no longer romantic about child-bearing, had apparently tried, in vain, to put an end to the nightly diversions of her husband's lust, with the result that she was now on Ward 6A, Public. "Then there is this young-young thing, scarcely seeing her menses yet, and the nurses tell me, in confidence, that she been in here for the second time this year, already. Darling, you see this modern young generation growing up? With all their pills and things? Well, in my time, my mother would have tarred" — she shot a glance at Bernice to see if she had used the wrong word; and she hastily added — "would have *painted* my tail, you hear me, darling, had she caught me in such a state." And there was Mrs. Jones who came in bleeding; and a Mrs. Vefferman, who ("Nobody would think she was such a rich and proper lady, furthermore a Jew! judging by her name, because I was under the impression that all Jews was very religious and that they had their own means and piles of money for getting rid of these problems!"), who came in, in a coma.

"So you're this girl's sister?" Mrs. Macmillan said, getting back to the present. She sat on Estelle's bed. She told

Bernice, "Sit down, darling. Draw up that chair and be my guest." And Bernice sat down, wondering whether Mrs. Macmillan had already made up her mind to spend the entire visiting hour with them; whether Mrs. Macmillan didn't have, nor expect, any visitors of her own, and had therefore decided to share Estelle's. Bernice didn't like her. Mrs. Macmillan struck her as a very nosy and aggressive and strong-willed woman. There were muscles showing at the sides of her neck, and her arms were developed, probably by the repetition of beating her children, Bernice imagined; or by raising them from cradle to knee, to toilet. Bernice kept her perpetual, public smile of geniality. She even was smiling when there was nothing to smile about. That way, she didn't have to talk — if Mrs. Macmillan had thought of giving her a chance to say a word. "Your sister is a clever girl, you hear me, darling?" she said to Bernice. Bernice smiled and nodded. It was the first time a stranger had said this to her about Estelle; the first time she had ever thought of Estelle as being clever. Estelle, meanwhile, dropped her head, and picked a piece of broken fingernail from a finger. "She promised to visit with me when she gets out next week, or the week after. Isn't that so, Ess, darling?"

"Yeah," Estelle said, a bit embarrassed, and wanting Mrs. Macmillan to leave. "Yeah, I said so."

"That's good," Bernice said. In her heart, she felt it was good, damn good Estelle would be away from Toronto — (although she could not then have known that Mrs. Macmillan lived outside the city) — but she felt it was better than having her recuperate too near to the evil influence of Henry, of Agatha, of Dots and of Brigitte, and of course too close to Mr. Burrmann. "I hope it wouldn' put you out, Mistress Macmillans. But as I always say, a little rest and a little holidays do not do any harm to anybody."

"The *very* thing I been telling this child! You hear me,

darling? Come up to Timmins with me, I says. Up there
you will get a lot of swimming in the lakes, I says to her.
We could go to the provincial parks, we could go fishing, I
says, and you see me here, darling? I am a better fisherman
than my old man, my husband, than most men. And I
betcha ya never had a taste of moose-meat where you come
from? Jamaica, ain't it?"

"Barbados," Bernice corrected her.

"The Barbados!" Mrs. Macmillan laughed heartily; her
two hundred-odd pounds shook from her breasts down to
the barrels of thick fat round her waist. The chintz housedress rippled like waves. "I'm forgetting. Sometimes, I'm
forgetful as hell, you hear me, darling?"

Other visitors had come in. Stealthily, as if their patient-
friends, or patient-wives or patient-girlfriends were still in
the clandestine act of aborting; as if the ward was some
section of a prison, or an isolation ward for incurable con-
tagious diseases. A minister of the church came in, looked
round at the three women, bowed and made the sign of the
cross for their benefit. He smiled. He came over to them.
He handed each a small religious pamphlet. And he moved
on to see after the spiritual well-being of the other patients.

The moment he was out of hearing distance, Mrs. Macmillan swore and then tore up her pamphlet, dropped it
into Estelle's wastepaper basket, and said, still heaving with
joviality, "Excuse me for butting in on your visit, darling. I
have to go to the john. And then I gotta call my old man."
She eased herself down, like a gigantic form of Jell-O, from
the bed. She grabbed Bernice's arms and said, "Let me see
you again before you leave, you hear me, darling?" And
then she left.

"Well?" It was a long time before Bernice spoke. And
when she did, it was like a foghorn. Estelle had been sitting

silently for some time, longer than a normal conversation break allows. "I see you mekking friends already. Right and left." She put as much sarcasm in her words as she could. And Estelle recognized the tone of disapproval in her manner. But for the time being she ignored it. She felt that Bernice's presence signified, threatened even, gloomier news, so she would wait and hear it. On Bernice's part, there was still the heavy terrible immorality of abortion, even though it was she who had suggested it, and even though she was therefore responsible, to a large extent, for Estelle's being on this hospital bed. Bernice was such a woman, of such ambivalent and puritanical disposition, that she would not have criticized Estelle or anybody else had the abortion been successfully performed. What worried her, what was immoral to her, was that Estelle had to be taken to the hospital in an ambulance and that the public had to know; that Priscilla, a nurse on this ward, had to know. The public knowledge and the public exhibition worried her much much more than the private commission of the immorality.

Estelle did not see it this way. To her, it was "just blasted bad luck, one hell of a mistake," as she had told Mrs. Macmillan when instead of Priscilla's head and face hovering over her, as she came out of the coma, it was Mrs. Macmillan's. "One hell of a mistake that I hope never in my life to make again!"

"Well, how you feeling, Estelle?"

"Not too bad, Bernice."

"What the doctor say?"

"About what, Bernice?"

"Well, did he tell you if, and when, you coming out? This costs money, yuh know? You didn' come in here with no Blue Cross, nor no Physicians-and-Surgeons benefits! And every blasted day that you laying down here and licking your mouth with that woman, Mistress Macmillans, it is costing Bernice money. It is money outta my pocket. That is why I asked you what the doctor say?"

"The doctor say Thursday."

"Good! That is only a few days off. He say Thursdee, eh? Good." Bernice then thought of having to spend so much time waiting for Estelle to get dressed on Thursday, of all the money it would take to get her back to Forest Hill by taxicab, of all the time and the money she would have to spend on Estelle as she crept back to good health. And for one spiteful moment, she saw Estelle travelling by foot all the way to Marina Boulevard. But she soon put that brutality out of her head. "What else the doctor say, Estelle?"

"Like what?"

"Well, Jesus Christ!" Bernice did not realize that her voice was so loud, until a few patients and visitors nearby turned to look. She lowered her voice, and hissed, "Did he say if you are going to have the baby? Did he say you not going to have the baby? Did he say if you damage your womb? What what what? What the hell did he say to you, Estelle?"

"Nothing like that, Bernice."

"Nothing like that! Nothing like that! But you still haven' told me one damn thing, Estelle. What's your condition? If you do not tell me, who is going to inform me? Mistress Macmillans? Or do you want me to go and ask Priscilla, and make myself more 'shamed than I was when I brought you in here, bleeding like a, like a damn . . ."

"Bernice, the doctor say I am all right, man. All that happened is that I caused slight damage down here," and she patted herself below the abdomen, to indicate. "And that was fixed from the night I was admitted."

"You not pregnunt no more? Is that it?"

"No, Bernice."

"You not pregnunt no more with the baby, then?"

"No."

"Praise God! Praise God for that! But you sure? Well, that's good!" And for the first time during her visit, she felt she could relax and smile a genuine smile. "I can't tell you how good I feel to hear that you lost that child, girl. I don't think you're able to understand the trouble you was letting yourself in for, in this place. And the winter soon come, too. No open-air clotheslines to hang-out diapers on, baby carriage to think of and buy, and those things so blasted dear and expensive! Child? And then there is baby food, 'cause the mothers in this country don't breast-feed no children these days. That is old-fashion, things of yesteryear that people back home are still doing. But not up here in Canada. And you can't work when you have the baby, small. You don't have no job, no baby-benefits; and even so, the paltry six dollars or so a month that the government puts in your hand for upkeep and having the child isn' enough for child-support. You won't be able to afford to pay baby-sitter and nursery school at the same time, and on top o' that, with no man to support you . . ."

Here she paused to think. And Estelle thought she saw the thought forming itself. She worried that Bernice would ask her about Sam Burrmann. The thought flashed across Bernice's brows, and her brows took on a deep worrying furrow. It was coming at last, Estelle was certain. And she prepared herself for it. But all Bernice said was, "Estelle, you remember me telling you that this place is not fit for a single woman who is black to live in, all by herself? Well, now you understand. You would understand it more if that child was still in your womb. And though I would have liked you to get this experience, because you couldn' blame nobody but yourself for bringing this experience on yourself, still as your sister, I couldn' wish such a terrible judgment on you." She took a deep breath and continued, "You see all the adoption agencies they have in this city? Well, I will tell you the reasoning behind them. They is Caffolick, Anglican, Jewish and Protestants. And *all* of them are full-up to the top with unwanted kids. That's what they call them in this country, *unwanted children.* Back home we calls them *outside-children.* Back home we does cherish children! never mind they born outside wedlock, but be-Christ, they born *inside love!* Now, in spite of all these agencies being full-up to the brink, the Canadian girls're still going out on the streets and getting pregnunt with *more* unwanted children and bringing them and putting them on the doorstep o' these adoption places. Or else they throwing their children in lakes, or as I read in the papers the other day, in sewers. You can find some in garbage pails, in incinderators in the big big luxuriant apartment buildings all over this city. All this I read in the papers. And now that I am on the subject, I may as well confess to you, that one day you had me so vex with you and your bad behaviour, that I wished God would have put such a burden on you, just because of your damn own-wayness. But God is a good God!" She wagged her head from side to side, as she said that. "God don't like ugly, Estelle. I am sure sure that if I could talk to God, if I had that power o' speech to speak to God, and if I was really sure that God was listening, if I was a real christian-minded person, I know He would tell me that what I wished for you wasn' no unfair wish at all, because you was heading that way anyhow." Estelle wasn't listening. She had learned how to plug her ears and her attentiveness against Bernice's harangues. "But I am glad that you come out the way you have come out, clean."

"I glad too, Bernice."

"Look what I brought for you." And she opened the
large shopping bag with Eaton's printed on it; and she
showed Estelle six large juicy-looking red apples, a dozen
grapefruits, two large bars of Cadbury chocolate, a carton
of cigarettes and a package of chewing gum. "I bring these,"
she said, somewhat unnecessarily. "Where you want me to
put them?" She was already unloading them on the table
beside the bed, when she noticed the vase of red roses. "A
dozen roses?" she said surprised, though impressed. "Wait,
who could be wasting their money on you? A dozen roses
cost a fortune! I buy them sometimes for Mistress Burrmann . . . a whole dozen? Who send them for you?" Before Estelle answered (and she didn't know what to say),
Bernice was searching the table to see if a card had come
with the roses. A card did come. But Estelle had already destroyed it. "Estelle, who senning these roses to you? Who
else know that you are in here? . . . besides me and Brigitte, who knows?"

"Brigitte send the roses, Bernice."

"Christ, I told Dots that Brigitte was a real friend!
That's nice o' Brigitte." She was relieved. "But I thought
it was *he*. Anyhow, I don't want to upset you by talking
'bout him. You's a sick girl. But when you get better, I
hope you would think-up something, some plan or some
action concerning your life and what you intends to make
out of it in Canada. And I trust I won't have to ask you,
nor tell you, what that action is going to be. You understand me?"

"Yes, Bernice."

"You really understand what I driving at?"

"I understand, Bernice."

"Good!"

Estelle wished Bernice would drop dead, would leave,
disappear, and never come back. She wished this afternoon

was that afternoon she was to leave for Timmins with Mrs. Macmillan.

"Henry get beaten-up." Bernice introduced this new subject because she felt she had gained enough compliance from her sister; and being herself a woman of a sensitive nature, although she could be very hard and heartless at times, she thought that this new gossip would provide some consolation for Estelle. "Henry got beaten-up."

"No! By who?"

"Running after somebody-else woman. Fooling round with the wrong woman, a man's woman. Heh-heh-heeee! he got some good lashes too!" She said it as if it was a blessing, long overdue.

"We Henry?" Estelle asked. "*Our* Henry?" she said, correcting her grammar.

"Two police. Not one. Two! And I sure he get a good stiff, cut-arse from them. Because, if what I see on television is true, and the television don't lie, Estelle, it don't lie . . . if them two police beat him *half* as proper as that television shows me is the manner that police does beat coloured people in Canada and in the States, well, be-Christ, Estelle, Henry got a *thorough* cut-arse!"

"Yuh lie!"

"I can't say it didn' serve him right. Them two police tarred his backside proper. One eye swell-up big big big, the other one black-and-blue, and Henry stiff from head to foot, all over." She paused to permit Estelle time to take in all this violence, and to relish it, before she added, "It took place in front o' me, on Marina, the same night you was bleeding your poor self to death. Opposite. That's where this stradegy take place. Brigitte had him up in her room. Doing what she likes to do with men. And no sooner than Henry put back on his trousers, I guess, no sooner than he peeped out through that alleyway leading from the stairs to that harlot's bedroom, and he reached the road, bram! the two police jumped him and commence to paint his arse, blam! blam! *blam!* . . . Christ, Estelle, I think I still hearing them blows right now."

"Did you know it was Henry all the time?" The question took Bernice by surprise.

"Well, I don't mean to say I actually heard the beating," she said, "but what I mean is that he got such a proper licking, and the damage done to his face and features is so brutal and so bad to look at, that anybody seeing his face in this situation would swear that they was seeing it when it happened."

"Oh!" Estelle said. Bernice was relieved.

"According to Dots, and you can't always take everything Dots say as the gospel, but Dots did say that Henry borrow a car from Boysie, and went up there unknown to Boysie, smelling round Brigitte. Seems, if you put two and two together, that cut-arse was earmarked for nobody else but Boysie. But God works in a damn mysterious way. Boysie born lucky. But it ought to teach him a lesson."

"This is a terrible place." She grabbed her stomach, feeling for the child she hoped was still there.

"That isn' the word for it, darling."

"Toronto is a cruel place."

"Though still, if a man is going with a woman, and that woman turned out to be deceitful and unfaithful to him, it still don't stand to reason that that man, if he is any human-being at all, if he have a *ounce* o' blood in his veins, he still shouldn' take up himself and lay-wait for the other man and beat him so unmercifully as I saw how them two white police beat Henry and nearly slaughter that poor man . . . man, they pounce down on top o' Henry, kicked Henry down to the ground, and when they see that they had Henry down, down down down, good-Jesus-Christ-have-mercy! the man was in the gutter panting from the blows and begging for mercy from the *whomps*, still those two heartless Toronto police went on beating Henry as if he was a snake . . . one police turned his heel round and round on Henry chest, and the next bastard stomped him in his in-gut . . . regardless who the man was, a Jew, a DP-immigrant, a coloured man, a Wessindian, even the worst nigger, I still say that white people is nothing but . . ."

"You said you saw it happen?"

"You calling me a liar, Estelle? I never said such a thing."

"You said a minute ago, correct me if I am wrong, but you said *and beat him so unmercifully as I saw how them two white police beat Henry and nearly slaughter that poor man*, and you said he *was in the gutter panting from the blows and begging for mercy from the whomps* . . ."

"Well, I didn' mean it that way," Bernice lied. She knew she was slipping. She knew also she couldn't afford the disclosure that she had sat at her window and had witnessed the two homosexuals pass, without their dogs, late that night; that she had seen Boysie's car park in front of the house, opposite, where Brigitte worked; that she had seen the police cruiser park behind Boysie's car; that she had seen the two policemen waiting in the shadows; and that she had seen them beat Henry, drag him from the alleyway, drop him in his car, and then drive away. And she had seen one of the policemen return in the cruiser, she saw him go up to Brigitte's room, and come back outside; and she had even called Brigitte late that same night to find out whether it was really Boysie down there in the beaten car. She had done this because she thought she heard the man being mauled by the policemen scream, "*Goddamn!*" and it was only then that she knew the man could not be Boysie, or was it Henry . . . because Henry was the only person she knew who said goddamn like that. Anyhow, she was determined to hide all this from Estelle. All this evidence of fear. Fear of implication. Fear of disclosure. Fear of criticism. Fear of allegiance. And relating the story to Estelle, she knew she had to conceal her participation in the beating, her observation of it from her window because of a new reason, a new fear: the fear of deceit. "I didn't mean it that way, Estelle."

"All right, Bernice. I understand." Bernice knew Estelle was too perceptive to be deceived. She felt she should change the conversation; and did, but Estelle wasn't paying attention. She was thinking of the days ahead.

It is the early hours of morning. In most of the taxicabs near the Toronto General Hospital, the drivers are loitering or dozing until the tap-tap-tap of drunken or late-night workers rouses them. The hospital is quiet. It is as inbred and unloquacious as Chinatown nearby, as stealthy and secretive as the male orderly who kisses the night nurse behind the medicine cabinet, in the security of the lowered lights on the sixth floor ward. There is an occasional tiptap-tip of a nurse reluctantly and sleepily going to a bed to take a bedpan for the bed-ridden; or administering medicine for the health-ridden. A woman snores. A woman cries out loud in her distant sleep from the harmless bottom of a dream, dreamed in the dungeons of fever and delirium. A radio is humming, reminding the night nurse through her passion that it is now off the air. Outside the ward, the noise of taxicabs comes up with the breeze and does not quite enter the uneasiness of the resting sick. A woman sleeps with the sheets over her head, imitating and anticipating the time when the night nurse will do that last decency for her when her hour is up, when her life and night are like death. Another woman sleeps with the reading lamp as strong as a candle, burning above a whispering, gargling head. If the nurse whose duty it is to be on duty, and who is coming to the head of her violent, hectic and stolen boredom with the orderly, had a better vision or a stronger sense of responsibility, she would see that at the west end of the ward, there are two women lying in their neighbouring beds, holding over to be closer to their whispering, so as not to wake the light, malicious sleeper on the left, so as not to rouse the night nurse and have her come and cross-examine them as to their history and convalescence and insomnia. The two women are Mrs. Joseph Macmillan and Estelle. They are talking in low voices, in a kind of abbreviated, note-taking conspiracy.

"Didn't tell her?" Mrs. Macmillan whispered, referring to Bernice. Estelle shook her head, to signify no; and Mrs. Macmillan continued to whisper, "Sensible thing to do, hear me, darling? You was wise not to."

"Bound to hear some time, though. She must."

"Leave that till when it happens. And the doctor? Didn't say what the doctor said?"

"Nothing 'bout the doctor."

"Sensible thing too. Now, listen. I getting outta this slaughter-house in two days. Going home. Timmins. You promised. Coming up day after me, right?" Estelle wasn't too certain about the wisdom or the practicality of this suggestion to go to Timmins with Mrs. Macmillan. She couldn't picture herself so far up north, even more north than Toronto already was from her Barbados. And having to live among all those children? Mrs. Macmillan's ten children, who because they were born in thirteen years would still be very screaming, peeing, clawing children for such a long time! After so many months, since she had arrived by Air Canada, she still couldn't wipe the memory of that jeering child's face from her mind. She would lie in bed sometimes, long after the other patients were subdued by pain and sleep, and she would see that small boy's face as clearly as that cold winter day when he looked up and called her *Aunt Jerimima*. It did not soften her hurt that the child meant "Jemima." The name had been reinforced with a certain obvious perniciousness since she had been living in Canada, reiterated by the constant visual references to it on the television programmes which dealt with the racial disturbances in Harlem and Chicago and Watts during that summer. Estelle could not therefore allow herself to be exposed to a situation where she could conceivably come up against this incident without having the psychological buffet of the nearness of Bernice and Dots and Boysie and Henry, and the other hundreds of unknown West Indians she met on the street and at the West Indies Federated Club, which everybody called the WIF. They were complete strangers, but friends by the common origin of their colour. ("Any blasted nasty nigger on the street, is a friend o' mine, *just* because I am black?" Perhaps yes; perhaps no.) And a simple thing like having Priscilla, the black nurse on this ward, so close to her made all the difference to Estelle. Priscilla's presence gave her more strength than anybody on that ward, including Mrs. Macmillan, could imagine. For the fact was, this was the first time white hands had ever touched her black body in the function and the performance of cleaning it, or even giving it food. *Priscilla herself never once attended to me; never once asked me if I want a bedpan; she make damn sure that there is always another nurse, a white nurse, to administer medicine and advice to me, blind her! that Priscilla touches only white patients . . .* There were no white nurses in Barbados.

Estelle was ruminating on all these new things in her life

here while Mrs. Macmillan was getting anxious, worried
that she hadn't heard her talking to her. "You promised,
darling," Mrs. Macmillan was saying, adhering to the short-
hand of her way of speech. "Timmins, best place for you.
Summer, there. Fish cheap. Fresh air. Lots o' rest. That's
what your doctor want you to have." For a moment, Estelle
thought she was telling her about the West Indies, but Mrs.
Macmillan had neglected to mention, or had never considered, the sun, and Estelle knew she was hearing about
the north again. She could not make up her mind. She knew
she couldn't go back to live with Bernice, and in Mr. Burrmann's home. Oh no, she couldn't do that. Mr. Burrmann
hadn't even come to visit her, although he called every day
at six o'clock, and he had sent the bouquet of red roses
which Bernice had seen. Estelle knew it was all over between she and Sam Burrmann. It had happened so many
times in her life in Barbados, and in the lives of her sisters,
or aunts, or cousins, as many times in history. Once reading
a book she found somewhere she came across the identical
case. A Barbadian case. The book was talking about the
early life of Sir Conrad Reeves, the "first black Chief Justice
of Barbados." And that was back in the days when Sir Conrad's father was a white doctor, and his mother a black slave
woman, back in the days when . . . *it was the lot of most
West Indian women in general who form part of matri-
archal societies, that Peggy had to find some means of keeping the boy alive on her meagre resources. There was no poor
and bastardy laws; and it was inconceivable and illegal to
think of taking the doctor to court for maintainance of
young Conrad. Both she and Conrad were simply expected
to exist. Dr. Phillip Reeves was a bachelor, and he lived
alone. Peggy would have welcomed going to bed with the
master of the house inasmuch as it had meant the customary
promotion from the cane fields. Catching the doctor's eyes*

was easy for a young buxom slave like Peggy. Already she had possessed most of the characteristics which all white men had traditionally fancied in coloured women. Jesus Christ! she thought, what a terrible truth! The truth does really hurt. Remembering this passage now, after so many years, she shuddered with the terrible heavy knowledge of fact that Peggy's case was identical to hers, except in one detail. Whereas Peggy worked for the master, Dr. Reeves, she, Estelle, was the sister of the master's slave, Bernice. "Jesus Jesus Jesus!" she said, and Mrs. Macmillan heard.

"What *did* you say?"

"I was just thinking, just thinking. 'Bout life. Repeating itself. Like a circle, a small circle."

"You right as hell, you hear me, darling?" The first light of morning was coming through the windows of the ward. Two nurses were already sponging the immovably sick with washrags and warm water; and some who could creep and shuffle to the washrooms were throwing their housecoats on their shoulders, and fumbling into their new slippers. Mrs. Macmillan felt she could talk louder now that there was more activity in the ward, and she began to repeat much of what she had said earlier when it was only dawn, because Estelle might have been listening only between the uncertain pauses between sleep and waking. Estelle was thinking: why did she tell Bernice she was not still pregnant? and why did she not tell Bernice she was really being discharged in two days on Wednesday instead of on Thursday? and why did she seriously tell Mrs. Macmillan she would consider going to Timmins to convalesce? And to all these things Estelle wondered why she had to lie; although she was sure, in fact she was positive, she would never go to Timmins.

Satisfied that drowsiness had done nothing to take away Estelle's attentiveness, Mrs. Macmillan raised her two hun-

dred pounds from the moaning bed and sat up, leaving her
feet, bare and white as two small ghosts, hanging a few feet
above the floor. Her mouth was stiff and her palate dry, so
she drank some of the stale water in a glass on her bedside
table, wallowed it round and round noisily in her mouth,
and then swallowed it. "Now!" she said, ready for Estelle
and for a long heart-to-heart talk. "You listen to what I
have to say, girl. I been down here much longer than you.
And a woman like me who went through childbirth twelve
times and who experienced pregnancy four more times
above those twelve, well after all, she isn't a person without
some experience and common sense. And because I happen
to have a wedding band on this hand" (she held it up to
Estelle's face like an accusation of spinsterhood and tainted
virginity), "it does not mean that I didn't get in a mess the
same way you did. You hear me, darling? I will bet you anything you name, that there is more married whores in here
with wedding bands, than single girls like you. And that is
the long and the short of it. You have all your life still in
front of you. You are young. One mistake do not equal a
death, or failure. Without mistakes, a woman isn't a woman.
And mistakes is experience. What you told me about your
sister and the situation where she works made me conclude
that you have to find somewhere else to live until you are on
your feet again. And girl, you hear me, darling? This country
is not a place where you could exist without a little help.
You hear me? And it is help that I am offering you. You
hear me? You ain't the first and like hell! you won't be the
last woman to have a child for a man who you love and
who turned round and pissed on your love afterwards, and
who tell you that he intends to marry you, and to do this
and do that for you, and then pissed on you after he put you
this way." (Estelle could not endure the double indemnity
of her mistake by admitting to Mrs. Macmillan, who after

all was a stranger, that the man was already married. She told her only that he was her sister's employer. But it didn't fool Mrs. Macmillan, although she never let on that she knew more than Estelle told her.) "Look, I know a few people in Timmins. Timmins is a small town. I was born and raised in Halifax myself, but I know more people in Timmins because it is a friendly little town. I make you a promise that by the time you come up, in two days, after you come by train, I make you a promise that I will have a job waiting for you in one of the hotels, or at one of the resort places, or even in a restaurant run by a friend of mine, a friend of my old man's. Girl, look, you are *different* from the rest of the people in Timmins. You look exotic, and you aren't exactly what you might call a bad-looking girl neither. In fact, you're beautiful as hell. And the way that men in the north look at beautiful and exotic women, like the Indian women! I swear to you that if you work behind a counter selling coffee, or even at the cash register as the cashier, that restaurant or that hotel or that resort would make more money, more business than it ever made in a whole summer full of American tourists! And you must get through, then . . . you understand what I say?"

All this impending adventure, all this strangeness, all this new life about to open in the north frightened Estelle. It went right down to the bottom of her guts like a stomachache. She didn't have chick nor child in Canada, except her sister Bernice, who although she would not welcome Estelle on her discharge from the hospital, yet she would scream like hell should she hear that Estelle was really going up to Timmins to spend time with a complete stranger. Bernice would see more visions of northern men and beasts and mooses and bears raping Estelle, and taking advantage of her, than the Grimm brothers could imagine in a ghost story! Bernice would not believe that Estelle was grown up

enough to be able to take care of herself — although Estelle
was twenty-nine years old — mainly because of what had
happened to her already, and because of what had laid her
out in this hospital bed with her present problem. Estelle
was a child to Bernice; and a child she would always remain,
so long as she lived in Canada. But Bernice didn't know
that Estelle was now a landed immigrant, meaning she was
free to go and come as she pleased, free to take any job she
could get. Estelle had kept this trump card hidden the same
way she hid the date of her discharge. It had taken Sam
Burrmann only two days after her admittance to the hospital to work out the immigration difficulties with his con-
tact in the Bedford Road immigration office. Normally, it
took a West Indian months, and in some cases years. But
he said he would do it for her, and he did. It was a side of
his character Estelle had not known before; and she was
sorry that she could not have found out more good qualities
about him. She had condemned him completely, not merely
because he had got her pregnant — she was partly to blame
for that too — but mainly because he had tried to convince
her that it was Boysie or Henry who had got her pregnant.
Estelle detested Boysie; and she was too close to Agatha to
horn in on Henry.

Meanwhile, Mrs. Macmillan made another effort to influence her. "I know things are hard as hell, you hear me?"
Estelle nodded. "And it has nothing to do with the fact that
you aren't a Canadian like me. I was born here. This country is mine. And by-God, sometimes, I have to sit down
and wonder if it is really so. Bloody foreigners and the
Italians particularly, in a small town, own this country, you
hear me, darling? Foreign people in charge of the mines up
north. They take charge of the resort areas. They own the
clubs, the hotels, and by-God, today in Timmins you can
see as many foreign faces on the city council as you can see

local faces. I was born in Halifax, in a place next door, jutting and butting on Africville where your people, coloured people, been living for generations. And the little amount of high school I managed to get before I found myself with my first child I was playing with coloured children at school. I grew up with coloured children. They was decent coloured folks, too! Some of them even made good in life, and I know one fellow who is a lawyer today in Halifax. Lemme tell you something about my life. When I was pregnant with Nancy, that's my first child, I was seventeen. Joe was eighteen. Neither he nor me had ever worked for a living 'cepting summer jobs, which as you know, or may not know, is the custom in this country being that most high school kids work during the summer months, July, August and September. Well, anyways. I was living at Joe's people. My own mother and father threw me out. But today we own the house we live in. Joe drives a truck for a large firm. The first three of my kids, Nancy, Peter and Anne, all are going to Timmins Collegiate. I worked in a factory for ninety cents an hour. Joe at that time was bringing in a dollar fifteen, eight hours a day, six days a week. But praise God, today, today he could come home anytime and sit down in front of his television and watch hockey with a bottle of beer in his hand, without worrying where the next meal is going to come from to feed twelve mouths. That's what I call being free. I love a large family, darling. I hope you get a large one too. There's no more fun in this world than to sit down when those supper dishes are done and everybody is warm and stuffed-full with food, it could even be potatoes! And you hear your kids talking and playing and arguing — or as we often do, in the winter, get round that old piano and have a sing-song. There's television in Timmins now, we have our own station — don't mind half of what you hear is in French! But the north is a bright country, and if you don't know French, well by-God, you would have to learn French then, eh? Anybody can learn French. If you don't want to learn French, well, don't watch television in French and don't learn French." She passed her hand under the belly of her housecoat, and slid down from the bed. "I am going to wash up. When I come back, tell me that you decide to come up north with me, you hear me, darling?" And she left in a clean action, as if there was no reference to what had been talked before.

Estelle admired her. Such a powerful, determined, sure woman! She saw some of Bernice's aggressiveness in her. Perhaps that was why Bernice didn't take to her when they first met. On Bernice's part, however, there was no obligation of friendliness nor of friendship: she was not in need of the kind of advice and moral support Mrs. Macmillan was resourceful in, and which was a great consolation, if not assistance, to Estelle. With Mrs. Macmillan gone merely a few yards away, merely on a visit to the washroom, a great loneliness came over Estelle. She had come to depend so much upon her; and her dependence was the greater since Mrs. Macmillan was the first woman in Canada in this hospital, white or black, who offered friendship based upon nothing more than the fact that she liked Estelle. "Girl, you are in a hell of a mess!" she had said, when they got talking the first time. "And you look like a straight kid. I could tell from the instant you came in." Estelle did not know that she had screamed in her sleep that first night, when they brought her back from the operating room, and after the sedative had worn off. It was Priscilla who had given it to her, following the emergency operation. Bernice had left by then.

With Mrs. Macmillan still away washing up, Estelle had time to face herself, and to try to remember and redraw that part of her life which began that night she hemorrhaged. She made an attempt to get up and go to the wash-room herself, but realizing that this was a subconscious desire to be near to Mrs. Macmillan, she lay back down instead and pulled the covers high, up to her chest. She looked at the ceiling of the ward, and saw that it was spot-less. She would spend many hours staring at the ceiling: *This ceiling is clean, everything about this hospital is clean. But it is dead, and the people in this ward are dead although they are living. I don't know what it would be like if I was in this place in the winter! I have to thank God for that at least.* (She recognized an echo of Mrs. Macmillan's words in her own self-conversation; and she changed it to:) *I am going to pack up and head straight back to Barbados where I come from, for home, as soon as I get out of this place. Imagine coming to Toronto on a holiday, and ending up in a blasted hospital cot! A woman gets herself in some-thing, like going out with a man, and then she finds out he is a married man and she tells herself that she is too good, too decent, too well-brought-up, she is too much to con-tinue seeing that man, when deep down in her heart she knows she loves him still, and anyhow there is a certain thing, a certain something, a daring, a security that Sam was a married man; and he knows about women, that he would treat me nice, and understand, because he didn't put a ring on my finger, and I know that, and I could have al-ways hurt him and reminded him when he got on damn fresh with me about anything that I was not his goddamn wife. I was not Mistress Burrmann, the bitch he left at home. I could have done all this to him. But it is too late now, too damn late now to start to think about these things. Crying over spilt milk, as Mrs. Macmillan would say, don't solve nothing. But when I get out, I am going straight back to Barbados where I come from. Or I could remain a little longer here, and work as a nurse's aide since Sam already fixed up my papers for me. That was good of him. I can't understand that man at all, at all. One minute he treats me like a whore, the next minute he treats me like the Queen. That bastard even sent me three silk nightgowns, slippers and a housecoat. And some money. Well, it must be his blasted conscience! And the roses* . . . (She looked at the roses, and she rearranged them although the nurse who had brought them in from the outside where they always spent the night had done that already. She ran her fingers lightly, affectionately, over the roses, all twelve, as she used to run her fingers over Sam's face, with deep affection and deep love. Her next thoughts were on her unborn child. Thinking about its life, and its death: did she already deform it? Did she tamper with its natural growth? *Wonder if he will look like his damn father? Christ, I hope I don't born no damn red-nigger-child! I couldn't stand my child to have no blasted picky-picky red hair. Rather he come out light-skinned, and with hard hair like Bernice-own, heh-heh* . . . *my son, my son! imagine me having a son in Canada, my son, my child* . . . and she broke off, and broke down crying, sobbing and crying with spasms of sadness and happiness mingled with the tears streaming down her face.

"Oh my poor girl!" It was Mrs. Macmillan. "Why're you doing that to yourself?"

"My son, my son . . . I want to have my son . . . my little child, my first child . . . I hope my child forgive me . . ."

"You want a damn good spanking. Why not take your chance and go in the washroom now that that Catholick bitch ain't in there smelling up the place? Come, get up, get up! It still in there," she said, kindly, patting Estelle's stomach.

And she helped her to the washroom.

Boysie chuckled as if he was choking, and then he gave Henry an affectionate slap on his shoulder. "Gorblummuh! man, you is my real friend, in true. You even took a stiff cut-arse in my behalfs!" He chuckled again. Henry did not see it as a joke. His pains were still paining, and the bandages were on his head, one covering his right eye. "And look, since you's such a damn real friend, I am not even sorry, and I am not mad at all at all, that you was screwing my woman, Brigitte, behind my back, man!"

"Stop!" Henry warned him. He held the rum bottle poised, threatening to throw it at Boysie's head.

Boysie chuckled, and said, "Man, you's a bitch." He chuckled again, and imitating the blows which Henry got from the two policemen, he said, "*Whupp! Whhop! Whh-happ!*"

"Stop!"

"Man, I gotta tell you something. I am going to tell you something now, man. Gorblummuh! if them licks was in my arse, instead of in yourn, be-Christ, I would be in a damn funny position now, in regards to my wife, Dots. Man, but look at you, though! You's my friend, and screwing your own friend's woman? Man, I think you deserved to get them blows."

"Stop!"

"Okay, man, I going to stop. But before I stop, let me ask you one thing. What happened to all the story and the pictures you tell me the papers was going to print concerning you and the beating? I been watching every paper for three days now, and I haven' seen nothing appear 'bout a black man getting beaten up. Them papers-people fooling you, yuh! And I understand that you pay that lawyer-man a lot o' money already. One hundred dollars you gave the lawyer-man for doing nothing for you with the papers. You better go back for the money, boy."

"Who the hell are you calling *boy?*"

"Sorry, *man.*"

"The papers will print that story, Boysie. The papers got to print my story. They *have* to. That is justice. And justice got to be done, goddamn, or I will do something about it."

The pains in his head sent a throbbing of fury through his whole body. Delirium had kept him restless on his spinning bed last night. Hope was not yet dead, although the newspaper had not used the story the day after, as Mr. Turnbull, the reporter Agatha's lawyer had introduced to him, had assured him. Hope was the only thing he had to keep him going. And pride. But the fear of disappointment was deep-seated, more real than the hope or the pride. He had known many men who drank at the Paramount Tavern who had been beaten up by the cops; and some in the elevator in the main station on King Street East, near Church. One fellow told how the detectives stopped the elevator between floors and poured more licks in Sonny from Nova Scotia than what John the Baptist preached about. Henry told this to Boysie one night, when Boysie whistled across Spadina Avenue at a white woman who looked like a whore. That was soon after he had arrived in Canada. Henry warned him that if he was in any part of the South, he could be shot, lynched for even looking at that kind of a woman, even if she was a whore. And there was the case of the West Indian man, "I can't remember his fucking name," Henry was saying, "but that ain't fucking important, what is fucking important is that that fucking man stopped one fucking night when a fucking cop was giving a man a fucking ticket for speeding, or something. And when the fucking West Indian asked what's happening, that fucking cop left the man and walked over from the fucking cruiser and tell this West Indian, *Mind your fucking business, nigger! Get going! or I run you in!* And the fucking stupid West Indian, being a West Indian, asked the cop, 'Who the hell you calling a nigger, man?' Well, straightway, the cop pushed the man in the fucking cruiser, lock-on them handcuffs 'pon the man's fucking hand, went back and parked the man's car and drove off. And gorblummuh, when he brought back the West Indian to his own car, after half an hour, the West Indian's arse was black-and-blue with fucking licks. This is fucking Toronto, boy. The same as South Africa, cops-wise!"

"You know something?" Boysie said. "You said *fucking* fifteen times just to tell me this story."

"That's my fucking business, you motherfucker!"

"Sixteen and a half times, now!"

"Ffff-fuck off!"

Boysie was going to say seventeen times but he thought better of it.

Henry said it happened all the time. Henry knew. Many more people knew about it, but they kept quiet, because they were not involved. And there was another fellow, a sailor in the Canadian navy. This man came down the stairs from his wedding party, the same night he got married; and the cops took him in for "being drunk" and "causing a disturbance." And the licks again, it was licks again in that poor sailor's backside, Henry said. "The cops in this place is criminals, savages, they're worse than the fucking Nazzis, but godblindthem! let one of them touch me!" He had forgotten, in his anger, that he had already been touched, and not by one, but by two. As they were drinking in Henry's room, with Henry lying on the bed, he said, "You want to know something? I feel like getting up outta this bed right now, and walking down Yonge Street and smashing every goddamn store window down there. Then, I'm heading for

Queen's Park, and I killing every blasted politician there. And when I finish doing that, I have my gun, and be-Jesus Christ, I am killing every fucking cop that pass, and . . ."

"One more!" Boysie said, counting and chuckling.

"That is the way I feel. Goddamn! No goddamn cop should hit a man. No fucking police should ever put his hands on a man. And when he hit a black man, godblindme! he should be killed instantly. *Killed*. Right on the fucking spot!"

"You's a cruel bitch, Henry."

"Cruel? You ain' see me cruel, yet. All the time you see me laying-down here, drinking this rum, well this rum's putting a blasted demon in my brains, and it telling me things, more cruel than the things I just say to you, things that I tell myself I intend to do. You think I making fun? You think I'm not serious? Well, wait. Wait, Boysie. You will see, you will be reading all about me in the fucking papers, godblindthem! one o' these days. And on that day, they won't forget to print *me*, this time."

"You're cruel as arse."

"Have you ever heard about the Mafias? Well, since two or three days ago, I joined the Mafias. You can never know when a Mafia kill somebody. You never know that. It does be too clean a killing. Not until you read about it in the papers, the next year, and sometimes you never read about it at all. Boysie, there's a lot o' crime in this fucking city, and a lot o' murders that nobody don't know nothing about. And you telling me, godblindyou, Boysie, because you are talking like a fucking white man now . . . you're telling me that it isn't time for a black man to get some fun from killing people? Wait, you mean we so inferior? Everybody does it. Every day a white man does kill another white man and get away with it. And be-Christ, they never stopped killing black people. And nobody ever ask them about that corpse. Well, I am joining in that fun now. I's a black Mafias!"

"Gorblummuh, you's a black murderer."

"Man, how the hell you expect me to feel? You think I could take this lying down?"

"I expect you to feel bad, that is the truth. But you must realize that you bring it on yourself. You know, you are so damn cruel and hateful that you forget to admit even to me and not counting-in Dots now (because we is mens and there is certain things a man can't even express to his wife or his woman), but between men everything is usually in the open. And as I was saying, you haven't even admit to me that there was two police who put them blows in your behind."

"Two? Who tell you there was two, when I say there was three?"

"Bernice said two."

"How the hell would Bernice know? Anyway, Bernice is nothing but a bitch."

"Bernice admit to Dots on the 'phone yesterday that she was at the window and she saw you, and she saw two police. And she even told Dots she thought the man was me! Because it was my car . . ."

"Bernice is a fuck . . . is a liar."

"Not this time, boy, not this time! I was laying down beside Dots when I hear the phone ring and Dots get up angry as arse because Dots is one ignorant woman when she's sleeping. Man, for instance, if I come close to Dots when she is sleeping and say I start kissing-up Dots, for instance, which is a thing I stop doing long long ago, man, be-Christ don't you know Dots would start one big worthless screeling as if her own husband raping her? That is the kind o' woman, the kind o' stupid-arse woman Dots is when she's sleeping. So that when Dots wake up in the night, every-blasted-body must know. And I telling you now, that on that particular night when Bernice call, late late, past one o'clock, Dots was cussing Bernice stink-stink-stink. And I heard Dots say, '*But Bernice, Boysie right here 'side o' me, snoring like a damn hog.*' So Bernice might be a liar, but not this time."

"Bernice is a fool."

"She may be that."

"A blasted liar too!"

"Now, that she ain't. Not in this instant, boy, not in this instance." Boysie took another drink, a large one, because Henry had paid for the bottle, and he wanted to put a stiff financial lash in both Henry and the bottle. "It don't matter, gorblummuh! It do not matter to me, at all, at all, that you was getting a piece offa Brigitte on the sly and behind my back. But the lies, man, the lies. The blasted fabrications, as it is called. You was telling me lies all the time you was embracing me in friendship."

"I didn' tell you no lies, Boysie. Goddamn, what I say to you, if it sound like a lie and even if it is a lie, it is not a lie to me because I want it to turn out exactly just as I tell you. You understand what I saying? A man sits down in his bed at night, or during the day, and he sees his whole goddamn upside-down life skin a fucking somersault before his eyes. Goddamn, it take a fucking strong son of a bitch to admit failure, that he is a failure, and continue living in the middle o' that blasted failure. You is the first and only person living or goddamn dead that I ever had the guts to admit this much to. Goddamn, Boysie, a man don't admit he is a failure to his wife. He does lie, he lies like hell. And she does have to find out for sheself. He tells her he's working, that he's drawing money every week from some job; goddamn, sometimes, if he is a real failure, he even invents a

job and tells her every two months that he got a raise. That
kind o' man is me.

"It start with the bank accounts. I opened three, about
two or three bank accounts with two dollars in each. That
way I felt rich as shite. With all them bank books. And I
would make my own deposits . . . every week I would
write-in $1,000 with my own hand. One thousand! And it
end-up with this. But it ain't no lie, Boysie. As far as I understand my actions, and as far as my woman Agatha explain
them to me, because she is the one schooled and educated
in all these actions and things of the brain and mind, she is
what she calls an amateur psychologist . . . and as far as
I understand what she was telling me 'bout the way I been
acting lately, goddamn, it is no lie! A man goes through
these changes. Sometimes all the time, till he kicks the
bucket and dies; sometimes, for a space o' time, a short time.
I invented things, she says, because my imagination is too
powerful for my subconscious and for my social position at
the present time. It is not simply telling lies, man. I inten-
tionally invented these things because something out there
is keeping me from getting at these very things, and that
thing keeping me back isn't powerful enough to keep back
my imagination and my subconscious and convince me that
I don't already possess them things. I's a goddamn failure.
But I imagine that I ain't no goddamn failure. I am a man
with one hundred and forty thousand dollars in fucking
imaginary bank accounts! That is me! An imaginary man.
So, when I say that there wasn't two police but *three* who
throw them lashes in my backside that night, it means that
I am so fucking strong that it would have take three police,
not two o' them, three o' them fascist bastards to beat me.
You understand?

"And I am going to tell you something now, even if this

is a way of admitting that I did taste a piece o' Brigitte, even if I have to admit this bitter truth in your presence, Boysie, you my real bosom friend; I tell you, that had I not been a bit shaky from doing the two things I did in that blasted woman's room, namely, drinking and you-know-what, gorblummuh! them two sadistic bastards couldn't have licked me. Oh no! I would have given one o' them criminals a judo chop, *blam!*" (The bottle of rum bounced off when Henry struck the table. Boysie reached out and caught it. The rum did not fall: none was spilled. Boysie was frightened: and not only by the suddenness of the noise.) "You understand now?"

"I understand, and I don't understand."

"Long's you understand."

They poured themselves new drinks. And they drank in silence.

"You notice how fast this damn summer come and gone?" Boysie said, when the silence was too much for him. He was a very restless man. And silence to him was like undressing in front of a new woman he was going to screw. Silence exposed him against his will, also. "Before you look round, the summer gone. Winter here now, boy. Winter coming. Was a good summer, though."

"We did a lot o' things together this summer."

"Yeah. But now that the summer all but gone, I feel as if there is somebody up there, telling every man to prepare for the indoors. I even notice in the relatively short time I living in this country, that the winter does bring a neverending everlasting vexatiousness on all the white people faces. Be-Jesus Christ, I never knew a whole race o' people could appear and remain vexed and unhappy, all at the same time, all the time, all goddamn winter! For that one reason, I hope I never would be a white man, gorblummuh! I like my women and my drinks too much for that. Whatever they got that we don't have, and probably never would get, be-Jesus Christ, they could keep it! I don't want it. Boysie Cumberbatch, this ugly half-ignorant Bajan man, sitting down here with you firing this steam, I do not want one blast of their life. Let me live my life, with my people, because there is more fun in that."

Henry smiled, and said, "I have to agree."

And since there was agreement on such a fundamental issue, the silence descended again upon them, just as the leaves were falling.

"You hear Dots is leaving the Hunters?" Boysie said, when it was silent enough.

"Agatha told me."

"What you think?"

"She's free now. She could behave and feel free. Fuck the domestic scheme. No woman should have to leave the West Indies to come up here in this prejudiced, unfair, two-mouth, cold country to work as a servant for Jews and anglosaxons or whatever the hell they call them, wasps? What I saying is this. No black woman should work in a serving job for no fucking white man, in a white country, and in the same country these fucking white people don't want to rent you a room, or give you a job. All them West Indian politicians who arrange this scheme should be strung-up by their balls, or have their balls cut off, and then shot."

"You talking violence again. You getting back to the same thing you was talking when I first came here," Boysie said, pouring himself a drink. "But I tell you simply, that Dots is leaving the job. She looking for a new job now. Five days, five days Dots is looking in the *Star* and the *Tely*. She don't like the *Globe*. Says it is too much a white man paper. No kiss-me-arse job for her, a black woman, saving these notices put in by the Jews and the rich white people, asking for help. Tell me something now, why is it that only the Jews does put ads in the papers asking for help? You could answer that? Now, I don't want to be unfair to anybody, because there is good and rotten in every kiss-me-arse race and tribe. But why so many Jews willing to have black people slave for them, and so few ahmm . . . what you call them? . . . anglosections? Do you think it is the Jews who want to keep us in this shit, for good? I can't really believe that. Because they is a race who themselves see shit, at the hands o' Hitler and many others, kings and queens, and according to Brigitte, who as you know, is a German Nazzi herself, the Jews been seeing shit for as long as the world began. And Brigitte say something else too. Brigitte say that the people who squeeze the Jews balls was right to squeeze the Jews balls. And I tell her, that that couldn't be true, because it is the Jews who give the black man the first break, the Jew who, because o' the knowledge o' sufferation at the hands of the anglosections, help the black man in his struggle, against the present-day anglosections. I argued strong strong in favour of the Jew. Brigitte argued damn strong in favour 'gainst the Jew. I am ashamed as arse to tell you the bad things and names she call the Jews by, even the woman she works for, Mistress Gasstein."

"Brigitte knows what she talking about," Henry said. With his eyes, Boysie inquired what he meant by that; but Henry said no more in the way of explanation. "Brigitte is a German woman. She knows the Jews. Listen to what she telling you, boy. Perhaps, you are going to learn something 'bout the city o' Toronto, if you learn something 'bout the Jew. But it is a good thing that Dots leaving Rosedale. You don't belong up there. They're too fucking phony up there."

"Brigitte say Rosedale is the home of anglosections."

"But what about you? How's the job situation?"

"Well, I hope I wouldn' be idle for the whole winter. I

been talking to some fellas, who say things *is* really hard.
But they can't kill you. You gotta have a job, even if it is
collecting garbage. A man must get a job. I went round so
far to a paper-box-making place, a paint factory, a publish-
ing place for a job in the storeroom, and you know where I
went too? Gorblummuh, that morning, I dressed-off real
sharp, and I put on that white shirt after my wife spend
two hours ironing it, and gorblummuh, the seams in my
pants would cut down a maple tree in half. And I go into
that man's office, in the Maclean-Hunter building. On
Avenue Road . . . no, University Avenue. Jesus Christ,
Henry, I barely had time to get in the man's office, and before I could sit down, this kiss-me-arse white man tell me,
'Sorry, Mr. Cumberbatch. But we haven' no openings on
our janitorial staff or our cleaning staff.' God blind him in
hell! Who told him I was looking for a cleaning job on his
fucking staff? And I want to ask you now, I want to ask you
if by looking at me, you could see that I am a born cleaner?
Gorblummuh, no! You know what I mean? A man could
look at a complete stranger, and the way that stranger is
dressed, how he wearing his jacket, or his tie, or the way he
walks or talks, and you can say and be almost a hundred
per-cent correct that that man is a doctor or a lawyer or a
dentist, or a school teacher, and you would be right, judging
from that man's appearance. But be-Jesus Christ, that white
man from Maclean-Hunter didn' have that kind o' knowledge in regards to my appearance. And still, he was brave
enough, certain that I was a cleaner by appearance. And I
was dress-off in a kiss-me-arse collar and tie! Man, road-
sweepers and scavengers back home in Barbados don't wear
no fucking collar and tie."

"That is your image, baby," Henry said. "Your image.
And though he only offered you a cleaner's job, the image
you give him still did frighten his arse! You see, Boysie, by

your coming out to meet that man in white shirt and collar
and tie, you frightened his arse, because you's like a crab
crawling outta your fucking shell. You confront that man
in a new shell, and your shell-less image sent such a fear in
his arse, that he had to refer you back to the only image he
ever had of you, namely, that you is a cleaner-crab. Dots,
your wife is a . . . was a cleaner-crab, until recently. And
you just told me that she decide to stop being a cleaner-crab.
Estelle, God help her! when she does come outta the hospital, she too will be a cleaner-crab. And it don't matter if
them women is maids, domestics, nurses' nurssaides, cooks,
kitchen-helpers, be-Christ, they is all cleaner-crabs. That is
the image."

Mrs. Macmillan was excited the whole morning. She was
to be discharged at two in the afternoon. And she had spent
the whole of this Wednesday morning packing her clothes
and talking to Estelle, reassuring her that the best thing
to do, the best decision she could ever make, was to come
to Timmins straightaway. Estelle was now to be discharged
on Thursday, instead of Wednesday. Even Mrs. Macmillan's discharge had been delayed.

Estelle nodded her head, said, "Yes, yes," as many times
as Mrs. Macmillan asked her if she was really coming up on
Thursday, and inwardly she felt isolated even although it
was still a few hours before two o'clock.

"I feel bad leaving you all by your lonesome in this
dump," Mrs. Macmillan said, noticing the beginnings of
grief in Estelle's expression. "I feel bad, you hear me darling?
But if you take my advice, first thing tomorrow morning,
you take a cab to the railway station, Union Station, and
you ask anybody in a uniform where to take a train going
north to North Bay and Timmins. And you get on that
train. It ain't going to take you more than twelve hours or

so to leave all this damn hospital smell and this unfriendly city of Toronto behind you. Don't forget. The train you want is the CN going to North Bay. At North Bay, you will transfer on a next train called the ONR, that is the Ontario Northland Rails. I am taking that same train now. Joe couldn't come all the way down here in the car because that costs money, and anyways, I am not too weak that I can't go by train. Furthermore, I have this to give me strength," she said, turning back her housecoat in the corner of her valise, and showing Estelle the bottle. "You see that? A bottle of gin." And she laughed. "If it wasn't against regulations, I would pour half in your water jug. Come, let me pour half of this in that jug for you. It is the same colour. And it is a damn sight better." She read Estelle's thoughts correctly. She moved swiftly like a thief, and in no time, half of the bottle of Gordon's Dry Gin was in Estelle's water jug, exposed to the public eye of nurse and patient and visitor. "Leave it there, darling. Nobody won't suspect that it is what it isn't, and not what it is."

"I'm sorry you going."

"Estelle, don't be sorry. Be glad. You must be glad. Because that way, you would want to come up to Timmins much much more. And don't forget that when you arrive at Timmins, I'll be there. Take the night train. The one leaving Union Station at midnight. That way, you can sleep most of the journey and wake up fresh and see some of our beautiful north country. I will be at the railway station with the car." After that, she had to go to the nurses' office, just off the ward in the hallway, to check certain things: sign a piece of paper admitting that she was leaving, and that she was taking all her clothes and other things she bought and had brought with her, and check on the dosage and the correct name of the medicine the doctor had prescribed.

Estelle remained sitting in bed, watching the gin in the

bottle mixed with the water, wondering when she would
have the chance to sip some of it, whether she would have
the courage to break the hospital regulation.

Mrs. Macmillan came back just in time to be discharged.
Estelle waited with her lunch to share that last intercourse
of friendship with her; but Mrs. Macmillan scorned the
lunch, at the same time being careful not to hurt Estelle's
feelings. "Girl, I am discharged now. And I discharge this
damn tasteless hospital food, too. You yourself won't be
eating it much longer. I will have some trout fish waiting
for you in Timmins. And some moose steaks." But she still
had time to wait, to sit for a while and talk with Estelle.
They didn't discuss the trip to Timmins anymore, they
merely talked little things that women sometimes talk when
they are waiting for a bigger event than the one during
which this kind of talk is taking place.

They gossiped about the nurses: who were the mean ones,
who were the kind ones, and who were the good ones; and
who, among the patients, in their opinion, unmedical but
certain, would not live to be carried out of this ward in a
wheelchair. And Mrs. Macmillan said something which
stunned Estelle. It contradicted a basic belief of hers, based
on the presumption that white people, because they were
over there, on one side, did not notice (they didn't have the
time) what was happening on the other side, on her side,
on Bernice's side, on Nurse Priscilla's side. Mrs. Macmillan
said, making her statement sound like a question, "But tell
me girl, honestly, why that coloured nurse never once in the
week you've been here so far, why she never once came to
your bedside and said goodmorning, or goodnight? She
never even brought you a bloody bedpan!" Estelle wasn't
sure she could tell Mrs. Macmillan the real reason. And
even after Mrs. Macmillan left, and while Estelle watched
her being wheeled out of the ward, and watched the elevator

indicator going down down down into the lounge, and when she saw her from the window on the sixth floor, get into the taxicab on Gerrard Street, and move off; and when she waved, although she knew that Mrs. Macmillan was thinking of her home in Timmins, still Estelle was not certain she herself knew the reason. But she promised, before she was herself discharged, to find it out.

The rest of this Wednesday afternoon reminded her of the hours she had been detained in the inner glass-walled office in the immigration section up at Malton International Airport, the night she arrived in this country. This was a sad afternoon. That night was no less sad. Mrs. Macmillan knew what she was doing when she offered her the gin. Before Estelle drank any, she made sure that there was chewing gum in the drawer of her bedside table. "That woman!" she said, full of admiration for Mrs. Macmillan. "That blasted woman! I feel I lost her, now!" A tear escaped from her eyes. "She's the only friend I can say I have."

Dots had it all planned. The fertility of her plan startled her own husband. Bernice, when she was told about it on the telephone, was no less astonished. Neither Bernice nor Boysie had ever considered Dots to be a woman of such imagination. And perhaps she wasn't, and had never herself felt she had this facility. Not because she did not have the inherent ability, but rather because she had never in the five years she worked as a domestic in this country been called upon to make a decision for herself: a decision such as choosing between a can of peas that cost thirty-nine cents and one that cost thirty-five cents — the dearer one being two ounces heavier than the cheaper one. Everything of this sort was done for her through the functions of her domestic job: Mrs. Hunter ordered the groceries on the telephone, and she herself paid the bills. Dots merely cooked the groceries, wasted them, pinched some for the private parties she had in her rooms, or saved them through her industriousness.

It was this prospect of a new life: the possibility that she would have to be going out in the summer heat and the cold of winter, lining up with the other housewives, shopping for her own groceries in those brightly lit frightening supermarkets, where everything was so silent, and so stark and so clean and so businesslike; where, if she had collected too many groceries in her cart for the money she had in her purse, the cashier would ring in the amount and she standing there in the long nervous line would faint before she could think of what to say or do. She was going into a new way of life after five years of seclusion and riding on the back of Mrs. Hunter's wealth. But this she knew. And she was prepared for it.

Her first plan was based on self-preservation. Dots always said, "I have to watch my health, gal. I have to make sure that there's always health in my body. This country is so damn rough and hard-hearted that a person is *nothing*, if one morning he finds himself without good health." And with this medical philosophy rivetted home, she arranged a thorough medical examination from Dr. Hunter; and because she was his maid, she paid nothing for it. "Mister Hunter, sir," she said to him one morning, on entering the office he had in his home where he did part of his part-time examinations of his rich friends and other clients. "Mister Hunter, if you please, and if you ain' too busy at the present moment, I would like you to look at this thing I have on my shoulder, because all the time, standing up in that kitchen and in front of that hot stove, I can feel this pain working itself down from my shoulder-blade, right cross my whole body . . ." Dr. Hunter was impressed by her complaint. And without Dots having to be more specific, if in fact he felt there was anything wrong with her, specifically, the doctor came to the door (he was dozing when she knocked) and gave her a thorough examination. Nothing had been wrong with her. But she wanted to be sure.

"You're as strong as an ox, Cumberbatch. An ox, Cumberbatch," he said. He did not realize what he had said when he gave her this clean slate of health.

Next, Dots arranged for an examination equally thorough, for Boysie. Once or twice, the doctor had remarked that Boysie should "see a doctor with that cough of his." It was a cough brought on by the lack of sleep, more than by anything else. When Boysie was examined, and found to be in perfect health, Dots said simply, "Plan number one, completed! I working on plan number two now, in her arse!" Plan number two was more involved. It was to get Mrs. Hunter to arrange a loan in order that Dots might make a down payment on a secondhand station wagon of a late model, for which she was trading in the old Chevrolet. Dots knew that if she was out of work (and she knew she would be when she left Mrs. Hunter; and she knew it would be a long time getting the job she wanted — although at this time, with the plans in her head, she didn't know which job exactly), she would not get any credit in the whole of Toronto, either from a bank or from a finance company. "They ain' like black people at finance companies." Mrs. Hunter would have to supply this service, therefore.

And this is exactly what she did, gratefully, because she knew that to keep her maid satisfied, and working for her as long as possible, she would have to keep her happy, too. Dots knew this. The loan was arranged. But when Dots went to the bank to sign and receive the certified cheque of five hundred dollars, she changed her mind about trading in the old Chevrolet for the station wagon. Straight from

the bank (the Toronto-Dominion Bank on the corner of
Sherbourne and Bloor), she walked farther along Bloor
Street, and opened a new account with the Bank of Nova
Scotia, in her own name, and deposited the five hundred
dollars in it. "When I leave that queen," she told the new
bank book, "we will see. I have watched that woman and
that man for months now, Mistress Hunter and Doctor
Hunter, and I have see how they operate, and now I'm
taking a page outta their book. Let them take that!" She
was laughing all the way on the subway to Bernice's place.
"I can move mountains, I can move mountains if only Boysie would cooperate and work with me. If only, if only that
bastard would join-in with me. And I not even *half* finished
with that queen, yet!"

Plan number three, the most daring and difficult of all,
was still brewing in her mind, as she journeyed on the almost deserted three-o'clock subway to Marina Boulevard.
In both of her plans which were completed, Dots had not
once been challenged by Mrs. Hunter. Dots didn't expect
she would be challenged in her third plan. "One thing I
find damn strange 'bout these people," Dots was telling
Bernice, "one thing puzzling me 'bout Mistress Hunter and
it is that that bitch hasn' even asked me one question in regards o' my check-up her husband gave me. She isn' suspicious at all. She ain' curious. She even isn' frightened that
I leave her backside one o' these days with half o' the supper dishes left-back in the sink, or her supper left-back in
the oven, burn-up. I just told you 'bout the check-up her
husband gave me and Boysie? Nothing at all, nothing she
didn' ask me. She didn' even ask, 'Dots, what you want all
this money for?' She didn' utter one blasted word in doubt.
And all this now have me feeling sort o' frightened. Because she must have something up her sleeve. I confess to
you, Bernice, it got me on pins and needles. That is what I

mean when I tell you that these blasted people is funny
bitches. Now, if it was a coloured person I was working for,
do you think I could play them two tricks so fast in succes-
sion, on her? Oh Christ, no, gal! That coloured bitch would
have taken out all sort o' search warrant and detectives on
me, already." Dots thought more of the situation, and said,
"But then, you know Bernice, I would have to admit that
Mistress Hunter is a woman who don't ask questions. That
man her husband, he comes in all hours o' the night and
day. And he don't say where he now come from. And she
don't pick her teeth to him in question. Now, if that was
Boysie, oh Christ, I would be tearing-loose in Boysie's backside! But not her. She's too damn quiet. And she is too
damn lady-like for him. And that got me frightened."

"You think though, that she could be laying a trap for
you?"

"Bernice, the way I feel, she could lay *two* traps!"

"Be careful, darling," Bernice pleaded. Now that they
had shared their loneliness together in the form of physical love, Bernice was more open and more obvious in urg-
ing Dots to be careful, and in using terms of endearment.
Dots, on her part, though not so expressive in this regard,
accepted it and made as if she was a bit shy, now that
everything about their formerly suppressed love was un-
covered. They had spoken nothing about it since. They had
accepted it as if it was their periodic exasperating flow. But
of course, it was always very close to the surface in all their
subsequent meetings.

"She can't trick me, be-Christ, no! I am too smart for
her, Bernice!"

"Be careful, though. You be careful, darling."

Dots ignored this nauseating protectiveness. She was beginning to regret that she had allowed herself to be taken
up in such an open expression of love with Bernice. Bernice

was the type of woman who was oppressively and very oozily romantic. Perhaps, this romanticness, as Dots called it, would someday expose them to Boysie, and that would be the end of her happiness. Perhaps, Boysie would kill her. She knew he would, because she knew his feelings and attitudes towards female homosexuals.

"Them blasted kiss-me-arse wickers!" he screamed once, when Dots and another West Indian woman were discussing the subject. They had heard that some West Indian women working as maids and domestics had been resorting to this diversion as an outlet for their frustrations and fears of loneliness. Boysie couldn't believe that any woman, so long as she still had an urge, would resort to anything but going to bed with a man, any man, if she was thirsty, as he called it. "Them blasted wickers! If I ever come across one o' them, be-Jesus Christ, I would hold she by that very thing she uses, and gorblummuh, I would kill her!" Dots shuddered. The woman (who was not a female homosexual herself) caught fright and left soon afterwards; and she never visited Dots again.

Dots was not therefore ignorant of the way Boysie felt about this subject and she could almost feel the violence of his hand on her body, the moment he found out. He would beat her like a snake, she knew. And if Henry heard first (and Henry had a habit of hearing all the gossip about women before anybody else), then he would surely tell Boysie, not to inform him, but rather to laugh at him.

"But still be careful, though."

"As a black woman, you think if I wasn' already careful for five years I would be sitting down here with you this afternoon? The moment I stop being careful, I am a dead woman. *Dead.* I been thinking a damn lot, lately. 'Bout this place and my position in this place. You know that I am leaving Mistress Hunter, that bitch. She has never told me a harsh word. She has never treat me mean. But I still have to leave her arse! It struck me sudden one night whilst I was laying down in that bed o' mine in Rosedale. I jumped up trembling like a blasted leaf. To think, Bernice, that after five years, five long years that queen haven' as much as taken out Blue Cross for me. I don't have no Blue Cross, Bernice! The same thing with Physicians and Services. Tomorrow morning if I am so unlucked as to fall down them staircases in her home, be-Christ, the poor house and welfare would take me. Suppose, one o' these nights I get drunk as hell and tell that woman what I really think of her, and tell her husband and her friends during one o' her cocktail parties! Suppose I cuss her backside, stink-stink-stink, which I have had in mind to do many a time, where would I be?

"So, darling, I decided that since this is the way my subconscious working, I will have to put a couple o' plans in her arse. God don't like ugly." She shook her head in a heavy sad gesture. The contagion smote Bernice. "This is what I planned to do, after plan number three's in operation. I getting more older every day, not younger. And after five years I am ashamed to tell you Bernice that I do not have a bank account. I am as poor as a bird's backside in winter, heh-heh-heh, bank-account-wise. Bank-account-wise is where you have beat me coming and going. I am thirty-eight going 'pon thirty-nine. Thirty-eight is old. That is old in any country. It is true that I married. But my being married isn' no benefit. The man who put this ring on my finger isn' worth shit, sometimes. That is my lot. I am not complaining, I am barely mentioning. But as I say, I am a person thirty-eight. Three-eight. It is not a pleasant thought. I know I haven' come from no mansion back in Barbados as some o' these worthless bitches on the domestic scheme let-on they come from. My father wasn' no civil servant. My mother never wear a ring yet, furthermore a wedding ring. I didn' leave no acre o' ground and land back in Barbados. And be-Christ, I didn' leave no money on Barclay's Bank there, neither. That is my history. A thirty-eight-year-old whore like me soon will reach her change-o'-life, mini-pause as these people here calls it. So you see, life will soon come to a full stop, as far as I am concern. And with that in mind, I want to take up something. I want to succeed. I want to become something. I been thinking of it and I been losing sleep at night merely thinking of it.

"Bernice, I want to be a nurssaide. I not only want to be a nurssaide, I intend to be one. Look, I even went down at the Doctor's Hospital place to ask the nursing director how I could become a nurssaide."

"More than a year ago I told you to do this same thing."

"A man says many things, Bernice. A man says many things in advice to a person, and that man don't take none o' that advice. But it don't always mean that that advice fall on stony ground. All it mean is that that advice have not struck a note. But it strike a note in me now, though. That note is Henry. When I see how a police could come and beat up a man the way those cruel bastards beat up Henry, well, the time for taking advice not only has come, but be-Christ, darling, it come and nearly gone, too! Yes. Come September, I stepping high like anybody else, because I would be *self-employ*. That is our only salvation in this country, darling. To be self-employ. We must be self-employed. Self-employment. Come when you want to come, and go when the hell you wish to depart. Heh-heh-heh! And this is how I want you to fix Mistress Burrmann. *Leave!* Leave Mistress Burrmann. She could always get a next maid. Everyday there is boat-loads and train-loads and plane-loads of Eyetalians, Hungarians, Portuguese people, all sorts and brands o' European people coming into this

country. Let *them* servant for Mistress Burrmann. But you?
Leave! Leave, yuh hear? *Leff* this bitch! Leff, leff, leff . . ."

"How could I do a thing like that, Dots?" Bernice said.
"I don't think a thing like that would be right, or christian-
minded to do." But in truth, Bernice had thought before of
leaving Mrs. Burrmann, but it was because of Mr. Burrmann's involvement with Estelle. She blamed Mr. Burrmann for bringing the temptation into her mind. He would
have to bear the guilt and the conscience for her unchris-
tian act. She was not open-minded enough to see it otherwise. There was enough hostility in her to make it impossible for her to recognize that he could not on his own have
tied Estelle down to the bedsprings and raped her. Estelle
would never have consented to that, Bernice felt sure. Mr.
Burrmann was to blame. But in spite of all this (and Dots
was privy to it now), Bernice still tried to hide the real reason she had considered for not leaving Mrs. Burrmann.
"They treats me well here."

"Oh come! What the hell you telling me? Ninety stink-
ing dollars a month for clear three years now?"

"I am still living, Dots," Bernice said. What Dots didn't
know was that as the storm of scandal burst, Mr. Burrmann
had raised her wages to three hundred dollars a month. She
knew that the coincidence of the increase with Estelle's ill-
ness was not insignificant. But she was not going to expose
this to Dots. Although Dots would appreciate the increase
in wages, and would say, "Gal, it over-due, it due and over-
due long long long time!" and would be very happy for Bernice's sake, yet she would be resentful and would talk about
the motive for the increase.

"You forgetting everything, already?"

"Like what?"

"Like Estelle. When that girl arrived, Mistress Burrmann
didn' even want to give you time off to go to the airport to

meet your own sister. The children been rude as hell to you, a grown woman. Mr. Burrmann came into this apartment and do what the hell he did to your sister. Mash her up. Henry get beat up, brutalized on this same street. And you are telling me that you don't understand what this same street symbolize to you? It don't symbolize something nasty to you?"

"I still have to live, child."

Bernice said it simply, and like an afterthought. Dots could think of nothing suitably angry to tell her. Instead, she went back to her original conversation about plans. "Anyhow," she said, "we have to plan." She settled herself comfortably on the chesterfield which was now covered with the Mexican cloth, and which was tidy. "Look, let me and you live together."

The suggestion took Bernice by surprise.

"What?"

"Me and you. And Estelle. We could live together. That way, we could save some money. Even if you still want to work for Mistress Burrmann you don't have to live in. Consider it."

"But Dots, after what we did . . ."

Bernice became very embarrassed when she said this. Before Dots could answer (if indeed she intended answering), Bernice looked away. She mentioned the kissing incident again, and Dots shook her head, signifying that she hadn't forgotten, and could never probably forget as long as she lived.

"Look, it would be cheaper," Dots urged her, getting away at the same time from the embarrassment of the memory. "It would be cheaper. I wouldn't have to journey all the way up here to see you when I want to see you. Boysie wouldn't be any wiser, neither. Instead o' me having to pay for the apartment by my one, you will chip in, and

Boysie would be working soon." Bernice refused. Dots began to think of Boysie. "Christ, I feel that the most ignorant man in the world must be able to get a job in Canada. This place have jobs. No man could be so stupid as not to be able to find a job in Toronto."

"But you must admit it, Dots, that it already take Boysie eight months to try to put his hands on something to do. I know Europeans that come to this country today, say, and tomorrow morning they have sick benefits, a bank account, credit and a job plus a motor car. Boysie should try harder and he should stop listening to Henry. Henry is a lost cause, a very lost cause. Furthermore, Henry have white woman to look after him. Boysie don't."

"Still, yuh have to give the devil his due. Look, two or three mornings ago, I pressed Boysie's white shirt, his trousers legs was like two razor blades, sharp! and he had-on a tie and dress-off real nice, and he went down at the unemployment place downtown. The man down there at that job centre must have ask Boysie if he want a job in the cleaning department. And child! you should have heard the way Boysie cussed that man! Well, Jesus Christ, we is black people in a white man land. What therefore is so blasted wrong with a white man suggesting to a black man that he should be a janitor? Eh? What is wrong with Boysie, a stupid-arse man like him; if I have to be honest, what is so contrary that he couldn' take that cleaning job? God, it wasn' even a cleaning job outside. I could have understand if he was ashamed to let people see him collecting garbage in the street. I could have understood that sperspective, as Mistress Hunter would say. But *a inside cleaning job?* Jesus Christ, I know hundreds o' Europeans, white people who come here and they work the first five or six years as cleaners. Be-Christ, Boysie ain't went as far as grade four in school, and all he intend to do is to listen to the shit that Henry

fills his head with, day in and day out. Henry tell him don't
look for no work. Darling, this is one country where it does
not matter what kind o' job a man have. The only thing
that matters in this place is what size a man's pay cheque
is when Friday evening comes. If you could push a heavy
bundle-buggy o' groceries with a couple thick porterhouse
steaks in it, with a case o' beer, and if your refrigerator full
up with food for Sarduh night, your blasted foots cocked up
on a chair and you sitting down in front o' that thirty-inch
television watching coloured television, child, *you is people.*
But in this country, if you don't possess them material
thing, you ain' people. You ain' nobody. That is all that
counts in this place. I heard my doctor-boss say them same
things. Canada is a poor man's country, too. This is a country o' advantages. The common labouring-man does drive a
brand-new-brand Buick car and the manager or the boss or
the president does only go to work in a 1929 Ford car!
What Boysie want a collar-and-tie job for?"

"You are not giving that man any credit for the months
he walked 'bout this Toronto, last summer knocking on
doors asking for a job. A man does get very tired begging.
Boysie ain't no different. Christ, Dots, is it any wonder then
that Boysie gone mad? Or that he gone now walking behind white woman?"

"Do you love Boysie better than you love me?" And Dots
got up and went across the room to where Bernice was sitting, and she embraced her and kissed her squarely on her
mouth. Bernice returned the embrace, the feeling, the affection and the kiss. And three hours later, when they were
dressing, after having eaten two of Mrs. Burrmann's largest
porterhouse steaks, and having drunk a quarter of a twenty-
six-ounce bottle of Haig & Haig Pinch, Bernice promised to
think over what Dots had suggested about their living together in a house or an apartment. She asked Dots to go to

the hospital with her, on Thursday, to bring Estelle home. Dots agreed and promised to meet her on Thursday afternoon at the corner of Yonge and College streets, in the Honeydew restaurant there.

"You have to leave Mistress Burrmann. Come and live with me."

"I am going to think about it, Dots."

"Think about it. But decide to do it."

"I promise."

"You don't have to tell him, Mr. Burrmann, that you're leaving. I suggest you leave sudden."

"He was in the house yesterday morning. I had my door locked." And they laughed, heartily, and Bernice said, still laughing, "If he ever come smelling round me, because he think I am alone in this unprotected house, be-Christ, I put you on him!" And Dots laughed again, and before her gaiety subsided, she was embracing Bernice in a close personal hug. They both felt very good about it. When Dots got ready to leave, Bernice, anticipating her loneliness and fear in this large house, where she would have to spend the night alone, held Dots's hand and said, "I am going to write you a letter, tonight, darling."

"Be careful, though."

"I know."

"No name, you hear?"

"No. Just my initials."

"Not even that. Boysie know you name," she reminded her. "He bound to know your initials."

"Not my handwriting, though."

"No, he don't know that."

"Well, I won't sign my name."

"Good."

"Okay."

"Goodbye, darling."

"Get home safe, honey."

" 'Bye, sugar."

" 'Bye, sweets."

"I want you to have these," Estelle told the beautiful blonde woman. The young woman smiled effusively; took the bouquet of red roses (the third bunch which Sam Burrmann had sent to the hospital), together with the vase, and she put it on her bedside table. "Get better soon, hear?" The young woman smiled again. Estelle and this young woman had spent the long previous evening the same way she had spent the nights when Mrs. Macmillan was there. The young woman had the bed on the other side of Estelle from the one Mrs. Macmillan had occupied, and she and Estelle quickly made friends during the long lonely afternoon following Mrs. Macmillan's departure. They watched the evening until it became dawn, and they did something new. They listened thirstily to CHUM radio station, and in that short time, learned and hummed all the tunes of the Top Ten tunes. But they did not talk about personal things; they did not become as close as Estelle and Mrs. Macmillan. This young woman talked mainly of the number of "guys who laid" her; and Estelle laughed, and listened hungrily to her frank way of saying things. She had more guts than Estelle, and Estelle liked her for that. Now she was leaving, and she would miss her. Still, Estelle knew that the moment she crossed the threshold of this ward, she would have to forget this young blonde woman.

"Take care of yourself, Ess," the young woman said, and smiled. "Next time, make sure he got a ring in his hand, or a rubber on his prick!"

"I will." Estelle blushed.

"Come and see me before I go."

"I will."

"Now, don't forget to come and visit me."

"I won't."

When the porter wheeled Estelle out, past Priscilla fuming about something, or somebody, and into the waiting elevator which was being held especially for her, Estelle sighed, and promised never to come back. Perhaps the young woman knew this. Once she had said, "Hospitals, Ess, are like morgues. I wouldn't even come to visit my mother, if she was dying." Estelle knew she wasn't ever coming back to Ward 6A. Just as the door was about to close, Nurse Priscilla shouted for the porter to come to her desk. "Give that to her!" she said. It was a letter with Estelle's name on it. And because of the urgency or the lateness of its delivery, Estelle felt she could not read it on the elevator going down with the orderly standing over her. It could not be an important letter, she surmised, else it would have been delivered before, even before she received her prescriptions and her appointments with her doctor. Her doctor was as scarce as Sam Burrmann. The taxi was waiting. She got into it, settled herself in the back seat, said, "Praise God!" and told the driver, "Union Station, please."

The shortest way from the hospital to Union Station is straight south on University Avenue, turn left, and you're there. It is about a seventy-five-cent ride. But Estelle did not know this. And the driver knew she did not know this. So he turned round, went back north along University Avenue, and turned east on College. When he reached Yonge Street he remembered with great exclamation and pity in his voice that he couldn't make a right turn onto Yonge Street ("They're screwing up this city everyday, that's what they're doing," he said, between the soggy cigar and his teeth; but Estelle didn't understand him. She was trying to find her bearings without admitting that she had lost them); so he had to continue a block on to Church Street, and by the time he abused the city some more, and the mayor some more, and the public works department, and the red traffic lights which seemed to stop only him, he reached Front Street and Union Station. The meter in the taxicab was reading one hundred and twenty cents! But Estelle paid him; and like a tourist, thinking she would have done the journey for much more money in any other taxicab, she gave him a fifty-cent tip. The man thanked her, very profusely, commented upon the summer now being short-lived ("Soon have to take me a trip down to Florida! This crazy weather in this crazy country!"), and walked all the way through the large windless yawning cold terminal (even in the summer) with Estelle's valise in his hand, and deposited it in front of a man selling train tickets to any part of Canada. "Have a good trip, lady!" he said, and before she could look round and thank him, he was merely one of the hundreds of silent, lost-and-rambled scampering, yet organized white people in this large concrete womb-tomb.

"Thanks," she said, nevertheless, although she was now looking into the face of the ticket seller.

It took her a few more seconds to get her bearings, not of geography but of mental attitude, before she asked, "How much please, for a ticket to Timmins, going and coming back?"

The ticket seller, like a geographer, consulted a very confusing book and said things like, "Overnight?" and "the fast train?" and the "ten-fifty-five?" and "or the nine-forty-five?" and when he had completely confused Estelle, he advised her to take the train leaving at eleven-thirty-five, "That way you can rest on the train, Miss, and arrive in Timmins early Thursday morning . . ." (she thought of Mrs. Macmillan). "Coach or compartment? You have to sit up in a coach all the way; in a compartment you can have your bed made up by the porter, and sleep . . . which one? The compartment cost only a few dollars more, and for all that comfort . . ." And he persuaded her to take the compartment.

Estelle paid for the tickets (she did not pay for the information) and walked down the heel-clicking, half-slippering incline to get the train. A man dressed in a black suit, and risking a smile on his corned-beef face, said, "You're early, aren't you?"

"Rather early than late."

"Well, the train ain't leaving for another eleven hours, lady. What are you gonna do meanwhile, wait till then? I don't think passengers can board so early, or if they've taken out the train yet. . . . You could check your bags in one of the lockers, and come back at about eleven when you can board for sure, or why don't you take a walk around the city, or a tour on a Grey Coach bus, or maybe take in a movie, or if you rather. . . . If I were you, I would leave your bag in the lockers and that way you don't have to take a cab to bring you back here at eleven this evening. You're an American Negress, aren't you? First time in our country?"

"Thanks," she said, and left. It was the second time she was asked if she was an American black woman: negro? coloured? Southerner? The taxi driver had asked her that. Was there something about Americans in Toronto? Did the people of Toronto like American negroes? When she told the taxicab driver she was a West Indian, he was visibly disappointed. With her new consciousness of blackness, conditioned through Bernice's recent preoccupation with Africa and the Muslims in America, Estelle was disappointed that no one ever asked her if she was an African princess. Perhaps, she felt, to be asked, "Are you an African?" was a question a Canadian was not prepared to hear the answer to. Perhaps, it was a deep, a too-deep confrontation of an image of his fear.

"Thanks, thank you very much," she said, always too late. For the man in the black uniform was already talking to a woman who spoke Italian and who had no one to translate her confusion for her. The train man did his best, which was bad.

Estelle walked back to the wall of lockers and selected one, and then found she couldn't operate it. She was conscious of eyes watching her, and overcome by this, she fumbled and fumbled with the locker and its key until a man came and helped her. "I don't know why they don't make these things sensible," he said. "As if they don't really want people to use them!" And he taught her how to operate it: take out the key, insert the twenty-five-cent piece, slam the door; now, you understand? He gave her the key and helped her to locate the locker by the distance it was from the door in relation to the nearest ticket seller.

"Thanks, thanks," she said, not too late this time.

The man said, "The way out is that way." She was pointed to a door which took her through tombs of underground passages and people, past people in shops, past a barber shop, past people coming towards her with heavy bags, past people just coming, past shop windows with souvenirs of Canada, an artificial Niagara Falls like the one Bernice had in her apartment, and three Royal Canadian Mounties carved from wood, walking a short distance in the snow in some part of the Canadian north, up to a man selling tickets, to a passage through a turnstile, and since she did not know where she was going, and since she was frightened to go ahead, and frightened to turn back ("I think I am lost, or something"), and frightened by the fear of the stranger who knows he is lost but who is too proud to admit it too soon, she bought a ticket and went through the turnstile and found herself on the platform of the subway station at Union Station; and since there was nothing else, nothing better to do, nothing to which she was used, she stepped on the train one second before the doors closed.

The train moved. She was heading north on the subway. The train was empty when it left Union Station, and at each screech and stop and jerk it gradually filled up. The people who got in were silent people. They did not seem to be alive: they merely sat (nobody sat beside her, although the half-seat next to her was the only empty space) and listened to their minds, or to their worries (their expressions did not reflect that they had happiness or hope inside them), with their hands in their laps. A brave, occasional man looked steadily at her when she wasn't looking, and when she glanced at him and saw him looking at her, he lowered his eyes as if he was a sheep caught eating the wrong grass in a grazing pasture. A woman got in, and moved in the direction of Estelle, and when she saw who Estelle was (what did she see? what did she see in Estelle? what did she see on Estelle?), she veered off and decided to stand, holding on to the metal pole, instead. Estelle sensed the eyes in other passengers looking at her. There was some conspiracy, it seemed. And feeling this same fear of loneliness, of isolation, of being dirty, she took out the letter and discovered it was from Mrs. Macmillan.

Dear Ess (the letter said), *I did not give this to you personally, or leave it on your dresser when I was checking out, because I wanted you to have it just as you were leaving the hospital. I wanted you to be able to have something to read on the long trip up to Timmins. I grew very close to you when we were together in that slaughter-house, and I offered to help you — the word is not a good word but I am not good at words anyways — and see what I could do. I*

feel that if I was in your country, you would be doing the
same to me. If I didn't meet you, meaning you, Estelle that
I know, as the person I met in the General, it would be
somebody else like you. By now, I hope you already left
Union Station, and are on the train heading north. It is a
beautiful train ride, if you are not too tired. I have taken
this trip many times myself. The people on the train are
very friendly. You will see for yourself that the moment the
train pulls out of Union Station, the people sitting with
you will behave very different from those kooks, that's what
they are, who live in Toronto. You can ask anybody for
help or assistanse. And when you reach Timmins, if for
some reason I am not there at the station, you can ask any-
body, or any one of the boys on the trains, for directions to
my place. That is where I live. I am telling you this because
you can never tell, accidents do happens. But everything
will be all right. I am very happy that you are coming to
live with me, with us. I know Joe will accept you. He knows
many coloured boys from the American air base in Ramore,
a few miles from Timmins. The first thing I intend doing
when I reach home is to fix up a room for you. You will be
a bit crowded, but what the hell? So, until then, your lov-
ing friend, Mrs. Macmillan. PS. The enclosed is to help you
buy your train ticket, and for any little things you need on
the way up. Love, Mrs. Macmillan.

Estelle wondered if it was really necessary for Mrs. Macmillan to sign her name twice: *Mrs. Macmillan?* Was it a
reproach intended to stress the difference between Mrs.
Macmillan and herself; a warning, a hint even, that the
similarity of their misfortune had no other common feature
in their lives than the fact that they had spent some time in
the same hospital ward, for some "female complaint"?

But she was travelling alone now. She had to address her
mind to some direction and to some destination, even a

temporary destination. But because she was in a strange city, she would not know whether a destination was temporary or final. All direction on this subway train was puzzling. The subway train became more crowded: women looking young, but actually old, with the tan of misleading youth, and of some wealth, some wearing dresses that belonged on their teen-aged daughters; shouting, screaming merry children from school, of various whiteness of white, and various shorts and various hair styles and various shouts, and various cleanliness. And Estelle became tired now, travelling without direction, without a destination. But she got out of the subway through the underground passages again, past the man in a glass cage with TTC marked on his lapel, selling tokens and tickets; past the show windows in this long channel of a dungeon, wondering who would window-shop in this airless passage; through the cold (although it was only the beginning of the yellow and the brown and the brick of the fall season), down the inclining walk, into the noise of the railway terminal. And here she paused, deciding what to do next. She still had ten hours more before it was time for her to board the train to Timmins.

"He tried his best. You can't deny that. There's lots of other lawyers who wouldn't't've touched this case with a ten-foot pole. They know what it is like in Toronto with a racial case. Mr. Berginstein tried his best. And I think it is rather ungrateful of you, Henry, to say that nobody is interested in your welfare or your well-being. It is really selfish." What Agatha was really telling Henry, this afternoon, was that the case had fallen through: he had paid Mr. Berginstein his fees (actually Agatha had paid it with her own money, since Henry had none, and was still unemployed); the case was erased from the memory of the policemen involved, and from their files; the reporter had destroyed his

notebook with the yellow notes, and it was best for Henry
to admit and acknowledge defeat. But Henry refused to see
it that way. It was his body that was bruised.

"Welfare? Well-being?" he shouted at her. "Is that all
you could say? But I say that the lawyers in this goddamn
place don't have no morals."

"That is your opinion," Agatha said. "You are entitled to
your opinion."

"Fuck my opinion! I am talking the truth. That ain' no
goddamn opinion. That is the goddamn truth."

"That is your opinion. You are entitled to it. I am entitled to mine. Mr. Berginstein is entitled to his."

"Fuck Mr. Berginstein, Berweinstein, Berg-whoever-the-
hell-he-is!" He was trying to tidy his mind, and control his
anger. But he was already too overwrought with the fear of
failure. "All Jews are bastards, anyway!"

When the words struck her, Agatha fell dumb. There
was a change of colour in her cheeks, which registered not
so much hate as shock. And then, swiftly as the repercus-
sion of his hate hit her, so swiftly did she recover from it.
She pulled herself together, almost making a visible, physical action, and she looked at him with a searing coldness,
and said, "I am a Jew too. You fucked this Jew, remember?
Would you call me a bastard Jew, after that?"

"Oh, you're different."

"How am I different?"

"Oh shit, woman, you're *different!*"

"But I am a Jew, Henry."

"Well, hell, ain't you ever said *nigger?* Nigger bastard?
Not once? Even in your mind? And you still know me?
Haven't you? Goddamn woman, I'm talking to you! When
did Jews stop saying nasty things about niggers, when they
get up there together in Forest Hill?"

"You're missing the point, Henry. You are *always* missing the point." She said this with great scorn. She said it also with the superiority of what she herself would have called (had she been writing a paper or discussing this present problem in a seminar) "the sophistication characteristic of a higher civilization." And as she saw how her words hurt him, she lessened or tried to lessen the injury by adding, "Whenever you're losing in an argument, you always have to resort to abuses and, and, and raising your voice and abusing everybody who isn't a *precious* negro . . ."

"Not negro! *Black!*"

"I said negro. They're negroes!"

"And goddamn you, woman, I say *black*. I goddamn say you ain' calling my people negroes. Not in my goddamn room, not in my goddamn presence!"

"Negroes!"

"*Black*, goddammit!"

"Negroes, they're negroes, they're negroes, and you are a goddamn no-good, unemployed poor-ass negro!"

The moment the last word escaped her lips was the exact moment the slap landed on her jaw. He was shaking. She was shaking. Immediately afterward, he realized he was silly to hit her; and all sorts of images started to crowd his brain. He saw more cops beating him up; he saw other cops, cops from the southern United States, driving him far out of town in the night, and cutting out his balls; he saw himself hanging from a tree; he saw Agatha's father with a gun in his hand, with the muzzle pointing at his penis. But all these terrors, all these frights did nothing to stop the propulsion of his hand. His hand contained more terror than those fears. And his hand continued to strike her, left and right, *plax-plax-plax!* in a kind of warlike African hitting of stick upon wood, a savage rhythm, *plax-plax-plax-plaxxxx-*

plax! the slapping and the frustration from the slapping because she did not cry. She did not weep, did not make a
sound. The coldness in her eyes said what had to be said.

He stopped slapping her, and he started to shake her,
trying to shake up some retaliation in her. But she was superior to him in her apprehension of nonviolence. He
wanted her to do something: if only she would cry, or
hit him back, bite him, kick him, call him a negro, a nigger
or a shit, but do some goddam thing, something. And she
cheated him out of this victory: she continued sitting on
the bed, watching him, and this watching became more
devastating than blows. The coldness was in her eyes. When
he saw she would not react he put his arms round her, and
he kissed her, and it was then that his lips tasted the salt of
her tears; and he allowed his beaten arms and then his head
and finally his whole body to fall down, until he was weep-
ing like a child in her lap. She placed her hands on his head
and on his neck, and soothed him, and told him, "I love
you, Henry, God, I love you." It was a simple expression of
his punishment; and of his incarceration. And the more he
wept. And while he wept, Agatha was taking off her clothes.

Bernice had just switched off the vacuum cleaner. And
immediately the house became uncomfortably quiet. She
didn't imagine that the machine was so noisy. She switched
it on again to find out for herself; and she discovered that
while it was working and fuming and buzzing over the rugs
and the carpets in the seven downstairs rooms, she couldn't
hear the cars passing outside. She switched it off, curled the
long cord round the body of the machine, and rolled it
across the cleaned, shiny cat's fur of expensive rugs, back
to the cupboard in the kitchen. She had just filled the sink
with the foamy detergent and cleanser when Mr. Burrmann
entered. Hearing him close the front door (who else would

be entering this house with a key so early in the morning? "That bitch still down there tanning her arse in Mexico! And them brutes her children up north eating hot dogs offa a stick!"), she became very uncomfortable. All the fears she held for her sister's safety, on those Sunday mornings when she left Estelle alone in the apartment, came back to her. But they came with more intensity. It was not that she felt he was going to attempt to seduce her too, or force her, or rape her; it was rather like the feeling one gets in the presence of a man who had been found out to be a rapist.

Bernice made a greater noise with the plates and the cups in the sink than necessary, to let it be known that she was there. She wanted him to know she was working; she was busy; she wasn't sitting down on her backside waiting on him. But most of all, she wanted him to know that she both acknowledged his presence and ignored it. It was a trick she had learned from Mammy who always told her that in the face of danger, pretend you are busy with the job you had been doing before the danger arose. That way, Mammy said, a man would have to be worse than Satan to think of troubling you. And it seemed to work now, assuming that that was Mr. Burrmann's intention. He went straight upstairs to his bedroom. She made less noise with the washing now that the danger was out of sight, above, walking on leather heels on the bedroom floor. But she was still frightened. She thought of calling Dots to tell her that Mr. Burrmann was home. She had seen a movie once (she couldn't remember its name), in which a man was planning to murder his wife; and she shuddered now as she had shuddered then, in spite of the safety of the knowledge that it was merely a film, and far from her, on the screen: when the man moved about in an attic room, and how the gaslight went down every time he went up there, searching for whatever he was searching for. She never knew whether or not the man killed his wife. And that made her more frightened now. She went outside that night before the end of the film, and she refused to take a taxicab home (it was almost midnight) from Yonge Street, near the bright lights and the book shops that sold sex magazines every minute of the revolving sun and moon. She stood in the chilly night with a waiting crowd for the subway, and then meandered home to Marina Boulevard by the bus which hitched up with the last subway train.

The feet are moving now. She looks up to see if she can follow the noise with her eyes. She imagines he is searching for something, just as the man in the film was searching for something. She looks up at the electric lights, the electric bulb in the kitchen, to see whether the light is dying. But it is daytime now. And the lights are not burning. She went to the telephone to call Dots. Something was funny. Something was happening upstairs. Strange, strange that he would come home, in the middle of the morning (it was ten o'clock), when he was supposed to be up north fishing. *Be-Christ, Mister Burrmann, you aren't going to kill me, eh! Not me!* She had been watching too much television, which was her only companion in the long nights — when Dots did not come over.

"He here!"

"Who?" Dots asked, slightly peeved, because she had talked to Bernice only an hour ago, and they had agreed to meet at the Rosedale subway station at two o'clock to go to the hospital for Estelle. It was the day she was being discharged. "You sound frightened."

"He! Mister Burrmann! Here!"

"I thought he was up north hunting."

"He back! And no sooner than that brute come through the front door, than he made it straight upstairs, and now he up there walking and walking all over the bedroom, over my head like in that movie I told you about. I frightened for him, Dots."

"You is a coward?"

"I ain't no coward, man," Bernice said, trying to control her voice, and put more sureness into it. "You remember that movie I went to see one night at the Odeon? With that man who had make up his mind to kill-off his wife for the jewels her mother left back for her in her will? And how the gaslight went down every time he start his prowling? And how she used to sit alone, poor soul, by herself in the house, night after night, midnight turn into dawn, and that bastard her husband never did spend one hour with that poor girl . . ."

"Look, control your blasted self, woman! You dreaming, or what?"

"Myself controlled. I am not a child, Dots. But living in this big house by myself now has me scared as hell. You ever stayed in a house this big, twenty-one rooms, by yourself? and when the nights come you start hearing all kinds o' noise, people walking when you know there ain't one bloody soul in this house save you! the house creaking, doors closing . . ."

"It's the foundation shifting. That's all. It does happen in the best and newest homes. Down here in Rosedale, it is haunted as hell, too! These white people's houses all haunted as hell! if you ask me. It's your goddamn 'magination. So hurry up and get dressed. Rosedale station. I'm going to be there at one-forty-five. Not a minute after, you hear?" And Dots, who knew Bernice perhaps better than anyone else, put down the receiver.

Bernice began to think of a man, of Lonnie, the only man she knew, as a defense against thinking of Mr. Burrmann, who was still walking above her head. She had forgotten Lonnie for such a long time now; not since his last letter which came shortly before Estelle went into the hospital had she actually thought of him in the way she had permitted herself to when her loneliness swept itself into that strange soft-heartedness when she addressed him as *my darling Lonnie*. There was also a great urge which throbbed about her thighs, and brought a faint hunger, a yearning with it. Thinking of this sexual hunger, she had to remember what had happened between herself and Dots. But that was not satisfaction. That was merely a sort of jerking-off of a deeper hunger which her deprivation and Dots's availability had made possible. But it was Lonnie who gave her this deep insatiable hunger, a hunger built and intensified upon the time and distance and the miles of sea and memory, which made it more desirable than it was satisfying when it did happen. She was ready, her mind was adjusted, her body throbbing, every nerve filed and waiting for Lonnie. *Oh dear darling, darling, darling Lonnie, You been weighing heavy on my mind. Life in this country is a battle. I have lost the first battle so far, but I declared war. A woman my age should be resting on her oars in a nice three-roof house with a couple of chickens and a cow perhaps, to help give milk. Instead, I find myself in a country where every woman have to work until the day she enters her coffin. I heard a man on the television say one night that if people was to stop working for even a fraction of a minute in North America, which Canada is a part of, being in North America, this whole big powerful country will collapse, overnight. In Barbados, as you know, many men and many women do not work at all, because there is no work. Now I told you one time in a letter about a girlfriend of mine, Dots Cumberbatch. She is a Bajan like me. She have a husband, Boysie, who came up nine months or more, perhaps a year. Boysie have not lifted a finger in a honest day's work in support of Dots in all that time since he emigraded to this country. Boysie is lazy. Boysie was offered a job in a large company in the heart of Toronto, called Macleans-Hunter. Boysie refused that job because it was a job picking up paper from off the floor. Now, I do not know what your views are concerning working in a job like that. But in this country, a job is a job. But I hope that when you come up, as I intend to take out papers soon to bring you up, that you would not scorn a job because they do not make you the prime minister of Canada the day after you land in this country . . .* Mr. Burrmann's footsteps were now coming down the runway of the carpeted stairs. Bernice did not hear him. She was too deep in the reverie of her letter-writing. And Lonnie was too close to her, in mind, as was the letter she had been writing to him, for her to notice somebody else. Mr. Burrmann went into his study on the ground floor, along the hallway from the sitting room . . . *I stand here in my place and I think of the temptation and the wickedness in this world. You will have to work when you come up though, because you will have to pay me back for the money I spend on you for your plane ticket and other things to bring you up. I am offering marriage now, Lonnie. Think of it. I have plans for the future. I want to buy a house. I will wait till you come up before I decide the final plan. I have the money already saved up and keeping on the bank. I have taken all my money off the Royal Bank of Canada because they was not employing enough black people as bank clerks and other workers, as another bank here, the Bank of Nova Scotia does. So my money is now in the Bank of Nova Scotia. That is a good bank. I think that was the best decision I have make since I emigraded to this country . . .* Bernice heard the cat's paws of footsteps behind her, on the thick broadloom rug. She looked back and saw him standing behind her. Her fear for him returned and its intensity wiped all thoughts and words going across the telepathy of her imagination to Lonnie, from her brain.

"How's it going, Leach?"

She took some time before she answered, "Fine, sir. Just fine! I was just cleaning up these dishes, sir!" She felt the need to justify her standing up in the kitchen doing nothing, merely thinking, at this hour of the morning. Mr. Burrmann did not understand this confession, or its reason. As he approached, Bernice saw that he held her cheque (in the customary manila envelope) in his hand, although he was not offering it to her just then.

"How's it going?" Sometimes, in his absent-mindedness, and in his secret desire to be far away from this house, he forgot that he had asked the same question twice.

"Under control, sir."

"Here's your pay." He gave her the envelope. There was nothing he could think of saying to her, or doing, now that he had given her the envelope. But there seemed to be something resting uneasily on his mind. "How's your sister?" he said at last. He had tried to rob his inquiry of all concern, all feeling. But he was not entirely successful.

"She coming round all right, sir."

"She's coming around all right, eh?"

"She's coming round all right. She soon come out."

"That's good to hear." (But he had already found out from his family doctor, who was attending to Estelle.) "Have you been to visit her, lately?"

"Two or three days ago. And I'm going again this afternoon, sir. This afternoon she's coming out. She soon will be home again." It occurred to her, after she had said it, that perhaps he might not permit Estelle to come back to live with her. And she had used the word "home"! She had better find out now if it would be all right for Estelle to come back. "I would like to ask you a question," she began. "If it wouldn't be too much, could Estelle stay here a little longer, please, till I find a decent place for her to live?" She was not quite sure she had read the puzzled expression on his face correctly: was it concern for Estelle, or indecision about granting permission. She hastily added, "It won't be for too long, Mister Burrmann, 'cause I already started searching for some place . . ."

"That's all right, that's all right, Leach. If it is fine with her, it's fine with me, but I don't think she would like it here anymore . . . of course . . ." Bernice couldn't understand what he was saying. She knew it was wrong for Estelle to come back into this house, but there was nowhere else to go.

There seemed to be always a game being played by the two of them. Mr. Burrmann did not really hate Bernice, cither as a woman or as his maid. He could not honour her existence with such importance and thought. She did not exist for him beyond the image and the labour of a domestic. Bernice didn't know whether she hated him more than she hated Mrs. Burrmann. Here of late, she had actually made a tally of all the people she hated. It was her conflict. Her confusion. Her basis for blanket distrust of everybody white, and her mistrust of almost everybody who was black. But she felt secure living within the battlements of a friendless circle of "friends." It kept her always on her toes, always making decisions, similar to the decision she was thinking of making now, concerning bringing up her old boyfriend, Lonnie, with a proposal of marriage.

"Well, Leach, take care of everything." He gave his nervous little laugh, as if he was clearing his throat of a small precarious fish bone. And then he left.

She was now queen of this vast vacant Burrmann kingdom, sole ruler of an empty citizenless dominion, for at least ten days. Her new power overpowered her, and rendered her powerless. There was nothing to do. There was no one to give orders to. No one to give advice to. There was no one to give her orders or advice; and there was no one to witness her efficient caretakership. She could only write Lonnie and tell him what a large house she "lived" in; and she could do like her other Barbadian friend, Millie, had done: stand in front of the house in which she was a domestic, like a pillar of granite and assumed ownership, in front of the double garage with the Cadillac and the Mercedes-Benz, in full view of the viewfinding, lying camera lens, posing as if she was the black mistress, the black Jew, as if she was Mistress Bernice Burrmann, and send the photograph misrepresentingly on its way across the equivocal miles of blurred ocean and seas back to the little waterless, lightless, sewerless village among the hills and luscious breadfruit trees in Horse Hill, St. Joseph. And she knew (so far as Millie's mother had behaved when the photograph arrived, airmailed and registered in the red-white-and-blue envelope), she knew that her own mother would show the photograph throughout the entire village, circulating with dog-ears of comments, like a "hot" book from the public library. And they would say, "Look-look, man! This is *we* Bernice! We Bernice! Here she is! here is where Bernice living nowadays in that big country called Canada! What a pretty-pretty big house, though! Bernice really making it big up in Canada!" And her mother, who knew the truth, and who would hide the truth from the other villagers, would wave her head in pride like the Union Jack above their heads, above the elementary school, twenty yards of dust and road and flies and exposed rotting garbage away from the small house where she lived, as she lied.

Putting these dreams aside, Bernice began to address herself to the problem of the reunion with her sister. Up until now, she had not really thought seriously of reentering the topsy-turvy life in the small apartment with Estelle. For two healthy women, the apartment was really unhealthily small. Bernice could not forget the first torment of living with a sister (or with another person for that matter) whom she had outgrown and whose personal hygiene and ways she had hated twenty years ago when they shared the same small bedroom, as girls, back home. Bernice could not forget the first offense Estelle had committed: she had turned off the church service from the Andes Mountains on the large walnut-painted radio for a rock-'n'-roll station, CHUM. And Bernice never lived down the shock and the anger when she found out that Estelle had used *her* toothbrush to brush her teeth. These were a few of the physical inconveniences that resulted from their living together. Now, Estelle was coming back. She was coming back a different woman: a convalescent.

Bernice was to go now. She came down the stairs with the valise, and she rested it on the first landing. Always mindful of her responsibilities as a domestic, she went into each of the three bedrooms on the second floor (Mr. Burrmann's, which was really the guest room until his wife stopped sleeping with him; Mrs. Burrmann's, and the children's), and she checked to see that everything was in order.

Outside, she saw the cover of the garbage pail lying on the ground. She cursed the garbagemen, "You blasted worthliss dirty bitches!" and she carried the pail, covered down now, out of sight and placed it in the small green-painted shed. Then she walked across Marina Boulevard, as if she was the housewife, Mistress Bernice Burrmann, the owner of the largest mansion on this mansioned, luxurious, wealthy, upper-class Jewish conspicuous street. Brigitte held her head out of the window in her third-floor room and shouted, "Hey!" Bernice waved her hand and said, softly so Brigitte couldn't hear, "You bitch!"

Dots was waiting for her at the Rosedale station. They caught the next subway from Rosedale to take them south to College Street, from where they could walk to the Toronto General Hospital.

"I just had to cuss that bus-driver bastard," she complained to Dots. She had given the driver a ten-dollar bill for two thirty-five-cent tickets and he had been noticeably and vocally annoyed. It had been worrying her all the way down. It was hurtful that she had to quarrel always for her rights, that she had to be humiliated, and that she had to humiliate herself.

The subway train was making quite a lot of noise, and conversation was impossible to hear. Dots spent the interim picking dead skin from her fingernail and easing her wedding ring further up her finger to get at the white soft mark left by the closeness of the ring. The train slowed down for the Bloor Street station. Dots said, "Guess what happened this morning?" Before Bernice could inquire, she said, "I just gave that woman I work for the best cussing in her life! I gave her my notice, too!" She said it as if it was a great achievement.

When the train stopped again, she sighed and said, "If only I could get Boysie to go out and find a job! If only he would stop hanging round that Henry . . ."

"Henry is a bad influence."

"A bad influence."

"I don't know what that girl Agaffa sees in that bastard!"

"I was reading a book the other day and that book told me a mouthful 'bout white women and their craving after black men. That book says that one time, a white woman came across a nice black man that she liked and who used to screw her and foop her, and be-Christ, she was so happy to find this goodness in that black man, that she rented him out to all her five club-member-friends. Jesus Christ, gal! all them five bitches enjoyed that black man, too! heh-heh-haaa!"

"God, Dots! You just made that up!"

"No! I saw it in a book."

"But you believe that?"

"It's printed in a book, ain't it?"

"You can't believe everything you see printed in a book."

"Bernice, gal, them five bitches rented-out that black man as if he was Mistress Grimes ram-goat back home!" And she laughed out loud. And before she finished the laugh, she cut it short and sighed, not in comment but in embarrassment. For just as she was about to secure her handbag which was slipping as she laughed, and pull the valise near to her legs because the train was making it slide, she saw a white woman sitting immediately behind her, and this white woman had obviously heard everything she had told Bernice. She jabbed Bernice sharply in her ribs to put her on her guard of silence, and with a slight jerk of her head she indicated the enemy behind.

Just as they left the subway at College, the white woman got up deliberately a little before Dots and looked back straight in their faces and said, "Calvin C. Hernton wrote that book! I read it too." Dots looked at the woman, and didn't know what to say. So she kept her mouth shut, and wished she could disappear.

Feeling sad, with the terrible guilt and the collective shame of the entire black race heavy on her heart, and the anxious frightened inquiring eyes of the informed white woman still in her mind, Bernice thought what a cruel world she was living in. She did not talk until they had rambled and eventually extricated themselves from the budget floor of the Eaton's department store among the paint and the cheap clothing at cheap prices and the better quality merchandise on the floor above at higher prices.

"Wait," Bernice said, "I been thinking all this time of that book. The book you was reading about sex. Talking 'bout that . . . could that book be really talking about people we know . . . could that be the case with Henry and Agaffa?"

"I can see you will have to read that book for yourself, gal."

"I don't think that book was right, though." The possibility that Agatha loved Henry merely because he was a black man, because he could give her the most complete sexual satisfaction, bothered Bernice greatly. What about Mr. and Mrs. Burrmann, then? Who were both white. If what Dots said that book said, and if that book was telling the truth, would it not mean that Mr. Burrmann could not give Mrs. Burrmann the most complete sexual satisfaction? "It couldn' be that, Dots. It must be something else. It must be love. I believes it must be that white woman *really do love* black men. Just love. I believes in love. I believe it is love. Henry is so damn ugly though, that Agaffa *got* to love that bastard a whole lot more before she could even look at his blasted face."

"Love?" Dots said. And she laughed sarcastically and cruelly in Bernice's face. "*Love?*" And changing the subject she said, "We'll walk," although they were already walking the three blocks to the hospital. Dots put her hand on the back seam of her dress to keep it from sticking up in the crease of her behind. Her dresses always did that in the summer, and it was a miserable feeling.

No sooner had her hand touched her behind, fixing the

dress, no sooner had she slackened her pace, and shaken one leg as a horse would, to shake flies off its leg, no sooner had she done all this, than a man in a slowing car *pssssssssst* at her, and added, "Sweetness!"

It rankled Dots. She felt she had been caught doing a very personal thing, like picking stuff out of her nose and then eating it. "You bitch!" she called at him, in a voice she knew would never reach him; but she had to say it anyhow. "Heh-heh-heh!" she commented to Bernice, walking beside her but miles away in her thoughts. "Why does men always have to holler after women in this savage place? They don't even do with any decentness at all! They don't have no damn breeding, neither, heh-heh-haaaa!"

"You look good, that's why." It was a strange thing for Bernice to say. It was the first time she had ever said it. Dots took it exactly that way. She knew she looked good. "Really. You looking good as hell these days, woman. If I was a man now . . ."

"Haul your arse, Bernice!"

"Wait," Bernice said, and Dots waited aside while Bernice went up to the small glass-walled office on the sixth-floor hospital ward in which a nurse was writing things in a book that had charts in it. The nurse looked back and saw her. The nurse went back to her charting. The nurse did not ask her what she wanted. Bernice, always uneasy in hospitals as in banks, continued standing just outside the door, but within range of the charting-nurse's sight. Two other nurses came rushing into the office. They said something in a language that had to do with the world of medicine, which Bernice did not understand.

The nurse who was charting left off her charting to look back and attend to the cards the two nurses held. She said something about "Mrs. Carmichael is to have ten see-sees"; and to the other nurse, she said, "Thank you, Miss Worrell." Miss Worrell put her card on the charted table.

"Pssst! Pssssssst!"

Bernice looked round. It was Dots motioning, encouraging her to go inside the office. Bernice found no support in this encouragement. She rapped lightly on the door post and said, "Excuse me, lady. Miss?"

"What do you want?" the nurse said, still writing, still sitting, still not looking.

"I come to see my sister, Estelle Shepherd who . . ."

"Are you a relative?"

"But I just told you I come to see my sister . . ."

"Not visiting hour yet. Come back in fifteen minutes."

"But, Miss . . ."

"Visiting hour starts in fifteen minutes. Now, we're very busy."

Dots didn't like the nurse's manner; she couldn't hear what was being said but she could sense something was wrong. "What she say?"

Bernice walked closer to her, and said, "She say visiting hour hasn't begin yet. I must come back in fifteen minutes."

"Look, you wait here! Let me get at her arse! right now!" Dots swelled herself out, took a deep hostile breath, pushed past Bernice and walked straight up to the charting nurse. The nurse was still charting. She did not give the impression she had heard Dots enter. Dots waited one second to prepare herself, and to allow the nurse to acknowledge her presence.

"You did not hear what I told your friend? Fifteen minutes." The nurse, accustomed to giving the orders on this ward, because she was the Head Nurse, assumed that the woman standing in front of her would obey; and she assumed that her orders would affect Dots. So she went back

to her charting in her concentration. Two more seconds
passed.

Then Dots said, "Liss-ten to me!" Her voice was high.
Her voice was loud. Her voice was indignant. "Lisss-tennn
to me! We have come down here to look for a patient. That
patient is getting discharge today. We intends to see her.
Now, you hads better get up offa your backside right now,
you hear me? and be decent to the guests in this horsepital
if you want to know what's good for you! After all, you is
only a nurse, yuh know!" She shook these words out of her
head. Her voice had risen even higher. She was thinking of
her new freedom. She was thinking of Mistress Hunter. She
was thinking of Boysie. The feeling of freedom she had was
based on a feeling that she was right.

The nurse did not move, however. Perhaps Dots's voice
had transfixed her to her chair; perhaps she was deliberately
ignoring Dots. Dots went up farther. Dots pounded her
hand on the tabletop and shouted, "Get up, get up, man,
and attend to we! Be-Christ, we ain't waiting. We tired
waiting!"

This completely shocked the nurse. The nurse changed
colour. The nurse's ears looked very pale. Her lips were
trembling. Something like a burning uncontrollable, im-
possible-to-be-expressed hate burned her cheeks and made
them bloodless. Three other nurses (one of whom was
black) assembled at the door of the office. The black nurse
was trying to look serious, sympathetic to her profession and
her colleague: but there was a smile beneath her straight
face. She was not Priscilla. The Head Nurse became angry
after being shocked. But it was Dots in front of her like an
awful threatening black persistent presence. And she became flustered. And something strange, something that was
not deliberately done, happened: all the white nurses were
suddenly standing *beside* the Head Nurse. The one remain-

ing nurse, the black nurse, was standing in the neutral frame of the door.

"I waiting!" Dots said. She had not noticed the miraculous alignment of the nurses. And this time, she did not have long to wait. The Head Nurse, who could think of no other way to defeat Dots, moved away from her and went outside to speak to Bernice. She was still flustered. The other aligned nurses drifted away muttering comments.

The black nurse, before she too left, pretended she had to get something from a cupboard in the office, and on her way out, she brushed close to Dots, and when Dots looked at her, she said out of the corner of her partial mouth, "Give her shit! She born in Southafrica. I thank you. I's a Jamaican." And she drifted among the white of the beds and the sheets and the orderlies who were standing beside a cart.

"Now, what I can do for you?" the Head Nurse asked Bernice.

"My sister. She's getting discharge and I come for her."

"What's her name?"

"Leach . . . no, Shepherd. Estelle Shepherd."

"Don't you know her name! Make up your mind! We don't have anybody here named Shepherd."

"How you mean?"

"I just told you! We do not have anybody here by that name!" She was moving away back to the office. When she got close to Dots, who was not in her way, she said, "If you don't mind!" in perfect, overcivilized, cold politeness. She rustled some papers hanging on a clip against a clipboard. She found what she was looking for (even her appearance gave you the impression of her diligence and efficiency), and she went back to Bernice. Victory, unconditional defeat (for Bernice) was marked all over her lipstick. She said, "Your sister was discharged this morning. She left this morning. The nurse who was on duty then wrote out her discharge."

Bernice was thrown back upon the fat of her own mental resources to solve this problem. It was as if she was having to pay for something, some act she had done long ago in her past, and which had now accumulated into a large vengeance. Before she began to search over the pages of her life — beginning from her village days of youth and freedom within the poverty of sunshine and sea — she had argued with Dots about calling the police to search for Estelle. She imagined Estelle raped again, this time by a cruel man who afterwards killed her. She saw Estelle in the Toronto morgue on Gould Street, in the garbage-can section of the city. She saw Estelle dead in some back alley, like Sackville Street or Toronto Street, dragged there, probably, by some desire of hers which she could not wait to satisfy . . . she saw Estelle in her mind, dead.

But Dots was the more patient; the more intelligent. "Wait a day or two. Nothing don't happen in this city that the police don't know about at least a day after. I wouldn't call the police, if I was you. Wait. Have patience."

And Bernice decided to take Dots's advice; but this did not prevent her from worrying. Again, she had had to lose her temper (with the Head Nurse) to gain her respect. If she hadn't talked up to that Head Nurse; if Dots hadn't intervened in her behalf, she would have had to wait the fifteen minutes; and that would have meant fifteen minutes less with which to face this problem.

"What I do? What have I done? What the hell have I done in my life that I am getting all this bad luck, all the time? First thing, it is Estelle — mixing-up with that man! Then, the pregnancy! The hospital. The ambulance. And

be-Christ, now this! What have I done in my past, Dots,
that now I am reaping all these bad times?" Dots could find
no piece of evidence in the history of her life to console her
with. If she had, she would not have told her anyhow, for
that would have worsened the situation. "All this bad luck,
Dots! Who know where it is going to end? My job. My job
is all I got left; and I can't afford to lose that. With a job,
it is shit living in this man's place. And without a job,
well . . ."

   She had called Henry by this time. She had called Brigitte.
She had called Boysie. She had called Agatha. She had
eaten her pride and had called Priscilla. And surprisingly,
Priscilla was very courteous. She was courteous in order to
eke out all the details of Estelle's situation, so that the
moment Bernice put down the telephone, she took it up
again, and called Carmeeta Anne Bushell, the other West
Indian woman who had attended the welcoming party for
Estelle many months ago, and who was a university student.

   Dots was impatient to leave. Bernice was so insecure that
she felt Dots wanted to leave so she could telephone
Brigitte, and tell her, and laugh about it. "Don't leave yet.
Stay with me, eh?" she pleaded; and Dots satisfied her with
an hour more. And when the hour was up, her anxiety to
leave once more suggested to Bernice her eagerness to spread
the scandal even further.

Bernice was alone: thrown back upon her resources which,
at the beginning of this situation, were not too strong anyway. But she made up her mind not to break under its pressure. "I can't give up now; I can't crumple under this, no no
no." But the strength had to come from outside. There had
to be someone who she could trust. She enumerated those
persons she knew as "friends"; and she found no one suitably trustworthy. Dots was already saturated by her prob-

lems; and Bernice did not want to harness her with more anxiety. Apart from counting her "friends," Bernice made a tally of the people she hated: Mrs. Burrmann (for over-working her, and making her "slave for peanuts" so many months); Mr. Burrmann (because he was white: she could find no other reason than that; and although she hated him for the brutal way he treated his wife, and more recently, her own sister, she could not make up her mind whether to hate him more than she hated his wife. She did not care enough for her own sister or for Mrs. Burrmann to avenge their mistreatment at his hands); Brigitte (because she had betrayed her: she had exposed everything about the at-tempted abortion, which she herself had induced; and also because it was through her that Henry had been beaten up by the police); Boysie (because he was Boysie); and Henry (because after he had tried to seduce her and had succeeded in getting her to think of him as her man, he had ruthlessly renounced her intentions by going back to his white woman, Agatha). For some reason, Agatha was the only member of this family of friends who escaped Bernice's enmity.

Bernice couldn't make up her mind whether to hate Dots or love her. Their recent physical, explosive love did not altogether wipe out the deep suggestion of distrust and envy that crept into her mind. She had only Lonnie now. But Lonnie was far away, and she could not tell how close he was in his heart towards her. He kept her always on her toes. She had recently proposed to him in her mind: a serious step, for she was a woman who worked out her actions in thought and followed them for some considerable distance of logic and practicality before she would put them into the sphere of reality. She felt she could keep herself secure with-out the great responsibility of having to be friendly to her "friends," because as she knew "to have so many friends cost money." Bernice was a very selfish woman. Although she didn't know this about herself. What frightened her always was how her "friends" would come to her apartment, accept her hospitality, and her warnings about gossip with which she entertained them, and straightway, go back and spread it round in a hateful and compromising manner — to the very persons against whom she had appealed to them not to talk. This was her great fear, her terror of having "friends."

She decided to call Lonnie in Barbados, by long-distance telephone. The operator told her the transatlantic call would cost at least nineteen dollars and fifty-somebody cents. She decided to put through the call, disregarding the expense. This was an act essential to her continued sanity. It had to be done. *Money can't stop me now; money can't stand in my way; Lonnie is the purest person I know at this moment. If I hadda brought up Lonnie, instead o' that whore, Estelle, all this wouldn' have happen to me now. It ain't natural for one person to have all this happening to her; and it got me asking myself if God vexed with me because one time I had to kill a child, before childbirth? But that was a mistake and a long time ago . . . and because Lonnie refused marriage and wouldn't even acknowledge he was the child-father. Not until he learned I was to emigrade up here . . . but then it was too late, Lord, and I had already done what I didn't have your permission to do. It done already, Lord, and you should forget it, and stop punishing me, and I should be able to stop remembering it, as I try to do. That is in the past; like the time when:* it was the king's birthday celebrations, under the clammy-cherry tree in the school yard of St. Matthias Girls' School in 1937, and the custom was to pass old stale hot-cross-buns that were no longer hot (since they were leftovers from the Zephrins Bakery in Bridgetown) round from hungry hand to starving hand; pass them through a circle of two hundred hands, until each and every child had one bag full; and in the midst of this feast which came whenever a king or a queen of England ascended the throne in England, midst the happiness of those young black Barbadian school girls, some barefooted as they were born, some in uniforms, some in rags, some bareheaded with the grease from coconut oil mixing with the sweat from the sun, pouring little streams of shining thick water down their cheeks, some with bad teeth that they were born with, and which hurt for days and nights because there never was a school dentist in the district because there was no dentist on the school's list of staff members, because nobody in that village who had to send her daughter to that school, to take buns from a king of England, free, could afford dentist's fees, nobody in that village black-enough-rich-enough . . . *the time when I told that lie, when:* Isabelle, who lived beside Bernice, was a small emaciated black anemic girl, who never was full, who was always hungry; and Isabelle knew this, and Bernice knew this, and Miss Henderson knew this, although she was the headmistress and never was very close to her pupils; but the headmistress did nothing (did she do nothing because she could not?) to quench the thirst of Isabelle's hunger. And when the buns came round, from hand to hand, and the bag reached Bernice's hand, she dropped one bag behind her on the ground, and stood over it, hoping that no other girl or assistant mistress had seen. And when it was almost over — the passing of the buns — one bag of stale buns was short.

"One buns missing!" the headmistress screamed.

The white inspector of schools was standing close to her at this gala bun-giving ceremony of majestical rejoicing. "One bag o' buns missing! Who thiefed a bag of buns?"

No one had stolen the buns. Universal silence said so. Not Bernice. Not the girl beside her; not Isabelle, whose mother Bernice had intended to give the buns to, later in the afternoon, to feed the four remaining children, who were too weak to go to school, who had no clothes (no rags mended sufficiently to enable the rags to go to school where children's fingers of play and rough-housing would have made them rags again. After all, the school was not paying for the buns. They were given to the schoolchildren by the king. The teachers were given three bags each because they were teachers.) So Bernice decided to steal the bag of buns which would have been supper for Isabelle's family. But the headmistress found out. She always found out everything with the help of a leather strap which the children said she soaked each night in "a topsy of pee-water."

When Bernice got home, without the gift of stale buns for Isabelle's mother, she rushed into the house and screamed into her mother's ears: *"England expects every man to do his duty!"* quoting the inspector in his speech, who was in turn quoting Lord Nelson.

Her mother almost dropped the cou-cou stick with which she was turning the corn meal which was her dinner; and she stood like a woman turned into the salt of wallaba, into a statue like that of Lord Horatio Nelson, and she said after she had wiped a fingernail of sweat from the forehead of her toils, "Never, you hear me? *never* you come into this humble but decent abode again, and utter them obscene words in my hearing! God blind England! Who the hell England think she is, anyhow?"

Two chastisements for one crime, one crime of patriotism: the headmistress had given her six lashes with her urine-soaked leather strap, and it had torn her skin in welts and little long mounds where the correction of the strap had landed. And her mother had warned her about England. *It is done already, Lord, and you should forget it and stop punishing me, and I should be able to stop remembering it . . .*

Bernice had forgotten about calling Lonnie. Instead, she was thinking again of people she hated. Mrs. Burrmann remained at the head of her inventory. In the thirty-odd months she was employed by her, Bernice had killed Mrs. Burrmann on seven different occasions, in her mind. Always, it was a violentless death: killing that wiped out Mrs. Burrmann away from the present, and from Bernice's presence. Bernice would sometimes will Mrs. Burrmann dead like a fairy with a wand of evil-doing — although to Bernice, willing Mrs. Burrmann dead was not an evil. She elevated Brigitte to second place because she got more money for doing the same domestic job less efficiently than Bernice. And Bernice never understood how a Jewish lady like Mrs. Gasstein could employ a German maid!

"You don't seem to understand, Bernice, gal, that this life is a battle o' wits," Dots said, trying to explain Brigitte's presence in the Gasstein household. "You don't really understand it? Well, let me explain it, then. Now, Mistress Gasstein, being a born Jew, wouldn't think of hiring a black woman like you or me. No. That ain' a high enough social position for her, in terms o' domestics and maids, since every blasted little white woman with a husband making more than five-thousand dollars a year wages, and with a house, want to and could hire a blasted person as a living-in slave. But that do not bring prestige. You see the sperspective I driving at? But when she could spend her riches on a German woman, who she know is a German, and therefore a Nazzi, well, she could brag to all her Forest Hill friends that she have *one o' them* working *under* her. You understand now, the sperspective?"

"I don't understand it. Not that I don't understand the words you used, it isn't that. I do not understand it becausing it is the same thing as a woman like me, let's say, with riches and class like the riches of a Mistress Burrmann

or a Mistress Gasstein or a Mistress Hunter down in Rosedale, turning round and refusing to hire a black person as
my maid, and instead, I hire a white woman who I know
beforehand is a member of the Klu-Klux-Klan."

"You got a point there!"

"Be-Christ, I have too."

"But still."

"Still, what?"

"Still."

"No still. That ain' true. It isn't a matter of still, or no
still. It splain. I would not, could not trust a Jewish person
who I know hates a German person and who still turn round
and employ one o' them, a German, simply because . . ."

"You will understand when you understand first that
white people think altogether different and *contrary* from
black people." Bernice was very attentive to this. "Be-Christ,
they have a different brand o' logic-machine in their head,
turning out the kind of logic you just discern concerning
Brigitte and Mistress Gasstein." And that was the only explanation that Bernice would accept.

In spite of a façade of friendship between Brigitte and
herself, Bernice had said some scandalous things about her,
and had ripped her reputation, which she could see sometimes through the window blinds, into threads: Brigitte had
two men visiting her at the same time, two white men, both
policemen; and she had a third man, a black man, Boysie.
Bernice said this. Gossiped about this. But she couldn't
understand it. All she knew was that one of the policemen
had a name like "Wallace-something . . . Wallace? or
Vallitz . . . ?" She wanted Boysie to put a "proper lashing"
on Brigitte and teach her sense. She wished that Boysie
would breed her, and leave her. She did not wish it in such
a way that Boysie would get into any trouble. She wanted
the sorrow and the misery to fall entirely on Brigitte.

But now it was time to repent, because she was certain that these hatreds had brought on the vengeance which she was now experiencing. There was a great superstition involved. More than a superstition considering how obsessive her problems had become to her. She wanted to repent, and being a christian-minded woman, she could think of only one pure way to do it. She had to pray. She wanted to read her Bible; for she was a woman who knew that only in the Bible would she find the exact word of advice or reprimand which her present crime demanded. As a matter of fact, Bernice used this book like a dictionary. She was searching for it now in its usual resting places: under her pillow, on the dresser, on the shelf among the soaps and the Modess boxes, under the chesterfield; she even went into the bathroom to see whether she had read it while peeing. But it was in no place she had searched. She was getting mad. "Where the hell is my Bible? Where it could gone to? It didn' walk out of here . . . Lord, forgive me for misplacing thy precious word." And with new God-given strength, and new vision, she felt stronger already: she could see things she had been accustomed to seeing, and therefore did not see, both due to her preoccupation with other things, and because of the repetition of these things in her vision, day in and day out, and their subsequent lessening significance. "Lord, he that hath eyes to see, seeth not. I asking you, God, for five minutes. Five minutes is all I need."

And then she remembered where it was. She had slipped it under Estelle's pillow on her hospital bed, the first day she visited her, when Estelle had to go to the washroom. Now, both Estelle and the Bible were gone. "I gotta find a blasted Bible, I gotta find a Bible." Grumbling going down the stairs, she ended up in the living room, to see if Mrs. Burrmann had one there. There wasn't a Bible in sight. She bounded back upstairs into Mrs. Burrmann's bedroom, and there was only a large bottle of Benedictine & Brandy liqueur on the table beside the bed. There were also two liqueur glasses. Bernice helped herself to two glassfuls of the strong drink. They did not give her any more strength. She saw some rubber things, like white balloons, small, wrapped and rolled carefully in paper cases, smelling like that part of the hospital where Estelle was. She took up one, smelled it, and saw written on it: *Ramses one genuine transparent TRADE MARK REG Rolled rubber prophylactic.* Bernice held it close to her eyes, examining it and smelling it and puzzling over it; and then she put it to her nostril, closer, and really smelled it; and for no reason, she started laughing, "Heh-heh-ho-ho-ho-ho-hoheh!" And she turned it on the other side, and saw: *sold only in drugstores for protection against disease. Printed in Canada. Distributed by Julius Schmid (Canada) Ltd.* "That is a German name, ain't it? Be-Christ, a German man like Brigitte made this thing, yuh!" *Toronto Canada, Always buy "Ramses" by the dozen and SAVE* "Shit!" She read this side again: . . . *for protection against disease* . . . "But wait, who in this house got the disease? Mister Burrmann? Or the mistress? But look at these two sinful bitches, though, eh? . . . *Ramses, Ramses* . . . heh-heh-haaaaaah!" And laughing with herself, and anticipating the amount of screaming this discovery was going to throw Dots into when she told her, Bernice went into Mr. Burrmann's bedroom next.

Her first impulse was to search his bedside table for more Ramses. But she felt that that was wrong. She was looking for a Bible. "These people want God in their hearts! Not a blasted Bible in this palace! Five television sets, four in colour, and not one blasted Bible?" But she found one, soon after. It was not the Bible Bernice called a Bible. It was green and red, like a school text, marked *The New English Bible, New Testament.* She didn't like it. It was presump-

tuousness on the part of somebody. "But wait, how many
Bibles they have nowadays? I only know 'bout one. And this
one in my hand ain' like the Bible in truth. This is a *book*."
It was the only one available. And rather than go without a
Bible at all, she condescended to read the passage she had
already chosen in her mind, the only passage which she felt
would give her the strength to carry on. She knew it had
something to do with Saul, *who used to be called Paul also;
that bad bad brute who went 'bout persecuting those blessed
disciples and getting-on like a real sinner with all his ras-
cality. But be-Christ, God stepped in though, and put a
finish to Paul's doings.* She found the passage: Acts 8, verse
9; and she began to read: *Meanwhile Saul was still breathing
murderous threats against the disciples of the Lord. He went
to the High Priest and applied for letters to the synagogues
at Damascus, authorizing him to arrest anyone he found,
men or women, who followed the new way* . . . "But this
thing ain' reading like a Bible, in truth! This isn't Bible-talk,
this isn't the way the Bible does say things, man!" She was
furious. "And what the hell this book mean by saying *who
followed the new way.* Which way that is? Are they telling
me something 'bout a road or a street, or something like
that?" Someone had tampered with the golden words in
her Bible, the one with which she grew up, and which she
read every night before she went to bed. "This is rudeness
on this man's part, whoever he is that write this book and
calling it a Bible!" But she still perused the passage and then
found out that she didn't even understand how the verses
and the chapters were arranged in this strange book. For she
had seen Acts 8, 9, and had mistaken it for chapter 8 verse
9; whereas it meant, that on that page, chapter 8 was concluded and chapter 9 started — on the same page. What she
had read was therefore Act 9, verses 1, onwards. *While he
was still on the road and nearing Damascus, suddenly a light*

*flashed from the sky all round him. He fell to the ground
and heard a voice saying, Saul, Saul, why do you persecute
me? Tell me, Lord, he said, who are you. The voice answered, I am Jesus, whom you are persecuting. But get up
and go into the city and you will be told what you have to
do. Meanwhile the men who were travelling with him stood
speechless; and they heard the voice but could see no one.
Saul got up from the ground, but when he opened his eyes
he could not see; so they led him by the hand and brought
him into Damascus. He was blind for three days, and took
no food or drink.* Bernice got up from the floor, brushed the
circulation back into her knees, put down Mr. Burrmann's
strange Bible, and left. She liked the message, but she disliked the way it was written. She knew what she had to do,
however: it was no longer an instruction to Saul, it was a di-
rect order to her. "But I must buy a small cheap Bible when
I go out, and read this passage again, in the right Bible-
language."

Estelle had just finished the novel she was reading when the
trainman, dressed in black, placed a board with the notice
that the Canadian National train going to Timmins would
stop at Richmond Hill, Barrie, Orillia, Gravenhurst, Hunts-
ville, Sundridge, North Bay, Timagami, Redlake, Latchford,
Cobalt, Haileybury, Earlton, Englehart, Dane, Swastika,
Kirkland Lake, Bourkes, Ramore, Matheson, Monteith, Por-
quis Junction, Pamour, Porcupine, South Porcupine, Schu-
macher and Timmins. Estelle had no idea that the train had
to stop at so many places, and having to stop at so many
places before Timmins, she concluded that Timmins must
really be behind God's back. This was her first journey on a
train of any kind. She had thought the train would pull out
of the station, blow its whistle twice or so, and fast "as a
train" stop in Timmins, in a matter of hours. So that, in

the event of emergency, depression and boredom with the north, she could hop on to another train and come back to Toronto; spend the night in Toronto, and perhaps return to Timmins early the next morning, by train.

She did not really understand why she was on this train going to see Mrs. Macmillan in Timmins anyhow. "Just to give her a chance, just a chance!" When she reached a man at a door, she asked him how far away Timmins was.

"Five-hundred-odd miles," he told her, as if he was referring to the bus stop around the corner.

"*Five hundred?*" It rattled her. But the man of the train could not see the shock in his reply: he was already walking away beside the steam coming from under the belly of the train she was boarding, and he was too busy to hear. "Five hundred miles!" And she immediately thought of Barbados: it is only twenty-one miles long in the longest part, and sixteen miles broad in the broadest part. She stopped to check her arithmetic on the dust of the green train, writing with the inkless pen of her index finger. "Four hundred and seventy-nine miles I would be travelling out in the damn Atlantic Ocean, Christ! ha-ha-ha!"

She was still walking to find her coach, walking and meeting the hissing of the underbelly of the train, and meeting also a few inquisitive but not jeering faces printed at the glass windows like patterns; meeting a man, a porter, standing like a black proprietor beside a step, one flight high, near a door which was not really a door, but rather a passage between two coaches which joined them together, and through which a passenger could enter one of the coaches or fall off. Estelle didn't want to stop and board at the first black-uniformed-conducted coach she met; so she walked on, amongst the fumes and the rattling of carts loading baggage and luggage and mail . . . on to the next man, a white man, and there she stopped and stepped. He took her ticket, looked at it, motioned her on, gave her back her ticket; and she walked farther along the walk, going to the noise to the front of the monstrous train, near the smells of hops and ale and beer stale on the nostrils from the nearby breweries, and into the face of the smells of the railroad yard. All the time, humid and miserable and a little tired and lost in the vast crowd of people coming and going, she was thinking of four hundred miles, or was it five hundred? . . . four hundred miles and seventy-nine added on, all those blasted miles to get to some place at the end of which she did not know for sure whether the woman, Mrs. Macmillan, was going be there: for Mrs. Macmillan, whose idea it was to get her to journey to Timmins, might be a completely different person by now, Estelle thought; she was certainly no longer a next-door bed-sitting, bed-talking neighbour. She was a friend who became a friend under the special conditions of a sickbed.

Estelle selected a seat beside a window. She stood up by the seat. She looked at the other passengers, some making themselves comfortable in their nests of choice, like birds turning straw and twigs into dunlippillo mattresses for a long night; and some already reading, or pretending to be reading, so they wouldn't have to listen to the railroad history of some of their neighbours. She looked in front. And she looked behind. She found out where people put their bags — on the racks above them — and she put hers there too. And then she sat down. She must find something to do.

She got up, reached for her bag (her slip moved above her knees, and the backs of her knees were showing, and her thighs were riding up in sight too; and one man, three seats and rows behind, whistled under his breath and whinnied in a low whinny as if he had just seen heaven up her legs!), and she took her bag down. She must not lose her shaking composure. She should read Mrs. Macmillan's letter again: she wanted to read the novel she had just finished — although she had never before read a book twice, not even a school textbook. But this new environment, this new condition, was making her uncertain of herself, uncomfortable, nervous, tense, doing things she had never done before.

She got down the bag which wasn't cumbersome, and when it was beside her on the seat, she realized that the novel, *Cannery Row*, and the letter were in the handbag. Anticipating the horselaugh of her admirer behind, she just left the bag beside her. It served a double purpose: the man wouldn't whinny again, and she wouldn't have to feel self-conscious if all the other seats were taken up by two passengers, except hers. She could rule this seat, herself, rule it like a princess on a colonial colony of leprosy — if it came to that. Before she could settle herself in her seat and hide (like the others) behind the novel or the letter, a man entered and chose the seat opposite her. Immediately, he started to inspect her when he thought she wasn't watching. She tried to concentrate on the novel, which she wasn't reading, and the man noticed this too.

Estelle wasn't even considering him as a serious threat, although he was so objectionable to her. But he continued to stare and to watch. The train started to move in the opposite direction she had expected it to go; but it soon corrected this error of direction, and pulled out of the station, with the noise and the clanking and the turning which only the lowest-paying passengers knew about. The moment they were in motion, the man's attitude changed. Motion had apparently given him more courage, more daring, more liberality. He placed her suitcase on the overhead rack, smiled, and sat beside her.

"Do you mind?" he said.

Inwardly, she flinched; she thought she knew exactly the kind of conversation he would begin.

"Do you mind?" This time, he took out a package of cigarettes. He lit a cigarette. He took two deep puffs on it, and the smoke erupted and seemed to hide his boorishness from her for a second. When it cleared, he was saying, "Very good book." He had seen the title, and now he was giving her his comments. "Steinbeck is a great writer. Always thought he deserved the Nobel Prize."

Estelle didn't know what he was talking about. She had to glimpse at the title of the book to see if it was really written by the man named Steinbeck. And it was. This thing about a Nobel Prize: the book didn't tell her anything about that. She was beginning to feel inferior with this strange unwelcomed man, who knew so many things about a book she held in her hands, and which she had read from cover to cover, and of which she apparently remembered nothing.

"Where're you from? The States? Where're you heading?" he asked, without giving her the chance to answer the first question. But then again, she didn't think she had to answer him. She felt it was too personal a question for a stranger to ask: but she answered him nevertheless.

"Timmins."

"You're really going north!"

She did not answer him this time.

"Went there once myself. Great little mining community, and the local people're real friendly. Small town, you know." He puffed on his cigarette. "Say, would you like a drink in the club car?" She did not want to answer this question at all, but he was leaning over, commanding her to say something, so she felt she had to answer; it became one of those situations in which a lie would relieve the tension.

"Sorry. I don't drink." And she swallowed hard; for the greatest wish she had for that moment was for a drink.

"C'mon! A little drop never killed anybody! C'mon. We can have a drink, quietly, in the club car." She was saved from answering by the arrival of the conductor who was taking up the tickets. Estelle found his work interesting: he would look at the tickets, seeming to know all the various kinds and prices and colours in the brainbox of his head by heart; and then he would punch a hole in them, destroying them, no doubt; and then he would stick the punched-up ticket in a little crease above the passenger's head, on the side of the coach.

The man was going to Orillia. Estelle remembered this as being one of the early stops. She would be rid of him soon enough. Perhaps the drink, a free drink, wouldn't be a bad idea, after all, she thought. The tall conductor looked at her. Fleetingly she went back in time and attitude to the night of her cold arrival at Malton International Airport, when the immigration officer gave her such a hard, unnecessarily cross-examining look. But this man was friendly.

"You are travelling in the wrong class, lady." Estelle laughed to herself. Of course she was travelling in the wrong class! And in the wrong company! "You should be in a roomette. I'll come later, and arrange for your roomette."

"Lord, you saved me!" Estelle said in her heart. And to the man, who was waiting all this time for her answer, she said, "Well, one drink never killed nobody, eh?"

He almost fell over in a bundle of extreme pleasure. He got up swiftly (in case she changed her mind), and led her through the coaches, saying as they went along, "Let me!

Allow me! Let me! Allow me! Permit me! Let me! Allow me! Let me!" The man had opened eight doors for her. And then they went round a corner, their bodies touching the panel, their hands brushing against the smooth, balancing wood, and into the club car, where Estelle blinked her eyes twice, because there were two black men serving drinks.

She was self-conscious again.

"What would you like to drink, dear?" he asked her. It took her some time to decide: he suggested a dry martini as a good summer drink, "although summer's gone now! but the spirit's still here!"; or a gin and tom collins or tonic water. And she took that. "Beer for me, tonic and gin for the lady," he said.

The waiter smiled. ("Ain't got much bread, eh baby?" he said to himself.) The waiter was accustomed to this. ("Can't make no fucking tips this way, baby. Betcha this white bastard only got a five-dollar bill in his lousy wallet!") When the drinks came, the man took out a thick wad of money, and deliberately, but not with too much bravado, peeled off the smallest bill he had, a twenty-dollar bill, and paid for the drinks. The waiter's eyes became slightly bigger, as he stared. ("Gotta give this bastard real cool service now!")

"I was interested in seeing you reading Steinbeck," the man said, when the drinks were served, and he tipped the waiter one dollar ("Goddamn! this cat's Howard Hughes himself!"), and had mixed Estelle's drink for her. She waited for the conversation to approach the "Negro problem." "I do a bit of reading myself, when I get the chance. I can't think of anything, anything at all, as great as that." He had finished his beer in three large gulps. He wiped the foam from round his mouth with the tip of his tongue, like a cow would, fast and efficiently. He held up his hand to

order again, and the moment his hand was raised, the waiter
was upon him like a wasp.

"Yes, boss?" he asked. And before Mister Boss could say
a word, he asked, "Same again?" This was even before Mister Boss had said yes. "Good!" the waiter said. The drinks
came. He again mixed Estelle's, held it to her to taste, gave
the waiter another dollar tip ("Goddamn! this motherfucker's loaded, baby! He's sure itching for them pants tonight, too!"), and took a large mouthful of his beer.

"As we were saying . . ."

The conductor's voice boomed through the train, "Orillia! next stop Orillia! Next stop for Orillia!"

This was the man's stop. This saved her. This made him
finish his beer and his conversation. The passages along
which they had to walk were shaking, and often, he rested
his hand on her hips gently, to steady her, but he left it
there long after the train had straightened out on its long
parallel lines. "Allow me! Let me! Allow me!" and he
reached a passage that was dark; and the train was not
even heaving, only his heart and his lust and his desire and
his bravery; and he put his arms out, and grabbed her and
pulled her close to him. And he planted his mouth, smelling like beer kegs, over hers. In a flash, she could feel his
tongue searching for something inside her mouth. It had
happened so quickly, so unexpectedly, that she did not have
time to push him off. "C'mon, babe! Just a little one." But
she got him off her. And when he was off, she let loose a
slap which hit his fat cologned jowls like leather hitting cement. "You bitch!" he cried. "If, if-if-if, if you weren't a
woman . . ." She was frightened. The passage became des-
olate. But she tried to appear brave.

"Don't you have to get your bags?" she asked him. And
she walked away in the opposite direction. . . .

The conductor met her to say that he had been looking for her: her roomette had been selected. When she reached it, with the bed already pulled down and made, she dropped on the bed and cried. She was very sad and very frightened to be in this country. *But what does a bloody white man think he is? What he think a woman like me, is? What the hell he thinks I am, still a slavewoman, or a child, this day and age? Godblindthem-all!* She tried to pull herself together. She sat down and tried to enjoy the ride before getting into bed, to sleep. *That wasn't so bad a thing to cause me to sulk and make myself depressed and miserable from here to Timmins!* She unpacked her nightgown (the conductor, or somebody else, had brought her valise from the other part of the train), and prepared to read Mrs. Macmillan's letter since she did not want to hear any more about Mister Steinbeck; and since she would be meeting Mrs. Macmillan soon; and because too, she wanted to see if she had overlooked anything of importance to herself, any pointer of what living in Timmins would be like. She could find nothing in it to interest her, one way or the other.

Someone knocked on her door. It startled her. The person was trying to open the door. Estelle scrambled to put on her housecoat. "Just a minute, please."

The knocker shook the door lightly. She wondered whether it was the man who tried to kiss her, in the passageway. She opened the door. It was the black waiter who served them a while ago, in the club car. He stood foolishly in the doorway for a while, but soon he controlled his slight nervousness and smiled. Estelle smiled, sweetly and genuinely. She did not reject nor welcome the company. But it was good to know somebody was checking to see whether she was safe.

"I came to see if you need anything."

"Oh, that's all right."

"I saw you just now. In the car. Drinking. With that fellow. First, I thought you were his wife, or something." In his profession, in his job, he must have seen many similar situations, she thought. She decided to let him talk. If you let men talk, they would soon betray the wolf's nature beneath their gentleman's attire. "I am a West Indian. From Grenada. I think you're a West Indian, too. Heard your accent. Lemme guess. Not Jamaica!" But he had already guessed, and decided that she was from Barbados. He could not mistake the dialect. He knew all this, but he wanted to give the impression he was really thinking about her well-being. But he had come with one thing in his mind. He and his waiter-friend had wagered five dollars that he would "lash her tonight, man! it take me no more than one hour to get in her pants, man!" He was to bring back some thread of evidence to show his friend. His friend asked, "What kind o' proof you going give me, nigger?"

The waiter-nigger laughed in his face, and said, "I coming back in half-a-hour, with my hands smelling like pussy, 'cause I not going wash them off till I put them in your face to smell."

"Shit, nigger! that ain't true! Gorblummuh, you can't fool a old black bitch like me, nigger! You only got to scratch yourself, or your dicky, and you *gotta* smell funky!"

"You're not a Trinidadian, I know that. I could smell that accent a mile off!" He inspected her face; convinced himself she was very beautiful, and very desirable; and he watched her closely to see whether she would really be as beautiful in bed.

"You're a Bajan," he told her. And he smiled.

"How you know?" She knew how he knew.

"The accent. Besides, Bajan women is the best in the Wessindies! In the world. I should know. My mother is a

Bajan." (His mother, when he had one, before she died of acute tuberculosis, was a Trinidadian woman.)

He had now come inside the doorway. But he held his hand still on the post; the door was slightly open. He was still dressed in his porter's uniform.

"Well, for one thing, it is good to meet another West-indian in a place like this, behind-God's-back."

"This country hard. That's why I working on the trains to pay my university fees."

"That's good, boy, you're young, and it's more important for you to be a doctor or a lawyer, or whatever it is you're going through for, than to worry-out your brains about these white people, and this country, eh."

She was enjoying talking to him. She could lapse into her Barbadian dialect without feeling self-conscious, without feeling anything but pride, and a closeness to the man she was talking to. It was so different when she was talking to Sam Burrmann, with whom she had to be so particular. "Boy, a job is a job, yuh," she said, her voice rich with the dialect and with an assumed deep knowledge of this country. "You is a young man. A man with learning and education to boot! So save your money to pay them school-fees, you hear me?"

"I like you, I mean, I like the way you talk." He did not think it was quite time to confess, or express, his sex-feelings for her. "You mind if I come back? Look, I gotta do a few things, but I won't be long."

She was nodding her head, telling him, yes, come back, it will be all right. And nervous in his thighs and anxious in his ambition, he was smiling. She's fucking easy, he told himself.

"You had something to eat?"

"Wait! you mean to say they give you food on these trains, too?"

But he was away before she could say more to him. She felt good: it would be so good to sit down and talk with a fellow West Indian, on a lonely train, going where neither of them belonged. She touched her hair with her hands, and ducked her head this way and then that, like a boxer in the slowest motion evading punches; she passed her fingers under her armpits, to see if they smelled; and when she passed them under her nostrils, and they did not smell, she nevertheless passed the roll-on deodorant over the tufts of hair growing under her armpits. Hastily, she changed from her nightgown and housecoat, and slipped on her panties, her half slip (no brassiere: which she didn't need, because of the ripeness of her breasts), and put on a dress, cream in colour, which exposed the tantalizations in her hips every time she even breathed. It fitted her suggestively neatly round the waist. It had no sleeves. It accentuated her colour, light bronze; and it made her look even more beautiful. (The dress was one of Bernice's which she had altered to her fancy and size and fashion.)

She had just slipped on her slippers, when there was a knock on the door, and again, the waiter-porterman entered without waiting for her to invite him in. She had not even said, "Who is it?" But he was standing there, holding a bottle of gin (he had served her gin earlier, and he was told by his friends that gin did the job quickly), and three bottles of tonic in one hand; and in the other was a parcel of greaseproof paper, with the grease showing through it, which contained three large pieces of chicken springing juice and smell like a spring springing water.

"Brought you a little snack . . ."

"Man, you is the first kind man I meet on this train."

"I know you was hungry."

"As a horse, boy."

"Good! I hope you thirsty, too."

"A little taste never killed."

"Good!"

"Boy, pour the drink, do!"

"More tonic?" he asked, pouring the drink, without asking her if he had given her too much gin. "Good!" They were drinking. She was eating. He watched her, and he laid his plans. He sized her up. And he laid his webs in the parlour of his anxiety. He undressed her in his mind; and then he selected, mentally, the best position he would bend her into, in order to get the most juices out of her body. *Baked fowl!* was the position he chose to use with her.

"So you's a student, eh?"

"Yeah. Easy course, man! I studying economics, and then law. When a grajjuate, I think I going back home to Grenada and enter politics. In Grenada, man, I could be a king! So far, there ain't all that many Grenadians with degrees."

"I like the way you talking."

"Well, it don't make sense to come up here in Canada, work like a blasted dog, study books like hell, and then when you grajjuate, with a better degree than some o' these Canadian fellows, you still can't command the same salary or job."

"Now, you're not talking the way I like to hear you talk. *They* don't have to give you one damn thing. You have to take it! My little experience here already told me that."

"You right! I agree with your thesis."

They drank; and she ate and drank. The train was moving fast. Now and then he checked to see how she was faring under the drinks, which he had poured heavily for her, and lightly for himself. He was talking now, in a lowered voice, as if he was conscious of somebody outside listening. He knew he had to listen out for the conductor. His friend, the Barbadian married-man-of-war-porter, was on the watch at one end of the sleeping cars, but he couldn't be at both ends at the same time. To be caught in a woman's room meant dismissal.

They talked about everything under the sun. She knew his name, Matthew Woods (he didn't think it would hurt to tell her his correct name), his age (he was thirty), and his address ("I live in a rasshole slum house, as my Jamaican friend would say, somewhere on Bedford Road, near the university. It does pain my arse when I have to pay that bastard, pardon my language Estelle, but this country can do funny things to a man's vocabulary . . . twelve dollars every Friday," he told her).

He was merry. He was beginning to feel his drinks, and his oats. He exchanged his seat on the chair for a place beside her, on the bed. Estelle moved to give him a comfortable seat beside her. He brought the gin bottle and placed it near, beside her on the floor. Estelle rested her hand on his, and got up, and closed her valise, which she had left open, and in which she could see a pink brassiere, and which she feared the young man had seen. ("Don't want to give this blasted woman-hungry West Indian boy the wrong ideas!")

The young man had seen it; he had also seen the under-softness of her knees. The moment she came back, he rested his hand on her knee, as if he was about to tell her something very personal, something very confidential. But when she saw that he was not about to say anything at all, she removed it in such a way as not to hurt his feelings. He turned, and put his arm round her waist, and forced her close to him. "All right? All right? Eh, darling?" he was asking. Estelle trembled. She trembled because she was so fed up. To think that this could happen twice in one train ride! And the second time with a black man! Her own people! "All right?" He was forcing his face against her face, trying to force her to lie on the bed. She had not yet refused his kiss by turning her face. And he, hectic with heat and sex, did not have the wisdom to see that his actions were objectionable.

"I warning you, Matthew Woods, I warning you to stop behaving like a damn fool."

"Oh, you only playing shy. Why you let me come in here then, with you in a bare nightgown and housecoat, if you didn't want me to . . ."

And then the gin bottle crashed over his head. And the blood spurted. She had given him a thud of a blow. In a mad, frightened, single action, he leaped off the bed, ran to the door, unlocked the door, rushed out, and closed the door, without the slightest sound, without the slightest jerk of his body, all in one swift, noiseless, jaguarlike action. Estelle looked at the broken bottle (she was very sorry she had spilled the gin: it was such a good summer drink!), holding it in her hand; and absolutely fed up, with herself, with her life, with Matthew Woods and the white man who tried to kiss her, she threw the bottle against the wall. Then she pressed the buzzer and started packing her valise. When the porter came (it was the Barbadian, who had made the bet with Matthew Woods, but who did not know he had won the bet), she asked him what was the next stop.

"North Bay, ma'am," he said, politely. "But your stop is Timmins, ain't it, ma'am? Timmins's still a long pull."

"How do you get off this train?"

"Two coaches down, ma'am. But the next stop is North Bay, not Timmins. We coming into North Bay in a few minutes." (Was he worried about his bet; or about his "admittable" evidence?)

"Thanks." She walked towards him, forcing him backwards towards the door. "Thank you now, very much." He got the message.

"Goodnight, ma'am," he said, and closed the door behind him. Outside, half asleep and puzzled ("Where in hell is that nigger?"), he had to admit, "she's a real dish! and one hell of a she-cat! I shouldda tried my luck! That nigger, Matthew Woods lucky as hell."

When Estelle walked down the steps from the platform, in the distance, amidst the steam and the roar and the men scurrying with the baggage, she saw Matthew Woods, with a large white bandage on his head. Beside him, laughing loudly so that Estelle could hear, and know why, was the Barbadian married-man-of-love porter. She did not look back. Although North Bay was a strange town.

"Estelle is nothing but a little cheap whore!" Dots said.
"Once upon a time, I would have argued with you 'bout that," Bernice conceded. "But now, I have to be the first man to cast the first stone in regards to my sister's badness. God knows, God knows I try hard to help out that girl. And what I get for it? I get thanks? I get acknowledgments? I get anything but botheration for the kindness I showed that girl in bringing her up here from Barbados where she would have rotten-away? I have put my job in jeopardy. I went into my bank account to the tune of three hundred dollars. Paying off debts for Estelle."

Dots and Bernice are sitting in Bernice's quarters: they are drinking German beer. All of a sudden Bernice says, "I have to turn over a new leaf. When Estelle leave to go back to Barbados, I will still be here fighting this man to keep alive. If Estelle get married, if she even married Mr. Burrmann, I will still be a damn domestic. If Estelle drop down dead, right now, be-Jesus Christ, Dots, Bernice will still be servanting. And if not for the Burrmanns, up in Forest Hill, it will be for the McDermonts of Leaside, or

the Skinners up in the Bridal Path, or some-other-blasted
white man or white woman, in this city, or in a new city, or
perhaps in Montreal. No, Dots. I have to start looking-out
for Bernice now. Estelle will come home. Estelle will find
me. Estelle will find me if it is the last thing she can do. She
must run outta money. I don't think Mr. Burrmann is giving her money. He don't strike me as the man to have that
kind o' decencies. She must experience discrimination in
this city, and hafta find me, or you, or Henry, or Agaffa, to
ask if we know any landladies who don't discriminate too
much. Child, this city is such a funny place, that sooner or
later, Estelle, like any other black person, will understand
white people the moment they feel the pinch of prejudice.
It is the way it is. And I am not telling you any damn
'nancy story."

"Still," Dots pleaded.

"Still, what?"

"It is in your place to make the first move."

"I am guilty o' that already. I brought up Estelle. I should
have brought up Lonnie, or some other man to help make
my bed more comfortable at night, in the winter especially.
I already made the first move, a damn bad one too, and I
not making a second bad move, Dots."

After all the desolation and the beauty of the fleeting country of the northern Ontario, which she had seen through
the window of the train, Estelle was stunned by the liveli-
ness and the big-city spirit of North Bay. It was similar to
what she had heard tourists in Trinidad say about the Trinidadians, and their life and their gaiety, in contrast to the
drab British dullness of her own little island of Barbados.
North Bay, which was halfway to behind-God's-back on her
trip north, was like a new pleasant world. She liked North
Bay. If she wasn't in her present predicament, she thought,

she would consider settling in North Bay, instead of in Toronto. In Toronto were the causes of her problems, and she
was woman enough to know she had to face them; in Toronto was Bernice who would be furious with her; in Toronto was Sam Burrmann who would be hating her now; in
Toronto was Agatha, who was her only female friend, and
who would want to know. Agatha had visited her once
(which was more than Dots did, or Boysie, or Henry had
done), and had insisted on coming for her the day she was
to be discharged. But Estelle was so obsessed by the reli-
gion of Mrs. Macmillan's promises and by the nearness of
Mrs. Macmillan every minute of the day that she forgot to
telephone Agatha. It was this mesmerization, she thought
now, which was responsible for her presence at this time of
night (or was it morning already? She didn't have a watch)
in North Bay, in a taxicab, going to the nearest and cheapest hotel where she would spend the rest of the night.

"Here we are, miss!" The taxi driver seemed glad to end
this short journey from the train station. He came round,
opened the door, let her out, and then leaned over the seat
and took up her valise. "Straight up those steps." He did
not even surmise that she was lonely, alone, lost, a strange
woman in a strange town, a fit prey for preying men. "Sam,
this lady want a room. A cheap one. But a good one. With
a bath, and . . ."

She looked at Sam, expecting to find some resemblance
to the Sam she knew, wanting there to be this resemblance,
but feeling deep down the disappointment that the resemblance had to stop at the similarity of names. This Sam was
a jolly, red-faced man. The man Sam was just telling her
where to sign when a woman came rollicking through the
door behind the desk. She was alone. She saw Estelle. She
stood erect. She watched Estelle, from head to toe. Estelle
was waiting for the comments: she knew what they always

said. The woman was beginning to remember something; but before she could remember it, a smile was changing the haggard expression into a pleasanter face. Estelle tensed herself, waiting for the abuse, the exclamation, the challenge to her presence. The woman was smiling, and remembering. Sam was watching, but he could have been watching a fly or a carnival, it made no difference to him. Estelle tried to divert the woman's scrutiny by going closer to the desk to sign the register.

But the woman had remembered by this time. She walked right up, close, very close to Estelle, arms outstretched in the first arc of an embrace, or of attack. And when she got close enough to trap Estelle into the jowl-hanging arms of her two-hundred-pounds weight, she exclaimed, with the whiffing perfume of beer in her scream, "Oh my God, Estelle! Estelle! Estelle. Jesus God, Sam, this is *her!*" It was Mrs. Macmillan. In the hospital she had been a redhead. Now, her hair was blonde.

part two

To the very quality of friends

Bernice was so very happy to receive the letter. She switched off the electric vacuum cleaner, dropped the handle where it was, and ran upstairs, taking the stairs two steps at a time right into her quarters. She locked the door behind her. She untied the apron strings and flung the apron on the floor. She walked on it, by mistake; but when she realized that it was *her* apron, she walked on it again, and trampled it. The letter was from Lonnie. She had thought of writing him so long ago. And now he had written her, without being asked to do so. She lay on her bed, always tidy, always made up — now that Estelle was away — and she opened the letter, kissing the envelope as she did so. She prepared her mind and her body for the sweet words of the letter. My boyfriend write me, she was saying to herself; my boyfriend write me a love letter.

Dear Bernice, How are you? I am still here, in the name of the Lord, as you can see from the source this letter coming from. I am in Barbados. But Barbados is looking like a strange place to me these days. It look like a strange place to other people too, because I happened to be talking the same thing with a fellow, and he up and tell me that Barba-

*dos today is not the same Barbados he and me grow up
seeing. That will give you an idea of what I mean by
the transformation of this place, as the fellow said, using
that word to describe it to me. First thing, everybody who
isn't old, or who have a few dollars, pulling out for Britain
or for the States. And now that Britain don't want we
coloured people in Britain, and since the States never
wanted we, and it is more difficult to get inside of than
inside a virgin, if you will pardon the word, well the only
place left back is Canada. Canada is so popular nowadays in Barbados, that big girls who went to such places
like Queens College and St. Michaels whiching as you
know, happen to be the two most powerful girl schools
in the island, even that sort of girl is putting down her
name to go up in Canada as a common ordinary domestic,
meaning a servant. What kind of place is Canada, Bernice?
The Canadian people living in the island listen to a radio
programme called the Grey Cup Game. It comes on once
a year, and a fellow who works for a Canadian family down
here tell me that all he could hear was a damn lot of screaming and shouting for "Kill-him, kill-him! Flatten-him, and
kill-him!" and the Canadian family was so drunk afterwards
that they felled asleep with the radio still on. Out of every
ten white people you see walking 'bout in shorts in Bridgetown, exposing their funny looking legs and foots, well
eight or nine is Canadians. They taking over the place.
When once a man could walk on the beach, and if the
urge take him, and he had to go to the toilet in a hurry, he
could maybe stoop down behind a coconut tree or a grape
tree and ease his bowels, and the only person who could
see him doing that would be the big wide sea or the trees,
well now, the people who would see him easing his bowels
is Canadians. They are over all the beach and hotels like
ants. All that freedom that we used to know is stopped*

now. The hotels coming from all up in Canada and they putting up fence and wire round the hotels and a common person can't pass there no more, fatherless ease his bowels. Soon, if a man want to have a sea bath he is going to have to go to the sea with a bucket and take a bucket of sea water back home and pour it on himself through a sieve and splash-about and say Hey-hey-hey-heyhuh-huh-huh! like how you see little children used to play in the sea when there was a sea for them to play in. A man was buying some things one day in Busby Alley and a next man, a white man, not even a Bajan white man, come up to this man and tell him, Get away, you nigger! Bernice, that is the first time a white man ever called a Barbadian a nigger on his own soil. We don't do them things down here. And Bernice, you should have seen the federation of people that congregate in that small alley which as you know can't hold two fat women walking side by side. It was murder. It was federation in Bridgetown that morning. Well, some fellows pelt some licks in that white man arse, and the onliest thing that saved that white man from getting his behind more full of blows and maybe his death too, was the simple fact that Barbadians are hospitable people, plus the next fact that a police, a police who the people like, I mean Johnny Salt Bags, it was really Johnny Salt Bags that save that white man's arse that morning. The powers that be, in this place, have a lot of explaining to do to the poor people. I am one of them poor people. But I struggling in the name of the Lord. I have to tell you now, something that I know you will be very happy to hear. I get saved. I am a christian now, these days. And when you see next month come, I will be holding the morning service on Sunday mornings in the Ebenezer Church in Brittons Hill. I lives in Brittons Hill now. I had to give Terence a stiff cut arse with a tamarind rod only yesterday, for using bad words in my pres-

*ence. By the way, when I say that the powers that be in
this island have a lot of explaining to do to we poor people,
I mean everybody excepting Barrow, who as you know is
our number one man. Getting back to Terence. That boy,
don't mind he is your child and mine too, he must have
a devil inside him. Sometimes I think he take after the
mother. But if there is a will there is a way. I intend to
bring up Terence in the fear of the Lord. Or if he goes on
in the ways of Satan, well then his backbone will be breaken
some day by the rod of justice and mercy. By the way too,
coming first Sunday, I am getting married. My wife to be
is a sister in the same church. We met whilst we was walking up to the altar to get saved at the revival meeting. We
held hands going up to face the preacher and the Lord.
There was no more better way to meet the woman you
want to spend the rest of your days with, as a future wife.
We went up to the altar complete strangers. But we came
down as man and wife, washed in the precious blood of the
Lamb, Amen. I remain, Lonnie, your once upon a time
man. I pray to God that your life in that far distant country over there, call Canada, endureth forever and ever,
Amen. I will pray for you with the hope that one fine day,
one fine precious day you too will take God as your personal saviour and that he will wash your sins away and
make you white as snow. It is not too late to repent, Bernice. Yours in Christ, Brother Lonnie. PS. I am going to
take out a picture and send to you, showing you my wife to
be and myself holding the morning service, Sunday morning, the first Sunday of the month. Thought for today:*

Though your heart may be as hard as flint,
In that heart God can still make a dent.

Bernice wasn't quite sure she was not dreaming. She
read the final page again, the page that contained Lonnie's moral and spiritual transformation. And the meaning

of the page hit her as Lonnie's baptismal water must have cleansed him of all the sorrow and the hardship and sins that baptism is meant to do. She was shaking now. She was furious. Lonnie had served her a trick. She was alone again: this time, irrevocably alone. There was no one beyond the present difficulties of life in her new adopted country to help her bear those very difficulties brought on by the country itself. Estelle, first; now, Lonnie. She could think of nothing to do but call Dots on the telephone. Dots apparently was engaged in something more important. She said this by the brusque manner in which she answered the telephone.

When Bernice poured out her heart to Dots, including reading the entire letter (she read the final page of Lonnie's baptism and reformation twice for Dots, who wanted to hear it), all the consolation Dots gave was, "I wanted to warn you 'bout this a long time ago. I warned yuh, gal! I warned yuh. Instead of bringing up man to warm your nightgown, you went and bring up woman?"

"But I didn' know that Lonnie was thinking 'bout marriage, though."

"You know now!" And then Dots sought to lessen her unkindness. "Any man thinks 'bout marriage, Bernice, if the woman is sweet enough and if she can cook. You don't know that? You didn't know that? Well, be-Christ, you know it today!"

"And Lonnie get saved. Lonnie get saved. When I was living with Lonnie, Lonnie never ever, never ever went near a church, oh my God in all . . ."

"Well, he's going now. And you're lucky that you didn' send down that new suit for Lonnie, for he would be wearing it to his wedding as his bridegroom-suit, and you won't be his bride, neither."

"And she is a sister . . ."

"When it rain, it does pour, gal. Lonnie *gone!*" And the telephone was dropped in her ears.

The message went first to Boysie. Boysie told it to Dots. Immediately (before she even knew the circumstances, the particulars, the causes, the reasons, the date or the place), Dots got on the telephone and told it to Bernice. Bernice telephoned Brigitte who was still in her bad books of "people to hate"; but this news was so happy, that old grievances and hostilities could be put aside — for the time being — so she told her. Brigitte could not call Boysie at his home for fear that Dots would answer the telephone. She would have telephoned Henry (who she was seeing on the sly, even after the policemen had beat him up), but she wanted to find out first if it was true.

Henry and Agatha were getting married.

Everybody was happy. Bernice wished aloud on the telephone to Dots that Estelle was here to hear the good news. Dots wished she would reappear before the wedding day, two weeks from now, on a Saturday afternoon, at four, at St. Thomas Church on Huron Street. Everybody wished Henry and Agatha the best in marriage, and lots of children.

Bernice got on the phone to Henry, and shouted into it, "You big ugly black man! How come you getting such a lovely woman to be married to you? That woman have rocks in her blasted head, or something, yuh! She couldn' find no better man in the whole o' Toronto than you?"

And she laughed; and Henry laughed too, and said, "I is a Cassernover!" They laughed again. Bernice's well-wishing was profusely West Indian.

"I happy happy for you, though. You get a good woman. And I think you deserve it. So, look, see to it you hear me, niggerman, see to it that you bring Agaffa up here tonight.

Me and Dots have a little surprise something for you and
Agaffa. But don't tell she nothing, hear?" Henry agreed to
come. "Boy," Bernice said, seriously now; feeling as happy
for Henry as if Agatha was her own sister, "boy, you have
a damn good woman, there. Treat she good, you hear me?
Treat Agaffa good." And Henry promised to do just that.
Agatha was lying on the couch in his room on Baldwin
Street, when this conversation was going on; and she was
sending kisses to him, at him, all the time Bernice was bel-
lowing on the telephone about the surprise party. When
he was finished, he sat on the couch beside her, but miles
away from her in thought; a bit startled, a bit ruffled, like
a man in the dock who has just realized that he has been
sentenced to years instead of days.

The seriousness of his agreement to marry Agatha had
just hit him for the first time. It wasn't his idea to get married. If he had his way, he would have continued to live in
the pleasurable sin of common-law happiness; he would
never get married: there were too many willing women
around in Toronto, he always told Boysie, who at one time
in the ecstasy of his infatuation for Brigitte had threatened
to beat up Dots and then leave her for Brigitte. "Behave
yourself, boy," Henry had advised him, then. "Look, never
exchange a wife for a outside-woman, be-Christ, you don't
even know where she come from. You don't even know if
she bathes only once a week, you don't know if she is dirty,
you don't know if she's married already in Germany, you
don't know if she have another man with you, you don't
know if she have syphilis or some other disease. You don't
know nothing 'bout that woman. And you come telling me
you're leaving Dots, a woman you know like the back o'
your blasted hand for a woman . . ."

"But I love her, man, Henry," Boysie pleaded. "I love
her bad bad."

"Love? Love my arse! I tired telling you there ain' nothing called love!"

And now, it was Henry's turn to love, to be in love. He knew he was in love with Agatha, in spite of his constant denials; in spite of his front of hardness, of toughness, of callousness, he had always loved her, and he had always put up these fronts in the presence of Boysie.

"Well, I have you now for myself, you brute," Agatha said, jokingly. "Mrs. Henry White! Jesus God, what a name for me to have! Ha-ha!" She was laughing — as she always did — at her new surname: the way it would fit her, and the way she first looked at him that night in a room somewhere on Bedford Road, when he told her his name was White. "*White?*" she had asked him; and then she burst out laughing. "Whoever gave you a name like that?"

"What's so goddamn funny 'bout the name, *White?*"

"Nothing, nothing at all."

"What's so goddamn funny 'bout being called Mrs. White?" he asked her.

"I like it. I love it."

And they embraced some more, and kissed some more, and Henry wanted to go further; but Agatha said she was not in the mood. "Let's wait. I'm best after a party, remember? We have to dress to go up to Bernice's apartment." Never during the time she had known Bernice had Agatha ever referred to Bernice's place as her *quarters*. Henry always noticed this respect which she had for Bernice, and he marvelled at it. It was the more significant because the two women, Bernice and Dots, had never come to accept Agatha completely. She was always the "white woman," or "Henry's white woman"; she was never referred to as Henry's woman, or as *the* woman.

"Where do you think we should live?"

"Live?" Henry was still looking for a job. He had given

his consent "to be married to Agatha," without having first considered the probability that he might never again get a job. He was getting old. And Agatha was such a type of woman that she would want him (and he knew this) to have a job that she could tell her friends about, and she would want her friends to be impressed by it. He could hear her talking to them on the telephone, or during some coffee party, or at some other party, "My husband works here . . . and he does this, or that." Henry knew there would be a great strain on him trying to measure up to Agatha's intellectual level, and up to her social level. But he had decided from the start, when the talk had become serious, and marriage had been skirted as the best thing for them to do ("I am tired living in sin with you, Henry White. We have to get married. Or end it. Lots of people, lots of coloured men, some of them still students, marry white girls"), that he was going to get himself a good un-skilled job that brought in about one hundred dollars a week, or one hundred and ten, or twenty or thirty (with overtime). He was going to kill himself with overtime to bring his wages up to a respectable level, and *if that bitch as much as open her goddamn mouth telling me I should be this or I should be that, goddammit, gorblummuh! as Boysie would say, I am going to pour some stiff lashes in her backside as I would pour peas in a pot.*

"Why can't we rent a nice cheap apartment somewhere down here, where you would be near the university, and we could save some money for the first five years, and . . ."

"Five years? Five years? In five years I would be an old woman, Henry White! What would I be doing spending *five years* to save enough to move out of this slum?"

"It is not a slum, goddammit!" He had raised his voice at her. It was too soon for the landlady to hear them carrying on like this. "This is a nice neighbourhood. It's near to everything. It's the Spadina area, remember?" He meant that as a Jew, she should appreciate that lots of her own people had begun right here on this street. "Spadina. Anyway, I have to get my hands on a job first, before we could move out of this place. I don't want you supporting me, lady. In a few months you would be telling me how to live my goddamn life."

"But darling, if you don't have money, and I have it, and I am your wife . . ." This was a very sore point with him. Over the months of their topsy-turvy relationship, she had lent him money often: they had got drunk together on her money; she had bought Christmas presents for herself with her money (and sometimes she would give him the money to buy the presents with), and she would write his name on it, as the sender of the present; and when they had first talked about marriage, and had decided that it was not a bad idea, and they wanted to celebrate, it was her money which bought the two bottles of wine. It was her money which had bought the engagement ring from the International Jewellers on Yonge Street, conveniently close to the old Pilot Tavern where they spent the two hours following, drinking rye whiskies and ginger ale, because Agatha had the money and because "you don't drink beer, common beer on an occasion as beautiful as this, Henry, darling." She was now talking about money again. "I don't think you should adopt that attitude, darling. After all, I have money. And you are my husband, at least, soon will be . . ."

"I don't give a god-damn!"

"Well, would you love me if I was as poor as you are?"

"You don't have to insult me, woman! Goddamn you! I didn't beg you!"

"Well, tell me what I must say to you, Henry. What must I do? Must I allow us to starve simply because I have the money and you don't?"

"Us? Us? Us, shite!"

"All right, all right. Well, let's see you get that job." Henry disliked her so much when she said that, that had his hate for her been a degree less, so that he could speak, he would have told her something which would have found them in court, instead of in a chapel. "All right," she said, seeing the reaction her words had. "We won't talk anymore about it." By this time, she was completely fed up with the subject anyhow. But Henry was not satisfied, and he said so, as if he was trying to rebuild the quarrel on her rather harmless statement.

"What do you goddamn mean by telling me *we* won't talk anymore about it? What you mean by that? Because you goddamn say stop, we must stop? *I* must stop? I must stop talking because you goddamn say so? I must stop talking 'bout money because you say so! I must dress this way because you goddamn say so! I must get my hair cut short because you goddamn like to see my head like a goddamn bald-head man's head! I must wear the kind of clothes you goddamn like, because you fucking-well say so! Jesus-fucking-christ, woman, I am only getting hitched-up to you, I am not selling myself to you." But that was the end of the discussion. The end had petered out a long time ago. What he really wanted was the last word. He felt it belonged to him, because he was a man. Agatha was reduced to tears. He had said a lot that was unnecessary. She was hurt. Henry became sad about it, but he was determined to be a man. He was hurt even deeper because he knew (and she knew) that he hadn't the means (no money in the bank, no money in his pockets — she would be paying the taxi fare to go up to Bernice's right now — no job) to behave as a man. But he needed the respect; he needed the shell of respect for his emptiness.

Agatha was crying. And he got frightened that perhaps,

should he allow her to go on crying, and do nothing about it, she might change her mind about the marriage (which after all was going to bring him *some* money!) and walk out, and leave him, this very afternoon, without enough money to buy a fifteen-cent draught glass of beer at the Paramount Tavern. He didn't have his money for rent. The shoes he was wearing needed repairing to keep out the heat of the road and the dampness of the puddles. He decided he would have to eat his pride, and he went close to her, held her in his arms and ran his tongue over the saltiness of her cheeks and over that part of her lips where the tears settled, and told her, "I love you, I love you, I love you, I love you, woman . . ." And she prevented any further profession of affection by smothering him in bed, and making love to him with him underneath. ("Jesus God, I hope Boysie never hear 'bout this, goddamn! A woman doing this to me? Goddamn!") When they finished, they got dressed for the surprise party.

"Here comes the bride! Here comes the bride!" Bernice was clapping her hands and making lots of noise, and doing things that one reserved for the wedding day. (She even threw some stale confetti, from Mrs. Burrmann's drawer, into Agatha's face.) Dots was there, dressed as if indeed it was the day of the wedding. Boysie was in a mourning suit, so black and so old that it was turning green. But he looked martial in it, prim and more than proper, and very stiff. ("The arse-hole seat o' this pants hurting my balls, man!" he whispered to Henry when they were in a corner. "But my ignorant wife insist that I wear it. I must look decent for my best friend, she says. Godblindyou, best friend! But I happy as arse for you, though. Let we fire one, as man!") Brigitte was there. From the closeness and the general laughter in the room, you would not have suspected that

Dots, with whom she was laughing the most, and drinking and making toasts with, was the wife of the man with whom Brigitte was tied up, amorously; and you could not know that Dots knew that Brigitte knew that Dots knew that Brigitte was having an affair with Boysie. It was a peculiarly tight circle of friends. Animosities were dismissed from school for the day. Anything could happen tomorrow — part of which might transpire tonight even; but for tonight, there was only time and the place for close friendship.

"Here comes the bride!" Bernice sang, for the *n*th time. But nobody was counting. Nobody cared. She took Agatha close to her, and hugged her, and kissed her on her face. And Agatha did the same thing. "You look like something to eat, you look so good!" She spun round and faced Henry and shouted, "Looka, you! you brute, take good care o' this child, you hear? Or all o' we, be-Christ, will give you licks like hell . . . pardon me, Agaffa dear." Boysie was smiling. There was enough to drink. Dots had pinched two bottles of Dr. Hunter's Haig & Haig Pinch, a bottle of Tanqueray Gin, and she had eased Mrs. Hunter of a half bottle of Cointreau liqueur and a large bottle of brandy, whose name she could not pronounce. (It always made her guilty to think that the Hunters never missed any of the liquor she stole from them.) Bernice had spared the Burrmann's liquor cabinet no less. She had displayed on the table two bottles of white rum, three bottles of Scotch — the Burrmanns drank Ballantine's — two bottles of Gordon's Dry Gin, and three bottles of Italian vermouth. The food, which was West Indian, and which could not have come out of either Mrs. Hunter's or Mrs. Burrmann's kitchen, was regally laid out in hot delicious splendour.

The ham could have come from the Rosedale kitchen; the English muffins from Forest Hill. So too did the two

bottles of wine, Blanc de Blancs. White Irish linen nap-
kins covered this equatorial beautiful board. Bernice even
brought upstairs Mrs. Burrmann's tablecloths, her incense
("You think rose suit this kind o' party, Dots? I think so,
too"), and her candles and her beautiful candlesticks which
looked like hands of bananas turned upside down. Secretly,
she was saying to herself, "I hope that bitch don't come
back tonight! Not tonight, Lord!" But this fear was soon
forgotten the moment Dots began to dish the West Indian
food. It was exactly what she had yearned for, lately, when
Bernice was visiting her: black-eye peas, and rice cooked
with coconut oil, and with large hunks of salted pig tails in
it. There were green bananas floating like heavy logs in
pools of butter (the butter came from Mrs. Burrmann's
kitchen), and juicy pieces of smoked, boiled mackerel. On
one large platter there were sweet potatoes, also submerged
in butter. "God, look at all this food!" Bernice had said
when it was ready. And now that she was helping to serve
it, she said to Dots, "I wish my sister, Estelle, was here to
eat some o' this!" And water settled in her eye. She wiped
the tear away with the hand that held the serving spoon.

"Where's Estelle?" Agatha asked her, from across the
room.

Bernice swallowed hard. Dots glanced at her like a con-
spirator. "Estelle? Oh, Estelle out somewhere with a friend.
But she coming back before we finish . . ."

"Estelle has gone to a party that she had to go to, but
she promised that she coming back here before you leave,"
Dots said, helping with the lie.

"Last time I made the mistake of calling you and Bernice
born cooks," Agatha said, laughing this time. "But not this
time. I learned my lesson, man. You don't make them mistakes with you people twice, man," she added, trying to
talk like them.

"Child, what's wrong with you at all?" Dots teased her.
"She is one o' we now!" Bernice said. She was practically
shouting, she was so happy. "She is one o' we. Gal, the mo-
ment you take up with a Wessindian man, you turn into a
Wessindian woman, yourself, overnight. You is one o' we!
One o' we."

"Thanks," Agatha said, beaming, and losing little colour,
so embarrassingly complimentary was the compliment, and
so natural. "I is one of you," she said, trying to imitate the
dialect once more, the dialect which alone could throw her
irredeemably into the blood of being a West Indian. (But
what they really meant was that Agatha was now a black
person, since her husband-to-be was black. But the occasion
was too gay, too happy, to introduce this racial aspect.
Agatha understood it to mean just that. Bernice and Dots
said it to mean exactly that. Boysie and Henry knew. It
was only Brigitte, already busy with the drinks, who didn't
hear, and who probably didn't care.)

"What about children?" Dots asked. "You planning 'pon
children, ain't you?"

"Leave the woman!" Bernice told her. "She isn' on the
honeymoon yet. Leave Agaffa alone, please. She is my sister now!" Bernice had been tasting the Scotch since four
in the afternoon, when she and Dots sat waiting for the
mackerel to boil. It was now nine o'clock. She was getting
drunk. But she didn't care. She was happy. "Later on, darling, I will take you to one-side, and tell you certain ins-
and-outs concerning how to deal with a niggerman like
Henry. There is certain instructions you are going to have
to learn, early-o'clock."

"Have you choose your wedding things, yet, Agaffa?"
Dots asked her. It was becoming a discussion among women
now, three friends, almost; and only one person, Brigitte,
was left out. Brigitte had actually left herself out, because

she could not stomach Agatha: she had hated her from the
first meeting, and she hated her now. But she had come to
the party because of Henry. She was content to stand with
the men and drink with them, like them. "You wearing
white? I hope you wearing white, eh gal? and that you
ain't playing you is one o' these modernt women who feel
they could wear any colour, like pink or blue or turquoise,
on their wedding day. A wedding gown isn't a wedding
gown except it is white in colour and long to-boot, with a
nice white veil all over your face and down to your shoulders, and white satin shoes and white gloves. Child, just
telling you this make me remember the kind o' wedding
gown I wore to my wedding. You have to look like a virgin
on your wedding day, even if you stop being a virgin years
before you get married." Dots screamed with laughter.
Agatha blushed. She was not yet accustomed to this West
Indian straightforwardness. It was something she would
have to make a great effort to understand, and not get annoyed at.

Dots realized she had spoken too hard, and she tried to
soften it by adding, "You don't have to be ashamed at
what I say, gal. There isn't, is not one woman in this room,
and scarcely in *all* the other rooms in the whole o' Forest
Hill who went to their wedding day or on their honeymoon
as a virgin. Not one o' them. Them virgin-days done, gal.
Not one o' we in here, even counting in *that*" (here, she
lowered her voice, as she tilted her head, indicating Brigitte, still in a corner with the men), "not even that virgin
Mary there, is a virgin. You are in grown-up company now,
gal. You're talking with grown-ups."

Still, Agatha would have preferred this personal comment to be made more privately; or rather, that she had
been the one to volunteer this biological and social information. She started to get frightened: West Indian women

were too frank; perhaps, Henry had talked all their personal business already to Boysie; all their sex life, all their closest confidences were perhaps common knowledge among these women. "Not at all!" she said, not very convincingly, "I don't mind." But the comment was too late.

"Well, that's good, girl." This was Bernice. She was relieved that no feelings were hurt.

"Yes, we are women together," Dots said.

"Yes. We is women together," Bernice said. "I glad you feel that way. We is almost sisters now that you and Henry planning marriage."

"But would anybody in his right mind think that you and Henry wouldda get married? I mean, you can never tell how much a person means to a next person. You may see them looking simple on the street, and bram! the next day, you hear this report, big-big wedding and big wedding-reception planned, with a honeymoon! And in a twinkling of a eye, be-Christ, the two o' them settling down and raising a family."

"But who tell you that Agaffa wants any damn children?"

"Bernice, what are you talking about? Every woman, there ain' one woman alive who don't want a chick or child for them to hold and cuddle up to, and say them little foolish things, like boo-boo, coo-coo to. And furthermore, according to something I been reading lately, they say in this book I was reading recently, that the nicest feeling you could experience is the warm body of a child next to yours. I mean, I am a woman with no lot o' papers testifying to the fact that I have the high learning that Agaffa here possesses, but I am a human being. *I am a woman.* And as such, I can appreciate what that man in the book was trying to say to me. Well, tell me then, Bernice, how the hell do you think that a mother could love a child when everybody in her village, every other living soul in that village agree that the same child ugly as shite . . . pardon me, Agaffa dear, we does talk different to you . . . ugly as hell? It takes a mother to have that kind o' contrary feeling towards a ugly child. Don't you agree with me, Miss Agaffa?" And she laughed her sensuous laugh, like a chastisement.

Agatha shuddered; she was thinking of her child, that her child (from Henry) might be such an ugly child; and she was wondering whether everybody who knew her would hate the child; and she wondered too, if she had it in her body and in her soul, enough of the love that Dots was talking about, to love an ugly child. Particularly, a child that was half-Jewish, that is to say, half-white. But she brought her knowledge of anthropology and sociology — particularly her knowledge of anthropology — to the matter, and in this way, she tried to look at her personal life objectively, as she had been taught to do in the lecture rooms of the university. When Dots's laugh died down, she was still frightened. But she had at least consoled herself, through the case histories of many anthropological seminars, that her child would be no different from any other child.

"I hope Henry gives you lots o' children. A woman isn't a woman unless she have the experience o' childbirth. Something is lacking, something sadly lacking, unless she could boast o' giving birth, something coming out from inside her insides, and she looks at this thing and could say to the world, *This is mine. I borned it.*"

Unknown to herself, Dots had put such a scare into Agatha by her last words, that Agatha curdled inside. She did not feel too sure she could look at her child (from Henry) and say, "This is mine. I borned it."

But Dots went on talking about children, and about her

own desire to have one. "It does be fighting like hell betwixt me and that man standing up there in that corner talking to Henry and that woman, fighting like hell I tell you, when the nights come. I want a child. Boysie don't want no children. 'Children is blasted hindrances,' he says to me. You do not know, Agaffa dear, and neither does Bernice here, my closest friend, neither o' the two o' you know how badly I want a child. But can I get myself pregnant? Jesus Christ, man! I am not the Virgin Mary! Not in this day and age." The conversation continued to frighten Agatha. She waited for the right moment to move away, and sit by herself on the chesterfield, which for this occasion was covered with its Mexican blanket.

Left to themselves now, Bernice and Dots could feel the freedom of their intercourse. No matter how great an effort they had made to accommodate Agatha (and it was a sincere effort on their part tonight), still, with her so near, there was a reservation in their opinions. Perhaps it was that Agatha was more intelligent, more educated than anyone else in the room. Perhaps, it was her wealth, and the clothes she wore, which one glance told you were very expensive. And perhaps, too, it wasn't just one of these factors, but the combination of all. Agatha had everything that a woman could want. And to crown her superiority, she was beautiful — with the insult to injury that she had Henry now.

"But I didn' know you was yearning after chick and child, Dots!"

"Gal, what chick, eh? What child? I was only licking my mouth with Agaffa. I was only talking to make the girl feel at ease, 'cause she looks so blasted tense. And I don't intend to throw 'way all this food, like the last party we had here. If they believe every thing that a coloured person say to them, then it is their bloody business, not mine!"

She laughed softly, but you could still discern her sexy throat in the laugh. "But serious now, though. I would give anything to have my own child. I could depend on a child. A child don't let down a parent. At least, mine won't dare! Not the child I would have. But whereas a man could wander, a child doesn't."

"And how Boysie feel 'bout this?"

"Boysie? Boysie want woman, not child. Boysie want fun, not responsibility. Boysie wants a good time from life, not hindrances."

"You ever thought o' adopting one?"

"Adopting a child? Wait, don't I still look like a woman to you? A strong, healthy, juicy woman like me! I look so old and done-with that I can't find a man to breed me and give me a child? If it is a child I want. Man, Bernice, you talking just like these blasted white Canadian women! I is a West Indian. And Wessindians, the women, don't adopt no child. Rather than adopt somebody-else child I will tell Boysie, my own husband, to go outside and look for a nice clean-skin strong black woman, with nice hair, and screw her and breed her, and bring that child o' that union home for me to mother. Because this is the way I think. That is the way I feel. I feel so strong 'gainst adopting a child, that I would prefer a child that my husband have from a outside-woman, a child that is half mine by virtue o' Boysie being my husband, than a child I don't know nothing about at all."

"You won't do that. You couldn't live with a child in your home knowing that that child come outta an arrangement with a outside-woman and your own husband, that that . . . that your husband been sleeping with that outside-woman. Don't give me that."

"Bernice, I just told you I would take my husband's outside-child in preference to a adopted child. I mean it."

"Well, you brave."

"It ain't a matter o' being brave, good-Jesus-Christ, woman! don't you understand that? It is cutting and contribing. And a person does have to cut and contribe, *contrive*, when he can't do no better. Life is a choosing-thing, Bernice. Yuh can't get everything you want . . ."

"I couldn't do it."

Melda oh! you making wedding-plan, carrying my name to obeah-man, all you do, can't get through, I still ain't going married to you . . . It was Sparrow, calypsonian, singing on a record about a woman who tried to force a West Indian man to marry her by questionable means. When the record started, Bernice looked at Dots, and together they watched Agatha to see her reaction. Agatha had by now, however, been so accustomed to the way West Indians spoke, that she had no difficulty in following the words. Bernice wondered whose idea it was to choose this record, just at this time. But its irony didn't seem to bother Agatha. (It was actually Brigitte who chose it.)

First thing, Boysie held on to Brigitte and started showing everybody the latest steps he had picked up at the West Indian club, the Club Tropics on Queen and Yonge streets. The others didn't know it, but Boysie had been taking Brigitte there dancing every other Saturday night, when he was supposed to be playing dominoes with Henry and Freeness.

Henry wasn't going to make the same mistake twice: of not dancing with his hostess, and with Dots. So he walked over to the table where the food was, where Dots could always be found, and he held out his arms to her, invitingly. "Let we," he said, smiling, sure of himself this time.

Dots turned her back on him. He felt the first pricks of a long pin going through his body. He felt Agatha's eyes on him, on them. Dots turned her back towards him, and went back to choosing some food. "You don't see your fiancée sitting down there? You is almost a married man now, boy, so left me out!"

The things that Henry said to her, in his heart, could not be reproduced. But he could not move away. Not now. He could not let this defeat and humiliation in front of Agatha be so complete for the second consecutive time. So he turned his attention to Bernice. He put his arm round her waist, affectionately, and said, "How Estclle these days, Bernice, love?" Dots was cackling with laughter now. She knew.

But before Bernice could say a word, Agatha was across the room, behind him, saying, "Darling, come and teach me how to dance the calypso. Come." And he did that. But when he turned in the dance, with his face to Dots, he gave her such a dirty, incisively foul look! and he winded his behind on Agatha's body implying that that was what he wanted to do to Dots: screw her up! And Dots knew. But she couldn't care. Sparrow was telling them in the calypso how dirty a woman Melda was; that she couldn't hope to get a man unless, at least, she bathed more regularly and wore clean clothes that were in fashion. Henry liked that part: he let go of Agatha, he held his hands in the air, and twisted his body one way, his head going the next, his body doing things with a glorious freedom which Dots had never before witnessed in him. Screw you, woman! Fuck you! you bitch! he was saying with his movement; and all this time, he was making more noise than was necessary, more noise than even Boysie and Brigitte were making — and they were by no means quiet and dignified in the dance.

And your perspiration smell so strong! Girl, you only wasting time . . . all you do, can't get through, I still ain't going married to you! . . . nastiness go' cause your death, girl no man can't stand your breath, you can't trap me with negromancy . . . Sparrow was talking to Dots? Henry said he was, in his heart. Dots knew. Henry flung his body into positions with a free movement. He was prancing up on Dots, he was screwing Dots, in his mind.

Dots turned from looking at him. She put down her plate. She said to Bernice, "Gal, let we dance, do!" And Bernice became bewildered by the request; but she did not resist, could not resist, for Dots was already holding her round the waist and by the left hand, and was whirling her round in the dance. She was going to compete with Henry and beat him at his game. Sparrow was in good form, too. And Dots, easily overcome by this kind of musical power, released Bernice (who was not a little embarrassed to be seen dancing with a woman, in the company of Agatha and Brigitte, when there were men present), and flung her dress high over her head.

For a second, Henry couldn't think. His entire mind and body were paralysed. There was a freshness and an entice-ment under those skirts that he had not imagined possible. He saw the colour of her panties, and he saw the torment of their distance. Henry wondered then how Boysie could even look at another woman, even a woman like Brigitte (who was tall and thin), when his wife possessed such power in her thighs. He shook his head (not to the rhythm of the calypso, this time), and said aloud, "Rass!"

Dots was in her briar patch. "Come to me! Come to me! Come to me!" she was yelling to the beat, talking really to Henry, and not to Bernice, her desultory dancing partner. Henry knew. Dots knew. "Come! Ugh!-ugh!ugh!" she was saying, in spasms, like short, painful overburdening, over-ecstatic orgasms. Henry at once felt he was a fool to have thought of marrying a white woman. He at once thought of the myths (although he didn't recognize them in his mind as myths) and the facts and the fancies and the facts and the desires and the facts of making love with a black woman. ("Is a long-arse time since I last screwed a black piece, Boysie! And is 'bout time, too!") And he knew then that even if he did marry this white woman, Agatha, he would have to find the primitive, real, funky, passionate passion and bodily satisfaction in the tightening thighs of a black woman like Dots. Dots knew.

"*All you do, still can't get through, I still ain't going married to you!*" It was Dots singing along with the calypso. Henry knew. When the calypso finished, Henry himself turned the record player off.

"What you do that for, man?" Boysie wanted to know.

"I want a waltz," Henry said. His manner was so simple and so absurd that no one, apart from Dots, realized how deep were the silent psychologies at work in the room. But Dots knew. And she had beaten him. Henry knew.

"*All you do, still can't get through, boy* . . . *ain't going married to you!*" Dots sang, and then laughed out loud, and sexily. And she tapped Agatha on her leg and asked her, "Yuh like that one, gal?"

Henry knew. Agatha was sweating from the exertion in the dance. She was the only one in the room sweating. *Goddamn! at a time like this, Dots playing the arse! Agatha is still a better woman, though. Agatha is more learned, got better schooling; Agatha could put any one o' these bitches in here in her pocket. She got a lot o' money, too; and she dresses better than any one o' them. Dots is only good-looking, but I couldn't be tied down with a woman like Dots. I would have to go out to work, couldn't stay home, even if I couldn't find a job. Dots won't think 'bout helping out a man, a man would have to support Dots. Agatha is a better woman, better in everything. The only thing I think Dots have on Agatha is that Dots could maybe give me a better screw, and that makes me glad as hell that Boysie don't love the bitch, that he has Brigitte . . . but just the same, pussy isn't everything, it isn't the end-all and the be-all in life, goddammit!* But the doubt was already planted. It would haunt him for a long time to come.

They had talked long into the night, that first night in North Bay. And even after Mrs. Macmillan had confessed that she had deceived Estelle with all her grand promises of living with her in Timmins, and had confessed that she didn't know why she had done it, still Estelle harboured no hard feelings against her. The greatest irony in the whole affair was that she should meet Mrs. Macmillan again, for the second time, when she really needed someone she could trust.

They had walked from the hotel, through a side street, then for about two more blocks, to a small prefabricated-looking house, where Mrs. Macmillan said she lived, "Alone, honey!" She hadn't the money to pay a taxicab. And Estelle didn't want to suggest taking one and having to pay for it, because she felt that the circumstances of their second meeting were really the circumstances of Mrs. Macmillan's finances and wealth. Estelle promised herself to leave the money Mrs. Macmillan had left with her somewhere in the house, before she left for Toronto again. She would put it in the kitchen: there must be some place there. In a teapot, for instance. And she was sensitive enough to surmise that Mrs. Macmillan was flat broke; and now, for her to hint at her straightened circumstances after her promises of easy living in Timmins would inflict an unnecessary wound upon this woman's sensibilities. But although Estelle was dog-tired, she did not resent having to walk. It was a short walk. A walk in the early morning, in a strange town, with a deep insistence of a dream.

"Enter my parlour," Mrs. Macmillan said, unlocking the

front door. "Said the spider to the fly!" Estelle resented the allusion, and the metaphor.

The house was small. It had a small living room: there was one couch, two stuffed chairs and a coffee table made out of a flimsy shiny wood that did not look like wood at all. From the living room, Estelle could see through a passageway into the kitchen. On either side of the passageway was a door. Presumably, there were rooms leading off the doors. On the wall, facing them, was a large cheap technicolour print of a man with a very pallid complexion, brown silky hair, and a brown full-length beard; he was dressed in something resembling a nightgown with a red robe covering it. The man's heart was exposed. It came out of his insides and was planted outside, on top of his chest. Something like flames were surrounding the man's heart. His eyes seemed as if he were drugged; as if he had been smoking marijuana from the time of his birth. One palm (Estelle had difficulty in determining whether it was his right palm or his left) was raised outward, as if this man intended to bless somebody. A drop of blood was caught in the slow motion of the painter's realism, and it was suspended an inch below the heart. She could find no hole in the heart out of which the blood might have come. The picture bothered Estelle.

Mrs. Macmillan was turning on lamps: she turned on one lamp that was on the coffee table. She turned on a second one on the television. Beside this lamp was a flowerpot made of porcelain, and in the flowerpot was a bunch of plastic flowers. Mrs. Macmillan then turned on a table lamp, the largest in her collection, which was sitting on the floor beside one of the overstuffed chairs — because there was no table on which it could sit. The room was burning with lamps. She had turned on five lamps in all.

"Well!" she said, like a woman regaining her breath.

"I am so pleased to see you again, Mrs. Macmillan."

"You hungry?"

"Well, I had a little something on the train . . ."

"I'll whip you up something."

"I'm not really hungry."

"Child, if you're hungry, say you're hungry. If I didn't have anything to offer you, I wouldn't put myself out in the first place and I wouldn't have offered you nothing in the first place."

"Well, thank you."

"Don't be too polite, either. That isn't a polite place we just walked from. And it ain't a polite world out there, either." Mrs. Macmillan was smiling now. She had a great searching power in her eyes. And though her eyes tonight were carrying the glare and the colour of alcohol, they were still piercing. Something about her eyes: they looked at you with a feeling that was divorced from the feeling of the particular topic of conversation, a feeling altogether strange and foreign from the feeling of the silence that lay between her words in conversation. Estelle had noticed this before. But she had mistaken it for periodic lapses in memory, or pauses in attention. Mrs. Macmillan was looking straight at her now, as one would look at something wondrous, that is to say, at something unexpected. It was making Estelle uncomfortable. She hoped Mrs. Macmillan would leave and go to the kitchen.

"Won't take a minute. I'll whip you up something. A belly-stopper. Beggars can't be choosers!" Estelle wondered what she meant by that. That was not what a hostess said to her guest. There was something sinister in the observation. Could there be something altogether sinister in this woman? She had never before confronted anybody as complex, and apparently as easy to read, as Mrs. Macmillan. And what made her even more uncomfortable was that up till now, Mrs. Macmillan had said nothing about her presence in North Bay, although she was supposed to be in Timmins; and she hadn't explained her presence in this house: there was no noise of sleeping children, no sign of comfort, the kind of comfort Mrs. Macmillan had talked about while they were in the hospital; there was no semblance of a man in the house, either. And Estelle was too scared to mention anything about the holiday she had been seduced into coming north to have.

"How's that slaughter-house?" Her voice came from the kitchen like a shout. Something was fizzing in a pan. "People still having abortions illegally?"

"You have a lovely place here."

"It's a shack!"

"I like it."

"My mother died last year. This is all she had. This is all she left. This is all I have. I haven't even moved her things outta the bedroom, as yet."

"How're the kids, the children, Mrs. Macmillan?"

"When you saw me tonight in that cheap hotel, I was just talking about you. Says I to the fella who buyed me a couple of beers, says I, 'I met the prettiest coloured girl in Toronto.' You're damn pretty, you know that, don't ya?"

"Are the children sleeping, Mrs. Macmillan?"

"You want to know something? When a woman has to go out in the night and hustle, child, it is not what I call easy living. Is it? You hustle all night, and the trash you have to take, well, I hope your horoscope has something better for you."

Mrs. Macmillan came back into the living room with a red, diminutive apron round her waist. It was the kind of apron waitresses in exclusive restaurants wore. It was delicate in its weaving, and it transformed her shabby appearance. She looked like a very real housewife. She came in, looked at Estelle, with no consistent expression on her face or in her eyes, and then she went back into the kitchen. Estelle had time to look around. There was a pile of magazines on the coffee table. She walked over and saw they were copies of the *Watchtower*. She thought of Bernice. Bernice and this woman would make good friends over these magazines, she thought. Estelle leafed through some of the *Watchtowers*. At the bottom of the pile were two old editions of *True Confessions*. She remembered that as a schoolgirl at St. Michael's Girls' School in Barbados, which she attended for three terms before Mammy's ambition for her higher education and Bernice's slight salary ran out, she and a few other girls used to read all about the sex and film-star lives in America from these same magazines. It was strange, exciting, to see one of those magazines right here in Canada. And she was here now. She made a mental note to buy one when she got back to Toronto.

She could not bring herself to live anywhere else. Certainly not in the north, not in North Bay. The north she found too unreal: like a picture postcard of a town which looked more beautiful and brighter in the picture than in the reality of visiting. And she had already experienced this deceit of communication: she had seen colour photographs of coconut trees, and of the Mauby-woman who sold that refreshing drink in the hot streets of Bridgetown; she had seen these colour photographs in Agatha's apartment (Henry had given them to her), and she could not recognize that what the camera and the photographers saw and what was said, and printed on the cards, was the same thing, the same people, the same colours even, as that with which she had grown up seeing around her.

"Lots of pepper?" The question pulled Estelle out of her reverie. "You people from the south always like pepper and hot things. I never been south of Toronto."

"Not much pepper, thanks."

The television was the most expensive and the newest piece of furniture in the living room. The stuffed chairs were old and dirty. The arms, or where the human arms rested on the arms of the chair, were coated with the dispositions of many visitors. The couch was dirty. You could see forms of movements on it; you could see the remembrances of emotions in the middle of the seat; you could smell some of the attitudes that had been present on it. On the coffee table was a carton of cigarettes, Macdonalds. The carton was opened, and three packs of cigarettes were already removed from it. The ashtray on the coffee table was full of butts, halves of cigarettes that had been left there for many days now. The other ashtrays in the room were crammed.

"Hope you like what I'm fixing for ya!"

Estelle wondered how to take that. She wondered what Mrs. Macmillan was fixing, and whether she should eat it. People, here of late, were bringing gifts of food and drink to her; and they were accompanying these kindnesses with the strangest unkindest requests. Perhaps, Mrs. Macmillan was now spitting in the frying pan, even as she was talking to her. Perhaps she is coughing over the pan. Or perhaps she is doing what Boysie told her that *they* always did when they served *us:* "fuck we up!" by breaking the plate.

But Mrs. Macmillan would have to bring the food on the plate first, and then afterwards, break it, if she was like *them*. Then she thought how ridiculous an idea it was! How stupid to think these things of someone like Mrs. Macmillan who had been so kind to her in the hospital. And at that moment, *she* brought in a plate breathing steam, and when the steam blew away, there was a mound of beans and sliding down the debris of the beans-mountain was a piece of pork, the size of a pair of dice, divided by two. She brought also a cup of coffee. There was a bottom lip from the mouth that had used the cup before, a lip from a mouth of lipstick still visible on the white pyrex cup. At least *she* had used the same cup once!

"Ya like beans?" She said it as if she was telling Estelle it was good to like beans, or as if she was saying, "Ya better like these beans!"

"Oh, beans!" Estelle beamed, because she could think of nothing else to say.

"Good. Cheapest food with the richest things in them. Good for the bowels, too."

Estelle started to eat. It was one way of stopping Mrs. Macmillan's questions. Mrs. Macmillan sat down for a while, watching her eat, moving her lips as if she wanted to ask another question, but never saying a word. Then as if a second thought had come to her from outside in the kitchen, she got up and left. Estelle never liked beans. But the operatic tension and quality of the situation and of the atmosphere told her that these beans must be eaten be they Boston beans or jail beans. They must be eaten. And she set about doing that. She was thinking of what it would have been like had she gone along with the desires of the strange white man who bought her the two gin-and-tonics in the club car of the train; what it would have been like had she allowed the porter-student to have his way with her; whatever the aftertastes of resentment and conscience, of guilt and regret, she was sure that it would have been better than these beans: beans were the lowest fare a man could climb down to, from any position of welfare; beans! "I haven't got a bloody bean!"

Mrs. Macmillan came back with a handful of bed linen: new linen, fresh linen. Estelle was sitting uncomfortably in one of the stuffed chairs. Mrs. Macmillan tossed the bed linen onto the other stuffed chair, and without saying why, she ran her hands, palms down, over the old bottoms and sides and legs and feet and backs of the ghosts of people who had sat on her chesterfield-couch; and when she could see no more imprints, she beat their ghosts off the seat of the chesterfield, and began to transform it into a bed. She spread the sheets, two of them, she stuffed the cushions into one pillowcase, and beat the pillowcase with the cushions in it, as if she was beating a man. Estelle had to look up to see whether there was really a man inside the pillowcase. But of course, there was none: only Mrs. Macmillan's personal thoughts and imaginations of souls and ghosts and men she wanted to beat, but couldn't beat, because they were men and not pillowcases. She did all this without saying a word to Estelle, without looking at Estelle.

Estelle held the empty plate in her hands for a long time, not knowing whether she should go into the kitchen and put it down, with the empty cup (she had turned the mouth of the cup away from the lipstick-mouth that was on it, so that her own mouth made a new imprint upon the mouth of the red-mouthed cup), or whether to leave them on the coffee table, which didn't have any room left on it, anyhow. She was still in this stupid position, holding the plate in one hand, and the cup in the other, with the knife and the fork held in the same hand as the cup, when Mrs. Macmillan appeared between the jalousies of the room in which she had taken refuge with a halo of light behind her, to say, "I gotta hit the sack, now. Put out the lights before you turn in, please."

She nodded her head; and the apparition of Mrs. Macmillan's head in aluminum curlers, covered by the meshes of iron that looked like cloth, nodded; and the jalousies closed like long parallel eyes. Estelle was now even more confused. If she had the strength, she would have remained forever, at least for the eternity of the remainder of the night, sitting with the plate and the cup and the knife and fork in her hands, waiting to see whether she was dreaming, whether she was mad, whether it was Mrs. Macmillan who was mad: for if it was not she who was mad, then she owed it to herself, and to the security of others not mad, to open her mouth and tell Mrs. Macmillan, "Are you goddamn mad?"

She put the plate and the cup and the knife and the fork on the floor ("If this was in Barbados, by morning this whole house would be crawling with ants!"); and she went to the chesterfield to lie down. She inspected the bed: it was really clean; Mrs. Macmillan knew how to make a bed.

She must have been sleeping a long time, for she did not hear the beginning of the loud knocking on the front door. Gradually, a conversation became clearer:

MAN'S VOICE: . . . and what the hell've you got here, Glo?

MRS. MACMILLAN'S VOICE: A friend.

MAN'S VOICE: You sure as hell know how to pick some lu lues! This is a strange one! I not kidding ya! Where's you find this one, this time?

MRS. MACMILLAN: Oh, she's a good egg. Not like the last one. Was my next-door neighbour in that slaughter-house in Toronto, where I been for the last four weeks. Paying me a visit.

MAN'S VOICE: C'mon! hurry-up, it's late. I been late three times already this week. The boss's mad as hell, too.

MRS. MACMILLAN: Won't be a sec, Joe. Gimme two more seconds. Gotta leave a note for Estelle here, tell her that I gone . . .

MAN'S VOICE: That's her name? Estelle? That's a damn nice name! I like nice names. Estelle. Estelle! Don't ya think Estelle's a nice name, Glo?

MRS. MACMILLAN: Prettier than Glo? than Gloria? You know something, Joe? I think you're nuts. I think somebody ought to look at that head o' yours. And soon, too. What's the difference between Estelle and Gloriana? A queen was named Gloriana . . . anyways, here I am. I am ready now. I'll just put this note where she can find it, first thing when she gets up. 'Bye, Estelle. Sleep till ya wake up.

MAN'S VOICE: 'Bye, Estelle. Nighty-nighty, and have a good nice sleep.

MRS. MACMILLAN: You got a crush on Estelle? Or you're nuts, Joe?

MAN'S VOICE: I got a crush on Estelle, or I'm nuts, Joe? I got a crush on Estelle, or you're nuts, Glo? 'Bye-bye, Estelle, nice sleep, sleep tighty-tighty . . .

When it was safe, when the curtain of Mrs. Macmillan's departure with the man had fallen, Estelle put on one of the many lamps in the living room and looked about her, to reassure herself that it was only a small part of her real life she was in the midst of, and not what people call "the drama of life," or "life's drama." It was she. Estelle. There. In a room in North Bay. And there was a man in the room, there had been a man in the room. And he was talking to Mrs. Macmillan. The plate and the cup and the knife and the fork were still there, on the floor. There were no ants crawling over them. So she was not dreaming she was in Barbados. She was not in Barbados. The *Watchtowers* were still there on the towering coffee table with its pile of magazines, watching her. But she had to find more proof: so she looked at the bottom of the pile of *Watchtowers*, and there were the *True Confessions*. She was on the chesterfield-couch-bed. Her valise was there. The coffee had been spilled, and hidden under the plate. The stain was still there. If all these things were there, before she went to sleep (if she did go to sleep and was not watching her own life on the stage of this dream), and they are still there, then it was "the drama of life" — it was not life that was a drama.

Estelle found the note waiting on the table. *Dear Friend, Wash the plate and the cup and the knife and the fork for me. Put them in the dish wreck. Hang up the towel on the nail above the sink. Leave the bed as it is, I will sleep there tonight. You were tense last night. Asprins are in the cupboard above the sink. Love, Mrs. Macmillan.*

Estelle did not feel safe until she was sitting at the back of the bus, five minutes later. She did not wash the plate.

She asked two bus conductors twice, "This going to Toronto?" And twice they said, "Sure thing, miss!" A woman who looked like a traveller, seasoned and pickled by custom and the sun, got in. Estelle turned to her and said, " 'Scuse me, lady. Is this the bus that going to Toronto, in truth?"

The woman, whose voice was younger than her face, said, "Sure is, miss!" And then she added, for her own private reasons, "Wouldn't be on it, if it weren't!"

It was only then that Estelle sat back, breathed freely and tried to put together the drama of Mrs. Macmillan; because now, for the first time since she had met her in the hotel, she was in a position of mental strength and health to look back and decide, with less fear of her own sanity, the answer to the question, "Is she goddamn mad?"

Boysie couldn't believe it. "Imagine, man, that after almost one full year, gorblummuh! twelve months to be exact, that I been walking 'bout this blasted city unemploy, looking for a job, and I couldn't get no blasted job at all, no matter how hard I try! And now, gorblummuh, right outta the fucking blue, a man ups and gives me a job!" He was shout-

ing so much over the telephone that Henry, who himself
could not believe it, and who had come to believe that
Boysie, like himself, was unemployable, was finding it very
difficult to hear. "Man, look at this thing, though! A man,
it appears he is a Jamaican-man, who been working at this
place on Sin George Street for donkey years as a janitor and
cleaner and general Mr.-Fixit-kind-o'-man, and he want to
go home to Jamaica for a little rest from the hard work, so
he ups and tells Reverend Markham, who ups and calls
Dots, to ask me to hold-down this job till he come back.
And I had was to say to Dots, 'Dots, is a blasted good thing
that we didn't forget all-together to drop in 'pon Reverend
Markham church one Sundee last year, gorblummuh! Gorblummuh! and *all* I have to do is sweep-out fifteen rooms
every night, carry a little wastepaper and other slight garbage outside, by the side o' the building, post a few letters
after the people finish working, and be-Christ, I hauling-in
sixty-somebody dollars a week. Man, I am robbing them! I
robbing their arse in this job, Henry!" Boysie was actually
being paid eighty dollars a week, but knowing that Henry
was always broke, he foresaw the possibility of unpaid loans
and therefore thought first of protecting himself. It was his
victory over Henry, one of the few in the years they were
running together.

"Where you say the place is?"

"Sin George, I tell you. The Baptist church house. And
guess what else?"

"You have to water the garden, and clean out the closets
and polish the sign 'pon the door, and wash-off the windows, and . . ." And Henry broke into a ridiculing laugh.

"Kiss my arse! You think I is a slave? Nothing like that
at all, man. They have a special man to do them things. But
the special thing is that there have an apartment going free

with the job! You hear what I say? It have four rooms on one floor, and if you climb a stairs, the man tell me, you will find yourself in a next floor with two more big rooms. The whole place furnished too. The whole place is mine!"

"Boy, this is your year!" Henry stopped laughing now.

"Man, Canadian people real stupid. Real arse-hole stupid, in truth! You think a thing like this could happen to me back in the Wessindies?" Boysie sucked his teeth in a long rasping noise. "Man, *I* should be paying the Baptist-people to have this job. But *they* paying me!"

Henry was serious, and he was overjoyed to hear of Boysie's success. Although he could not report the same successful news, he held no grudge against his friend. As a matter of fact, he was so happy that he invited Boysie down that same evening to buy him a drink ("Goddamn, Boysie have so much luck that I want to touch him and let some o' that luck rub off on me. And I am going to buy the fucker *any* kind o' drink, beer, hard liquor, liqueur — anything he want. I just touched my woman for twenty bucks, and I am going to invest half 'pon Boysie, tonight. We celebrating his job, the first real kiss-me-arse *ipso facto* job in this white man country"). They would go to their favourite drinking place, the Paramount, where drinks could be washed down by the southern-fried chicken wings which the Chinese man behind the counter of steam and oil and fat and smokescreen whipped up in five minutes flat, together with generous coatings of flour.

Hastily, Boysie accepted the invitation. He even kissed his wife, on her lips. Kissing his wife was a thing which through negligence she had concluded he had forgotten how to do. He promised her he would be back early, in time to have a bath and a good night's rest. He wanted to face his job bright and early the morning after.

"I don't have to start work before tomorrow evening," he was telling Henry. He had found out that the job was an evening job. They were sitting at a round, salt-splattered beer-ringed black shining table in the Paramount, fifteen minutes later.

"Boy, you're goddamn lucky."

"But the man, Old Man Jonesy want me down there tomorrow morning to show me the ropes. He leaving for Jamaica the day after tomorrow."

"You are goddamn lucky, I say."

"That is the kind o' job I always was looking for in this fucking city, man."

"And it have enough room for two people to live in, too, judging by what you tell me on the phone. That place you just told me about, man, that apartment have enough space for two people to live in comfortable. And when you realize that you're not paying rent for that, nor for the place in the attick, man, Boysie, you're in a goddamn good position."

"Yeah."

"I don't feel a man should have to pay rent any-goddamn-how! Not in this socialistical day and age. And this place you talking 'bout is centrally located at Bloor and Sin George, ain't it, boy? Man, that will be a great place for the rest o' the summer, till Old Man Jonesy come back from Jamaica. Be-Christ, you should even wish that Old Man Jonesy drop dead down there . . . imagine the parties you could have! Jesus Christ, Boysie! You imagine that, yet? A big place. Nobody there at night to get in your arse, worrying you, or to see which goddamn broad you're taking in for the night. You could take in a broad at five in the afternoon, work on her for a few hours, take in a second goddamn skins at eight o'clock, and you will still have the rest o' the fucking night for Brigitte." Boysie's eyes began to reflect the sweetness of this conspiracy. He was beginning for the first time to see new large dimensions and universes of sexual activity surrounding his job. "You have the best goddamn job of the year. You deserve a goddamn medal, too!"

"I have to take Brigitte there, man! At least once! I not telling Dots 'bout the apartment before I get organized."

"What a person don't know . . ."

"Can't have bad-feels about!"

"For-fucking-sure, pardner!"

"And nowadays, my kiss-me-arse wife, Dots, having ideas about leaving Mistress Hunter . . . in a week or so. And she may want to move into the place with me, and live there till Old Man Jonesy come back from Jamaica."

"*Don't* let Dots move in."

"God, no."

"Do not tell Dots any-goddamn-thing 'bout this apartment, and free accommodation, man."

"God, no!"

"*Don't* let her know that the free apartment goes with the job, neither."

"God, no, man!"

"And if you haven't already tell Dots that an apartment exists, well this ain't the time to give her that information."

"God!"

"Think o' the parties, man! And the women! You will be *free!*"

"Jesus!"

"There's nothing like goddamn freedom for a man. A man have to be free. The word, '*man*,' sometimes means freedom. And you is a man who should be free."

"Christ!"

"You strike me as a man who, if he ain't goddamn free may as well be dead. And I want to say that you, Boysie Cumberbatch, is one man with a goddamn great desire o' freedom in your whole body and anatomy, in your entire make-up, in your head."

"Freeness, that is what I like!"

"Jesus Christ, Boysie, not *freeness,* but *freedom!*"

"Sorry, man. I make a mistake. I did mean freedom, though."

"I hope so."

"Yeah. Freedom. I am a man who must have a piece o' freedom."

"Not a piece, Boysie Cumberbatch. 'Cause I couldn't say to you, or to anybody behind your back, that you are a piece o' man, or a half o' man, even. I would have to confess that if you is the Boysie Cumberbatch I have known for almost twelve months now, I got to admit even if it hurts my arse, that you is a man. You is man. You are a man. All man."

"And I want *all* freedom."

"Right! Yeah!"

"Freedom like rass! as the Jamaicans would say."

"Jamaicans is men."

"And I is one, too, Godblindyou!"

"You talking like a man, now. God!"

"Freeness is what every man should have, and . . ."

"Jesus Christ, man, you slipping again. *Free*-dom, free-*dom*, free-*dom!*"

"I make a little slip, man. This beer going to my fucking head."

"That does happen."

And Henry stopped talking to concentrate on his beer. There were two full glasses and three empty ones before each of them. A ring of froth was extinguishing itself, bead by bead, from round Boysie's mouth. The beer was working a certain recklessness and a certain brand of courage into his system. He wanted Brigitte at that moment, very badly. Henry was observing.

A huge beautifully black, black man entered. He entered silently. Like a cat. But something surrounding him caused both Boysie and Henry to look up and notice. Other drinking drunkards noticed too. The mountain of a man walked as if each time his soles hit the sanded sandy floor, footprints of rubber were miraculously placed under each footfall. He bounced and he walked. His hair was slicked down and back and black with murmurs of waves. If you looked carefully, you would have seen that something like golden thoughts were whispering up from the blackness of his hair, in between the waves and some of the crests also. In the middle of this silent arrival, the huge beautifully black black man shouted across the room (to no one in particular, so far as Boysie and Henry could guess, at the moment of the shout), "Hey! Atlasssss, baby!" The words came out in a beautiful sonorous, kissing Harlem American inflection. "Atlas, baby! Shit, man, when'd you get outta jail?"

And eyes turned. For a man was walking through the sets of tables and drinkers. And they rested on a small jack-in-box of a man, neat and tight and immaculate in a tense-fitting Italian suit. It was a humid day but the man was wearing a fur hat that belonged by the origin of fashion and the vogue to the East and the black nationalists of New York City. Atlas was Jewish. He stood up with much spirit and waited. The mountain man approached him (Boysie and Henry were staring), and Atlas opened his arms and embraced one-quarter of the mountain's girth in the arc of a Russian-bearlike friendship. "Salaam!" the little Atlas said, with a pronounced accent which made you think automatically of Brooklyn, New York, and of Jews.

"Salaam, baby!" the mountain said, with his pronounced

accent. Harlem and black cats automatically came back to mind. "How you feel, Jeffrey, baby!" Atlas said, after the official greeting.

Before Jeffrey told Atlas how he felt, he looked back, and guiding Atlas's eyes by the direction of his own eyes, which were focused on Boysie and Henry (the only persons in the room who were finding this meeting interesting enough to stare at it), he said, "Let's beat the shit outta these two dumb West Indian monkeys! There's too much West Indians in *my* goddamn city, baby!" He made a step in their direction. But he was only pretending. He then sat down beside Atlas, and hid Atlas from part of the room by the bulk of his body. And he laughed as if there had been a particularly good dirty joke being told.

Atlas laughed and his whole body rackled like an old car. "These goddamn dumb West Indian dudes should be back in the canefields, sweating!" the mountain man said. In the next breath, he gave his order for drinks. "Double bourbon. On the rocks! For my friend here. And bring me a can o' tomaaato juice, a double bourbon, no ice, a Red Cap ale, and ahhh . . . you want anything else, baby? . . ." And he seemed to forget all about West Indians and his city and the other customers getting drunk in the room.

"Fucking American nigger!" Henry said.

"They frighten me sometimes, yuh know."

"No blasted wonder the white people in the States . . ."

"I have no love . . ."

"I hate them American negroes more than I hate white people, you don't know that?"

"Me, too. I am glad as arse I'm not a 'Merican negro."

"I prefer to be a fucking American *Indian* than to be an American negro."

"Me, too."

And with this agreement of their racial attitudes understood, Henry ordered three more glasses of beer for each of them. Boysie raised one of his new glasses to his head. When he took it away, there was only the reading of his beer-leaves and fortune in the bottom of the glass, twinkling like beads and foam, then dying. "Fucking Americans!" Boysie raised the second glass to his head; and as it touched his lips, Henry rested his hand on the glass-bearing hand, on Boysie's hand, and said, "Wait a minute." Boysie waited. Henry didn't do anything just then. Boysie put the glass down.

Then Henry began to talk. "You have known me as a man, who, gorblummuh, would tell you if a spade is really a fucking spade, right? Right!" He waited until Boysie nodded. But when Boysie nodded, his head fell out of control, slightly, lower than he had intended. "Right! And I mean to say to you, that in all the time we been firing rums together and having a beer, here and at the Pilot, in all that time, Saturday nights running down whores, or going to the Tropics, in all them things that we do together, I mean to say to you, you can't say in all honesty that I ever let you down in something that was important, or that was serious. Right?" Again, Boysie nodded. This time, however, he remembered the beer in his head. "Right! Now, this is what I want to put to you. I been listening to what you just tell me, and on the telephone too, concerning the job and the apartment that goes with the job. Now, don't get me wrong. 'Cause, I mean, if what I am going to put to you should sound wrong in a certain way to you, I expect you as a man to talk up and say to me, 'Henry, you wrong as shite!' I expect that much from you. But you have led me to understand, however, that this place is big enough for two people living together, to live in together, right?"

"Right!" This time, Boysie didn't have to nod.

"Right!" Henry was leaning forward, close enough to

kiss Boysie's face. But he smelled the beer-breath and the
stink of tobacco, and said to himself, "This bastard smell
stink as hell!" He went on to say, "Now you know that I
am thinking 'bout marriage for Agatha. You also know that
I is a man with hard luck, meaning that everybody in this
blasted place is against me, in a certain way, in regards to
getting employment, or getting a job. And you also know,
you can bear me out in this, that I is one man who try hard
as shite to find employment in this city. I isn't a lazy man.
A West Indian isn't a lazy immigrant, like some o' the
pricks sitting down right here in this room, drinking this
blasted cheap draught beer, from twelve when the tavern
opens to one o'clock in the fucking morning when it close.
You know all that, eh?"

"Yeah."

"Now, the position is this, Boysie. I want to get married
real bad to Agatha. Real bad. I know I am making the
biggest fucking mistake in my fucking life, but to err is
man. And goddamn, I am only a man. You can't kill me for
being a man. And *ergo, quod erat demonstration*, yuh can't
kill me nor hang me nor lynch my arse, because I err.
Right?"

"*Quod a rat demonstra . . .*"

"Gorblummuh, you know Latin, too?"

"I just pick it up."

"Continuing. I don't like the idea of marrying a white
woman with money, no more than any other man like the
idea, if he is as poor as me. It ain't wise marrying any
woman who have beans, particularly if the man don't have
a goddamn bean to his name, to back up her beans. You
follow?"

"*Quod a rat.*"

"As man! Now, I want to ask you something personal. But

you got to give me the green light to put this propersition to you before I could open my mouth and ask you."

"Put it, man! Put it! *Quod a rat*, so put it."

"Goddamn, boy! I like you. You *quodding* like hell to-night! You *quodding* real cool, baby!"

"Okay, I'm listening," Boysie said.

"Okay! I am going to *quod* just like you. I shall ask. I shall ask. The question is: I want you to let me and Agatha live in that apartment till I could get my hands 'pon some money, till we could get a place of our own, but remember! I am not trying to force myself on you, in no kind o' man-ner, and I am not trying to impose, or nothing so. It ain't nothing like that, it is only that I feel bad as hell that a woman got to support me in the essentials o' life, like even buying the toothpaste that I uses every morning, buying the cigarettes I smokes during the day, and goddammit, she even pays for the fucking frenchleathers I uses when I am screwing her! You see what I mean? This fucking woman have me enslaved, Boysie! I am a fucking slave to her, and she turning another screw a little bit more tighter every morning, because every morning, the first thing after I open my eye, and wipe the booby outta my goddamn eyes, there's something some-damn-thing that I got to want that day, and the onliest way I am going to get that thing is by asking Agatha for it. And that pains my arse to have to ask. I was not born asking, man . . ."

By this time, Boysie had heard enough of the request, which was contrary to the plans he had already laid for the use of the apartment. Henry's request was the kind to de-stroy any freedom which Boysie imagined he was going to have by living alone. He immediately, and expertly, there-fore, fell asleep. If he was asleep, Henry could not expect him to answer, could not expect him to hear, could not bind him to anything he might have said, because he couldn't be completely conscious while he was asleep. Boysie even started to snore; and the noise attracted the mountain of a man, who walked over, stood beside Boysie, and rested his hand affectionately on Boysie's shoulders. The waiter was already ready, willing and fuming to throw Boysie out of the tavern.

But the mountain man said, "It's all right, Bill. This here cat's my main man. He's cool."

But Henry intervened and took control of Boysie, who might have been really sleeping, and led him through the onlooking side entrance. Henry was so embarrassed (and very perturbed by the size of the muscles in the mountain man's arms, which looked like rippling mountains themselves) that he did not notice Boysie's miraculous transformation from the depths of drunkenness to articulate sobriety.

"Look, man," Boysie said, when they reached the sidewalk, "I gotta go home."

Henry did not even notice that it was the first time he had heard Boysie refer to his wife's living-in quarters in Mrs. Hunter's house as "home."

When Boysie left, Henry did not go straight home, where Agatha was waiting for him. She had skipped a seminar in her Ph.D. course in zoology, at the university. She had stopped at the Liquor Control Board store on Spadina Avenue, near the burlesque theatre which was not far from the Paramount Tavern. She bought a bottle of wine, Casal Mendes Rosé, and a twenty-six-ounce bottle of Seagram's VO rye whiskey. The whiskey was for Henry. She did not like whiskey. The wine was for dinner, and for herself. She stopped at the rundown variety store, two doors north, and bought him three packs of Pall Mall cigarettes. (She had made him stop smoking and accepting Rothmans, because of South Africa.) As she walked down from College to the liquor store, her mind returned to the happy days of first love and infatuation that she and Henry had shared in the Paramount, and other places. In those days, it was slumming for her, a liberal-minded girl of great wealth and social position, to go to "those places." She could enter her seminar room the morning after, still throbbing from love and the "experience" and Henry's small room, and tell the other "sheltered students from rich middle-class homes" what real life was.

But today, the Paramount was not a place for her. The tension of this rejection did something to quicken her steps, and she didn't even breathe easily until she had passed the building. She walked back more leisurely going home, because she always liked Spadina Avenue. It was on this street that her father, and his father before him, had laid the foundation of their fortune in the clothing business. It started with secondhand clothing in the terrible days of the Depression. It was now in a large building, with renovated front, with many employees, in the hardstoned, brown-brick heart of the shopping district, in the heart of Yonge Street between King and Dundas.

But she liked Spadina Avenue most. It was a beautiful street: it anchored her to something grand, something solid, something *there* in her past. And now that it was autumn, with the colours of dresses and skirts and blouses and shirts and trousers matching the colours of the leaves falling in that paused stage of overripeness and rot; and because there was space on Spadina Avenue, space and a feeling of freedom, on the jousting ground of immigrants and ambitions, Spadina Avenue was one of the few places left where people behaved as if they were loving and living and enjoying the thing called life . . . Spadina Avenue was after all, the street on which she and Henry had made their first date.

But she forgot all this and hurried home, hurrying her steps, wanting to justify her skipping the zoology seminar by making Henry a very good meal, and having drinks and making love after the drinks. She thought of a surprise for him. She would cook him a Jewish meal, a Jewish meal from Poland, where her father's father's father came from. "I'd better stop in the Kensington Market," she told herself — meaning the Jewish Market. She never called the Jewish Market the Jewish Market, because she was Jewish. And Henry noticed this, and he noticed too, that when Jews were present, people who were not Jews always said, "the Kensington Market." The Kensington-Jewish Market in recent years had become an exciting, exotic place to shop, filled with the faces and languages and abuses and customs of people from all over the world: with certain foodstuffs from the West Indies, like salt fish, ackee, avocado pears, tamarind, and even Barbadian "heavy-sweets," a homemade bread with coconut and currants and spice and egg and vanilla baked in it. But it was a white woman who sold "heavy-sweets" in the market.

Agatha headed for the Kensington Market. She bought the ingredients for the Polish-Jewish meal and headed for Henry's room, which she was now in the habit of calling home. At this moment, Henry was on a streetcar going along College Street towards Yonge. He had not yet made up his mind where he was going. He was trying to get the disappointment of Boysie's refusal, or rather the disappointment surrounding the suggestion, and Boysie's behaviour in the Paramount, out of his system. He had spent five dollars on Boysie, and he had got nothing for it. He was getting married shortly. He hadn't set the date yet, because he saw no signs and no hope of having enough money for his part of the reception expenses. And he wanted a new suit for his wedding. He hadn't yet bought Agatha a wedding present. He couldn't rely on Agatha's friends. He hadn't met Agatha's parents. He wanted to be able to pay at least the bus fare or the train fare (he hadn't even considered planes) to the honeymoon spot — probably Niagara Falls. He had been accusing himself recently, saying, "But I am too damn old to go on a honeymoon, anyhow! I won't know what to do with such a young woman. Why we don't save the goddamn money and buy furnitures with it?"

He caught himself from these thoughts when the streetcar reached Church Street. He ran up the corridor to the conductor, and asked for a transfer ticket; and he jumped on the Church Street bus going south. He wanted to change again to the Dundas streetcar, but he remembered that the same transfer wouldn't take him in the same direction from which he had come. He would have to pay another fare. The bus rambled along Church. He saw some old men and old women loitering from their age and their leisure on benches in front of a large church. It could have been a cathedral. A man was sleeping with a copy of the *Telegram* over his face. The sun was not shining. There was a vacant lot between two buildings in which were about a dozen secondhand Citroens. He always liked these French cars. ("Two great things the French invented, Boysie, boy. Frenchleathers and the Citroen!")

Looking now on the other side of Church Street, the east side, Henry noticed the pawnbrokers' shops. Jewelry, cameras, guitars, rings, watches . . . "Watches? Watches! Jesus Christ, why didn' I think of this before?" He got off the bus and entered a pawnshop. Before he went in, he looked right and left to see whether any of his Paramount friends were among the loiterers on the benches nearby. He laid his gold pocket watch, with its heavy gold-painted chain, noisily on the glass-topped counter.

A man came smiling. "What can we do for you, sir? Nice day, isn't it?"

When Henry went out through the door, into the autumn freshness of the street and the late afternoon, he had thirty dollars in his pocket, apart from the five left over from Agatha's gift. He was without his heavy golden pocket watch. He was also without his ring, his mother's wedding ring, which she had given him more years ago than he wanted to remember now. And he was without a silver dollar, made in 18-something. He had further plans. He walked along Church Street, and found his way on Jarvis Street, at the Crippled Civilians bargain store. Here, they sold everything: including junk. Henry was braver here, because there were more people buying cheaply. He selected a black suit of a worsted material and a lighter weight suit that was fawn-coloured. He paid six dollars for them. He even got the waistcoats with the suits. His next stop was at the Invisible Mending & Alteration Tailoring While-U-Wait shop, at the corner of College and Beverley streets. He knew the old European man with the rimless glasses and the weak eyes which were producing almost as invisible light and eyesight as was his mending.

"Look, Vladdy, I got me these two three-piece suits a long time. They're damn good suits, Vladdy . . ." (Old Vladdy was nodding his head and saying, "Yah-yah! Yah-yah!") ". . . and I feel it would be a sin . . . man, they're too good to throw out, so I want you to make them into younger suits for me, man. Eh? Take this padding outta the shoulders, and make the jackets more shorter than they is now, at present. Make them like the ones you see the Eyetalians up by Spadina wear."

Old Vladdy was still saying, "Yah-yah! Yah-yah! I do good job for you. I do even better job than last job, no? And you like last job, no?"

Henry stared Vladdy in the eye, and added, "And I want the trousers to be without cuffs, the bottoms sixteen inches, and make the trousers legs more slimmer than they look now. Eh, Vladdy, man?" And he patted Vladdy on his back to make him feel better. Old Vladdy was looking steadily at him, over his rimless glasses. Henry wondered whether he was actually seeing him, or anything else. But he was a blasted good tailor! Henry knew that. Vladdy had served him excellently in the past. "Now, Vladdy, as you know, I is one man who always pays his debts, punctual. And I know you appreciate that. Now, I want you to make-up these three-pieces real good for me, and real fast. Now, another thing, Vladdy, old bean, as you also know, I is a man not working at the present moment, but that don't matter, 'cause you are going to get every fucking penny you charge me for the alteration job. The only thing is that I want you to treat me real nice, this time." And there the bargaining began.

"Forty!" Vladdy almost overshouted his enthusiasm.

"But Jesus Christ, Vladdy, man! I am not buying-out this bloody tailor shop!"

"Forty! I take off twenty even before I say forty."

"Goddamn, Vladdy! Man, wait, you want to send me on welfare, or something? Thirty, Vladdy, and not one bloody red penny more! I give you a lotta good work . . ."

"Thirty-five!" Old Vladdy was looking at him through the pincers of his rimless eyes. "Business, she is not too good this time of year, my friend. You see, look, my friend. You see all these suits? I make them in February, March, May. Now, is October. The people who own them, they bring them, I don't see them no more. I have suits. I don't get the money. You see, my friend, business she is not too good." Old Vladdy was the champion shrugger when it came to telling a hard-luck story. Henry could spend a whole afternoon watching Vladdy, just to catch him shrugging his overclothed, overstuffed, padded shoulders. Henry wondered whether Vladdy wore the suits which were left with a down payment of their alteration costs, and which their owners never remembered to claim. Perhaps this rich brown suit with the shrugging shoulders was a suit that was owned, once upon a down payment, by a customer of Vladdy's. "So, you see, Mr. White, the business? What I need suits for? I am tailor, not dandy."

"Look, Vladdy, man, I have always deal fair and square with you. You know that. And I sorry as hell to hear that you not making a million dollars a week in your business. But you can't blame me for all these unclaimed suits hanging up in your shop, man."

"Thirty-five. The rent, it is due today. I have to pay it. The Hydro . . ."

"I am going to tell you something, Vladdy! Look, I got here with me . . ." And Henry made a big dramatic production of reaching into his leather wallet and fingering the bills ("Gimme the thirty in ones, please," he had told the clerk at McTamney's Pawnbrokers). Vladdy saw money and he saw blood. The first cash he had seen for the day; and he looked harder over his rimless glasses. Henry knew. *"Look, ten dollars!"*

And he dropped the ten one-dollar bills on the scissors-scarred counter, and they seemed to make a great noise in Vladdy's invisible eyesight, so much so that Vladdy said, "All right, my friend. All right. Fifteen! And you leave my establishment this minute!" Something like a smile broke through the thickness of the rimless lenses.

"Fifteen, godblindyuh, Vladds, my friend!" And he almost jumped over the counter to embrace Vladdy. The next five one-dollar bills fell like a harvest of rain on the counter. "Now, Vladdy, boy. I want these suits real fast. And because you doing them in special speed, I still want a first-rate job, eh, Vladdy?"

"You come next week. You get suits."

"In *three* days?"

"I am first class tailor, Mr. . . ."

"Okay, okay! Don't get angry, Vladdy old bean!"

Henry walked the rest of the way home, to Agatha and love and the happiness of the Jewish-Polish meal. He had fourteen dollars left.

"Thanks," he told her, repaying her the five dollars. When she saw the five dollars, in bills, she wondered. But Henry was too happy now, too excited for her to express what she was really wondering. And if Henry had told her that he was smiling because he had nine dollars left, in his wallet, that he could now join the crap game already in progress in the East End; if he had disclosed this to her, she would not have objected to his going, because she was so happy. "I love you," he told her.

"I love you," she said. She really loved him.

"I am the best man in the world, baby. So, you better be cool."

"I don't know 'bout the world, but you sure as hell are in bed!"

"A Barbadian man is the best man in the goddamn world! Ask any Barbadian."

"Now that you're in such a good mood, I may as well tell you that I have a seminar tonight at eight. And after that, I have to go visit mother . . . if you don't mind. She's not well . . ."

"Fine, fine, *fine!*"
Agatha continued to wonder. But she dared not ask him
what he was wondering.
"*Fine!*"

Huron Street is beautiful in the autumn. The houses have
just come through the scathing summer heat; the ivy on
the walls of some houses changes its colour gradually, and
if you had not walked along this street for three months
before, you would not recognize it now. The street is marvellous from Bloor Street going north, but it ceases to be
marvellous after you pass Bernard Avenue. After Lowther
Avenue there is the noise of young ethnic children screaming from the Huron Street Public School, Junior. Estelle
could see all this in her walk along the street, reading house
numbers and front windows for Room-for-Rent signs, and
reading the faces of ethnic landladies and landlords and
men whose faces were pale and square, and whose English
was strange if spoken at all. She was searching these faces
and houses for a sign that the "room" printed on the sign
in the window was really a room in the house which they
were willing to rent to her. She had heard somebody say
(perhaps it was Henry, who knew this district well) that if
a black man couldn't get a room on Huron Street, then his
chances of getting a room anywhere else in Toronto were
nil. Huron used to be the international street in 1955, when
the first flood of West Indians arrived to attend the university a block away. Estelle saw a sign in a window, just one
block north of Bloor Street. But as she was walking up the
path to the front door, she happened to notice a woman
wearing glasses, peeping through another window, beside
the door. The woman hastily pulled the transparent white
curtains and covered herself from Estelle's presence, and

from Estelle's request. Estelle turned back. Her courage fell. It was her first trial. Her first defeat: but she was not certain that it was not herself defeating herself.

Estelle felt the dejection of this first, probable, self-inflicted defeat: and she knew also that there would be other defeats not brought on by her self-consciousness. She walked, and she looked and she walked: left and right; but she looked in such a way so as not to let on to the people passing, or the people loitering on small cement porches, that she was really looking for a room to rent. She wanted very much that her other defeats not be witnessed by *them*. It was too personal an adventure she was on, too personal to expose her quest to any-and-everybody. She was out to get a room. This was her own problem: she must find a room before the night became too old. Her valise she had left in a locker in the Gray Coach bus terminal on Bay Street. The advice given her by the man in Union Station when she was setting out for Timmins came in very handy. She knew something now about life in a big city: you didn't have to load yourself down and lug your load all over the place: you could rest it behind you. There should have been some of these lockers in Barbados, she mused; and straightway went on that journey and fantasy of memory through distance: those country women in Barbados, who came to Bridgetown early in the heavy dew-dropping, damp mornings with the weight of their labourious backbending existence on their heads. Only a few lockers, and those women wouldn't have to walk with such loads on their heads! Boysie once had something to say about this, too. "It is all-right for certain eddicated people to talk a lot o' shite 'bout Wessindian women having good shapes and good-looking backsides because of the heavy loads they have to carry on their head. But I would

say it is plain simple, arse-hole hard work! Wessindian
women know more 'bout hard work than a snake know
'bout grass!"

"I need a blasted room," she reminded herself, when
she got to St. George Street. "Today." She had just turned
across Bedford Road, looking for signs and a sign. The first
house with a sign said Furnished Room. The house itself
was an imposing structure, and Estelle felt it was too good
for her. There was ivy on its walls. Estelle thought she saw
five levels of windows. The front door was open. She walked
up the walk, and just as she was about to press the button
marked Press ("What else could you do with a button?
Eh?"), a man came forward out of the broadloomed twi-
light of the house.

"Yes." Was he telling her something was all right?

"I was just passing, and I noticed your sign . . ."

"For how many? I have three vacant rooms going. Furnished or unfurnished?" Estelle didn't have the experience
to understand then that not all rooms had to be furnished
before they could be rented. It was another absurdity about
life in this country. She felt that all rooms had to have furniture; she didn't bring any with her, from Barbados!

"Come, come with me," the man said. On the second
floor, somebody was playing a kind of music she had heard
often in Sam Burrmann's house, when Mrs. Burrmann was
absent. It was Sam's music; and it was played as loudly as
Sam played it. She thought of Sam. The landlord informed
her what the music was, and what his attitude to it was, as
he said, with great history-assured confidence, "That damn
jazz! They call it music?" On the third floor there was a
different music, the music of guitars, and she liked this kind
better. The landlord didn't tell her what his attitude to this
kind of music was, but led her up the broadloomed steps of
the short staircase to the fourth floor. "Here it is, miss."

She was in a coffin of a room. There was a bed, a narrow couch like the one she had slept on in North Bay. There was a cupboard made of metal, painted white to look like wood. There was a stuffed chair which took up most of the head-part of the coffin. And there was a bentwood upright, uprighteous-looking chair, and a table whose top showed how many and how often glasses and hot plates and cigarettes and staining things had been put on it. The landlord was moving out of the coffin. "Now, out here, in the hallway, is a hotplate . . ."

"A what?"

"Hotplate! You know, a small stove-thing for boiling yourself a cup of tea in the mornings, or cooking little meals like weiners and eggs. Snacks and so forth . . ."

"Oh yes."

"You will be sharing it with the other lady who lives on this floor with you. There are only the two of you up here." Estelle tried to picture what the lady looked like: and whether she was a lady. "She's an old lady, so you won't get much noise from her," he said. But Estelle was thinking of other old ladies: those who usually pissed in their beds and groaned and grumbled all night. Thinking about this old lady made her think of her own mother, Mammy: "Christ, that was why I had to put Mammy in the poorhouse, poor Mammy, before I left Barbados." But she needed a room, and this was her first experience, and the landlord didn't seem too interested in her colour or her race — only in her money, eight dollars a week; so she decided to take it, and forget the old lady; and also Mammy.

"I take it." And immediately she saw many reasons why she had made the wrong decision.

Estelle left soon after, feeling relieved, and at the same time depressed, that she had a room. No matter how small, no matter how grim parts of the house looked, no matter

she had to share the passageway with an old woman, it was
going to be her castle; no matter she didn't have a private
bathroom as she had in Bernice's servant-quarters, it was
going to be her dominion, so long as she paid her rent. And
when she found a job, she would move into a better place.
Her present worry was to find Gray Coach terminal by
means of the subway or the streetcar, and get back to her
room before dark.

When she returned to Bloor Street from the Gray Coach
terminal on Bay, with her valise, she realized with terror
that in her excitement to get the room she had neglected
to take down the address of the house. Her fear of present
poverty and of future hunger must have done something to
her senses and her judgment and her intellect. However,
before she had time to think and guess again, she was
standing before the house: the right house, her rooming
house.

There was an envelope with her name, *Miss E. Leech*,
written in lead pencil in a scratchy hand. On the back of
the envelope was the information: *from Mr. Wassermann,
landlord. Key to front door plus key to your room. No du-
plicat keys must be made of these keys. By order of the
landlord. Thank you.* He had, unwittingly, put an idea into
Estelle's schemes. She made a mental note to do something
about it, sometime. When she reached the landing, on the
second floor, she could smell the same smell that came
from Harvey's restaurant on Bloor Street: a student, or an
artist, was having hamburger meat for supper. It filled the
whole house with its aroma; but the more she got accustomed to it, the more it nauseated her. She trembled to
think that the old woman on the fourth floor with her
might be cooking hamburger meat for her supper.

In her room, there was nothing on the wall — none of
the furniture, the smell, the colour of the bedspread and

the bed itself — that belonged even remotely in character to her. It was her prison. She thought of it again as a coffin. There was a framed picture torn from some magazine, depicting a scene in winter. There was handwriting on the wall; and she laughed at this handwriting which she could read and understand, which was different from *the writing on that wall* in biblical times presaging destruction. She read the writing: names of women, accompanied by their telephone numbers: *Marta*, 922–1111, *Greta*, *LE* 2–2001, *Eloise*, 922–1112, *Nadia*, 921–0084. Estelle wished there was a man's name and his telephone number, but soon she regretted the thought and started to unpack her valise. There were black dots of sand in the drawers of the chest of drawers, running round on the stale, yellow newspaper pages which lined the drawers. It was rat-shit sand. She knocked this onto the floor, put her few belongings into the drawers, and her comb and brush and toothbrush into a glass, and put them on top of the chest. She lifted back the bedspread and the pink blanket which had LORD SIM-COE HOTEL printed on it, and she saw pools of dried sexual avariciousness. "Oh my God!"

It was becoming dark outside. In the West Indies it would be night, and Mammy would be going to bed, shaking out the sun and the dust and the bed-wetting of the straw mattress, and shaking it into a comfortable body-fitting body-rest for her old bones to rest on for the long unsleepable painful night. Mammy coughed throughout the night, and she punctuated her coughing with talk. Would this old woman, her new neighbour, be the same?

Perhaps the old woman is doing just what Mammy is doing now, miles away; perhaps, like Mammy, she is down on her tired knees, her old useless knees praying to God or to somebody about how nice it is to be alive another day. Mammy would be finished now; and she would be taking her kerosene lamp with the sparkling crystal ball of a lamp-shade into her small coffin of a bedroom to die for the night, her Bible in one hand, and her kerosene lamp in the other, smiling and happy about some secret of old age which the young can never quite understand. Perhaps this old woman is the same age as Mammy: all old women are the same age when they start forgetting.

To think of this old woman: to bring back the memories of the past bad treatment she had given her own mother; to rent the one room in the whole of Toronto, a city of two million white, black, Chinese, Indians from India and Indians from Canada, Eskimo and the rest and to find that her neighbour is an old woman; to be reminded of her own mother, probably wetting herself in the alms-house; to be reminded of her past and to see a glimpse of her future each time she should hear a moan or a groan; and to smell her, even before she knew she was there . . .

Estelle could hardly see the words on Mrs. Macmillan's letter for the tears in her eyes. She had taken the letter out, and read it again, to try to understand what kind of a woman Mrs. Macmillan was. She hadn't the time to think of her before now.

The letter itself did not explain any more about Mrs. Macmillan. *Dear Ess, I did not give this to you personally, or leave it on your dresser when I was leaving, because I wanted you to have it just as you were leaving the hospital* ("because she knew she was lying like hell, and she couldn't face me, that's why!"), *I wanted you to have something to read on the long trip from Toronto to Timmins* ("This woman's crazy as hell! Something for me to read?"). Estelle skipped the next few useless pages of the letter, folded it, and tried to sleep. She left the light burning because she was scared of the strange house and of the old woman mumbling in her sleep next door . . .

One afternoon, as Estelle was dragging her feet in the dead leaves of autumn and Bedford Road, about six days after she moved into the rooming house, she all of a sudden got the idea that she should write Sam Burrmann, and tell him she needed some money for rent. Rent was due the next day. She had left the money which Mrs. Macmillan had given her in the teapot in her kitchen in North Bay, and now she had very little left. In her new condition of having to take care of herself, of having to supply the immediate and essential means of her livelihood, she was a bit inexperienced. For example, that first night, six nights ago, she had overspent: but it was nothing more than hamburgers which she hated, potatoes and a little milk. Sometimes, she had to use one teabag more than twice the same day. And very often she had to drink her tea without milk or cream. She was worrying about her health. The sugar she had brought from the hospital in little sacks which advertised the name of the hospital on them. These little thefts she had been talked into committing and encouraged into continuing by Mrs. Macmillan, who, with her, had made tea every night when the nurses weren't looking from the hot water tap in the washroom. It was a good thing, Estelle now realized, that she had met Mrs. Macmillan. A simple thing like a teabag, a teabag which normally Estelle would have walked over, had she met one of them on the street; and sugar sacks, such as she was served on the plane coming up from Barbados; in restaurants when she went out with Bernice, she had never imagined that a sugar sack would come in so useful. But now it was time to live above the sugar-sack level. Sam Burrmann would have to give her money. As she walked in the dead leaves, she wondered how she would ever reach him.

There was little strength and fewer vitamins to be got from her daily diet of hamburgers and potatoes. Her pride made her refuse five invitations to go for a coffee with the student who lived on the first floor, and who had been pestering her for a date: "A wha'? *Date?* At my blasted age, and in my condition, you asking me for date? I am a pregnant woman! I don't want no date, boy, I looking for a man to father my child," she told him once.

"Or can I take you to the movies?" he pleaded. "There's a party a Wessindian is holding tomorrow night. You want to go? Would you like some coffee — in my room?"

With these things on her mind this afternoon, she walked with her head down, consciously looking and hoping to find money. But it hadn't happened. And she was starving. Her hate for the old woman, who she had seen only once, slipping out of the smelling washroom, increased every night when she smelled the hamburger meat she was cooking, and it did not matter that she herself was reduced to eating the same hamburger. Once she told herself that the smell had changed to that of frying pork chops; and this caused her to remember the way her mother used to fry them back home, with lard oil running out of them when you put a piece in your mouth, and with the fat burned, but not too much, turning into crackling, and the sting of black pepper and the cloves and the onion. The old woman's food was driving her crazy.

She had thought many times of writing Sam Burrmann a letter. But she ruled out the wisdom of the letter since Bernice might see it when it arrived. It was better to telephone him. And arrange to meet him some place. Or should she threaten him? "Should I scare the bastard? Who am I kidding? Me? Trying to scare a lawyer?"

Estelle was walking back through the dead leaves on her way back from the phone booth at the corner of Bedford Road and Bloor Street, wondering whether the secretary who answered the call had told her a lie: "Mr. Burrmann is away from the office, ma'am." When Estelle raised her voice, in frustration, the secretary explained that Mr. Burrmann was fishing in northern Ontario. She felt now that she should have been strong enough to have written Mr. Burrmann the letter.

The first day Old Man Jonesy showed Boysie the job at the Baptist church house, Boysie was sorry he had taken it. Jonesy lectured him about cleanliness, saying, "This is a important job you doing here, Boysie. It is a responsible job, too. There is gentlemen and ladies working downstairs on the first floor, who are doing some very important work for our people in Africa. The boss-man is a man with great education himself. That is Doctor Glimmermann, a real important gentleman. And a nice one, too. Now, the first thing I do on evenings when those gentlemen and ladies leave, is to go through each and every office, making sure they haven' left something behind, by mistake, such as a comb or a wallet and so forth. Then I come back up here, if they haven' left any such valuables behind, and I begin sweeping each room with this broom, cleaning the toilet bowls, doing the rug, and fixing the desses. Now, the first thing for you to know is never touch nothing that you see or find in them desses. I been doing this job for ten years now, and I never take up nothing that didn' belong to me, so these people come now to trust me with such a great trust that I can even go to their bank at the corner and cash their salaries. And they also allow me to take out the letters, all important letters going all over the world. Man, only yesterday evening I take out a big big bag o' mails and I notice while I was putting them in the bag in the office, that some was address to Ethiopia, Ghana, Tanzinnia,

South Africa . . . man, I even see one letter going to a place named Timbuktu, and my God! I thought that that was a name we in the islands had invent to make a certain point with, and not a real name of a real place in Africa. Now, you see the kind o' important job I leaving you to handle in my behalfs, whilst I am in Jamaica on holidays? Good."

Boysie had nodded his head, because he didn't have the strength or the energy to waste in the effort of speaking. Old Man Jonesy had made him vexed by his talk. He was superior, his actions and his important way of speaking simple things to Boysie expressed this. It was a feeling that went with the job: an important job that had to do with the important gentlemen and ladies downstairs in the church house. He wanted Boysie to know this. He wanted Boysie . . . could he tell him? . . . to know that he knew certain inside-things about these gentlemen and ladies, things they had leaked to him about Africa. But he didn't have time to tell him right now: he was preparing for his holidays in Jamaica where he was born, where he hadn't visited in the twenty-five years he had been living in this country as an immigrant. Like Henry, Old Man Jonesy had begun on the railroad; and had moved up, in prestige but not in salary, to the janitorial job in the more exclusive church house.

"But I have been putting my money in the bank, Boysie. I heard from your wife that you don't do that. I haven' been licking it out on women and liquor, like you young generation o' Wessindians. Every Fridee, for the ten years I been on this job, I been banking my money. Because o' the presence o' mind I had ten years ago, and the sense to put my wages on the bank, boy, today I could *go* into the Air Canada place and pay *cash* for a two-way ticket home to Jamaica. Ain't that something? That's a great achievement, ain't it?"

"But Mr. Jones, it take you ten years? Ten years is a lot o' time, man."

"Ten years may be a lot o' time to some people. But I know there is many who came here to this country with me in the Depression and they can't even pay rent for a dirty room today, furthermore buy a cash ticket to Jamaica!"

"But, but-but . . . but godblindme! Mr. Jones, if it is going to take me ten years to save a couple hundred bucks on the bank, be-Jesus Christ, this is the wrong brand o' job and the wrong place for me, man! Ten years? Man, you know what I could do in ten years? You know how kiss-me-arse old I would be in ten years?"

"That is something I want to tell you about, Boysie. On this job, you have to watch your mouth and your language, boy. Your language is not the language those gentlemen and ladies downstairs want to hear! As long as you are working 'mongst these gentlemen and ladies, you will . . ."

"All right, man, all right . . ." Boysie was thinking of having his first night alone with Brigitte, in the large apartment. Otherwise he would have put some more language on Old Man Jonesy.

"Good." And Old Man Jonesy went on to explain further eccentricities about the job: going through each room with Boysie, pointing out the corners into which the broom had difficulty getting at the dust; showing Boysie the expensive glass-topped "desses" in the offices of the important people; making him walk on tiptoe in the office of the boss-man, Dr. Glimmermann; and making him use the vacuum cleaner in this office only, running the vacuum cleaner with the grain of the rug and not against it, leaving the rug regular and fluffy like a sprightly growing field of thick guinea grass in Africa, bent in one direction by the kiss of an afternoon breeze.

Boysie admired Old Man Jonesy's diligence, but he hated him. He knew he wouldn't waste such time cleaning a mere rug, regardless of whose office it was in: "Gorblummuh! it could belong to Jesus Christ, himself!" he told himself, watching Jonesy work.

Old Man Jonesy showed him which room to clean first, which to clean last. He showed him how to take the garbage pail from the basement, and how to lift it. Jonesy had pinned to the wall in the basement, inside the closet for the brooms and the mops, a regulation put out by the safety branch of some organization, which showed with pictures how workmen should lift heavy loads. "Find time to read them regulations, Boysie!" He gave him a tour of the rest of the basement. "Sometimes, off and on, you will be called upon to fix these cups and saucers, when the gentlemen and ladies upstairs have a party or a important conference. Now, don't break none. You would have to pay for breakages outta your wages. Ten years I working here, and never have my hand faltered in this regards. And I is a older man than you. When I come back in three weeks, I want my work record to be still spotless. I can't lose this job now!"

Boysie was impressed by the size of the basement. It was well decorated. When Jonesy was doing something else, Boysie looked for signs of bottles, or even wine. But he remembered that he was in a church house, and that such drinks would not be there. He made a wish to have one hell of a party the moment Old Man Jonesy left: next weekend, in this same basement. Back upstairs, in his living quarters, Old Man Jonesy showed him where to sleep.

Boysie thought he was going to sleep in Jonesy's large feather bed.

But Jonesy cleared up that point early. "My madam gone on ahead as you know. She left yesterday. I had to remain to straighten up a few important things such as taking out today's mails. Now this is our bed. Don't sleep in it. You isn' to sleep in it. I will show you where you going sleep. Come, up here." And he took Boysie up into something, a room with dust and spiders and cobwebs and probably ghosts at night, that looked like a belfry. It was musty too. It was smelly. It was not a belfry. "This is a very nice place, Boysie. You have your own quarters up here. You can use the things in my kitchen. But wash them up after you use them, please. I am going to lend you my alarm clock, and you keep it up here so you won't tarry in bed and be late for the job. This is a very important job. This is all."

"That man is a blasted slave!" Boysie was telling Henry, half an hour later. "Ten blasted years it take him to raise two or three hundred dollars! And he telling me all the time 'bout my generation, that my generation o' Wessindians is too worthliss!"

"Jonesy came to Canada when things was rough. He is a pioneer."

"Pioneer my arse! He is a slave!"

"Don't say that, Boysie. Old Man Jonesy represent a certain brand o' black man who had to creep before they could stand up or walk or even talk. Gorblummuh, it wasn' no bed o' roses in Canada in the year 1930-something, as far as a black man was concerned, you understand that?"

"But man, the way that man talked to me! The way he show me round that place, he made me feel he was proud as shite to be a cleaner. And that thing hurt me. Because, man, now suppose I don't do the job good, and I hate the blasted job . . . I already hate it . . . but suppose something happen in Jonesy's absence, he will think I let him down. First thing I can hear Jonesy saying is, that . . ."

"You can't trust coloured people!"

"Gorblummuh!"

Boysie could change instantly from lightheartedness to deepest depression, and this is what happened now. Henry had something else for him to consider, and knowing Boysie, knowing that this depression could go on for many hours, Henry quickly presented his business. "Look here, Boys, old man," he said going into the clothes cupboard and parting clothes with his hands, like a man opening a window blind, with a flourish. Boysie liked clothes. He had always liked them. But in Canada, without a job, he was unable to afford many of them. "You know I'm getting hitch-up with Agatha in a week or so, and I have to have a good suit for the thing. You know too, old man, that you's my best man, gorblummuh! and you have a obligation to look damn sharp, too! Well, I have a transaction which I hope you are going to be interested in. Now, I don't want to tie you down to nothing, old man, because that ain't the way friends should get on with friends. Not at all. I just want to show you this." And Henry held the suit in front of Boysie's eyes like a matador teasing a charging bull. "This suit. And see if you like it enough to want to own one like it."

Henry knew Boysie didn't have a suit good enough for the wedding. Dots was saving every penny these days, both for her course in nursing and for the apartment which she wanted to rent as soon as she moved out of Mrs. Hunter's place. Up until a few days ago, Boysie was hopelessly unemployed. He was down and out and Henry knew this. "Look at this suit, man. Expensive as arse, old man. I am

a married-man about-to-be and I can't be going round
wearing a lot o' damn expensive threads and getting on
as if I'm still the greatest bachelor he-man in Toronto. So,
I want to give you a good deal. Now this one, the sharp-
looking one, is the one I like best. But you is my friend. I
think it is a perfect suit for the wedding, too." That was
enough to whet Boysie's appetite. He sprang up and was
standing before the open doors of the cupboard, running
his hands over the material of the suits as if they were
Brigitte's luscious thighs and breasts.

"Gorblummuh! this is the material I see one time down
in Eaton's!"

"First class."

"You not telling me nothing I don't know, boy."

"Eighty dollars!"

Boysie had the suit in his hands now. He was pleased
that it had a vest too. Henry followed his thoughts as they
expressed themselves in his hands as his hands ran over the
material.

"Fifty, and not one kiss-me-arse dollar . . ."

"All right!" Henry said, seeing the bargaining getting
out of hand. "I am going to tell you what I am going to
do. This fawn-coloured suit is just the thing for a wedding.
I know how you would look in it. Man, try-on the suit right
now. I want you to feel yourself in a good suit for a change.
Every man should have a good suit. A good suit, at least
one, that cost over a hundred dollars. Try on this other
one, too." He took down the black worsted suit. He was
trembling. He had to have his money today. He had lost
thirty dollars that belonged to Agatha. Again he had lost in
a crap game. He had to have his money today. After having
bought these two suits from the Crippled Civilians used
store for six dollars, after having paid Vladdy, the invisible
tailor and mender, fifteen to alter them, he was out twenty-

one dollars. He wanted to make thirty more, off Boysie. Twenty-one and thirty is fifty-one, he said, making a fast calculation in his mind. "And I got to make a little profit on the side, too," he told himself. Boysie felt good in the fawn-coloured suit. He looked good, too. He wanted to see himself in the black suit, too.

"I prefer the black one for the wedding, though," he told Henry, after he had put it on.

"Black is your colour."

"Yeah."

"It is yours now. The fawn-one, too. Try-on the other one again. They is yours, man."

The gleam of possession overpowered Boysie. He shrugged his shoulders into the jacket of the black worsted, as if he had just paid cash for it; as if he was born in it. Henry did not fail to notice this pride of possession.

"Made-to-fucking-measure!" Henry said. And indeed, Boysie looked like a black male model from the pages of the *New Yorker* magazine. "Goddamn, boy! if only you was a touch less black, you would have a whole fortune in front o' you, by just wearing clothes and letting people take pictures of you in them clothes. You's a born model!"

"You think so?"

"Eighty, and both is yours!"

And that was what Boysie agreed to. Henry was amazed: where the hell did he get all this cash from? But Boysie merely laughed, and hinted at something about "a loan from Brigitte." Boysie paid him cash, then and there: eighty dollars, in tens!

Henry put the thirty dollars earmarked for Agatha's business in the left back trousers pocket; fifteen for next week's groceries in his left side-pocket; and the remaining thirty-five in his wallet. ("I gotta remember to get this changed-up into ones for that crap game this evening!")

He could now return to the match with Freeness and the boys, at Freeness's house in the West End. When he saw Boysie walking through the door, wearing the fawn-coloured suit (his own clothes that he had worn to Henry's, his jacket and his worn-out grey flannel trousers, were in a paper bag, and the black wedding-suit-to-be in the laundry bag in which it had been hanging since Vladdy gave it to Henry), and Henry looked at him, it made him feel a little sad.

But that sadness was nothing like the sadness he later experienced that night, when he lost his thirty-five one-dollar bills in the crap game; and then, "damn! I might as well spend this next fifteen that is for food to try to get back that thirty-five. Can't stop now, not now, baby!"; and then when the food-dollar-bills had disappeared like autumn leaves in the wind, it was then that he had, in despair, felt his back trousers pocket and discovered Agatha's thirty. In three wild bets, betting ten dollars each time that Freeness could not throw a four (it was then Freeness's fifth "four-main"), and collapsing each time that Freeness threw a four . . . Henry shook his head, and had to borrow taxicab fare from Freeness in order to get out of the desolation of the West End.

"Man, I can throw a four-main in my sleep," Freeness said, "you stupid old Bajan. Go home and tell your woman Agatha to send you back with some more dollar-bills!"

The first week, Boysie cleaned the fifteen rooms at the Baptist church house by sweeping them with the broom, as Old Man Jonesy had told him to do. It was hard work. He knew he had taken the wrong job. Dots had come down one night to help him clean and had never returned. She didn't even press the point about living in the church house apartment that was rent-free. It was too musty. And all the religious books and religious tracts upset her. When she found out that Boysie was to sleep in the attic room, in which the double bed took up most of the space, she decided to continue at the Hunters' a little longer until she was ready to rent the cheap apartment on Ontario Street.

Boysie was glad that she disliked the job and the quarters. Brigitte had come down every night after work and she would remain in the living quarters, lying on Jonesy's bed, and Jonesy's wife's bed, in her panties, cocking up her feet, reading the religious tracts which Jonesy had stolen from the offices of the gentlemen and ladies downstairs. She would hold the religious tract in one hand and a bottle of German imported beer in the other. The cigarette smoke coming through her nostrils was the only thing that told you that she was alive in this posture, which she could hold, unmoving, for minutes and minutes . . .

Once, on her day off (which she would spend with him), she made a stain the size of a full moon on Jonesy's white sheets. It took Boysie three hours washing it and then five dollars to get it cleaned professionally by the New Method Laundry. But Boysie enjoyed Brigitte's company. When he returned upstairs to his quarters (he spent most of his time in Jonesy's kitchen, where Brigitte cooked him all the German meals she could think of on her days off), sweating and cursing and regretting that he had ever known Jonesy, she would be there, almost naked, ready to take him on another, different, but more pleasurable journey of work.

But one weekend Boysie held the party he had been dreaming of for years: a party at which his wife would be absent, and not thought of, at which he would have all his friends, Henry (without Agatha), and Freeness, and all the men he knew and all their outside-women.

The party began one Friday, about two hours after Dr. Glimmermann left, and when the last guest left, it was seven o'clock Monday morning. It was then, in a stupor of drunkenness and sexual satiety, that Boysie remembered the fifteen offices to be cleaned. The church house opened at eight o'clock. He had often timed himself cleaning the offices: the first night he did them in two hours, the second night in one and a half hours: he had not cleaned all the toilets. "I am no blasted shit-cleaner, man!" And as time passed, it was done in progressively less time. He had it down now to a clean eighty minutes, but he felt all the time it could be done in twenty-five minutes. And it was this morning of anxiety and a bit of terror that the test had to be made.

He found the solution easily enough. He would clean the offices by using the vacuum cleaner only. No time for sweeping and picking up dust and bits of paper and paper tissues and chewing gum stuck under the hidden desks. He would empty the vacuum cleaner in the toilet bowls, and send them swirling to thy-kingdom-come, to the accompaniment of Drano.

He was shocked to find how fast he had cleaned the offices on the third floor: all five of them in five minutes! He went through the second floor like a tornado. And the last office on that floor, apparently the office of one of the important gentlemen or ladies that Jonesy talked so much about (it had a broadloom rug on the floor, and glass on the top of the desk), he thought he should give this office some extra time. He wiped the glass with the wet rag which he had soaked in the toilet bowl ("Heh-heh-heh-hahh! shit!"); he was laughing and working, singing and working, giggling at his wisdom and cleverness and dusting; and Brigitte might still be upstairs, panting and yearning and tingling like a she-dog for him (she had to reach her job in Forest Hill at eight-fifteen, at the latest). There was a lot of Friday afternoon wastepaper in this last office. Boysie went through the office like a madman. He emptied the vacuum cleaner into the toilet which served the entire floor, flushed the toilet, and went down into the *"sanctum santimonium,"* as he called the first-floor office where Dr. Glimmermann spent his rimless, glassed time. He was whistling "Brown Skin Gal, Stay Home and Mind Baby" as he walked down the carpeted stairway and as he plugged in the vacuum cleaner. He did the three secretaries' offices first, then the boss-man's office, being careful to let the grain of the rug flow in one direction only, as Old Man Jonesy had taught him, and after this *"sanctum"* was sanctified by his cleansing, he started to go into the board room. But at that moment, the first stages and signs of diarrhea erupted in his bowels, and he fled upstairs to the second-floor toilet. Time was now released against him. So he emptied the dustpan into the bowl when he was finished, flushed it, and ran back downstairs. The diarrhea had done something to his spirits.

In the board room were mahogany chairs, and a large mahogany table large enough for a first and last supper, given even by Baptists. There were large technicolour pictures of Christ, with Christ dressed as a shepherd, on the wall; and a Bible in front of each man, in front of each chair. There were twelve chairs. Boysie had amazingly adopted a possessive, a family-or-cousin-like air of propriety over this table. It was his table. He gauged his efficiency in cleaning the offices by the amount of brilliance, the degree of cleanliness he could see coming forth from this table, with its sun-shining top of glass. This morning, now weakened by the weekend and the diarrhea, he had not strength left to be efficient. Nor was he observant.

He had just pushed the door of the board room open when he heard something that almost made him drop the vacuum cleaner. Voices were in the room. He listened and found out that the voices were voices of worry, of questioning, of wonder and doubt.

"But where could it be coming from?" one voice was saying. No voice answered this voice. Boysie pushed the door farther open. The board members were unexpectedly early. Five of them were standing round the table, which for some reason did not have its glass top on, looking up. Boysie looked down and saw the water dripping down, brown: not plain clear water, but water with a brownish colour, dripping, dropping. The toilet had overflowed.

"A plunger! A plunger! A plunger!" Boysie was saying, imitating Dr. Glimmermann's anger. "The man lost his bloody temper, and all the time he was shouting all he was shouting was 'Plunger! plunger! plunger!' "

"And you didn' know what the hell a plunger is?"

"It is a serious thing, man. A big hard-back man like me, walking 'bout that Baptist church house like if I own the blasted missionaries working there, I playing all kinds o' music on Jonesy's high-fi, all day, godblummuh! and I didn't know what a plunger is!"

"And nobody won't even believe you never laid eyes on one o' them things in all your born days! They sure as hell won't believe it!"

"Be-Christ, I thought old Glimmermann was going to change into a cherry, he turned so blasted red. Like the plume of a fowl-cock, man! Glimmers looked at me, be-Jesus-Christ, Henry, he looked at me as if he was looking at a real, true-true African from somewhere in the jungles where all them letters they write goes to. Plunger, plunger, plunger! he saying all the time, and the more I tell that overeducated bastard I don't know what a plunger is, the more redder he turning, and he looking at me as if I is a piece o' shit. He walked past me and stomping in them big boots that look like army boots that he wears, he marched himself down in the fucking basement closet, and come back upstairs holding this thing, with a rubber bowl turned upside-down on it, and gorblummuh! that was the big important plunger he was screaming so much shit about!"

Boysie then took a dirty piece of paper out of his pocket, and he unfolded it, deliberately slowly, and then handed it to Henry. Henry looked at it seriously, creases of concentration marking his face, and he nodded something like agreement, and then he handed the piece of paper, after folding it back in its old creases, to Boysie. Boysie took a deep breath through his nostrils and his mouth at the same time, giving the impression that he had passed some very important educational test. The paper contained a drawing of a plunger which Dr. Glimmermann had made for Boysie's benefit, after the event, and which he had included in his pay envelope. "A plunger! Godblindyou, Dr. Glimmers! Old Man Jonesy didn't remember to show me the blasted plunger, at all!"

"And you couldn't even admit you never see one o' them things before! You couldn't admit to Glimmermann the real reason and motivation concerning your ignorance of this instrument. And you couldn't Boysie, merely because you never had the experience back home of doing your number-one and your number-two in no blasted indoor-water-closet, hah-hah-hehhhhhh!"

"Gorblummuh, I didn' know it was as serious as that!" But he tried to think about it, in this serious manner, for a second or two, and he said, "A simple thing like a plunger made that man know my whole arse-hole background! But look at that . . ."

"And that boss-man, a big Doctor of Religious and Theological Studies, goddamn, he bent down and used the blasted plunger with his own hands! And you, Boysie, the office-boy, because that is what you are, a goddamn office-boy, you didn't know the top of the plunger from the goddamn bottom o' the plunger! That is life, boy."

"And look," Boysie said, weakly. He took two other pieces of paper from his other pocket, and he unfolded them, and showed them, one after the other, to Henry. Henry looked at each one, shook his head in approval, and returned them to Boysie. One was drawn with blue colouring pencil, the other with red. They were two drawings of a plunger. Boysie had drawn them, following the model he received from Dr. Glimmermann that sad afternoon in his pay envelope. His pay envelope contained ten dollars less: the cost of repairing the damaged mahogany table, and probably also what Dr. Glimmermann considered compensation for the rise in his blood pressure. "A fucking plunger cost me a job. The first *ipso facto* job, as that bitch Dr. Glimmermann himself used to say, that I ever had on my own."

"A plunger for a job, a plunger for a goddamn job! This is Canada, baby."

But deep down, Boysie was not too disturbed that he had lost the job cleaning the offices at the Baptist church house. The only disappointment was that he had promised Henry he could use the basement to hold his wedding reception. Cleaning the fifteen offices was a harder job than he had expected; and the iron ruled precedent laid down by Old Man Jonesy was the precedent of slavery.

Boysie would be so tired at the end of each day, even before he started to clean the offices, that many times he lay beside Brigitte, panting like the sides of a thirsty dog in the sun, useless, fagged out, limber as a piece of melting rubber.

When he did move out, and back in with Dots, he was glad of his decision. It had not been an actual separation between Boysie and Dots: merely that husband worked one place, and wife worked another place. His wife used her free time from him to visit Bernice and talk; and once or twice during this hiatus, she romped and rollicked in bed, naked with Bernice. They did not make love. They merely kissed, because Bernice insisted that "God would be vexed with the two o' we for doing *that*."

Boysie now began to see his wife as more beautiful than he had ever noticed before: if indeed he had ever paid her any attention. He noticed that Dots was a better cook than Brigitte. He realized that his own West Indian meals were more interesting, more appetizing than the German meals Brigitte had been cooking for him. He found out with a great amount of amazement and some guilt, and also with sexual gratification, that his wife was more sweetly maneuverably agile and pleasing in bed than Brigitte. He noticed that his wife wore cleaner panties than Brigitte, that she was cleaner than Brigitte in those personal areas of the underarms and underthighs. He noticed that his wife took better care of money (hers, and his little amount from the cleaning job) than he had come to give Brigitte credit for. He noticed that his wife dressed better, in more style and taste, than Brigitte. Boysie opened his eyes and noticed and saw his wife for the first time.

To assure her of this new attention, he made love to her, twice the first night. And when morning came, he was still locked amidst her thighs. Dots was smiling in her sleep; and Boysie ("Is this bitch really sleeping, or she playing tricks on an old bastard like me? Gorblummuh, never in a certain amount of months of marriage have I seen this woman so damn happy! And all it cost me was a little regular dicky! Gorblummuh! as Henry say, life real funny"), he was strong, felt strong, and walked around the apartment in his shorts giving orders for his breakfast. Dots was still smiling even when she woke up that first morning. And she tiptoed round the apartment, silent as a mouse, obedient as a worm, satisfied as a woman.

"Bernice," she whispered on the telephone later that day when she got the chance, "Bernice, well, heh-heh-hehhhhhhh . . ."

The first piece of clothing Henry took off was his tie. His jacket went next. Then his vest. He was still losing. The dice were running against him. So he took off his shoes. "Goddamn, man, I gotta throw *some*-thing tonight, baby! These dice is like women, *whores!* Nasty!" Henry was playing with money that belonged to Agatha. Nervousness was working itself all through his body; and it was going to his mind. He felt he would lose Agatha's sixty dollars.

After an hour of playing, Henry was still losing. There was terror in his hands, and in his mind, and in his body. He saw himself losing all his money; and he saw himself losing Agatha; and he saw himself having to beg in his characteristically childlike manner for taxicab fare from Freeness. Freeness always pretended that he was more embarrassed about this than Henry was about his indigence.

It was getting late. The dice came back to him after he lost ten dollars — five to a man they called Stumpy, and five to Freeness. His hands started to sweat. He had fifteen dollars left. He was praying to throw a "main"; he was praying to throw two or three "nicks"; he was praying for luck. The dice felt like hot cubes of sugar in his hand.

Freeness looked up from the pillow on which he was sitting and snapped, "Rass-hole bet, man! Bet, man! I not here for my health!"

And jolted by this command, Henry took the dice once more, rattlingly together in his hand, placed a two-dollar bill on the carpet, and said, "Two dollars." It was spoken as if it was an apology. Boysie, all this time, concerned about his own luck and winnings, noticed for the first time the tension and the fear in his friend's eyes and in his movements. And he felt sorry for him. Their eyes met, and they transmitted (Henry's more than Boysie's) terror. Boysie noticed it there, and he lowered his head. It was his turn to place a bet against Henry; and he purposely bet five dollars that Henry wouldn't throw the "eight main" so that if Henry won, he would at least get back some of his money.

But an "eight main," according to Freeness, who was an expert in these things, "was the rass-hole easiest main to throw. Jesus Christ, a dead man could throw a eight! Look, you have six-two, five-three, double-four, good Jesus Christ, man, a little child could throw a eight main!" Henry knew this too. But today, he was not sure. He held the dice a long time; throwing all the time, but each time the dice landed on the carpet it was not an "eight." Four times he threw a "nine." Freeness, coaxing him (for Freeness really liked him in a strange way), said, "One too much, Henry. Nine minus one is eight, man! Christ, you can't count?"

And then Henry felt some courage in his hand. He rattled the dice, closed his eyes, said a silent prayer, and threw. When he opened his eyes, Boysie was taking up the fourteen dollars — seven of which belonged to Henry. And the dice passed him. Freeness avoided his appealing eyes. In this short revolution, more than twenty-four hours of life, more than one day and one night of terror, passed through his consciousness. Passage of time and dice made him talk to himself, grumbling and mumbling about his luck.

"You's a rass-hole old man, or what?" Freeness shouted. "You talking to yourself, a young rass-hole man like you? Boy, are you getting stupid?"

And Stumpy erupted from his characteristic gentleness and silence and said, "*Getting*, sah?"

Henry was involved in arguing with himself for the benefit of convincing himself of his own logic: "Money don't mean no big deal to me . . ."

He had the dice again. His first throw showed a "four." A "four" is, to most crap players, the most difficult "main" to make. "But if it's on the fucking dice, as it is," Freeness said, "you can throw a kiss-me-arse four-main! You can throw *anything*. They're on the dice, man."

But Henry, already convinced within himself that money didn't mean a great deal to him, bet his last ten dollars that he could throw the "four." He did not believe within himself that he could throw it. But he was frantic. He wanted his bad luck to break. Or he wanted to break himself.

Freeness's eyes opened wide, as if they had opened by themselves, and they spotted the ten dollars on the floor. "Boy, are you crazy? Ten dollars is a lot o' money, you idiot! *Ten* dollars? On a *four?* Man, you have rocks in your rass-hole head, or what?" And he started laughing at Henry. He himself never bet ten dollars on a "four." "Ten dollars is a lot o' bread, you arse! If you had ten dollars this afternoon and you was in Barbados, you don't know you could be the rass-hole governor o' that place? You could own Barbados with ten dollars!"

But Henry kept on mumbling . . . "*money ain' no big thing to me, man*" . . . and the first throw he made he showed "seven" — and therefore *crapped-out!*

"That fucking white woman who marrieding you, *she* got rocks in her fucking head! Not you! Only a foolish woman would want you, man!" Freeness said, a bit unkindly; but after all, judging from Henry's behaviour, more than a large grain of truth lay in Freeness's harsh pronouncement.

Sanity now abandoned Henry. Sanity (or "rocks," as Freeness termed it), or whatever it was that was inside his head, and which held him together, and only allowed him to grumble and talk and mutter these things about money not being a big thing to him; this little mechanism, this controlling mechanism apparently snapped loose. Henry flew up, and grabbed Freeness by his shirt front, and shook Freeness vigorously five or six times, and then threw him flat on the floor, before anybody knew what was happening. Henry was screaming, "Don't make me tear-up your arse, nigger!"

It was the first time anybody had ever heard Freeness called by that name. It was a name Freeness himself never used. It was the first time a black man had ever called him by that name. It was a name Freeness never liked. And in truth, Freeness did bounce back up from the floor at the sound of the word, "nigger." But it was not so much from the shock of the fall, as from the shock of the name, *nigger*, that he caught himself so quickly. It was not a physical reverberation. He bounced back up, through rage and through the shock of being thrown down by Henry his old friend. And when he bounced back up, he ran straight into his kitchen, and came back with a long bread knife, swearing, "Get to rass-hole outta my fucking place, or lemme push this in your goddamn guts!" And he meant it. Henry saw this clearly. And he did not stay to find out the seriousness of the threat. So while Freeness was still raging, going back and forth from the kitchen, with the long bread knife still in his hand (all the time, Boysie and Stumpy moving out of his way, drawing up their legs even though he stepped over them), Henry was already long gone.

"Why he do that, eh, sah?"

Boysie shook his head. His head didn't contain the knowledge nor the motivation for Henry's behaviour.

"That man have rocks in his rass-hole head!" Freeness said, when he sat back down to continue playing the crap game with Boysie and Stumpy. But the game had lost interest. "That fucking white woman is turning his rass-hole head! That white woman is so blasted ugly anyhow, that I know, *I know* if she was black, be-Jesus-Christ, Henry wouldn't walk 'bout with her, except it was a dark night, be-Christ! Except he *eating it!*"

They all agreed. But they agreed in silence. It was a chastisement, a judgment, which touched each one of them, including Freeness himself. It touched them all with a terrible heaviness of truth.

Agatha received the letter (written in a hand strange to her), and because she could not recognize the handwriting at a first glance, she placed it casually on the top of the knife-marked, old-age table in Henry's room.

She was ironing a shirt for Henry. The wedding was two days off. She finished the shirt, and then found four others in a bag, a blue plastic bag, which he had taken from the coin laundry on Spadina Avenue, near where he lived.

Something about the way the writer of the letter made his A's bothered Agatha. And both her patience and her curiosity for the contents of the letter drove her to open it. She immediately had the feeling that it was a dirty letter: a letter of abuse, even; a letter from a crank, someone who might have seen her with Henry: perhaps it was from his landlady, Miss Diamond, who recently was out of the house very regularly and who never seemed too pleased to find Agatha there so early in the morning. The letter had no signature, no address of the sender and no date. And that is what made it such a frightening letter. It said: *Your wed-*

ding day — I know this won't reach you on the actual day, but I am writing this nevertheless and sending out my thoughts to wish you all the bad luck and unhappiness, and hoping that the years ahead will hold much bitterness for you, for many, many returning anniversaries.

And so Agatha — you are to marry a coloured man — God help you! He will murder you, he will adore you — he will deify you, he will humiliate you — he will bully you, he will protect you — he will put you in hell, he will lift you up to the heaven — and if he should make you cry a lot, at least he will show you the essence of laughter and tears too — take notice of his EGOTISM — it is a protective shell, a chip on his shoulder to cover a lost exceedingly neurotic child underneath . . . It was at this point, based upon her knowledge of Bernice, Dots, Boysie and Henry, and their friends; and mainly on her knowledge of their intelligence, that Agatha made her first conclusion about the author of the letter. They were all too stupid to write this kind of letter. This conclusion drove her out of her mind: who then could have thought of writing it; and she was the more worried now because she could not pinpoint the motive nor the mind of the sender whose anonymity therefore rendered motive more difficult to comprehend. . . . *Marry Henry, Agatha, and you will never know normality again, as the world understands normality; but a crazy kind of fulfillment you certainly would know. I am holding you responsible. Love him Agatha, and know that your close friends will be delighted to know that you have at last ceased to embarrass them; and his friends would be delighted to know that you have joined their coterie, their fortune, their storm of fortune. My warmest wishes and I hope to meet you one day. Some-one Who Loves You.*

Her first instinct and her first impulse was to tear up the letter. And she followed them both. But when the drops fell into the wastepaper basket, she took them out again; and spent the next fifteen minutes sticking them together. She sat down at the table, and cried as she read the letter, over and over, seeking the motive out of the words. She could find nothing. She continued reading it: sometimes, as she well knew, things, problems, solutions came when she was least expecting her mind to focus and give her the light. How would she tell this to Henry? How could she tell him, when she knew how he felt about marrying her, a rich woman? How could she ever show this letter to the man she was going to marry, when the man himself had thought, and had been worried about, some of the very points made in this letter?

"Oh my God! so much trouble when you associate with a black man, a negro! So much trouble! and nobody will ever leave you alone to work out your own bloody problems!" The only person she felt she could commiserate with was Estelle, but she hadn't seen Estelle for a long time.

She called Bernice to find out where Estelle was these days. She felt better when she thought of Estelle. But Bernice didn't know where to find her. And Agatha, tormented beyond reason, beyond her strongest rationalizations about marrying a black man, found herself thrown deep into a pit of self-argument. One argument would tell her that such a letter was nothing more than a symptom, an example of the insane people living in this city, in this world — a gesture, but a clear explicit gesture, of bigotry, or sickness even. She liked to tell herself that all those people who stared at her when she walked beside her black, her loving black man, were not merely angry at her with their glances, they were sick. Sometimes she told herself it was their envy. During that time of trouble and of embarrassment and loss of money deposited on apartments, when she had to vacate those apartments when landlords found out she was being visited by a black man, she always insisted she was the only healthy person: everybody else was sick.

She was healthy in her body too, and would always try to make herself more beautiful for Henry. She was strongly built with a small face, and a mouth full of teeth, her own teeth, for which apparently small fact Henry was exuberantly grateful. Her ankles were strong, the ankles of someone who had walked many miles through the manure of fields, or through the slush of a spring day on a farm, long long ago in the history of her genes. She loved Henry, and something in her makeup, perhaps her arrogance, told her she could give him happiness. She was conscious of being suspected by Bernice and Dots, and by Boysie, but she still felt she could give Henry more happiness in his life than any other woman.

Now, the letter . . . for this letter to come and spoil all this beauty, all this happiness; for a letter from an unknown person to come and bring about such unhappiness, and such doubt!

Boysie was blowing the horn from a way down at the bottom of Baldwin Street. Some women looked out their windows, imagining the noise was the noise of an idiot, a crank; that a car horn was stuck; that a child perhaps, was stuck between the steering wheel and the seat or some other part of a parked car; but when they saw who it was driving the car and making all this noise, they slammed their windows down; blammed their front doors and went back inside their gloomy parlours.

Boysie was driving his new station wagon. It was not really a new model. But it was a model new to him. He had Dots in the front seat with him. The pride of possession on Dots's face was as loud as the noise of the horn, if her pride and her expression could talk or could scream. Already she was a new woman, a free woman; a woman with her own apartment, her own key; she could take the elevator and go up up up to the seventh floor now; she could open her front door any hour she liked; her dark blue Princess telephone with the light, to illuminate the darkness of the numbers of the dial when the lights in the living room weren't on, and when the bedroom was darkened just prior to nightly sex with her rejuvenated husband . . . she was free and new in these ways. All these things she could do now; all these things she couldn't do in the living-in quarters in Mrs. Hunter's home on Binscarth Road in Rosedale, just a spit's throw from where she was now living on Ontario Street. Dots was free. It had been a day of rejoicing. Boysie was sitting behind the steering wheel!

Dots is the first to get out of the station wagon. She bends down, and inspects her face in the shining side of the car. There is a spot there. She looks at her face in the mirror of the door and she wets a Kleenex tissue with her saliva, and she wipes the spot off. Nobody could have seen that spot with a naked eye. All this time, Boysie is blowing the horn. His hat is pushed back on his head. His forehead is shining like the car. A cigarette is in his mouth, and he carries it just like those well-tanned men at the races who have won heavily on a horse that is a "long shot." One hand is relaxed through the window; the other is running along the top of the seat, and his legs are on the seat. He is smiling. Dots gets back into the station wagon; but she has left the door open. More people come to their windows, look out, see who the *madre* it is out there, close their windows with a bang, and disappear. Boysie is still blowing the horn.

"You think he's there, though?"

"Oh hell, Dots! He's in there, man. Only thing he don't know the blowing is for him. Put your hand here, *not* there, woman! Christ I tell you here! Here! Yes, there! I say put your hand here, yes, right here, and press this silver thing slightly and feel how nice she sounds."

"It sound nice, in truth, Boysie." Dots was blowing the horn now. Boysie leaned back and the upholstery of the seat creaked, and leaned back with him. "I hope Henry come out soon, and see how nice she look, man." Dots was becoming impatient. Although she liked the sensation of feeling and blowing the horn, she still felt it was making too much noise unnecessarily.

"I am only sorry that she ain't a sedan or a convertible, though. 'Cause, she being a sedan or a convertible, we could go to Henry's wedding in her, with a real good wash and a shine, inside and out, and have her shine real bright, man! and some pretty coloured paper 'pon she, like how them Eyetalians dresses up their motor cars for a wedding. Dots, girl, don't you see that we are 'bliged and bound to bring in the first prize . . ."

"But don't begrudge she, though, Boysie. This automobile that me and you sitting down in on this nice afternoon in late summer, this is a investment. It bought because we have plans. And so, I say, don't begrudge she, because she is a station wagon and won't be proper enough to follow Henry to his wedding in tomorrow morning."

"Oh Christ, girl! do you think my gratitude is buried? My gratitude ain' buried, Dots. I acknowledge what you did for me to get this. I proud as arse I could sit down behind a steering wheel in this white man country. 'Cause Jesus-christmas! I didn't born here."

Dots was looking back while Boysie was talking. She wasn't sure that the man she saw get out of the car at the far end of Baldwin Street was in the uniform she thought he was wearing. "Look back there, Boysie, a sec, and see if you think that man, the one in the uniform, is a Salvation

Army man. Ain't he?" The man had just got back into his light green car. Boysie looked hard, and then he saw the aerial on the roof of the car. The car was coming towards them. And without waiting anymore, Boysie slammed the station wagon into gear, and without knowing it, roared off in second gear, although the salesman at Ted Davy Used Car lot had warned him to "take it easy, sir, in the gears. Move off in first, and then break her in . . ."

"Is a fucking police! A police! You think somebody called the police . . ." Boysie was trembling. Dots wasn't concerned about whether anyone had called the police. She was already shaken up by the quick getaway. And the door had slammed itself shut, without her help. And through the jerk forward she had heard a little noise in her neck say *snep!* But she wasn't hurt. She only got her dress caught in the door.

"I wish Henry could have seen the car, though."

"Dots, do you know that that blasted police still following we, just because we blow our car horn, our blasted car horn that we just bought . . . that blasted cop who do not have nothing better to do, he is still following we . . . there is a lot o' crime in this blasted city, all downtown . . . the bastard been following we since Baldwin, and we just passed Danforth and Broadview, two miles from the apartment . . ."

The traffic policeman had already taken down Boysie's licence number. When Boysie swung out into the crowded hawking foreign-language street of Augusta, and then into College, the policeman made a note of the station wagon, its colour (guessed at its year of make), and the red letters printed on the side of the wagon, in amateur lettering: BOYSIE CUMBERBATCH LIMITED, CLEANERS. It was then that the traffic policeman had turned back to other police and private business. It was a different policeman driving behind

Boysie now, along Danforth Avenue. He was actually going to the East General Hospital where a woman had tried to kill herself, after having first successfully killed a nurse. This policeman thought of stopping Boysie for speeding, but he had to think of reaching his call before the woman killed another nurse.

Suddenly the house was filled with Beethoven's Sixth Symphony. Mrs. Burrmann was home. And she had brought Mexico back with her. She was tanned and she was lovely, and she looked wealthy and healthy and younger. And judging by her quietness in the house, Bernice imagined that she had come back a different woman.

She *had* returned a different woman. When Bernice heard the noise of the music, she came hurriedly downstairs, and before she went into the room where Mrs. Burrmann was, she noticed that a smudge of fatigue and worry was on Mrs. Burrmann's face. Bernice then tiptoed into the sitting room, expecting to hear a quarrel. She could see Mrs. Burrmann in full now, and Mrs. Burrmann saw her, and rushed to her and embraced her, while Bernice said to herself: *but to think that this woman had to sneak into her own house! and suppose I was entertaining friends!* but she went to Mrs. Burrmann and entered the offering of embrace and friendship.

"Oh Bernice! Bernice! a wonderful time! and how are you? and how are the children?"

"Mistress!"

"Bernice, I'm never going to be unhappy again, as long as I live! How're the children? When're they coming back? I am so glad I got back before the children and before my husband." It was not often that Mrs. Burrmann called Bernice, "Bernice"; not often that she called Mr. Burrmann, "my husband." Bernice wondered what goodness had happened to her in Mexico. But she knew she could not ask what had happened. She was happy that Mrs. Burrmann was happy; the house would be happy.

"Look what I've brought for you!"

"But, Mistress!"

"It's for you! For you! For you, Bernice!" It was a shawl. "Aztec . . . the first people in Mexico, real artists, they made it. Rather, it was made by an artist who practices the arts of the Aztecs. It is pure art, Bernice. And I want you to have it."

"Oh, Mistress Burrmann . . ."

Beethoven was raging over some topic of a theme that had nothing absolutely to do with the warmth in this sitting room. "And oh! here's a letter for you. A local letter."

"Thanks, Mistress."

"Well, I'm home! *Een mi casa!* I am home!" And she breathed in the air of Toronto, all the time giving the impression that it was really the air of freedom and the air of Mexico she had been breathing and enjoying. "Please draw me a bath, and then you are free." Bernice got worried: *this woman ain' come back different! she come back crazy as hell! what freedom she telling me 'bout?* And as Bernice moved away with the suspicious letter in her hand, thinking of Mrs. Burrmann's use of the word, "free," before she was out of earshot, she heard Mrs. Burrmann say, heavy with nostalgia and longing and happiness, and perhaps with love, "*Free, free, free, libre! libre! libertad . . .*" By the time Bernice got halfway up the stairs to her quarters, after having started the bath, Mrs. Burrmann was on the telephone, to her friend and neighbour Mrs. Gasstein, telling her, "*Coma esta usted? como esta usted, Irenina? Diga*-something, darling, *diga*-something, I have come back, *oh-May-he-co! May-he-co!*" And then there was a pause in the conversation. And then there was a complete change in the

expression of Mrs. Burrmann's voice. You knew that something not quite as warm as Mexico was being discussed.
Mrs. Burrmann sighed, and said, "Yes, and I must thank
you for writing to me . . . yes, you can never tell. You
think these things happen only in books, in novels, and on
television . . . and I want to talk to you about it as well
. . . well, I always had my suspicions, Irene. After all, a
married woman is always suspicious of these things . . .
though she tells herself they won't touch her, won't happen
to her, because . . ."

My dear Bernice (the local letter began), *I don't know
how to say this, or what to say really. So much has happened. So, I had better just come to the point, and tell you
what I want to tell you. As you can guess from the letter,
I am living in Toronto. I was always in Toronto. I couldn't
face you on that Thursday when I knew you were coming
to get me. I could not face you because of many things. But
I am fine now. I would like to see you, when you have a
chance. I do not want anybody else, Dots or Boysie or
Henry or Agatha to know what happened to me, and where
I am living. I give you the address on this separate piece of
paper, so you can keep it in your purse. If you don't intend
to come, just burn it. But I wish you would come. Your
dear sister, Estelle.*

It was much later in the afternoon, almost nighttime, before
Bernice felt she had the strength to go downstairs to see if
Mrs. Burrmann needed anything done. Her valises were
still unpacked, lying on the settee in the hallway from the
entrance. Mrs. Burrmann had meantime gone across the
street, and had been telling Irene Gasstein all about her
Mexican trip firsthand with personal experiences, some of
which included "strong brown Mexican men, oh, darling

you should have come with me!"; and after the enthusiasm
of those reminiscences had worn off, and after Irene Gasstein had drunk three medium-strong vodkas-and-orange
with Mrs. Burrmann, the conversation got round to the real
topic for which the visit was made: Mr. Burrmann and
Estelle.

"I know how badly you feel about this, dear." They were
sitting in Mrs. Gasstein's bedroom. No other room in the
large three-storeyed mansion seemed safe and secretive
enough to bear witness to these personal words of advice.
There was a lamp burning on the dressing table, although
it did not add much more to the natural light of the dying
afternoon. "That night when it happened . . . it was the
first time in the twelve years I've been living on this street
that an ambulance ever had to enter this neighbourhood . . ." She sighed. "I made up my mind to get it out
of her," she said, talking of Brigitte. "And I damn-well did!
The bitch! I was like a judge at the Nuremburg trials, I tell
you." And Mrs. Gasstein went on to relate everything she
knew: the parties in the house while Mrs. Burrmann was
away; Mr. Burrmann's comings and goings, which she had
recorded in her diary after she heard of the scandal; about
Brigitte ("Soon's I get a person from an agency, I intend
to get rid of that! You must do the same with Bernice! You
have no other choice"), and about the two police officers,
"Gentiles, god-damn Brigitte!" She was careful to call them
"gentiles" and not the other more derogatory name, for she
was a woman of some sophistication. "Well, what in the
hell would my children think?"

A film of tears and sorrow that came to Mrs. Burrmann's
face was now wiping away the earlier happiness which
Mexico had brought back to Toronto with her. When Irene
Gasstein saw it, she stopped talking for a while. Children
were shaking the door to get in. Brigitte had told them a

harsh word in German. Nobody in the Gasstein house knew German but Brigitte. "Go away, you goddamn brats!" Mrs. Gasstein shouted. And the shaking at the door faded, and faded into steps running down the thick broadloomed passageway. "I'm sorry, Glad, darling, that this should upset you." Then cars flowed across the boulevard; and then it was quiet again, as that night of the beating, before the ambulance invaded the shaded privacy of this exclusive street.

"What am I going to do? Suppose there's more trouble from *them*."

"What the hell could *they* do?"

"You don't understand. Supposing . . ."

"Two goddamn black bitches, niggers? What is the law there for, eh? Eh? Your husband is a lawyer. My husband is a lawyer."

"You don't understand . . ."

" 'Course I understand. And you understand what I mean, too. You have to do something. Something. Soon. This is Forest Hill, Gladys, not the West Indies. Not Spadina Avenue and Dundas!"

"What *can* I do?"

"Something! And soon. But whatever you do, for God's sake, keep it from the children. And don't let anybody else know."

"What would you suggest? I can't think about this now, Irene. I haven't got the strength. I was so glad to be back home, even after what you wrote in your letter . . . it was redirected, so I just read it before I came over . . ."

"Get rid of that nig- . . . get that negro out. But do it nicely. I know I can trust you to do it nicely. Even give her some money when you do it. She doesn't have to know what's happening; she doesn't have to know the truth. In her place, get yourself a nice, middle-aged European Jewish woman. There's scores of them, refugees and people like that . . . coming to this country every day."

"It's strange! Life's strange!" And the silence returned to the bedroom. Brigitte was shouting at the children again, in German. Cars were coming home from the office, bringing husbands and daughters; and some daughters and sons were coming home from the university. "I had decided to leave Sam. My mind was made up to leave him. I went to Mexico and I thought about it. I thought about it a lot. I tried to live without getting myself to think about him. And for a time, I succeeded. I even succeeded living there for almost one week without thinking about the children. And it was during that week that I took a lover. A Mexican boy. A beautiful young man. Twenty-eight years old. Christ, Irene, he was a child to me! And after I had him make love to me, and I was laying down there in that goddamn cheap hotel bed, what I saw in his face and his eyes frightened me so much, that I thought he was going to kill me. I actually felt he was going to kill me. I saw such hate in that boy's face, Irene!" Mrs. Burrmann started to cry again; and she took up her glass and sipped it. "Such deep hate! His eyes told me that in his heart, he was saying, 'I am going to fuck you, rich woman, I am going to fuck you till thy kingdom come. You exploiter!' "

And again, the pause, the silence of new thoughts about to be born, of old thoughts being recollected, being reorganized. All this silent mechanism possessed the bedroom. Irene Gasstein could think of nothing sensible to say to relieve the tension. So she sipped her drink. The children, in some other part of the dungeoned house, were singing. A car with a heavy engine pulled into the driveway. Mrs. Gasstein became visibly tense. "Milt's here!" Mrs. Burrmann rose, or tried to rise, to go. "Don't go. That's all right, Glad. He won't come in here." The silence again. And then Mr. Gasstein's voice teasing the children, and teasing Brigitte, in broken German; and Brigitte cackling like a hen in German and then in English — but saying two different things in two languages; and then, back in the bedroom of thoughts, Mrs. Gasstein, registering something on her face to suggest, though not too strongly, that she disapproved of what she heard through the closed bedroom door, that Mr. Gasstein was the same bastard as Mr. Burr-mann.

"You know, Irene, that trip to Mexico . . . and I've gone there many times now . . . but this last trip was like a new experience. It has taught me so much! I learned so much!"

"All travel teaches you a lot. Mexico is no fucking different, if you'll pardon the pun!"

"But Mexico *is* different. In Mexico, people, the people who belong to Mexico are different people from us, from me and from you . . . that is what I mean when I told you that when I looked into that Mexican boy's eyes, and I saw what his eyes were telling me, even against his whole body, even when he held my body and said he loved it. Irene you don't understand . . . you don't really understand why everybody hates us Jews. Everybody hates people who are as wealthy as us. *Everybody.* But why, why, why? *Por que?* . . ."

An emptiness, a hollowness. The fast taxicab ride down from Marina Boulevard late that sad afternoon did nothing to make Bernice think she was moving fast enough to get out of Marina Boulevard. At the same time, she was thinking she was travelling again in an airplane punctuated by clouds and air pockets. She was nauseous. The sting of

Mrs. Burrmann's decision took her by the balls of her surprise.

"Mistress Burrmann, I just was thinking that maybe,
since Estelle will be coming out of the hos——— . . . since
Estelle will be coming back from a little vacation she took
in New York, that maybe you won't mind, seeing that you
didn' in the first place, if she could stay with me a little
more longer," Bernice had begun, aware of the first slip of
the tongue, and aware moreover because of this, that she
would have to clothe her request in the most diplomatic
and softest of manners. "I know that it isn' exactly the kind
of subject to bring up to you at this moment, seeing as how
you have just come back from a trip to Mexico, but . . ."

Mrs. Burrmann did not let her go farther. It was here that
Mrs. Burrmann had stopped her. Not rudely, not so harshly
as she sometimes had done, before Mexico and the mecca
of her new understanding of the relationship of the poor to
the rich Jew. She did not even raise her voice. She did not
show any enmity. What she showed was that sophistication
which Dots always referred to as "These blasted bitches'
way o' doing things with honey in their words!" Mrs. Burr
mann said what she had to say with the greatest kindness
in her voice. It was the same voice she used when she hired
Bernice; the same voice when she gave her a hand-me-down
dress. Had it been a different topic of conversation discussed, or concluded; had it been a different person being
sentenced, Bernice herself would have enjoyed hearing it,
so civilized was the manner in which Mrs. Burrmann
handled the situation.

"As a matter of fact, Bernice, dear," she had begun,
"that is exactly what I had on my mind. Now, you know,
that in the four years you've been *helping us* . . ."

It had taken the guts out of Bernice's stomach. Bernice
was lost. "As from now," Mrs. Burrmann had said, as if she

was asking for a drink, or commenting on the weather, or asking Bernice to run a bath for her, or raise the thermostat.

Just like that? just like that? Bernice was saying to herself and to the taxicab driver, and to the people on the street; and to God. *Just like that? So cold-blooded, like a machine or something? A person who you have served for months upon months could take up her hand and in a whiff of time, in a twinkling of an eye, you are nothing to them, at all, at all? Just like that, as if she playing she is God?* "And you know something, you know something funny about this whole thing?" (Here the taxicab driver turned his head because Bernice was talking loud enough for him to hear, and felt he had to answer. Bernice disregarded him, just as he ignored a couple of amber lights.) "You know something? I don't even hate her."

The taxicab stopped at 700 Ontario Street. The minute Bernice entered the lobby, she felt hate, a deep hate for Mrs. Burrmann. Entering the lobby of this apartment building brought her mind to the reality of her position: she would have to start looking for an apartment herself.

She entered the main door just as someone was coming out, and therefore forgot to ring Dots on the intercom. The elevator was going up and up and Bernice wondered how best to break this sad news to Dots. Perhaps, at this moment, Dots was having her own problems with Boysie; perhaps Dots, from her new height, was looking through one of her four windows which gave her four "sperspectives" of Toronto; perhaps Dots was busy cooking Boysie his meal before he got home from his new job as contract cleaner and janitor in the offices of Macintosh and Company, Stock Brokers on Bay Street; perhaps Dots didn't want to hear anybody's troubles; perhaps Dots, now no longer a domestic, was fed up with all this black and white business. The elevator stopped. Bernice remained inside, checking the number she had pressed, and checking her wisdom of intruding upon Dots. And as she stepped out, the door, already with its mind made up for it, by the pressing of a button on a different floor, came at her like a large black slap, with the side of the hand. Bernice got out just in time before the door struck her body. Her handbag strap was caught in the door. But she pulled it out before the elevator left without too much difficulty.

She walked to Dots's apartment door (she had memorized the number from the panel of names and numbers in the lobby), and she knocked. Immediately, the noise of the television inside went down. Then water stopped running. Bernice was still knocking at the door. Someone had been laughing as if he owned the building just before her second knock, but when he heard the knock, the laughing stopped. There was a shuffling, and then silence. Bernice knocked the third time. No one came to answer the door. In a rage, she went back to the elevator. And just as she was entering it, and the flat hand was coming at her to tell her, get out of the damn way and keep inside the elevator, she heard the noise of guns roaring and people laughing — both in the television and in the apartment she had just left. She thought she heard dishes talking as if food was being put in them. ("That bitch thinks somebody's coming to beg her for food, or what?" Bernice said to the closed elevator.)

In the lobby once more, she checked the number of Dots's apartment against the number she had carried in her head. And she found it was the identical one. She pressed the buzzer beneath Dots's name: DOTS AND BOYSIE CUMBERBATCH. A voice unaccustomed to the mechanism bellowed through the speaker, at the top of the panel of names and buzzers and numbers, "Who is it?"

Dots home, Bernice thought with deep relief and satisfaction. Bernice bellowed back, "Me!"

"Come up, man, come up!" And buzzers were pressed, and buzzers were answered, some of them the wrong ones, and they sounded like small farting boys. And in the midst of this new noise, Bernice took some time before she could organize herself, and open the door when the right buzzer was pressed, before all the farting buzzers stopped.

When she reached the door of the apartment, she noticed it was the same door with the western noises at which she had knocked a minute before. There were still western noises. The door was open now. The noises were coming out. The plates were being laden with the beautiful smell and sight of West Indian cooking: pork chops, black-eye peas and rice, salad with hard-boiled eggs and avocado pear cut up in it. They were on a heavy breathing table at which Boysie sat sweating with the steamed rice, his jaws moving in a delightful rhythm.

"Come in, come in," Dots said, laughing, holding out her arms to greet her friend. "I thought you never was going to come and see where we living these days! Come, sit down here at the table and have some o' this food, gal. Boysie, go in the pantry and bring a clean plate for Bernice, boy. Oh Christ, gal, I am too glad to see you!"

"You damn right!" Boysie said, with food in his mouth.

"A minute ago, Boysie and I had to say that you didn' look as if you was still friends with me. Ain't it, Boysie, boy? But you come, at last. And we glad we have you now."

"You damn right! The prodigal girl come home!" Boysie said, his jaws moving in a constant rhythm. "Want some wine, Bernice? We eat wine with our meals every evening."

"Man, get up! Stop asking the girl if she want some wine, and *give* the girl some wine, do!"

"I had to find out first, Dots. Perhaps, Bernice might

want to have some whiskey, or rum, or stout, or beer. Take your pick, Bernice. We have everything. Come, sit down, man! This plate is yours. Dots put another pork chop on Bernice plate, and some more o' them black-eye things for me, man, and give Bernice piece o' pig tail . . ."

Dots was dressed in an apron, not one from her days of domestication and service with the Hunters, but a red lace one which looked like a large heart. Her hair had recently been done by Azan (she told Bernice), the hairdresser of Beauty World. And she was wearing pinkish cream-coloured tights that fitted her so closely, that had Dots's own colour not been pure black, Bernice would have thought she was naked from the waist down. And she was wearing Indian sandals, sandals from India of the East. Something that looked like a black sky with small silver stars was glistening on her body. This was her armless bodice. Bernice could not help staring at her. All this transformation in such a short time! Perhaps, there was something good about not being a domestic. Boysie now seemed her master, Bernice observed. Boysie was now Dots's employer, and Dots, the dutiful, happy maid. Although dinner was on the table, Dots held a filter-tipped cigarette in her hand. And her fingernails were bright, vulgar, whoringly red.

A great insecurity came over Bernice. Envy warned her she could not be happy in this company. But she was hungry, and so she sat down at the table; and she accepted the wine, Canadian sauterne, which Boysie poured correctly in a wine glass. Bernice noticed this, because it was her profession. Glancing up from the wine, and from the second heaping plate of food which Dots had just placed before her, she saw, on the counter in the kitchen, a long line of bottles of different denominations, different influences, different hangovers and different prices — all liquor.

"So, how's Mistress Burrmann?" Dots asked. And for no

reason, she added, "Tell Mistress Burrmann that Mistress Cumberbatch send her best regards, heh-hah-haaaaa . . ."

"And how old Burrmann himself?" Boysie asked. "I want to talk to that man. I have some business to throw his way, something legal I want him to do for me." Was there some conspiracy, Bernice wondered. This was not the time, and it hardly appeared to be the place to confess to them that Mrs. Burrmann had just fired her.

"Eat, girl. Eat," Dots encouraged her. "And drink the wine. Boysie spend a hell of a lot o' money on this wine, so drink it up, gal." Bernice stopped thinking of their new life because of their invitation to eat and drink. She did not know she was so hungry, but she could not put her whole mind on eating, not when the present fact of eating, and eating such good food, reminded her that tomorrow either she wouldn't eat at all or she would have to eat out of her own pocket for the first time in over three years. It was too much for her. She put down the wine glass. She put her hands on the edge of the table and pushed herself from the table. Boysie's head was mixed in the steam coming from his plate; but Dots had been watching Bernice all the time, scrutinizing her carefully. Bernice moved away from the table, and it was only then that Boysie looked up. She was standing at the window looking west; the only window through which Dots hadn't given her, over the 'phone, a "sperspective" of the Toronto skyline. Dots was about to say something about the view and the "sperspective," and the window itself, at which was hanging an expensive piece of material that was made of Indian silk, when Bernice began sobbing.

"I loss my job."

It was some time before either Boysie, who had stopped eating meanwhile, or Dots fully realized what was meant. And what it meant to Bernice. They never thought Bernice

could lose a job. They never thought Mrs. Burrmann could
do without Bernice. They did not understand even the superficial meaning of Bernice's words. But it took them a
much shorter time after that, once the superficial meaning
was clear, to comprehend the deeper psychological implica-
tions of Bernice's firing.

"Jesus Christ, and winter coming!" Boysie said.

"Look, gal! come here, do! Sit down and finish eating.
Eat your guts full. Drink till you drunk. And forget the
bitch!" Dots wasn't even mad. She was smiling all the time
she said this, and this manner greatly helped Bernice over
the embarrassment that firing from a job meant to her sensibilities. It did not console her about her loss of income.
She had always held on to a job; she was not to be fired
from a job, ever. "I suppose that she would be hiring a
servant-girl from Mexico, now! A Mexican domestic." Nobody noticed Dots's sarcasm.

"It could be about Estelle, though," Boysie suggested.
Nobody commented upon this. Everybody knew it was
possible. "But I always used to tell you women, remember? Remember? Gorblummuh . . . and I can swear and
use profine language as much as I like now! even though
we don't generally swear as much now we stopped living in
the Hunters place . . . 'cause we does pay for this! But
you know something, Bernice? We don't as a rule, curse
half as much as when we was living round white people.
We don't curse at all since we move here, 'cause there ain't
no more tension. And there ain't no tension in here because
there ain't no blasted white people sneaking 'bout in here!"
Boysie had forgotten what he began to say. But he was a
new man now. And he waved his hand, his left hand which
had a large piece of dripping, juicy, delicious pork chop in
it, all round the apartment, with its new, shining furniture
which you could see, colour for colour, design for design,

price tag for price tag, and time-payment schedules for time-payment schedules, in many similar apartments all over Toronto, urban, suburban, laboururban and snobburban.

"But I always told you and Dots that today Mistress Hunter, or Mistress Burrmann is going to smile with you or with Dots, but be-Jesus Christ, tomorrow morning that smile may turn into a blasted skin-teet and a sneer! I know what I was talking about then. So, Bernice, I don't see what the hell you're depressing yourself over. You're damn lucky you come outta that mess whilst you's relatively still a young woman, with strength left back to start scratching out a livelihood in your own behalf." Boysie put half of the large pork chop into his mouth; and much of the gravy was left outside. He used his tongue expertly to wipe it away; and then he gripped the white lily-white Irish linen napkin from somewhere in his lap, and wiped his mouth and his face and the corners of his eyes clean; and then he said, "Bernice, pour yourself a next wine, man."

"Gal, stop this damn crying in my apartment!" Dots said, and then laughed. She went to Bernice, and gave her a playful slap on her behind. "You should be ashamed, *damn 'shamed* to let me and Boysie, two black people, see you shedding tears over a white woman!"

"All white people is bitches, if you ask me. And we, as black people, ain't much different, neither. But we have one thing that they ain' got, and never will get. And that is *love*. It may be all we got, but be-Christ, it is still something. So, gorblummuh, we have to love. We have so much love in our heart for them bitches and bastards, that you see with your own two eyes, right now, a black woman, Bernice, look! here is a black woman, Bernice, gorblummuh and she is crying because Mistress Burrmann . . ."

"No, Boysie! No no no!" Dots said, and she had to stand

up to make her point. "Not all white bitches is bitches. Agaffa is white, but she is one exception to that rule. Agaffa is a lady in *any* colour."

"But Agaffa isn't white no more! I regard Agaffa as a black woman now, because tomorrow morning bright and early, Agaffa will be going up that aisle with that black bastard Henry, and when she walk down, be-Christ, her fate will be sealed as a black woman. There ain' half dozen white women I know, in all my days in this city, who would do a thing like that for a man like Henry, *unemploy'*, gor-blummuh, for the past year and a half! A woman like that *can't* be white. She *bound* to be a black woman. 'Cause that is love to the heights."

"You talked a mouthful."

" 'Course, I just said a mouthful."

"Come, Bernice, sit down, gal. We can't be leaving back this food. We ain't servants now, so we can't throw away all this food. We ain't white people neither that we could afford the luxuries and the wastages of throwing this good food into a garbage can. Sit down, sit down."

Bernice did that. And instantly, she felt she was among friends. She ate the second plateful before her, and before she could be honest and ask for more, Dots, who was reading her mind, refilled the plate. Bernice was halfway through this one when a great belch escaped her. She looked round, frightened; embarrassed because had this happened in Mrs. Burrmann's presence, she would have had to beg pardon many times, to hope for forgiveness, with the many "pardons" calculated to hide the fact that she had belched. But Mrs. Burrmann "burped" many times in Bernice's presence, and *she* didn't say, "Excuse me, Bernice." Bernice saw the difference in her life. A simple thing like this had changed it. She was among friends. Not that she didn't have to say "pardon" among these friends, but saying "pardon" was not the same as it had been in Forest Hill. Could there be many more things she had been forced to do because of her nearness to the Burrmanns and the Gassteins and to Brigitte, and the children all over the streets in Forest Hill, and other places and other people all over Marina Boulevard? Did Dots have to force herself to do certain things in Rosedale, when she was close to white people? Could there be things about her behaviour, which because of her proximity through employment, though not through social equality, in Forest Hill that she had sacrificed or had forgotten to do through lack of practice? When was the last time, even in her room eating alone, had she had the guts to put down a fork and pick up a pork chop in her hand, and eat it and chomp on it, and suck out all the juices, holding it in her greasy fingers as Boysie was doing now? When was the last time she really laughed, *like she was people*, as Dots always used to say? When was the last time she could sit down comfortably, in a streetcar or in the subway train, with her legs stretched out, and enjoy the ride and ignore the stares? When was the last time she talked with food in her mouth, manners-or-no-goddamn-manners? When was the last time she could guide a hot ironing comb through her hair, without thinking that every housefly in her quarters was Mrs. Burrmann reincarnated?

All of a sudden she was laughing. She was happy. And she was envious. She could not help watching the clothes Dots was wearing. Boysie himself was dressed differently. He was wearing a sports shirt with the colours of the tropics, the rainbow and the exuberance of the West Indies all worked into it. There were sandals (new ones, brown and creaky and noisy and shiny from the first polish or stain put on them in the factory) on his feet. In all the months she had known Boysie, she had never seen his feet; she had never seen the colour of Boysie's feet, although she knew what colour they had to be. And because she had never visited the home of a real black man, a real coloured man, a real negro man, but only the homes of a few "farts" as Dots called them, she did not even notice that Boysie was now wearing a moe-joe on his head — not before Dots mentioned it. Boysie's moe-joe was the top of a woman's nylon stocking. It helped to press down his hair close to his scalp. At first, Bernice was laughing scornfully at it, until she realized that this stocking-top was not a bit different from the skullcap which Mr. Burrmann sometimes wore, even when he was eating.

"But wait," she said, pointing at Boysie's head. "Boysie turn into a Jew?" Dots recognized the source of her curiosity; and they all three started to laugh.

"How you like Boysie's moe-joe? Child, every self-respecting black man who calls himself a black man won't be seen *living* without his moe-joe, honey. That is *ours*. Be-Christ, the Jews have their skullcaps, but this is ours! *Our-own*. And they can't take it from we, can they, Boysie, boy?"

"I must get Dots to make you one o' these, Bernice."

"Look, man, I have my own stockings! When I was wearing moe-joes or stocking-tops, as a little girl in Barbados, where the hell you was?" And there and then, Boysie and Dots knew that at last Bernice had relaxed. That at least, for the time being, she had stopped thinking of her dismissal from Mrs. Burrmann's kitchen as a great setback in her life.

"But how it happen, Bernice?" Dots asked, much later. "How it happen, all of a sudden, that that princess could dismiss you, a woman who have slaved for her, and in ways that had nothing to do with the regulations o' your job?" Bernice noticed that there was even a change in the way Dots was thinking and expressing her thoughts. She was really using less curse words, and her language was almost grammatically spotless. She also had a kind of distinguishable accent, which was neither Barbadian nor quite Canadian. "Did Mistress Burrmann find out something?"

"I think so."

"Estelle, I suppose."

"I suppose."

"And how is Estelle these days? You don't say nothing about your sister, here of late."

"Child, I heard from Estelle today! This afternoon. One thing came just as the other struck me!" Boysie and Dots exchanged glances. "Estelle living here all this time, gal! I ꞏhave the phone number. Right here in Toronto with we! But she don't want anybody to know."

"I can understand that," Boysie said, picking something from between his teeth. "When a man is down, he don't want nobody, particularly his family or his friends, to witness his downfall. Isn't that right, Dots?"

"Where? Where exactly Estelle staying?"

"She don't want anybody to know . . ."

"How you mean she doesn't want anybody to know? We are one, Bernice! The time for playing the fool is finished! She is your sister. And we are her friends. And she is the same flesh and blood as me. And one black woman in the gutter, one black woman out on the street picking fares and hustling men, whoring, is a reflection on you and on me, Bernice. I can't really be Mistress Cumberbatch if all the rest o' black women are madams! Even although everybody else knows that we, you and me, never brought ourselves to that degradation. You don't see it through this sperspective?"

"Read this letter and see for yourself, then," Bernice said, feeling a trifle guilty.

" 'My dear Bernice, I don't know what to say . . . so much happened . . . I couldn't face you . . . (She ought to be blasted ashamed, indeed!) . . . but I am fine now . . . (That's good to hear) . . . I would like to see you . . . (Of course! Just what I was telling you. A sister is a sister. And sometimes, you have given me the impression that Mistress Burrmann was more your sister than your real sister, Estelle) . . . I would like to see you when you have a chance, I do not want anybody else, Dots or Boysie . . .' Boysie boy, she's naming you and me as the people she don't want to see, boy!" Dots read that line again, and then said, "But I see that she didn't mention Brigitte as one of the persons she doesn't want to see! I see that, and I wonder why? I wonder why?"

Nobody answered. Nobody apparently knew what to say.

"And Agaffa coming here tonight, gal! With Henry, to talk over plans for holding their wedding reception in my apartment! Oh God, heh-heh-heh! Life!" This was another embarrassment to Bernice. Boysie merely sniggered. Dots put the letter in her pants pocket, absentmindedly, and said, "Come, come! Boysie go down and warm up the station wagon. Come, Bernice, drink-up the little wine and get ready!" It was after Boysie had left for the underground garage and Bernice and Dots were standing in the corridor, waiting for the illuminated numbers on the elevator panel above their heads to change from M to 1, 2, 3, 4, 5, 5, 5, 5, and to 7 — all that time elapsed before Dots told Bernice where she was heading. "We going for Estelle!"

"A police coming into a man's house, and at a wedding reception, to-boot! and breaking up the party? Just because some old can't-sleep bitch next door or down-below can't find a man to keep her more occupied, or something? What kind o' place, what sort o' country is this? It never happened in Barbados, and it never could. Imagine a police in Barbados coming into a man's house, during a party, and a wedding party at that, to tell that man he's making too much noise!"

Boysie never got over the shock of seeing the policeman at the apartment door, standing like a monument to something, with an untranslatable expression on his face, with one hand resting, perhaps absentmindedly, on the holster of his gun, and the other, raised and caught in the slow-motion paralysis of knocking on the apartment door again. The wedding guests were at that time in the middle of the speeches; and Boysie, who was master of ceremonies, had been saying some amusing things about marriages. It was at the point when he was saying (in his best stentorian, oratorical Barbadian dialect), "Ladies and gentlemen! ladies and gentlemen too! greetings and salutations. On this most auspicious of evenings, on the aurora of long and felicitous matrimony, I say to you, to you ladies and gentlemen, I say *ecce homo*, behold the man! *ecce homo*, here I stand!" Freeness was there, dressed to kill, in a three-piece suit, which he told everybody he bought from Lou Myles Designitore; Estelle, beautiful as a virgin in white, and many others, crammed into the happy apartment, all screamed for joy when Boysie thus began his speech. It was his fifth for the evening's festivities. He was very proud of Henry on this day. Every wedding guest, including Agatha and Henry, had made a speech, some twice. Boysie had made his first about an hour after the wedding party returned to the apartment from the church. It was five o'clock then. The wedding had been delayed. (Henry couldn't find cufflinks for his formal white shirt; and he couldn't find the old courage he had for marriage. Boysie had to telephone Dots to ask Agatha to arrive late, because Henry had to be induced into appearing at the church.) Now, after many toasts and speeches and eats and drinks, Boysie was captivating his audience again. The time was midnight. The guests liked it. They bawled. And they told Boysie they liked it.

Henry, sober and married; Agatha, turning red, and flushed and happy, and drunk as Dots was, held her head back and exposed her silver-filled cavities and said, "I could have another wedding reception like this tomorrow! One like this every month!"

"I say to you, ladies and gentlemen, too! I say, *ecce homo!* behold the man, *ecce homo*, here I stand! Here I stand, ladies and gentlemen, with a glass of Mount Gay rum in my hand, wherewithal for to mitigate the aridity of my thirst. And as I have arisen from my esteemed seat this fifth time, and as I have quoth to you, *bonswarr* or good-evening, my dear Agaffa — goodevening, Henry you lucky old Bajan bastard!"

It was here, in the roar of acceptance by each person in the room, when they held their glasses up, that the knock brutalized the apartment. Its suddenness made them notice it. But they had no suspicions. Boysie said, still with his glass raised, "Perhaps, ladies and gentlemen, it is some poor suppliant wanting the warmth of this nocturnal congregation." And he moved away, towards the door, his drink still in his unsteady poetic hand, to invite the person inside to partake of the hospitality. Bernice went to Agatha to fix the veil on her dress. She therefore, fortunately, blocked Agatha's vision of the police officer at the door, with his hand on his holster. Boysie didn't lose his aplomb.

The police officer was very polite to him. "Break it up soon, buddy. The neighbours are complaining about the noise. And it's past midnight."

Boysie was going to offer the officer a drink, but he thought better of it.

"Don't let me get another report to come back here, or hear that you making noise, eh? Break it up, soon."

Boysie did not move from the door until the officer of the law walked back to the elevator; and he did not move until the officer got into it; and Dots, by this time (she had put on a record on the player the moment she heard the officer's warning), was standing beside Boysie like a doorpost.

"And the poor girl's enjoying herself so much. And on her wedding day? Jesus Christ, these people is real savages, man! You mean to tell me that they could do this on the girl's wedding day?"

Boysie put his arm round Dots's new shiny, almost bare shoulder, and he squeezed her a little bit, and said, "This party can't done! Let that son of a bitch come back!" Boysie left her. He went to Bernice and whispered something in her ear.

"The police?" Bernice said, almost too loud; and immediately she grew tense. "Only me — and now you — and Dots know. So keep it dark. We *got* to go on. How the hell could we ask people to leave. Not now. How would Agaffa feel? How would Henry feel on his wedding day, to boot?"

But Boysie and Dots and Bernice made certain that Henry and Agatha did not feel the tension that had begun to creep into the party. It was impossible to recapture the gaiety and the enjoyment that was present before the policeman knocked on the door. Dots would have had the guests leave immediately, just to save a disgrace; even after a respectable time, the time it would take to serve another drink, she would have insisted on it, because Agatha and Henry had to leave for their honeymoon in Niagara Falls. But Boysie said no. "This is a wedding. Not any damn party with hippies! This party going done when *I* say it done!" (In her heart, Dots said, *"As man!"*) And he left her standing there, arguing the wisdom of his suggestion with Bernice; and he went to the record player (the record player had arrived two hours before the wedding reception was to begin: delivered on a hire-purchase, the monthly payments of which were fifty-five dollars and twenty-five cents), and he selected a calypso by the mighty Sparrow, "Shanty Town People": in which Sparrow was complaining of having to move out of his comfortable apartment in Trinidad because people from the slums came and inhabited his precious location on the hill.

The music raged as the spirits in the guests and in the drinks raged. Estelle was still beautiful in her long white wedding dress. She was thinking of when she would get married. And more than once, during the hectic afternoon and night, she wondered where Sam Burrmann, her unborn child's father, was at this happy time. But by this time, she had put him out of her enjoyment; and she devoted all her body and energy to the dancing which shook her body as if she was in some mad trance. *Sunday morning, they fighting, they drinking, they beating pan . . . send for the police, still the bacchanal won't cease . . .* It was a royal time; and as Dots said, "A person can only get married one time. Even if he divorce after that first time, the second time round can't be like the first time. You can't even do it in a church, then. Not the second time round. So the first time is *the* time!"

Boysie was dancing with Dots. Brigette had held on to Freeness the whole day (probably because of Boysie who,

now in his castle, in his role of host, wedding-giver and
master of ceremonies, had no time for outside-women);
and Bernice was dancing with a man who nobody knew,
who nobody invited, who just heard the music and had
knocked and had been invited inside and had come in, and
who was treated with the same courtesy and hospitality as
the bridegroom.

Agatha's father hadn't arrived yet. Agatha's mother
hadn't arrived yet. Agatha's many white friends from the
university, and her lawyer-friend (all of whom were sent
invitations — that was Boysie's personal gift to the couple), hadn't arrived yet. It was a sorrowful sight at the
church when it was discovered that no one was sitting on
the bride's side. Dots saw quickly the embarrassment setting up, and how it would rain on Agatha's sensitive feelings, when she arrived sweet and young, virginal and white
in her long dress; and Dots reushered half of the church
over to Agatha's side.

When the organ roared and snorted through the wedding march, everybody was laughing, even Agatha. Reverend Markham was happy. The choir was in good voice,
loud when it was supposed to be loud, soft when the organist breathed upon the keys of the organ. But when they
were in the office signing away their lives and their promises to one another, for better and for worse, Dots stood
like a mother hen on the top step of the church, directing
the people (those who didn't have lifts) to cars, and warning the photographer who had arrived late to "Look, don't
take the whole damn day here, hear? We have perishables
and other eatables waiting long at the reception place, heh-
heh-haiiii!" And after that, she whispered in Bernice's ears,
"Is a great burning shame that that bastard, Agaffa's father, what-the-hell-his-name-is, thinks he is too great to
come down here and witness his own daughter on her wed-

ding day. Well, we didn't expect him to behave as a bride's-father: nobody tell him he have to give the child away! But, Christ! Anyhow, Reverend Markham said such a nice prayer for them, too! That bastard didn't come to see his handsome black son-in-law. He didn't have the courage to come. White people is coward bitches, all o' them — your late Mistress Burrmann included! All o' them!"

"And the mother. I could just see her up there, taking a overdose o' sleeping pills and sleeping through *all this life, all this love* . . . She ain't turned up yet, neither."

"Their Cadillac break down, darling, heh-heh-haiiiii! Bernice, gal, you are witnessing on a certain high level o' life the ways o' white people. They would kill their own flesh-and-blood, *just* to prove a bloody point."

"And godblummuh, guess what they would do to us!" It was Boysie, throwing a lash too.

"It is sad, though."

"It is true, though."

Estelle had overheard, and she drew nearer, and said, "They love one another, though. Agatha and Henry. So, let them live." She was thinking of her turn to come.

"Still's a blasted shame!"

And now, at the reception, nobody appeared tired, after so many hours of eating and drinking and dancing with the problems of "Shanty Town People" reproduced for them by Sparrow on the record player, and their own problems represented for them by the visit of the policeman; these West Indians and one white woman were as one in joy . . . *I tired and I disgust . . . big Sunday evening, they cussing, they fighting, they gambling, they beating pan and bup-bup! iron-bolt and stone pelting, send for the police, still the bacchanal won't cease . . .*

There were fifty persons invited to the reception, plus the uninvited guest, all packed and sweating in the two-bedroom apartment from five o'clock. There are fifty-one persons in the apartment now, at one-thirty Sunday morning. Boysie has his arms in the air, and is dancing as if his body has been seized by some voodoo or St. Vitis dance-mood; and Dots has thrown one brocaded expensive slipper somewhere in a corner, and is jumping up. The record, a favourite with everybody in the room, is put on again. It is put on three times, four times, five times, six times; and Boysie says on the seventh time, "Man, play that thing a next time, do!" And it is put on the eighth time . . . *and big Sunday morning, they cussing they fighting they gambling; they beating pan and bup-bup! iron-bolt and stone pelting, send for the police, still the bacchanal won't cease, so they violent and they fast, they better go back to their mansions on the Labasse* . . .

A smudge of fatigue and sweat walked imperceptibly from under Estelle's arms. Bernice noticed it; and she took Estelle into Dots's bedroom, and rubbed some of Dots's underarm deodorant, Ban, on the story-telling odour. "Your time soon come, girl," she said, and smiled. Estelle smiled, and dashed back out to dance. Agatha, with the first signs of married-hood and possessiveness, sat and watched Henry dancing with Priscilla, the nurse ("But who in hell invited that whore? Who invited Princess Priscilla in my decent place, eh?" said Dots. "Boysie, did you invite Nurse Priscilla?"), and Boysie laughed; and Agatha watched Henry as she watched Priscilla's stylized and sterilized hips, as they did things with the rhythm that she herself, legal and wedded to Henry, for better and for worse, could not do.

Some men are in the kitchen eating, as they have been doing since five o'clock in the afternoon. There is a big argument going on about cricket. None of these men has seen a cricket match in five years — not since they left

the West Indies. But they are arguing about Sir Frank
Worrell, and the cover drive he made off an outswinger
from Alex Bedser the English fast bowler, at Lords in
1950, many many years ago. One man says, "The English
think they are great? They *playing* they great! Be-Jesus
Christ, when Worrell, when *Sir Frank* leaned into that outswinger from Bedser, it went straight through the fucking
covers for four! Right offa Worrell's kiss-me-arse wrist! And
as man, you know that Sir Frank is a man with more wrist-
work than, than-than . . . than Boysie in there have stones
in his underwears!" And like a contagion, everybody bawled,
and poured themselves another larger rum.

The record is changed. Sparrow is talking about his boy-
hood, in Trinidad. The men dropped their glasses and they
ran for the women. They reached out their hands, and
lifted the dripping shiningly dressed, rouged-and-perfumed-
smelling tired women off their chairs. Boysie is dancing with
Dots as if they are lovers: close. His brillantined head,
which had sweated four hours, four hours under his moe-
joe, is sleeked-down and shining; and Dots's hairdo, done
amidst pain and time, talk and gossip at Azan's beauty parlour on Bloor Street, the previous Thursday, when the shop
was noisy and talkative with domestics on their day off,
about "this rich-able Jewish girl who is marrieding some
Bajan black man, Christ, he really have his blasted head
full with rocks! Wait, he couldn't find nobody better than
she? Why they always have to go and look for white
woman?" Dots had listened and had held her peace and
her head down: they did not know all the facts. *Now, I
am a rebel, I seeking my revenge any kind o' way, I'm a
devil. I don't laugh, I don't smile, I don't play* . . . Boysie
is smiling. He is holding Dots so close, that she can feel
something between his legs: but she is his wife and he her
husband.

Estelle thinks of the day before when Bernice and Dots and Boysie came to the room on Bedford Road, and found her delirious with fever and misery and thoughts that could not be achieved; and how they dressed her; how they paid the landlord the rent she owed, the rent which Mr. Burrmann had eventually promised to pay, but which she finally told him not to pay because she didn't want to be obligated to him; and how they had driven her back down to this apartment; and here she had slept, the first good night's rest in such a long time. She is thinking of Bernice and her bad luck: ". . . that woman, Mistress Burrmann really thinks she is somebody precious, to treat my sister so! . . . one o' these days Ontario Street's going to move up in Forest Hill . . ." And Estelle wonders what Bernice is going to do with her life, what she herself is going to do about Sam Burrmann, or to him. She thinks of the future, and the future looks bleak; and this makes her think of the present. And before her like a threat, like a challenge, is the man who nobody invited. He wants to dance "with the prettiest lady in this house, ma'am." The compliment is sincere, and Estelle stands up just as Sparrow says: *They treat me like a savage, of me they took advantage; when I was young and growing up in town, all o' them bad-johns used to knock me down* . . . A tear is crawling like perspiration down Estelle's face. This man is not a bad man, she thinks; but nobody knows him. The man does not notice the tears. He has his mind on other parts of her anatomy.

Somebody was kicking down the apartment door. Boysie went to the door. The same policeman, plus another officer, were standing there. "Come on, I told ya, didn't I?" the first policeman said. There was a strange kind of anger in his voice. There was also a kind of disappointment. He seemed peeved that somebody would report noise twice in one night. Boysie knew what to do. The guests began leaving right away. Everybody except those who lived there, those who were sleeping there for the night: Boysie and Dots, Bernice and Estelle.

Henry looked at the policeman and said loudly in his heart, "Fuck you!" Had he said it aloud, he knew what would have happened to him: another beating and probably jail. Agatha started to cry. She was still wearing her wedding gown, Henry in his formal morning suit.

The policemen waited until every one of the guests left. As Agatha, walking beside Henry along the long corridor, as if she was still walking that interminable aisle to face the altar and the cross and the Maker and Reverend Markham, reached a certain point along the quiet broadloom, women with curlers in their hair peeped through open doors, and just as the two policemen entered the elevator and went down into the half-awake apartment building one of these white women in a torn pink nightgown sneered, "*You white bitch! You white trash!*" and slammed her apartment door. The others in the onlooking guard of honour and dishonour shook their heads, and did not slam their doors; and nobody knew what they said behind the closed doors of their minds and honesty.

In all this confusion, in all this disappointment and crying and embarrassment, Dots and Bernice and Estelle remained sitting on the large, new, unpaid-for couch, crying. Agatha had wished them goodnight with the kisses of her tears.

part three

Gathered into the ling

Boysie had the habit of putting his feet on the desk in the main office. This belonged to Mr. Macintosh. He was the president of Macintosh and Company, Stock Brokers since 1867. Dreams and ambitions would flood Boysie's head, and they would prevent him from finishing his work in the hour he had given himself as the time limit for this job. Cleaning the twenty offices in this company was his main contract. He had five other cleaning contracts in other parts of the city. But he liked doing Mr. Macintosh's offices first, when he was fresh. He liked Mr. Macintosh. Mr. Macintosh had met him late one night in the offices, when he was finishing some brokerage business, and he had talked to Boysie about hard work, savings, investments and making a killing on the stock market. Boysie liked him. He liked Boysie. And from that first meeting, and after several others, Boysie decided to make his life as close as possible an imitation of Mr. Macintosh's, for Mr. Macintosh was successful. Boysie started to smoke a pipe because Mr. Macintosh smoked a pipe. He even bought the same tobacco from a cigar store on King Street West. But soon he found he couldn't afford such expensive habits. And knowing he hadn't as much money as his idol, he used his head, and started to buy his tobacco supplies from a discount store on Bloor Street, near the subway entrance. He wore the same clothes as Mr. Macintosh — not while he was cleaning out his offices, of course — at least his suits were similar in appearance. He could not match the expensive material and expensive cuts Mr. Macintosh had, since he could not afford to have them tailored by Beauchamp & How Ltd. (Free Parking 2 Doors W of Store 94 King W — 364–4161; he had seen the label in one of Mr. Macintosh's jackets which was left on the rack in his office, and he had looked up the address in the telephone directory), Boysie therefore did the next best thing his pockets could afford. He got his clothes custommade at Tip Top Tailors. He had planned, when he did this, to get his hands on some old labels from Beauchamp & How Ltd. Free Parking 2 Doors W of Store 94 King W — 364–4161, but that chance had not yet arrived.

Dreams and ambitions would fill Boysie's head on those lonely hard-working fluorescent bright vacuum-humming nights, high in the sky overlooking Toronto, as he would pause to look into other buildings scrubbed and cleaned by European men-cleaners with heavy accents and their women with heavy ankles and blue veins and thick stockings. Once he thought he saw his apartment building from this height. The offices he cleaned had so much money in them, symbolized by the ticker-tape crawling like endless worms out of the wastepaper baskets; so much money represented on ledgers and cheques and notepaper torn up and thrown into the garbage with gobs of tense chewing gum smothered onto them! And Boysie would dream of making a million dollars. He had already started to read a lot of books to improve himself and to help him make some of this "easy-arse money the white people in Toronto have, man!" He read *Time* magazine and *Life;* and once he looked into the pages of the *Atlantic,* but he didn't see anything in there to hold his errant interest long enough. So he closed it. These magazines he took from the brokerage offices and from other offices he cleaned at night. He tore off the addresses on them and put them, in full view of Bernice and Estelle and other West Indian friends, on his coffee table in his apartment, as if they were his private subscriptions. He also took home, a month late, copies of *Marketing, The Financial Post, The Economist* and the *Stock Broker.* He glanced into these, but like the *Atlantic,* they did not hold his interest long enough for him to learn their value so far as money was concerned.

But his great chance came when, one night, on one of his contract-cleaning jobs, he came upon an old set of Knowledge-of-the-World books. Fifteen volumes in all. They were in the wastepaper basket. "How the hell could anybody in their right mind throw-away all this good knowledge?" But he didn't wait for the answer. He cleaned them off, put them in the front seat of his station wagon, away from the vacuum cleaner and the soaps and the cleaning wax and the brooms and the mops, and finally arranged them to rest, unopened, undisturbed and decorative, in the built-in bookshelves in his living room, where previously Dots had put Bernice's replicas of the Royal Canadian Mounted Police walking without horses and the imitation of Niagara Falls, with some artificial small forests of coniferous and deciduous trees. Dots packed Bernice's symbols of military history and geography in a Javex box and put them, with the rest of Bernice's belongings, in the basement locker. "Education, darling," Dots bragged to Bernice, with the same sudden concern as Boysie for more education. "Education. *That* is what makes the world go round! We have to have education on display. Everybody know about the damn RCMP and Niagara Falls already! Education must take first place, gal!"

Whenever Boysie was home, he was reading. Dots had just started her practical course as a Nurse's Aide at the Doctors Hospital on Brunswick Avenue; and she was too busy to read, and too tired, too. But she was happy. For the first time in her life in Canada she thought she was doing something worthwhile. "Something with dignity, gal." And she more than once encouraged Bernice to stop wasting her time and postage stamps applying for living-in jobs in the rich kitchens of Cooksville and Oakville and Montreal, and instead learn to do something "more dignified than a damn domestic slave." Estelle was saved from an equally searing tongue because she was just beginning to show her pregnancy. They all knew it was hopeless for a woman "with a belly" to get a job in Toronto. Estelle would have to wait until after the baby came.

Estelle and Bernice were still staying with Dots and Boysie in the apartment, and the arrangement worked well. Bernice would be out all day looking for work; Estelle would do the housekeeping, and cook the meals; and Boysie would sleep in the daytime, while Dots would be at the Doctors Hospital, lifting old decrepit men and women, mostly Jews and Italians, learning how to aid a nurse, and learning a lot about the habits of these two ethnic groups. So far her course was more interesting than it was backbreaking, or scornful.

"Live along with us a little longer, till you can catch yourself, gal. Boysie don't mind. And you and Estelle are helping me," she said to Bernice one night when she found her sitting in a corner of the bedroom. Bernice was beginning to become self-conscious about her position in Dots's household at such things as not being able to change the record from a calypso to a gospel hymn. She had to listen every day, and on weekends especially, to the noise of the calypso and the shrieking of the rhythm-and-blues singers which Boysie and Estelle liked so much. And she was thinking of moving out because of it.

"I can't impose," she said.

Dots could see nothing wrong with her living with them. She had even given it her blessing. Once they even drank a rum to seal and celebrate it. Boysie, when he heard, was sorry they were going to leave. He was getting used to Estelle; he was getting to know Estelle: he and she would sit together in the late mornings and talk about Barbados, and about life in Canada, and Boysie began to give her advice about getting a job, even although he was no expert in this department.

Agatha repeatedly told Estelle she must give her baby up for adoption. "You have to think of the future of the baby. After all, Estelle, the baby didn't ask to be born. And with no father in the home . . ." Not once during the long discussions on this subject did Agatha mention the responsibility of the baby's father, Sam Burrmann.

Estelle merely shook her head, and smiled. Finally, when Agatha persisted, Estelle simply said, "What's in my belly is mine. Wherever I go, he goes!" Agatha automatically sensed a strong resentment in Estelle.

"I was just doing my duty as a socially conscious friend. I was just telling you what I have told hundreds of unwed mothers with unwanted children, when I did field work with the Big Sister Organization." It was at this point that Estelle really lost her temper.

"Listen to me! You have come in here, telling me a lot o' blasted foolishness 'bout adoption and responsibility. But I want to tell *you* something now. The man who breed me and got me pregnant and who hasn't looked back yet to see if I'm dead or alive is not a West Indian, yuh know? He ain't a negro, Agatha! And he isn't a black man! He's a fucking white man, just like you! And he is the same blasted Jew as you, too! Now, I want you to go and talk to him, and tell him about *his* responsibilities."

That happened two weeks ago. Agatha never called again. She never came back to visit. But Estelle didn't care.

During the afternoon discussions and coffee drinking, which Boysie learned to drink through his imitation of Mr. Macintosh and which Estelle made for him, the two of them would play lots of calypso records and dance together. Estelle would tease, "This little bitch inside me is kicking like hell!" Once Boysie held her close, and for a second of reckless infatuation he saw himself lying on top of her, making love to her. But when he considered that she had already been made love to, and by a white man at that, and was now protruberantly repentant from that love-making, the thought became repulsive. And he apologised to himself for having thought it. Estelle was now almost five months pregnant, just beginning to be obvious. Boysie felt sorry for her. Sorry that such a beautiful, kind-hearted young woman could not go out to dances and to clubs and private parties and meet a man without the men trying to take advantage of her. And he wished he had the nerve to take her dancing.

One morning, just as he came out of his bedroom, and walked towards the bathroom, he saw Estelle coming out. She had only a towel round her. She did not expect him to be awake so early. It was only ten o'clock. He usually got up around two in the afternoon, since he came home after cleaning at about four in the morning. Here he was, standing an inch from her. In pyjamas, with the pants hanging under his waist, his fly completely open, with no pyjama top on. And she, in a towel, with her round slightly pointed belly showing. And he saw that her breasts were full now, with round black spots circling their nipples; she, as desirable as when she was not pregnant, water dripping from her breasts like jewels.

"Goodmorning, Boysie, boy!"

"Hi!" He had got this too, from Mr. Macintosh.

"Boy, I didn't know you was up so early, eh! Excuse me, man, for walking round your place dressed like this."

"All right, it's A–OK!" He was talking like Mr. Macintosh again. And something inside him started to work an unquenchable desire from his spine, from the top of his spine all through his body down to his thighs into a stiffening.

"The bathroom is yours now, boy."

She had not been able to move since she first saw him.

"I know."

He was standing still an inch from her; and the way he was standing made her know she could not completely come out of the bathroom without touching him with her belly, or he touching her with his stiffened jointed desire. But she knew there could be no touching.

"I left back a lot o' hot water for you, man."

"It don't make no difference. Hot or cold, the same thing."

"Well, you better go and catch your bath. I am going to make your breakfast for you."

"It's all right, it's A–OK," he said, waiting for the minutest sign from her that she was as willing as he was to do what was on his mind.

He thought how frustrated he was, how "thirsty"; for he had come home late, this morning, and Dots was in a nasty mood, and he had had a few drinks with the boys, and a few hands of poker, and everything had worked a great passion and a great desire for Dots in him. But Dots was tired too, and she had turned over on her belly, as a sign that she didn't want him. And before he could get up, foreday morning, to go into the bathroom to spit out some of the awful saliva of rum-drinking, Dots was dressed and putting the cup of half-full tea on the hasty table, and rushing through the door "to see what these bitches got up their sleeves for me this blessed morning. I gone, Boysie, boy!" And she left him more thirsty. Now, as if someone was sending him a blessing, here was Estelle before him. But he had to wait for a sign, the sign. *If only this goddamn woman would give me the signal!* "You sure you have finished bathing? I could wait back in the bedroom."

"Oh no, man! You go in, and get your bath, man!" And she held him round his shining stocking-capped head, and drew his head close to her belly, and she kissed him on his stocking-cap, and said, "Feel! Feel there, man. And feel how this little half-black bitch kicking inside of me, already. Be-Christ, and he even isn't born yet! You feel it, Boysie? You are going to be the godfather, yuh know!"

Boysie thought he felt the movements of a terrible chastisement in Estelle's belly. And he felt dirty. And with his eyes averted from hers, and from her belly, he went into the bathroom and remained standing in there for a long time, trying to find out for the sake of his own guilt and conscience whether she knew that he wanted to have a quick screw off her. He got into the tub and turned on the tap. It was the shower tap. And it was the hot water tap. "Shite!" he cried, beneath his breath.

Estelle went into the bedroom which she shared with Bernice. She sat on the unmade bed and cried.

"Estelle and Bernice have to leave!" Boysie was screaming. "Estelle and Bernice gotta go! Right now! Tomorrow morning, at the latest." He was talking so loud that Dots felt sure the neighbours were hearing him. Estelle and Bernice were out. "What the hell kind o' home you running at all, woman? A woman almost ready to drop a child, and you have her in here? Suppose the child come and she don't want to move out? Don't you know that the city or the health people or the welfare people or somebody could prosecute me for throwing out a pregnant woman at the last minute? So she gotta go now!"

"Jesus Christ, man, hold your horses! I heard yuh. It always was me telling Bernice she should go, and it was you, Boysie, remember? who always say, 'Wait a little longer.' "

"That's different now."

"All right. I will tell them tonight when they came in. I will tell them."

"*Tell* them."

"All right, all right."

He was so filled with anger, the anger of guilt and frustration, that he wanted to tell somebody, anybody, why all of a sudden he wanted Estelle and her sister to leave the apartment. But of course, he couldn't tell Dots; neither could he tell anybody else. He worked himself relentlessly into this anger; and he felt that Dots with her remarkable sensitivity would soon discover his motives. But how could she? She was no fortune-teller! And he did not think she was studying psychology in her nursing aid course at the hospital. Still something worried him: it was his manner of bringing up the subject. Perhaps, he ought to have hinted at it, and let Dots make the open statement of their leaving. It should have been her entire desire. Suppose Estelle was to talk about what he did to her that morning at the bathroom door!

"Well, after all, they didn't invite themselves here," Boysie said, lamely.

"I glad as hell you come to see that! The way you been carrying on 'bout Estelle, a poor girl, pregnant, I swear to

God something must have happened! And her sister, Bernice, who haven't done you one blasted thing in the weeks they been living here. Eh? Doesn't Estelle make my home tidy for me? Cooks your meals? Washes your blasted clothes as if she is a servant? Whilst I am at that damn hospital learning my course? Isn't Bernice always ironing, always ironing and washing too? And now for you to come and say what you said about them in my hearing, well, Boysie, I tell you, you haven't got as much gratitudes and niceness as what a blasted dog borned with. And I know that a dog don't have none!"

"That's true. That's damn true, Dots. Perhaps it is something else bothering me. Perhaps, it is all this night work, all this damn night work and late hours that's getting me down. Man, I never worked so hard in all my born days! I can now understand why Henry don't want to look too hard for work since he married to that rich woman, Agatha."

"That is Henry's blasted business!"

"It's mine, too!"

"Estelle is a damn good woman. I have said a lot o' bad things 'gainst that girl, since she came here to this country. And just in a few weeks having her living here I now come to understand what a priceless girl she is. She is a lady. And once I even thought, what a nice wife she would have been for Henry, but, well . . ."

"That's true. Estelle is a princess."

"And so is Bernice."

"She had a blasted hard break from that bitch Mistress Burrmann, though."

"Bernice told me last night whilst you were out working that she intends to rent a place in this same building just because she wants to be near to me and to you, to help you with your meals whilst I am up there on Brunswick Avenue, at the Doctors. That is what I call kindness. You don't know nothing about kindness, Boysie. Sometimes, I swear that when you was born, kindness dropped dead. Bernice intends to buy a house too. That is what I really call using your head. I always had it in my mind to buy a house. But a certain somebody I know always said, 'House hell! house hell! We happy living at the Hunters.' Well, you see what the Hunters give now, eh? You see what the Burrmanns give now? Bernice is a wise woman. Once stung, twice shy. Estelle will be dropping child in the middle o' winter, and that will be an added burden. That bastard Burrmann hasn't remembered to look back yet, to see if Estelle living or dead. And Agatha been fulling her head with a lot o' damn foolishness 'bout adoption. Estelle told me. And you want to know something? You haven't told me yet, why *you* of all people, all of a sudden, you of all people, who only yesterday was singing the praises of both the Estelle and the Bernice, why now, sudden so, you want them to leave?"

Boysie could feel it coming: Dots might have diagnosed the correct motive. Women have this peculiarity, he knew, this ability to smell things.

"I think I know what's bothering you, Boysie," she said. Boysie froze. "And I pray, every chance I get at that hospital, that it isn't so. You have no idea of the kind o' thoughts that pass through my head whilst I am in that course at the Doctors, maybe emptying a bedpan full o' some white man shit . . . half of my mind is always right here in this house. In this bedroom. Right here where me and you sitting down now. I always ask God, 'Lord, Jesus Christ, don't let it happen to me. Jesus Christ, no, God!' "

"Wha' you mean, Dots?" Boysie asked in a rough manner. He wanted to shock her off the subject: he was sure she was on the right track. And in a frame of self-flagellation, he wanted, too, to shock it out of her, and have it said and done with. "What the hell are you getting at, now? You are saying a damn lot, and you ain't saying one damn thing. You baiting me, or something, woman? What's on your mind?"

"Every minute I get. Whilst she is here. And I pray and pray Estelle won't do anything foolish. And with you here. You don't even know how to boil a saucepan o' hot water. Christ, for Estelle to attempt another abortion in anger over that man, Burrmann! Christ, it would be hell if you couldn't help her. And if in your ignorance, you had to call-on 'pon one o' these so-called neighbours in this building, God, look, how both you and Estelle would be landing-up in the Don Jail!" Tears were in her eyes, and she let them fall on her face, and Boysie, in a broken pathetic mood, moved her gently until she was resting on his chest. They were sitting very close now, on the bed in their bedroom. "That is what I worry about every spare minute I get from that course."

"Oh!" And he began to thaw, to breathe more comfortably. For the first time since they started discussing this topic did he remember that he had mixed himself a rum-and-Coke. He took the glass off the dressing table, where it had marked the newness of the shine, and he raised it to his lips with his eyelids closed. And in his confidence, he planned to confront Estelle again before she left.

Bernice frightened herself when she realized she had so much energy and versatility. She wanted a job in a very rich home, with the condition that she didn't have to sleep in on the premises. "One experience like that is good enough for me." She had suffered an almost complete mental and physical breakdown when Mrs. Burrmann fired her; and the terror of seeing herself going through her life savings so rapidly (which now totaled only two thousand dollars from the five thousand she had when Estelle arrived), and the prospect of spending the coming winter without a job was a future that looked fatal. But there was in her a great reserve of strength which she did not know she had. She had returned to Marina Boulevard for her belongings. She had seen the oldish Polish woman struggling with the housework. Mrs. Burrmann had the Polish woman washing the floors. That was a thing Bernice had refused to do when she worked there.

Mrs. Burmann tried to appear kind to Bernice on this occasion, hiding any animosity she might have felt. And she even invited Bernice into her sitting room for a drink. And Bernice accepted it too. Bernice saw many things in the sitting room as if for the first time. She was no longer a servant. She was now a guest. She even folded her legs as she chatted.

"I am sorry, Bernice," Mrs. Burrmann said. "I am truly sorry that it didn't work out as we had hoped. But then again, that is life, isn't it?"

"True! I don't mind, though," Bernice said, sipping the whiskey-and-soda as if she was born sipping it. "All I want from you now is what I have a right to. What I am entitled to. And that is a piece o' paper saying that I carried out my duties during my stay in your household to the best of my ability and to the best of your satisfaction."

"Of course, Leach . . . Bernice, I mean! I am so much in the habit of calling you Leach. But you aren't Leach to me any longer. Of course, Bernice. Where do you want it sent?"

Bernice didn't expect that it would have to be sent anywhere; she wanted to have it in her hand to present to her next employer. But seeing Mrs. Burrmann in such congenial, helpful spirits, she didn't worry to insist on taking the reference with her. "Well, I have a' appointment with a Mistress

Wolfe in the Bridal Path, tomorrow afternoon . . ." Bernice began. And she searched in her handbag for the address, and gave it to Mrs. Burrmann, who wrote it down and returned the paper to Bernice. "I already talked to her on the 'phone, and she seems interested. But she want to see a reference first before I can start the work next week."

It was a long time, a space of more than a week, before Bernice would remember this conversation. She had seen three other women, all in Rosedale, and had told them they could get her references from Mrs. Burrmann of Forest Hill. They never called her back. But she was happy. At last she had learned the truth about Mrs. Burrmann. In future she would give references that were from Barbados, and she would say she was in the country only a few months, or one year; and if she suspected reservations on their parts, she would show them her passport which had stamped on it (not *Domestic*) *Immigrant "Landed" Immigrant "Recu,"* and beneath these two lines, in a stamped box, an imperial crown of Great Britain, *Canada Immigration, Toronto,* in block letters and the date AUG 12 1960; and beside this, the scratches signifying that a human hand had witnessed it. "Live and learn, child!" Bernice said to herself, when she hit upon this plan. "Live and learn."

The very next day, she presented herself back in Rosedale, of all places, as Miss Bernice Leach. "Yes, ma'am, I am from Barbados originally, but I am living here now, let me see, ahhmmm, one year clear running into a year and a half. I have experience in this job stretching to many years in Barbados, having worked at Government House in Barbados, whiching as you know, mistress, is the same position as being chief cook and bottle-washer heh-heh-heh! for your governor-general of this province o' Ontario. Now, mistress, you would agree that it isn't everybody in Rosedale who have a maid with credentials to match mine . . ."

Bernice didn't have to say more. Mrs. Asquith Marlborough Breighington-Kelly was a young enough woman
to appreciate the importance of the snob value of having
black hands in her kitchen that had worked for royalty,
even if only in the West Indies; having a "coloured maid,
darling, who has worked for royalty and excellency in the
islands, in Jamaica, darling, would you believe it?" She was
wealthy as she was young as she was beautiful. And she was
very beautiful. And she gave Bernice three hundred and
seventy-five dollars a month; permission to sleep "wherever
the hell you want to sleep, darling, and with whom, too!
hah-hah!" and a large apartment in the basement, to rest
during the toils of the day.

"And Jesus Christ, look I already went to the expense of
renting an apartment!" Bernice regretted. "If only Estelle
wasn't here to weigh me down!" Mrs. A. M. Breighington-
Kelly even hinted that Bernice would be going with them
each year to the Bahamas. Mr. Asquith Marlborough
Breighington-Kelly was under forty, and was a millionaire
already.

Bernice went home to Dots, rejoicing. She was shaking
with nervousness to tell Dots and Boysie and Estelle the
good news. "Christ, if I could only get rid of Estelle, I
could save money like water! But after all, Estelle is . . ."

Mrs. Breighington-Kelly too waited excitedly to tell her
husband, with a martini in her hand and a martini in his
hand; and laughing, and ". . . what made me engage her,
darling, was that she's the most marvellous liar in the world!
She had just showed me her passport which said she entered
Canada in 1960, and she still insisted she has been here
only one and a half years! She's beautiful, she's marvellous!
I took her because I knew you would have done the same
thing, had you interviewed her . . . and darling, darling?
She's not young, hah-hah! . . . but all the time I was

thinking of that Jewish woman, Mrs. Burrmann, and the things she said . . . imagine calling me to tell me that . . . and I hired Bernice simply because of the things that bitch told me on the telephone. Oh, Bernice is marvellous! You must meet Bernice! . . . hah-hah-hah!"

What was it? What was it? Boysie kept looking round the room. He looked as carefully as he could, when Henry wasn't watching. And still he couldn't find the answer. What was it? What was it? he wondered, about this room that made it look so strange from the last time he dropped in here, just before Henry got married? The last time was soon after he had got his station wagon, and he had come back to drive Henry to his wedding in it, but there was so much excitement that afternoon that he hadn't noticed anything strange about the room. Now he glanced around the walls, and his eyes saw strange things but they did not register them. Then he knew. It was the walls, themselves: no longer walls, but walls painted by books in shelves and bookcases. Every available space was taken up by books in bookcases, made out of onion crates. Boysie was not only amazed at the number of books (books had so recently crept into his own life), but also by the fact that they could change the appearance of a room he was accustomed to visiting, a room he knew by heart, a room in which he had drunk a lot of rum and whiskey so many times in the past, on so many conditions, as he and Henry were now doing this chilly Saturday afternoon.

"Wait, who owns all these books, man?"

"The wife. She owns all these books."

"Wait, and who build them bookcases? and put them in them, all over the place, so?"

"The wife. She build the bookcases."

"She's a hell of a woman, a wife, you have, boy."

"Book have now become my fucking enemy in my old age, boy. Books, books, books everywhere. Books in the bathroom upstairs there, books under the bed, books all over the place. One day I was so mad I started to count these blasted books, and when I reached two thousand, I gave up, 'cause be-Christ, Boysie, as a old man, I am too fucking old now to start worrying 'bout books and education. And all these blasted books're written in a language that I can't understand or talk in, at all. Zoology-sociology-anthropology language! I don't know why *one* person — and a woman at that! — have to know so much just to live in this fucking twentieth-century world!"

"Education, boy! That's what I mean when I say you're lucky as hell. Agaffa is a highly educated woman. And she is your wife now. I wish my wife was a more learned woman."

"My wife. My wife? My fucking wife! Look at this fucking room, man. Man, these fucking books is stifling me, man! I can't breathe! Look at my room, Boysie. Boysie you know me a long time, a long time before I had this brilliant idea to marry a woman who breathes books! You know me when I had a television set in here, when I could come in here on a Saturday night, with you, and with a case o' beer on the floor between us, and watch the Montreal Canadiennes beat the shit outta the Toronto Maple Leaves. Boysie, this is one-room-apartment-room. It isn't no fucking luxury apartment in Rosedale or on Avenue Road. And I been living here comfortable as arse, for years, before my *wife, my* wife moved into my fucking parlour — said the spider to the fucking fly!"

"The books look good, though," Boysie said; and he meant it. "They have the place looking like a educated place."

"My wife did it, man. She is a very fucking educated

lady. I didn't tell you she just qualified for a fellowship? My wife just came first in her class. A fellowship worth four thousand dollars. Some goddamn foundation is giving my wife four *thousand* dollars to write a lot o' shite about dead animals, because that is what she tell me social zoology is all about. Man, be-Jesus Christ, in the West Indies, we *buries* dead animals!"

"I wish my wife could get a . . ."

"Shut your fucking mouth, boy! You don't know when you're lucky!" Henry then poured another glass of wine for Boysie and for himself. They were drinking Mommessin, a red wine. Agatha had bought the wine. She also bought the pure crystal glasses they were drinking the wine from.

Boysie looked round the room, marvelling at the number of books on the walls: all four walls. They were arranged in a certain order, for he could see all the books dealing with one branch of a particular animal and its instincts and behaviour were together; and there were many books about black people. Boysie touched the covers of the books; he opened some of them, and all of them bore Agatha's name, her maiden name: *Agatha Barbara Sellman, Zoology U of T, 5T9*; and in a recent mood, a hand of contemporary ballpoint writing, she had written on each book in the house (Boysie made a sample testing when he saw the name first in a book called *The Myth of the Negro Past*), she had written "née" before the *Agatha Barbara Sellman* line, and underneath that line she had written *Agatha Barbara Sellman-White*. Boysie liked it, and he laughed to himself. Only Englishmen from England, those who owned Rolls-Royces and large black Humber Hawks and those big Jaguars, had names like Agatha's, names joined together in holy matrimony by a hyphen.

He wondered what Henry's new name was? Was it Henry White-Sellman? But he was not foolish enough to ask.

Boysie sprang off the footstool. His wine spilled. "Man, hey! Man, that is you! That is you!" He was pointing at a piece of paper taken from a large notebook (the holes from the rings were visible, and visibly torn), on which was a drawing of a black man's head and shoulders, done in running smudging charcoal. The lips of this black man were very thick. The hair was very bushy: but in some way, the face looked like a white man's face, with the one difference that it was painted black. Boysie looked at it for a long time. "Man, this is you!"

"My wife! She is a fucking artist, too."

Boysie kept looking at the drawing and then at Henry: at the drawing, then at Henry. What is it, he wondered. And then, finally, he got it. The hair. Henry had started to grow his hair long, like an artist's or a black nationalist's, since he got married. The drawing had handed him over to Boysie.

"The hair, man! The hair!" Boysie was chuckling. "Man, you look like one o' them fellows, them beatniks from up in Yorkville, them hippies, or like that fellow from the States called Rap Brown . . ." And Boysie made that ridiculing luugh, laughing and holding his head to the floor, and then pointing at Henry, and then laughing some more. "Man, you need a haircut bad, man."

"My wife likes it long so. My wife says it makes me look like a real Afro-Canadian! Me, a fucking Afro-Canadian! Man, Boysie, I don't even like the word, 'Africa'!"

"That's it! This picture that Agaffa draw make you look like a African, a Watusi!"

"Heh-heh-hahhha-haaa!" And this was the first time Henry laughed since he got married. Agatha had said the same thing, exactly, word for word. And Henry had slapped her goddamn hard in the face. "Never a-fucking-gain call me a Nafrican, you hear me? I don't call you a Jew!" But this time, coming from Boysie, it had perhaps told him the truth; and if Boysie could see it, and Agatha, then it must be the truth. Henry was beginning to like the idea that he looked like an African. The tension, the guarded replies to Boysie's questions (after all they were still friends), and the sarcasm in his own voice about his wife — all this disappeared. Boysie got up from the footstool, and saw the framed pictures on the wall — in what little space was left back from the bookcases. They were all, each and every one, of black people. Agatha had clipped them from various magazines. She had framed them herself with cheap unpainted frames which she also painted. "What I want so many black people's faces in here for?" Henry had said. "Black people looking at me wherever the hell I turn. Even in the goddamn bathroom! Goddamn, woman, are you out of your cotton-picking mind?" The only previous picture Henry had on the walls of his room was one of himself in the uniform of a porter of the Canadian National Railways, as Porter of the Year — a picture which showed him shaking hands with the prime minister at the time, Lester Bowles Pearson. There were added three or four photographs of Agatha, at various stages of her academic development, in penguined white and black, intellectually unfashionable, so far as Henry was concerned.

"I see Elijah Muhammad, man! He is a great man for black people. For white people, too. And this is Malcolm X. He's a giant. Somebody tell me he is a West Indian, too. A great man! But who is these three black children?"

"Ask my wife."

"I mean, she knows them?"

"*Knows* them? Where the hell would she meet three black girls? Up in Forest Hill playing in her backyard, or in her swimming pool? She tore them out of that goddamn magazine, Boysie! Now, look at those three goddamn half-starved little bitches! You tell me, if you see anything beautiful in their goddamn undernourished faces? Because I want to know if I am going stark-fucking-crazy! . . . or my wife? All three of them girls are teethless, toothless. One is wearing rags. The other two are not dressed much better. And my wife tells me they're beautiful, 'What marvellous faces!' she says . . . and I want to kill her! Do you think that my wife is trying to tell me something, in a zoological way?"

"You mean that since you are black, a black man, and these children are black too . . ."

"Boysie, you're a fucking genius! You are more educated, *in my books*, than Agatha is, with all the Ph.D.s and M.A.s and B.A.s behind her fucking name. She is trying to give me a *inferiority* complex, Boysie! And she is calling it beauty. I don't see one fucking beautiful thing in being poor, or in being black, or in being hungry. I happen to be born black and poor — and perhaps ugly — and goddammit, don't mention it no more, 'cause I can't change that!" And he made a feigned grab for the framed picture of black infant beauty, making as if he wanted to tear it from the wall. But he had tried to do so before, even when he was alone, once, and he could not tear the picture from the wall. There was a greater power which Agatha had over him, a power that cancelled his ability to destroy the picture of the three little black girls. "Man, I feel I am under a fucking microscope twenty-five hours a-fucking-day! That woman *knows too much* 'bout black people, baby!"

"She is a good woman, though. You lucky as arse!"

"Lucky?" Henry took a piece of paper from his hip pocket. It was a page from an expensive writing pad. Agatha's name, her new name, *Agatha Barbara Sellman-White*, was printed on the top. Henry gave the piece of paper to Boysie. Boysie took it. Boysie read it. Boysie started laughing. Then he gave it back to Henry. "Read it, man. I asked you to read it, and I mean that you should read it out loud. Not to yourself. I could do that myself."

"You really want to hear it? Okay. *'I love you because you are black. I love your black black skin. I love your black hands. I love your black face. If you were lighter in complexion, like Estelle, I would not like you so much, because that would not be a perfect match of opposites. I love your thick wooly hair. I love your thick purple lips . . .'* Jesus Christ, I didn't know you was so *black?*" (Boysie was shaking with an enjoyable laughter. Henry was laughing too.) "'. . . *I love you, I love you, I love you, you big black beautiful black beast.'* Ohjesuschrist, man, ho-ho-ho-ho!"

"Does your wife write you love letters like that? Tell me, man. And tell me if this woman, my wife, doesn't have rocks in her goddamn head? Does Dots write you and tell you she loves you because you are a goddamn black beast?"

"But Henry, Dots black like me, man!" Boysie was still laughing. He couldn't read more; but between the mirth of film and laughter in his eyes, he saw: . . . *and I love the way you make love to me, and* . . . "Man, it must be a hell of an experience to be married to a white woman, eh?"

"You better believe it, you black beast!"

"Hah-hah-hah! black beast!"

"Boysie, you's a goddamn black beast!"

"Man, Henry, you was one first! Grrrrrrrr! you black beast! You is a black beast too!"

"How Brigitte, boy? You still lashing it?"

"Do you think you is the only beautiful black beast in this kiss-me-arse place, eh? I am throwing lashes left and right. In Estelle, too — but on the sly! Grrrrrrrrrr!"

Henry went to him, and embraced him, and applauded him, and patted him on the back. "Let we go to the Paramount, for some chicken wings and draught beer, man. We have to celebrate. We are the same fucking beasts, any-how!" He took up a twenty-dollar bill which Agatha kept in a jar on which was marked, on a piece of adhesive tape, in her firm clear printing: ENTERTAINMENT, LUXURIES, THE PARAMOUNT AND HENRY. Boysie noticed it, and laughed, but he also made a mental note to have Dots put a jar similar to this one, with the exact wording, on the top shelf of his built-in bookcase. The idea appealed to him as a good one. "I am going to spend twenty dollars on you."

"And I have a twenty to spend on you, too."

They left the station wagon parked in front of Henry's roominghouse, on Baldwin Street; and they walked, arms round each other, close as friends, close as rotten peas in rotten pod, clear and honestly friends. Henry even tipped his hat to the old man who came round begging for empty bottles. And Boysie gave him a quarter, and called him, "Friend."

They had not only become drunk together often, but more importantly, they had opened the most personal secrets and actions of their lives to each other. This was the kind of relationship there was between Henry and Boysie. Now, away from the influence of Agatha, as represented by her decoration of the room, they sat down with a few glasses of draught beer before them, and talked with candour as men sometimes found it necessary to do. Freely. There were many things bothering Henry, and it was some of these that he was telling Boysie about. Boysie, on his part, confessed some more about seeing Estelle, when she came over, in Dots's absence, to help with the housework. Dots had not yet smelled a rat, he told Henry, but he was sure she would, as she always did. And Boysie admitted that he was not as careful as he ought to be. He admitted still seeing Brigitte; although that close, belly-rubbing friendship had now withered into something like an occasional orgasm.

Henry, who could no longer pretend that he did not know Brigitte, either literally or biblically, confessed that since he was married he had "known her three times," on Marina Boulevard, where she still worked for the Gassteins. And it was from Henry that Boysie first learned that Brigitte had booked her passage home to West Germany: she was going to run out on the Gassteins. With all their past, certain aspects of which were identical, and which had often moved on a head-on collision path, they still remained friends. It was to this friendship that Henry was now addressing himself, his thoughts, his confessions of thoughts which were like monologues spoken to himself, within the privacy of his bathroom, as he sat on the closet seat.

"I been meaning to tell you all this a long long time, man," he was saying now. They had drunk about four glasses each of draught beer. "But I was catching my arse royally, as the Trinidadians say. It was pressure in my arse, man. And I couldn't breathe, man. First thing, was the police coming and breaking up the reception. Well, Agatha ain't forget that yet. And I don't blame her. I don't expect she ever would. 'Cause, look at it as it is, man, and you would have to agree with her, although I nearly killed her dead that night, for saying the same things as I saying now — but you have to agree with Agatha, that if the reception was held in another district, like Forest Hill, no fucking cop would be so stupid as to break up a wedding party. But that is life, and we have to see it and know it, and move on, boy! But after that quarrel, came the hunting for an apartment in this fucking place. Hunting for an apartment in this rass-hole city, boy, for a black man, and *with a white wife*, Jesus Christ! well, I don't have to tell you. Sometimes, I was angry as arse. Sometimes, I was embarrass. Sometimes, I just laughed. But I was thinking of my wife, my goddamn rich white woman, and she can't find a decent place to live, merely because she happened to be walking beside a man with the wrong brand o' colour, according to the landladies and landlords in this fucking Toronto. Just before you dropped in, I had just come back from walking up along Lowther Avenue, and I see some nice places in private homes up there, with good apartments. I would enter a door, or knock on a door and the first thing I see is this big change on the woman's face, or the man's face, and then there is this big explaining and excuses, and I can't get inside that fucking drawing room to sit down with a drink or a cup of tea or coffee, and discuss the terms o' renting and rent that the apartment involves. I can't get a chance to behave like a human-civilized-fucking-being. I gotta see an apartment, and before that man or that woman could change his goddamn eyelids, I gotta shout, 'I take it, I take it!' and hope, be-Christ, that the man get frightened as arse for me, and rent me the place, and then, because I haven't had time to look over the place, I then find out I have rented a fucking pigsty!

"I can live through this, because as you know, I am a goddamn Wessindian. But I couldn't live through it if this was the States and I was a black American. But sometimes I can't see no fucking difference between Toronto and Harlem! I mean, certain times, a certain time comes in your fucking life when you want to relax and ease-up offa hustling. You want a nice place to live."

"I was going to mention that they can't refuse you an apartment because o' colour no more, or race, creed or nothing. The government passed a law saying so. Only if it is a private house, or they have less than six places in that house or apartment."

"Man, the government talks a lot o' shite about six units and apartments! And they write more shite than that, too. If the government wants to find out, let the fucking government walk 'bout with me, one o' these nights, even tonight, and I will show the fucking government some apartments in this city, man, where no fucking law don't apply, at all, at all."

"That's a hard thing to say about your government, though, Henry."

"It is true, though." Henry then looked scrutinizingly at Boysie; and he noticed the way he was dressed: new suit, a pin-striped suit, he was wearing a tie, too; and his shoes, black, were polished; and there were cufflinks in his french cuffs, and he was smelling like a woman, with perfume. "You like you turning into a goddamn white man, boy! Or you become a conservative since you hustling that cleaning job!"

"Me? No, man."

"Well, don't talk bullshit, then! I am telling you a kind o' history and sociology that not even the great Doctor Agatha Barbara Sellman-White, hyphen, be-Jesus Christ, could contradict. One night. One night, I spit in a fucking white woman face, just because she was about to close her blasted door before I had time to talk. Another night! God-blummuh! Boysie, as I am sitting down here, I was so mad that I grabbed this bastard by the scruff of his European neck, and be-Jesus Christ, if my wife wasn't there as a witness, I would have *kill* that bastard dead dead dead be-Jesus Christ! *This thing*, man. This thing does some funny things to a man's mind, Boysie. I am talking about the effects, man, the *effects*. One night again. I was so mad that I went back to that house on Huron Street where the woman played the arse with me, on Huron Street near the corner of Lowther. And I painted a fucking red swastika sign on her front door. The front door! Fortunately, the door was shite!"

"You do *what?*" Boysie lost his breath.

"On the fucking door!"

"But was the woman a Jew?"

"No!"

"She didn't even have a Jewish name?"

"How the hell would I know her name?"

"And why you painted a Nazzi sign on the woman's door, then?"

"It was the only fucking sign or symbol I could think of to make her feel the way she made me feel, and to scare the shit outta her pants."

"A Nazzi sign? Ohmygod!"

"Red as shite! Like the communists. It was a goddamn pretty swastika I marked on that door!" And he laughed out. Some neighbours, only in distance but not in attentiveness, nor consciousness, held up their heads, but soon they held them back down, or had them pulled down by the weight in the drinks before them. "The very next day, I saw it in the papers . . ."

"I remember now. The papers was talking 'bout a Nazzi party and persecuting the Jews, and . . ."

"I laughed my goddamn head off!" He took a long draught on his beer glass. "And when you sit down soberlike, and face these things, Boysie, you don't like to know what's possessing you, or what's happening to you, you don't want to know. Living with that woman, Godbless-her! is like standing up in front of a life-sized looking glass that is behaving like an X-ray machine. You see things that make your goddamn heart bleed. I started to think so much these days Boysie, that the moment I sit down, I start thinking. I stand up and I am thinking. I go into the bathroom upstairs to fire a shit and still I am thinking as

I am shitting. I am sleeping and I am thinking. I am walking or talking to my wife, and I am thinking. Something inside me, *some thing*, big and terrible, man; there is some-damn-thing inside here, and I got to get it out. Or else it would kill me. It didn't come out that night I laughed when that European whore slammed the door in my face. Man, that thing made me walk to-rass to the College Street public library to look up one o' them election polls, rolls, with the names and streets and the people living in a certain electoral district! . . . and be-Christ, all the names on that street that slammed doors in my face, or won't open the fucking doors, all the names were mostly European names. *Chuck* or *Chich* or *Gowski* or *Shev*, God-blindthemall! Man, they're lucky I didn't burn the whole fucking street down! So, as I was telling you, I have to express these feelings . . ."

He paused to take a sip of his beer. Boysie took one too. They lighted cigarettes. "I don't want to make you feel that I is this big writer, this big writer like that fellow from Barbados, or the other two writers living in this fucked-up city, the one from Guyana and the other fellow from Jamaica. I don't even know if I got it in me to put two ideas side by side and make them make sense. But there is *some thing* in here that I have to let out in the way a writer, a real writer can let out things like these. Lemme show you something. I have a piece o' paper here . . . I been jotting down things like this now for a long time, whenever I think of *this thing* and of life. But don't laugh, man, because they are written down in a poetical form, like poetry . . ."

"Don't tell me you think you's a writer! You playing the arse now, if you think you is a Shakespeare the Second, or something!" And Boysie, the close friend, ridiculed Henry with a laugh which sent shivers up Henry's spine. But Henry was already taking out the piece of paper, folded by creases and marks, from his pocket.

"But you dedicate the thing to Agatha!"

"She is my wife, man."

"Oh!"

"That's exactly what I mean . . ."

"By dedicating the thing to Agatha?" Henry nodded. Boysie read the poem, which said:

> *But was it really time that killed*
> *The rose of our love? Was it time?*
> *And was it time to die? Is it time?*
> *This rose?*
> *It was not, could not, be time. Time*
> *Has no power over roses, or over love*
> *Or over me, or over you.*
> *Time has no gun over love and beauty.*

Boysie handed it back to Henry; and all he said was, "Man, I didn't know you like roses so much!"

"What you think of it? You think it is a poem?"

"A poem? Man, I look like a kiss-me-arse poet to you? Only a poet would know if a poem is a poem. I am only a cleaner. But I didn't know though, that you had this great feeling about a rose."

"How it sound, though, Boysie? How it read, man? It reads like one o' those we used to have to learn by heart, back in the old days, in school?"

"Man, in those days, the things we read as poems was printed in a book, man. They were poems. But this one, this poem that you show me, well, I can't rightly say if it is a poem or if it is not a poem, because as you know, the only poems we learned were printed in a English book sent

down by England. I just see this 'thing you show me as
something write-down on a piece o' paper talking a lotta
shite 'bout roses!"

"Where in hell did you pick up this zombie?" Sam Burrmann said one day, referring to the middle-aged Polish-
Jewish maid who had replaced Bernice. He had seen her
around the house during the day and night, but he was so
preoccupied that he never even stopped to consider whether
she was just a part-time help, a visitor, or a poor relation
from beyond the seas.

"She replaces Bernice," Mrs. Burrmann said, when Marta
left for the kitchen, silent and placid.

"*Replaces?*" And for a long time he was silent so she
might savour his sarcasm. "What *did* happen to Bernice?"
he asked, after swallowing the hot coffee. "I thought Bernice was a good maid."

"Oh nothing, really! Just itchy feet, restlessness. You
know these West Indians. She wanted to try another job,
so I told her it was all right for her to leave."

"Suppose you can't blame her for that."

"Course not. We can't blame her for that."

She was waiting for him to mention Estelle's name. She
was waiting, as she had waited for weeks now, to get the
chance to lose her temper, not only about Estelle and Bernice, but about many things she had in mind to quarrel
about. He had skillfully sidestepped the issue. He worried
about it himself, for many hours each day, since his return
from his vacation in the north: at the office; driving his automobile down to work along Avenue Road, and sometimes coming close, too close to the back fenders of a car
in front. Once, he forgot to stop at a Pedestrian Crosswalk,
and almost killed a child. He took sixty minutes to regain
his composure in Murray's Restaurant, where he stopped

to drink three cups of black coffee. The child he almost killed, back there, was a "coloured" child: this started him thinking about Estelle . . . what kind of coloured child would his be . . . he was thinking of it now . . .

Mrs. Burrmann had been grumbling all the time about what a diligent maid Marta was, how she would do things which Bernice felt too proud to do: "Sometimes, I have to remind Marta she's not a young person any longer . . . she is cleaning the floors, when I told her I have a cleaning woman, a char, to come in to do that . . . and the children, they just *adore* her . . . she allows them to ride on her back, at her age! . . ."

"Course!" He got up. He wiped something from his mouth with the paper napkin. He held over and kissed her on the hair. She closed her eyes, as if praying for a more passionate kiss. "See you." And then she opened her eyes.

On his way out, Mrs. Burrmann said, "Well, I'll do what I told you about the new furniture for Marta's rooms . . ." He was ducking down into the garage. "*Hasta la vista!*" she said. Marta was standing beside her, wondering who she was talking to, in this strange tongue. "*Hasta!*" And to Marta, she said, "That was Mr. Burrmann I was talking to . . ."

He stood outside the garage door catching a breath of fresh air from her stifling conversation. He had heard: enough, every word. "*Aster-la-veester? Aster-la-veeeester?*" he said, over and over again, as he went into the garage. "*Aster-la-fuckster! Aster-la-fuckster-la-haster! Vesster-la-fuckster . . .*"

It was some time before Henry realized he was being followed. When he found out it shocked him. He was terrified. He did not know when it had begun, but he told himself, as a way of preparing himself for the worst, that men had been following him from that night almost a year ago when he struck the policeman on Marina Boulevard. But that was such a long time ago: since then he had been beaten up by two policemen, again on Marina Boulevard. The cuts and bruises he had got from that beating were now healed; and usually, he forgot about them, and also about the newspaper report and the large photographs that were supposed to have been arranged by Mr. Turnbull. He would remember the cut on his face only when he shaved. But he had stopped shaving now, since he had taken up writing down his thoughts and his frustrations in verse form. And he had become so preoccupied with this recent literary diversion that he did not have much time to look behind, to understand what he had done in the past five or six months, and to see whether in fact someone was following him, or whether it was his imagination. He could not believe that anybody would want to follow him.

But someone did. There had always been a shadow. One night, Agatha came home late from the university library and told him, "Henry, there was a man out there in a car, parked. He was there when I left. He was there when I came in." And he said, "Oh?" There had always been men out there on the street, parked, in cars, and with women in their laps. It was near the car wash on Spadina Avenue; and some cars would park on Baldwin and on other side streets to get away from the traffic policemen. But this night, when he found out he was being followed, had been followed for some time, he was alone, and heading for the Embassy Coffee House on St. Nicholas Street.

Recently, he had started going to coffee houses, hanging around, trying to relax, trying to unwind, also to get away from his wife. He was now interested in poetry, and had heard that young men and women read their poetry there, on certain nights. He never told Boysie he was going to these places because he knew Boysie would laugh. It was not the thing that sane West Indians did; and West Indians, he knew, did not write poetry. And he did not tell Agatha because he wanted to keep this part of his life private . . . "except if I should get a poem published in a poetry magazine, then . . ." This was his first time going to read his poetry at the Embassy. He was hoping that no one would call on him to read. But he was going nevertheless. He was not sure if what he wrote was really poetry; there was no one he knew who knew anything about poetry; and he was self-conscious about beginning to write at his age. Recently, he had read many books of Canadian poetry. But he didn't like any of them. All the poets whose works he read were younger than he, except one old man with a beard from the days of the westerns and saloons.

He took another deep pull on his cigarette to steady his nerves; and he made to climb the long narrow flights of stairs to the darkened moaning voice above. Just as he put his hand on the door, a man came out of the darkness and stood in front of him, for a moment; having made his quick and brief identification, he moved on. Henry ignored him. Henry regarded him as a drunk, or perhaps he was a poet, so he went up and entered the coffee house. A man was telling someone on the telephone there was no reading tonight.

Henry started to go down the steps again. He stopped to light a cigarette. He walked on. He stopped because the cigarette was not burning. He thought of calling Boysie or visiting him; perhaps visit Bernice and Estelle. Henry had just stepped off the last step and onto the cobblestones in the street when he sensed there was someone nearby, in the shadows. He could not see very well because the street was narrow and flanked on both sides by tall red brick buildings and chimneys the same age as the cobbles in the street. It was now too late for him to turn left and go the few yards to Wellesley Street. His instinct told him it would be safer to turn right, and walk the farther distance to the other street, north. He could hear his footsteps echoing. He was trying not to give the impression he was more frightened than he was. But he was frightened. Many scenes from crime movies came back to him; and he realized with great terror that this street, St. Nicholas, was similar to a street that had something to do with waterfronts in New York. He was frightened.

He was terrified. He started to think of Agatha. He should have brought her along with him; at least there would be a witness. He made a promise that in future, no matter where the hell he was going, Agatha would have to come with him; she would have to come; she would have to put down her goddamn textbooks on zoology, and come . . .

Before he could make more promises, the man from the shadows was upon him. He held Henry firmly. He was close, very close to his face. He held him firmly, but not like a policeman would hold a suspect, or a murderer would hold a victim. He was holding him like a man would hold a woman he wants to kiss, against her wish. "Jeffrey, you bitch! Jeffrey, you weird old queer!" the man said, in a voice uncertainly feminine and masculine at the same time. "I knew one day I would catch you up there with him, letting him feel up your ass. If I waited long enough . . ." The man raised his hand to strike a blow, and it was then that he saw he had approached the wrong man. "Oh my God! oh my God!" he cried, in a woman's voice . . . and all that was left was Henry standing bewildered, and the man's running steps along the cobblestones.

Henry decided to keep this experience to himself. He turned and headed for home.

The following day, Saturday, in the morning, Boysie got up early. He did not clean any offices on Friday nights. He gave himself this night off for taking his wife to the Club Tropics or to the WIF Club. And when they didn't go there, they would go to the Park Plaza Hotel lounge to hear Jackie Davis, the blues organist, who came to town often, and who was a crowd-pleaser, a crowd-drawing performer; or it would be Junior Mance, the pianist, and his trio. Boysie had decided to go to these "damn white people places," as Dots called them, because he was conscious of going up in the world.

Saturday mornings he reserved for home. He would get up early and drive Dots and Estelle and Bernice (if she was off from her living-out domestic job with the Breighington-Kellys of Rosedale) to the St. Lawrence Market. He stopped shopping in the Jewish Market because there were too many immigrant people from the Wessindies going there these days. "I can't take on so much black people round me, these days!" he would say. The pork chops in the St. Lawrence Market were large and cheap; and the pigs' feet and the parts of the pig's head were also fresh and cheaper than in the Jewish Market. There were lots of fresh vegetables and fruits — tomatoes, lettuce, beets, carrots, sweet potatoes — as if still growing in the kitchen-gardens of the countryside, with the dew falling off them like perspiration of vitality. Bernice said the dew was really water from a hose to make the vegetables look as if they were fresh.

Boysie liked to walk through the laneways of greens and smells, and he liked to smell the fruits and sometimes he would steal a grape from a bunch on a tray, and the vendor-owner would smile and say, "Buy some grapes now, sir! You taste how good my grapes taste, sir. Buy some for the lady."

And Boysie would push his hand into his right-hand

trousers pocket and take out a wad of bills, and deliberately and slowly, peel off the largest bill, a twenty-dollar
note, and pay for the twenty-cents purchase of grapes. He
would spend more time counting his change; and when it
was correct, he would raise his head and smile with the
vendor-owner; and he would place the dollar bills in as-
cending order of denominations, and then place the wad
back into his right-hand trousers pocket before moving off,
and smiling and telling the man, who also would be smiling,
"Damn good grapes you got there, man!"

But especially he liked to drive the women out, and fuss
and wrap the steering wheel round and round and display
his marksmanship with parking in the narrowest spot available, which not even a driving instructor would do to im-
press his student. The station wagon would be gleaming
like the stones of a dog in the moonlight. Boysie would
have gone up to the car wash on Spadina at six in the
morning, while the women were fussing and forcing their
jellied overeating, overweight avoirdupois into skin-fitting
skin-teething ski pants, although the season was autumn.

This Saturday morning Bernice was present. She had got
paid the day before. She was going to cook a real meal for
Dots and Boysie, and Estelle was going to help her. She
was going to be Dots's "domestic for today, girl. I am playing domestic for you, to you, and you is my mistress, but
for today only, hear?" And then she laughed and said,
"Who do you want to be? Mistress Dotsstein or Mistress
Dotsmann? Heh-heh-haaaa!"

"Gal, you see me complaining?"

And they bought dried increase peas and lots of wild
rice. They bought five avocado pears, lettuce, small spring
tomatoes — "man-these-is-the-very-same-ones-we-have-back-
home!" — pickled pig's parts, including the snout, "which
is the sweetest part of a pig, except maybe the fowl-pooch

of a chicken!" And when they left, laden down with three straw baskets which had JAMAICA, NASSAU and BARBADOS stitched in straw on them in bright colours, Boysie was singing a James Brown number, "I Feel Good!"; and Dots and Estelle were smoking Benson and Hedges cigarettes in the back seat with the groceries, while Bernice, in the front seat beside Boysie, chewed Wrigley's chewing gum, making it snap and make other noises in her rebellious mouth.

"Liquor store next, man! Liquor store! There is one down here, 'pon Wellington."

When Boysie went into the liquor store, Bernice held over the seat, touched Dots's knee, and said, "Child you would kill yourself to see the things them people I working for does carry-on with, at night, especially Friday nights. Have you ever heard of a *paint-in?*"

"Course! gal, you don't see that I have some hanging up in my place? A painting? Estelle haven't you ever seen the painting I bought recently from Coles?"

"A painting is a . . ."

"No! not one o' them, man. I mean a *paint-in.* Pee ayc-eye-enn-tee . . . that's one word. Now . . . eye-enn. Paint! In! Two words, *Paint* and *in.* A paint-in."

"Oh! like a sit-in. Or pray-in," Dots said.

"Zactly! That is what them people up there in my house do all night long, last night. It would make a sinner ashamed."

"Well, Christ! what is the next thing these white people will copy from we black people? They copy the marching, they copy the picketing, they copy the dancing . . . I don't mean dance-in, gal. I mean plain, simple coloured folks dancing . . ."

"Well, let me tell you 'bout this thing they call a paint-in. Now, I told you that my mistress is a young woman, pretty as hell and with a nice figure and gait. Well, her husband

is a young man too. And most of their friends, at least the
ones I see coming to their parties on Friday nights and Saturday nights and Sunday nights, the Lord's day, they is all
young people, doctors, lawyers, CBC people, writers and
artists, and the women, child! the women wearing the lates'
fashion and behaviour. Dresses short-short-short, so short
that oh Christ! you could see the colour of their panties
without even trying to look!"

"Mods, gal!"

"I wouldn't be seen dead in one o' them!" Estelle said.
"They're even wearing paper these days. Tomorrow, they'll
be wearing fig leaves, or coconut leaves, or just plain nakid.
We passed out o' that stage long long ago in history. But
these people?"

"What the hell would you be doing in a mod dress, you
with such a damn big belly? Heh-heh! look, don't kill me,
eh, gal? You past that stage."

"For truth."

"Well, anyhow," Bernice went on. "I had to work like a
damn slave all day yesterday, Friday, preparing things. And
I must say she don't stand up over me whilst I am doing
her work, like Mistress Burrmann did. She tells you what
and what you have to do, and that is that. Well, after the
rum-punches . . . child, let me tell you about them! I one
day, introduced real punches in that house, and Christ!
who told me to do that? I must have been mad as hell to
do a thing like that! Last Friday gone is three weeks I introduced them to West Indian rum punch. And every day,
every lunchtime, she have a flask full of it in her hands, like
a baby taking a bottle, taking it upstairs for he and she,
heh-heh-heh! and I am downstairs, listening to every movement he and she make in the king-sized bed. The springs
tell me every-damn-thing! Well! And I am still damn surprised how they don't have chick nor child to call them

Mammy or Daddy, they *always* in bed, lovey-doveying-it-up!
But I am telling you a story . . ." Boysie had come back,
heard what was going on, and was sitting quietly listening.
". . . 'bout the paint-in, man! She told me it is the latest
things going. Now, all these rich and powerful people arrived in motor cars as long as hell, and they dress in this
mod-way, with short clothes, the men in funny-looking
clothes looking as if they were old men before they became
young, and with tics bright as hell, enough to make a blind
woman outta me, and the women, as I say, they are dressed-
off in these psychedel-something clothes . . ."

"Psychedelic!" Boysie told her.

"Thanks. And everybody happy as hell. That is the one
thing I grudge them for. They are blasted happy people, or
at least they look so, and they surely drink enough liquor every weekend to *be* so! Now, I am bringing in a new set of
food, and my rum punch, and right there in front o' me with
a pretty young white woman in his lap, *in his lap*, is this
black man!" Bernice paused now for emphasis, as she had
paused then, through utter shock. "Jesus God, I nearly
dropped everything I was carrying in the tray. And that
black bitch looked me in my eye and called me, 'Sister!' He
says to me that all them ladies and gentlemen in the room
could hear, 'How you feel, sister?' I was so 'shamed, Dots!
Boysie, Estelle, I was so blasted ashamed that I prayed
something would smite me from the face o' that nigger!
And all the time, my mistress laughing and enjoying it, as
if it is a blasted joke, in truth. When I am in her house, I
want her to know that I am there as a employee. Not as a
friend of her blasted beatnik friends!

"Well, that wasn't nothing at all. After a few drinks,
and more jazz music . . . they have this pretty thing
where you can't see nothing, you could just hear the music coming outta the walls at you, and she doesn't play Bee-

thoven at parties like Mistress Burrmann! She hardly plays that kind o' classics, at all. The Beatles and James Brown *all* the time! But I am telling you, child. All of a sudden somebody, I think it was my mistress, all of a sudden that young thing screamed, '*Paint-in! Let's have a paint-in!*' Well, stupid me, I thinking now they are going to draw pictures on a piece o' paper, 'cause they have a gallery-full o' nice priceless paintings in their home, and nice ones too, I mean that! So, I walk out of the room, 'cause I don't really like these modern paintings too much. Then all this laughing and giggling. All of a sudden from the kitchen I hear this laughing like how, if two people are in a room and you can't see them, but you know they is two people in there by the two different voices; you could know, Dots, you aren't a fool, you could know by the giggles coming out of that room what the hell they are up to! You understand what I mean? The sliding door to their big big sitting room, I closed that now. Bernice the servant don't want to see what goes on in this mansion, this, this . . . mansion o' vice and destruction.

"But be-Christ, when they think that I had locked myself out, oh no! Jesus God, I beat it round outside, yes! I went outside. Outside. And I took a box with me. And I stand up. In the shade o' the trees. On that box, you hear me? Yes, sir! And what my two eyes discerned, as she herself would use that word, what my eyes discerned as happening in that sitting room in the middle o' Rosedale, it almost made me break my blasted neck through shock! I almost fall off that blasted imported beer box I was standing on, and break my neck. Every man, every man, every individual man, naked as when he come outta the womb of his mother. *Naked.* Every woman, every woman as she would be in the bathtub. *Naked,* too! And the he's have a paintbrush in their hands. And the she's have brushes too.

And this big big ewer, which I had taken in, thinking they wanted it for water for their drinks. But no, do you think they wanted it for water for their drinks? Hell, no! Christ, they wanted it to dip them paintbrushes in! Now, I say to myself, all right now! All sport aside! There is one black man in there amongst all them whites.

"Well, a party with drinking only, is one thing. But stripping in front of a black man all o' them white women doing it — that is something else altogether completely different. And I intend to look for him in that gloomy place . . . the candles, only the candles they left burning . . . heh-heh-haiii! first time, soul, that I realized it is so blasted hard to find one o' we in darkness, in the dark. Heh-heh-haiii! And I am a black person myself, heh-heh-haiii! Well, I spot that brute. That bitch! And guess what he was doing? Guess!"

"Standing up in a corner!" Boysie said. The image of naked women was too much for him.

"*He was painting too!*"

"Christ, no!" Boysie breathed. The images of all those naked women overpowered him, and he started to dream.

"He was painting a black, *black*, mind you! . . . he was painting a *blasted black circle* round that girl's you-know-what . . . so help me God! . . . so I don't have to tell you . . ."

"Oh Jesus God! hah-hah-hah!"

"Ohhhhh-weeeeeeeeeeeceeeeee!"

"Lord God in heaven look down!"

"He! That black bitch! Was painting a black circle, round-round-round as a circle is, on that white girl's private parts! And everybody else was doing the same thing, as if they was born artists and painters. Girl, I almost had a heart failure. Well, I thought the parties at the Burrmanns in Forest Hill was something. But this paint-in-thing beats the cake. Now, I couldn't see my mistress too good. But I could see *he*. And who he was painting, and what he was painting, wasn't anything you would show a child in Sunday-school, neither! And he wasn't painting it on *her*, neither! The wretch! heh-heh-haiii! Dots, he wasn't painting *her!* Estelle, Boysie you listening to me? husband and wife don't paint the same person, they don't paint one another. Child, those people must really be what my mistress herself calls *liberated and freemissive*, or whatever the hell the word is . . ."

"Per-missive!" Boysie told her, not braggingly, as he once would have done.

"Thanks."

"Oh God, I wish I was there!" he said.

"You wish you was *what?*" Dots snapped.

"I wish I was there where Bernice was, peeping . . ."

"If you want to peep at woman, peep at *me*, you hear?" And she exploded in her sexy deep-throated laughter.

"Oh, Dots, he ain't mean . . ." Bernice said.

"Oh!" Dots said. "Go on Bernice, gal."

"Well, I am trembling at the time. But this is too much to miss. They paint and they paint. They paint this one and they laugh. And they run for that one, woman or man, man or woman, and they paint the next one. Husband painting somebody else's wife. And vice versa. Then I see that bastard again. The coloured man who shouldn't have any damn business in this thing, at all, at all, as far as I see . . ."

"Why, gal?"

"Because."

"Why? Why why why?"

"Because he ain't one o' them, that's why! He is a decent coloured man!"

"You are talking shit to me, now, Bernice. Pardon me, Boysie. Pardon me, Dots."

"You ought to know!" Bernice said very savagely. But she went on to say, "I saw that one, and a funny thing was happening. You remember I told you he was a jet-black black man? With pretty smooth soft skin? Well, a funny thing was happening. *No matter what colour they put on that bitch, him! still you couldn't see it!* And guess what this woman, his woman, his mistress, his wife — or *whore!* . . . guess what she did? She took up some paint in her hand from outta some place, and when she moved her hand from offa that man's skin, be-Christ, that man was painted *white!* White! White-white-white! White as . . ."

"Shite!" Boysie exclaimed.

It was difficult to keep the car on an even course. He was laughing all the time he drove along Yonge Street, north from King. Bernice and Dots and Estelle were rolling with laughter. "Let we pass round and pick up Henry."

"And Agaffa, too!" Dots suggested. "Don't leff out *her!*"

"Yeah," Bernice said, "she's all right."

"Henry hasn't come round to visit me since the wedding reception," Dots said.

"I wonder how they making out?" Bernice wondered.

"All right," Boysie told her, although he knew differently.

"You know something?" Dots asked, still heavy with the memory and the taste of the painting and the paint-in on her mind. "I can laugh at a thing like that, that paint-in thing. But I couldn't take part. I would be too ashamed to let anybody see me naked like that."

"I would *never* do a thing like that," Bernice said. There was animus in her words and in her breathing. "It is sinful. It is a shame. Sinful."

"Well, I don't see it as a sin. But I still won't do it in

front of all those people. And in my own house, and in front of my husband?"

"Gal, there ain' no better place to behave like a whore!"

"What I mean is, a thing like that, a thing like a woman and a man being naked, well, it should be in private. A man going with a woman should be in private."

"White people does that all the time!" Bernice said, as if she was sitting in judgment on the white race.

"Not all. Some."

"Some, or few. They're white."

"That is life, child. That is life. And what I think eating out your backside is that you can't do it," Dots said. "I looking this spade in its face and calling it a spade! Since I been working at the Doctors, I have seen many things that I have never seen before, that I never thought happened before, nor could happen. And it is all done by white people. If this place was inhabited by blacks, be-Christ, Bernice, do you think it would be different?"

"It would be different, Dots. A vast difference."

"Different? How?"

"Well . . ."

"You mean that the white people who would now be in the minority won't hear 'bout it? Because black people is the most prejudiced bitches and bastards I have ever come across, Bernice! Some of my best friends is black, too! oh-heh-heh-heh-haiii!"

"Black people aren't the same as white people."

"White people does foop. Black people does foop, too. White people is bullers — they call them queers in Toronto, but we call them bullers. They is the same bullers as the black people back home! Christ, the Sin James coast in Barbados is full-up with them, Bernice! Where were you born? White people is the same blasted wickers as black people." She realized she had said something she should

not have said to Bernice. She herself had had this homosexual experience with Bernice. And she saw Bernice stiffen,
preparing the anger in her return thrust. But Dots simply
added, "One o' these days, everybody here in this car will
be able to attend a paint-in in my apartment, if he wants
to. I going hold one! It ain't so damn permissive . . . that's
the word? . . . as everybody white or black think . . . But
I wonder if Agaffa would come . . ."

They had reached Henry's roominghouse on Baldwin.
Dots wanted Boysie to get out and call Henry. Boysie
wanted Bernice to get out. "Hey, Bernice! perhaps, Henry
and Agaffa are having a paint-in, right now, eh? You could
join that one."

"Haul your arse, Boysie, if you please," she said, and
then immediately begged his pardon; and begged Dots to
forgive her for using such words in her car, in her presence.

"That's between you and Boysie. Left me out, gal."

"I'll go," Estelle said. "I need the exercise."

"Be careful, darling, getting out on the curb. We don't
want you to lose that baby. That baby belong to all four o'
we in this car, so don't play the arse with it. Boysie and me
is godfather and godmother. And we even picked a nice
name for our god-son."

"What's that name you pick for me?"

"Boy."

"What?"

"*Boy*, you ain' hear. The name is *Boy*. Be-oh!-why! . . .
BOY!"

"Thanks." And Estelle got out, and walked up the path,
with the empty bottles and the dead flowers and the empty
rotting cigarette boxes lining her way, like fallen rosebuds.

"Estelle looking *good*, Bernice."

"Yes. And she's bearing her burden like a queen!"

"I glad she didn't do no damn foolishness like giving up

her child for adoption, as that blasted fresh doctor suggested. And he had the gall to tell her he is sending social-worker to my apartment to look for her! Be-Christ, some o' these white people think they rule the world!"

Estelle knocked on the door many times. There was no answer. She started to move away. Then the landlady came. The landlady said, "Mrs. White isn't home. He is sleeping, or out, or . . ." She examined Estelle from head to foot. "They had people in last night, late, so perhaps . . ." She thought some more about it, and said, "They must be sleeping in." And she smiled. And Estelle smiled, too. Because it was that kind of a morning.

"Any message?" she asked her. "I'm sure he's sleeping."

"Just tell him we came looking for him."

"Who?"

"Estelle and Bernice and Dots and Boysie."

"Fine."

They drove back to the apartment, laughing, and arguing about holding a paint-in when they got home. The car radio was playing beautiful rhythm-and-blues songs. And Boysie was singing and dancing while he was driving. Dots was too happy to notice his recklessness. She looked at her watch. It was nine o'clock. "Only that?"

"How much?" Bernice asked.

"Nine o'clock, gal. Every working man and woman should still be in bed — sleeping, heh-heh-haiii! Yuh can't be vexed that that lazy bastard is still sleeping. It's Sarturday. And he's a married man now, too."

"He might be sleeping alone, though," Boysie said, sniggering. "Kee-kee-kee-kee . . ."

The moment they got into the apartment, he put on his favourite record, "Shanty Town People," by the Mighty Sparrow. When Dots heard the first two bars, she laughed

out, in her sensuous way, and shouted from the kitchen
where she was preparing a late breakfast (before Bernice
cooked as she promised) for them all. "Christ, man! you
is one o' them? Are you one of them, so early this blessed
morning?"

"One of what?" Bernice asked her.

"Shanty-town people," Dots said. "The record he's playing in there."

"That's the same one we were playing and dancing to,
when the police came," Estelle said.

"Fuck the police!" Boysie said, under his breath.

"Blind them!" Dots shouted from the kitchen.

"It's a lovely record, Dots. It's a lovely record, and it is
our music. We music! We can't be ashamed to hear it, regardless of the hour!"

"But Bernice. Is that you that just say that 'bout calypso?
Girl, have you took a man last night? This is revolutionary
for you. Gal, you are blasted agreeable this morning, and
so early, too!"

*Bright Sunday morning, they cussing, they fighting, they
gambling! Beating pan, they beating bup-bup! iron-bolt
and stone pelting! Send for the police, still the bacchanal
won't cease! So they violent, so they fast, they better go
back to their mansion on the Labasse . . .*

"Wow! wai! wow! waaaaaii!" Dots was saying, as she
prepared breakfast, as she danced to the music by herself in
the kitchen. "Wow! wee! wow! wee! We living, gal! We
are living! Boysie, please turn up that thing a little more
louder, man. We only got one chance on this earth."

Boysie, who couldn't have been asked a better request,
turned the volume up so loud that the entire apartment
and perhaps the entire apartment building capsized with
the rhythms of the West Indies. Dots interrupted the making of breakfast to come into the living room and dance

with her husband; and when he was not available, when he was mixing drinks for the women, she danced with Estelle. "I can feel that little bitch inside o' you jumping, darling. Treat it nice. Treat Boy nice. I am the godmother, don't forget. And I don't want no cripple-up god-son, hear me?"

"Come here, man!" Bernice shouted from the kitchen. "Come in here and look after your business." Dots stopped dancing with Estelle, wondering what now was wrong with "this man-less bitch, Bernice?" But all Bernice did was to give Dots the large fork she was holding over the simmering scrambled eggs. She left Dots standing, still wondering, and went outside into the living room, and held on to Boysie, and began dancing as if dancing had just been invented, especially for her.

"Lord Lord!" Dots screamed. "Look, don't dance too close to my man, you blasted man-thirsty woman, you! Looka, Boysie, watch-out, boy! watch-out! Bernice horny now. Bernice is horny as hell since she been attending them, them paint-ins. Don't let that woman rape you, boy . . . guard thyself!" Amidst the noise from the scrambled eggs arriving in thick yellow freshness and the sound of Sparrow, still lamenting that the slumdwellers had invaded his privacy and middle-class comfort on the hill in Port-of-Spain, Trinidad, amidst the joy and the noise and the rackling of the ice cubes in the glass in Estelle's hand, Dots went on laughing, and talking to herself about Bernice, and warning Boysie of Bernice.

Nobody was listening to her; because it was all in a joke, all part of their new release from the prison of their earlier immigration regulations. Dots even mentioned that she didn't know it was possible to enjoy life so much, she didn't know the happiness of being free, living in her own apartment. ("Gal, it could be a room, or a flat, or a hole in

the blasted wall. But it is mine! I pay the rent here!")
*Beating pan, they beating bup-bup! iron-bolt, and stone
pelting . . .*

Dots could see the sun and feel the wind in the country
district of Barbados where she lived before coming to this
country. She could remember herself going across the street,
dusty with sun and the epitaphs of low-flying cars, as boys
used to say about speedsters, and she remembered how she
would stand in line, and wait until the butcher had par-
celled out the best pieces of the dead pig, pork chops for
Mistress Bannister, *first;* because Mistress Bannister is the
schoolmistress of the girl-school in the village; the gentleman from America, *next;* and so on and so, down the line
of the unspoken but sacred ladder of importance and money
and light complexions; until the butcher would look up,
and there would be little Dots, and he would see her, at
last! standing there with the large white enamel pail in her
hands, waiting for a half-pound of the cheap part o' the
pig, please, "and my mother ask you if you would mind
putting this on her bill, till next week, 'cause Daddy didn'
come home Fridee night." And depending upon whether
the butcher, Mr. Webster, had got up on the wrong side of
the bed, or of his wife, he would either cuss both Dots and
her mother, or he would *give* her two pounds of the second-
best part of the dead pig, free; and tell her, "Get loss! I ain'
give you nothing, you hear?"

And now, on the counter in front of her was all this
food: and also the inside-running water tap, beside the
large white refrigerator, beside the stove which could cook
a meal even when she was at the hospital, improving herself while Boysie was out with Henry and the boys, playing
crap or dominoes or drinking beer. *Today in Canada . . .
praise God! I thank you that you put it in my head to get
out of that blasted stiffling island called Barbados and emi-*

*grade, be-Christ, emigrade here, and it is the wisest thing
I have done* . . . (Still the bacchanal won't cease! Sparrow was saying) . . . *Don't let this bacchanal cease at all,
Lord! don't let it done, it is too sweet!* . . . She could hear
the others in the living room dancing and laughing and being happy. Her thoughts went to Henry and Agatha. Breakfast was almost ready. She was making the toast. And she
got the butter out of the refrigerator, and she had to comment on the fact that this morning she was eating real butter, real butter, which was a fact that she and Boysie and
Estelle and Bernice could appreciate, it being also a fact
that real butter cost very much (even now, in Canada)
when they were home in Barbados, especially during the
war years. *I wonder how Henry making out? Agatha is a
nice girl, it is true that she is white, but that doesn't kill
. . . poor Henry, poor fellow! he had such a rough break
in this country. Well, it agrees with one person and it is
like a dose o' salts or a dose o' castor oil to the next person.
And you is a good man, Henry, after all; and one gotta help
the other* . . . She had to shake these serious thoughts out
of her head before she could go into the living room with
the others. The music was in the room with the others. The
music was in the room adjoining, and she couldn't therefore concentrate on other people's problems while she had
only happiness in her life now. When she went into the
dining area with the breakfast, they noticed there were
tears in her eyes.

"What happen, Dots?" Bernice asked.

"Just happy. Just happy, gal. I am happy and I just realized it." Bernice patted her on her back; and the others
knew.

They were eating now. Boysie helped the women, and
Dots helped Boysie. It was a West Indian custom, sanctified in her mother's mother's home, and in her mother's

home, and now in her home, that a woman guest never helped, never served the man of the house. Dots was still thinking of her lot in this country. So much food, so much food, she was saying to herself, as she saw them eat; one day it is a damn famine, the next day, it is a feast. Tears came back to her eyes. She got up without making it obvious and went into the bathroom. She let the tears spring up. And she let them fall. And then she washed her face. Her thoughts strayed back to Henry: ". . . it strange he ain't even call . . ." But the water was running noisily into the porcelain blue wash basin. "We still have a long way to go, boy! Food isn't everything," she told the mirror in which she saw her reflection. She came out, going back to the table, with none of them really knowing what she was going through. That is life, too, she mused.

There was some transformation in Bernice, these days: she was happy. Dots couldn't understand how she could be so happy. She didn't have a man. But still Bernice was happy. She didn't notice it herself, at first; but after a while, she did notice that her behaviour and her actions, particularly her behaviour in front of and behind Mrs. Breighington-Kelly was more relaxed; there was not that old tension and that old hostility. It was merely work this time. And perhaps this transformation was due to Estelle, who was great company for Bernice, Dots felt. No matter how you curse and swear and say the worst things to your family, your family is still your flesh and blood, Dots said. Bernice was losing some of the excess weight she had when she worked in Forest Hill. Her dresses were fitting her well, now. And Estelle? She seemed happy, contented: although no one would believe that in her present condition, she could be a hundred percent happy.

All of a sudden, Bernice started to talk, as if she was making a speech. But the gist of what she said was something they all knew to be the truth. "And to imagine, that after almost four years, this is the very first time, the very first time that the four of us . . . well, Estelle wasn't here three years ago, but this is the first time in a long time, that the four o' we have sat down, like decent people, which we are, after all, and had a meal like anybody else this morning, in all of Toronto."

"I was saying that very thing to myself as I was making this breakfast, gal."

"It is like a re-union."

"It *is* a re-union, boy!" Bernice said. "Somebody told me, or I was reading it somewhere, or I probably saw it on television, somewhere . . . anyhow, there is people in New York who don't see their family until Saturday morning at the breakfast table, they are rushing rushing so much during the rest o' the week! Life in that country is such a constant rush, anyhow."

"It is like New York here, too, in this damn place, sometimes."

"Well, look, since you-all women thinking so much 'bout a re-union, why don't we call Henry?"

"*And* Agaffa! Don't forget her now, man. Whenever we invite Henry nowadays, we *have* to invite Agaffa too. They is one, now, Boysie. Don't forget that."

"But woman, you didn't let me finish what I was going to say. I was going to say Henry *and* Agaffa, and invite them down for breakfast, and then, afterwards we could listen to some records and drink some rum and generally have a good time this afternoon. Today is Sarturday! Nobody, except the police, godblindthem! — every time I think of a cop I want to kill all o' them — nobody should have to work on a Saturday."

They called Henry's number. But there was no answer. And just as quickly as they had remembered him, so quickly did they forget him. When breakfast was finished, they did what they said they would do had Agatha and Henry come.

Hours later, they were still dancing and having a good time, when a voice was heard at the door. "Paper boy!"

Boysie had to turn down the music which was saying, *they treat me like a savage* . . . He went to the door. He opened it, and paid the paper boy. He threw the bulky weekend paper on the couch. He went back to his dancing. Dots glanced at the paper, the front page, and she turned her attention back to Boysie and Estelle, on the floor. She was trying to think of the exact hour, the exact day when Estelle would have to be taken to the hospital. "I hope she isn't exerting herself too much!" The record came to an end. Dots got up and shouted, "My turn now, my turn!" Bernice, who was hoping it was her turn, merely sat back down and kept time with her hands, while Dots danced with Boysie.

Estelle was sitting beside the newspaper on the couch. She was tired. Perhaps she had exerted herself too much. There was a large photograph of a man on the bottom of the front page. She took up the paper, feeling she knew the man, and she read the line over the photograph: WEST IN-DIAN POET FOUND DEAD. She put it back down. Her mind could not conjure up or conceive of a West Indian poet she knew who would be found dead in Toronto. She never knew a West Indian poet. The poets she knew were in school books. Something however, about the face in the photograph had caught her curiosity; and she took a second look. She took up the paper, and looked at the photograph. "Wait! Boysie, come here." They thought she had had a pain. "Tell me if I should know this face?"

"I dancing. Wait till this thing finish, Estelle. Gimme one more minute with this woman!" He laughed and Estelle laughed, and so did Dots.

"Come, man! come and see if I should know this face, in truth. They have a big ugly black man with a beard and long hair like an African on the front page . . ." Boysie left Dots to dance by herself. Bernice got up and started to dance with Dots. "You know this face?"

"*Jesus Christ!*"

"I knew so!"

"*Henry!*"

And when Dots came, and Bernice followed, Boysie was reading the story which said in part: *Police today found the body of a West Indian poet, Henry White, in his boardinghouse room, on Baldwin Street, at 11:30. Mr. White, a Barbadian, was recently married to a Canadian woman, formerly Agatha Barbara Sellman. Mrs. White is a postdoctoral student in clinical zoology at the University of Toronto. At the time the body was found in the unmade bed, police reported, Mrs. White was not at home. The landlady, Miss Heather Diamond, who discovered the body some time after a carload of West Indian friends had inquired for him earlier this morning, told police Mr. White had been a tenant in her boardinghouse for the past fifteen years. "He was a decent quiet man," she told police, as she wrung her hands in grief. Police are searching for the missing wife for questioning. A poem, presumably one of Mr. White's unpublished last works, was found beside the body. (It is reproduced in the box below.) Police are investigating the theory that death might have been caused by suicide. An autopsy was ordered by Metro Chief Coroner Dr. Morgon Shrillman . . .*

Before Boysie read the poem, he tore it out of the paper. The women were all in tears. They were all on the couch. Somebody had turned off the record player.

"*She* killed him!" It was Dots, screaming all of a sudden. "She killed Henry as sure as I name Dots!" Bernice held over, and took Dots in her arms and patted her on her back, like a sobbing child. Estelle did not try to restrain her tears. Boysie was finding it difficult to read. He read the poem to himself first, and he recognized it as the one Henry had shown him in the Paramount Tavern. Then he read it aloud, for the women, in a shaking voice, his pronunciation as shaky as his voice:

> *But was it really time that killed*
> *That rose of our loves? Was it time?*
> *And was it time to die? Is it time?*
> *This rose?*
> *It was not, could not, be time. Time*
> *Has no power over roses, or over love*
> *Or over me, or over you.*
> *Time has no gun over love or over beauty.*

The women cried, in a wailing bawling tone, as Boysie had read the poem.

"She killed that man, she kill him, as good as anything," Dots said again, tears and snot running into her mouth. Bernice took out her handkerchief, and wiped Dots's face; and she held it to Dots's nose, and she blew into it. "She killed him! I was thinking about Henry a minute ago, inside there in the bathroom . . . it came to me like a feeling in the pit o' my guts . . . I could feel something was wrong this morning. I still say she kill Henry. Suicide? Ain't no suicide! . . . what suicide? Henry never had a blasted chance in this white man country . . ."

"But look! he get his chance now. He get it now. And he get it like a real hero, too. They have his poem *on the front page*, where it belongs."

"He get it now. But now, he is a dead man . . ."

"Read the part where Henry talk 'bout the roses again, please Boysie," Estelle asked. And Estelle listened, with her eyes closed with water, with her hands folded together in knots of fingers, while Dots screamed and accused; and Bernice wept and tried to comfort Dots.

Before Boysie began (he was more upset now, more upset than they knew), he sensed a great hate for Agatha come into his body. Henry was his friend. He could not picture Henry dead. Certainly not through taking his own life. Suddenly Dots screamed out. Terror and hate were in her scream. *"That white bitch Agatha killed our Henry! She kill-lim, she kill-lim, she kill-lim!"*

"Don't say that, Dots. Please. Don't say so. Nobody ain't know how Henry dead." It was Bernice asking her to be forgiving.

Boysie was reading the poem, and when he came to the passage Estelle had asked for, while Dots was still crying and condemning Agatha, Estelle whispered, along with Boysie's shaking voice, the lines:

> *Time*
> *Has no power over roses, or over love*
> *Or over me, or over you.*
> *Time has no gun over love or over beauty.*

Instead of an image of Henry or of Agatha, her thoughts conjured, in front of her sorrow, the image of Sam Burrmann, with the photograph of her own private wish: *with his throat cut!*